The Garland Library
of Medieval Literature

General Editor
James J. Wilhelm, Rutgers University

Literary Advisors
Ingeborg Glier, Yale University
Thomas R. Hart, University of Oregon
Guy Mermier, University of Michigan
Lowry Nelson, Jr., Yale University
Aldo Scaglione, University of North Carolina

Art Advisor
Elizabeth Parker McLachlan, Rutgers University

Music Advisor
Hendrik van der Werf, Eastman School of Music

Lancelot rides in a cart driven by a dwarf, while Kay is unhorsed to the right. Folio 170r from Manuscript 806 of the Pierpont Morgan Library, a fourteenth-century *Lancelot* written in a Picard dialect.

Chrétien de Troyes

Lancelot
or, The Knight of the Cart
(Le Chevalier de la Charrete)

edited and translated by
WILLIAM W. KIBLER

Volume 1
Series A
GARLAND LIBRARY OF MEDIEVAL LITERATURE

Garland Publishing, Inc.
New York and London
1981

Library of Congress Cataloging in Publication Data

Chrétien, de Troyes, 12th cent.
Lancelot, or, The knight of the cart.

(Garland library of medieval literature ; v. 1.
Series A)
Translation of Le Chevalier de la Charrette.
Bibliography: p.
Includes index
1. Lancelot—Romances.   I. Kibler, W.W.   II. Title.
III. Series: Garland library of medieval literature ;
v. 1.
PQ1447.E5   1981   841'.1   80-8960
ISBN 0-8240-9442-5   AACR2

Printed on acid-free, 250-year-life paper
Manufactured in the United States of America

For
NANCY
. . . ce est la dame qui passe
totes celes qui sont vivanz

Lancelot crosses the Sword Bridge to rescue Queen Guinevere, who watches from a tower with King Bademagu, who then welcomes the hero to the Land of Gorre. Folio 166r from Manuscript 806 of the Pierpont Morgan Library.

Preface of the General Editor

The Garland Library of Medieval Literature was established to make available to the general reader modern translations of texts in editions that conform to the highest academic standards. All of the translations are original, and were created especially for this series. The translations attempt to render the foreign works in a natural idiom that remains faithful to the originals.

The Library is divided into two sections: Series A, texts and translations; and Series B, translations alone. Those volumes containing texts have been prepared after consultation of the major previous editions and manuscripts. The aim in the editing has been to offer a reliable text with a minimum of editorial intervention. Significant variants accompany the original, and important problems are discussed in the Textual Notes. Volumes without texts contain translations based on the most scholarly texts available, which have been updated in terms of recent scholarship.

Most volumes contain Introductions with the following features: (1) a biography of the author or a discussion of the problem of authorship, with any pertinent historical or legendary information; (2) an objective discussion of the literary style of the original, emphasizing any individual features; (3) a consideration of sources for the work and its influence; and (4) a statement of the editorial policy for each edition and translation. There is also a Select Bibliography, which emphasizes recent criticism on the works. Critical writings are often accompanied by brief descriptions of their importance. Selective glossaries, indices, and footnotes are included where appropriate.

The Library covers a broad range of linguistic areas, including all of the major European languages with the exception of Middle English. All of the important literary forms and genres are considered, sometimes in anthologies or selections.

The General Editor hopes that these volumes will bring the general reader a closer awareness of a richly diversified area that has for too long been closed to everyone except those with precise academic training, an area that is well worth study and reflection.

James J. Wilhelm
Rutgers University

Contents

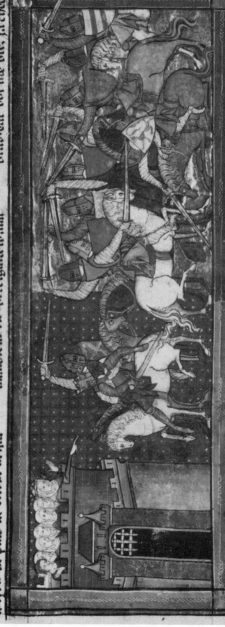

Lancelot contends in a tournament for the honor of Queen Guinevere, who signals from the tower. Folio 262r from Manuscript 806 of the Pierpont Morgan Library.

Introduction

Life of the Author

Lancelot or *The Knight of the Cart* is the third or fourth major work by the twelfth-century poet Chrétien de Troyes. It was preceded by *Erec and Enide*, *Cligés*, and possibly *The Knight with the Lion* (*Yvain*), and followed by *The Story of the Grail* (*Perceval*). Many critics, following Maurice Wilmotte,* also recognize Chrétien as the author of the hagiographical romance *William of England*. What little we know about Chrétien is drawn from allusions found in his works or from what can be surmised from a careful study of them. This information enables us to piece together an all too sketchy biography and arrive at all too uncertain dates for his romances.

In the prologue to his earliest romance, our author refers to himself as *Crestïens de Troies* (*Erec*, line 9), and this longer designation is also used by Gerbert of Montreuil in his continuation of Chrétien's unfinished *Perceval*. In *The Knight of the Cart* and his other romances, he refers to himself simply as *Crestïens*. It is thus likely that Chrétien was born or at least spent the better part of his formative years in Troyes, which was one of the leading cities in the region of Champagne, located some hundred miles along the Seine south of Paris. The language in which he composed his romances is also tinted with dialectal traits from the Champagne area.

At Troyes, Chrétien was most assuredly associated with the court of Marie of Champagne, one of the daughters of Eleanor of Aquitaine by her first marriage, to Louis VII of France. Marie's marriage to Henry the Liberal, Count of Champagne, furnishes us with one of the only dates which can be determined with any degree

---

* All names and page references are keyed to the Select Bibliography, which follows.

of certainty in Chrétien's biography. For many years it was thought to have occurred in 1164, but recent archival research by Holmes and Klenke (p. 18) and Misrahi (pp. 109–113) has pushed this date back to at least 1159. In the opening lines of *Lancelot* Chrétien informs us that he is undertaking the composition of this romance at the behest of "my lady of Champagne," and critics are in unanimous accord that this can only be the great literary patroness Marie. Chrétien could not have begun a romance for "his lady of Champagne" before 1159. At some time after Henry the Liberal's death in 1181 Chrétien shifted patrons and began his never-to-be-completed *Perceval* for Philip of Flanders. The *Perceval* was certainly begun prior to Philip's death in the Holy Land in 1191, and probably prior to his departure for the Third Crusade in September of 1190.

Apart from the dates 1159 and 1191, nothing else concerning Chrétien's biography can be fixed with certainty. At the beginning of his second romance, *Cligés*, Chrétien gives us a list of works which he had previously composed:

> Cil qui fist d'Erec et d'Enide,
> Et les comandemanz d'Ovide,
> Et l'art d'amors an romans mist
> Et le mors de l'espaule fist,
> Del roi Marc et d'Ysalt la blonde,
> Et de la hupe et de l'aronde
> Et del rossignol la muance,
> Un novel conte rancomance
> D'un vaslet qui an Grece fu
> Del linage le roi Artu.

> (He who wrote *Erec and Enide*, who translated Ovid's Commandments and the Art of Love, who wrote of the Shoulder Bite, of King Mark and Isolde the Blonde, of the metamorphosis of the hoopoe, swallow and nightingale, begins here a new story of a youth who, in Greece, was of Arthur's line.)

From this list it seems established that Chrétien began his career by perfecting his technique in practicing the current literary mode of translations and adaptations of tales from Latin into the vernacular. The *comandemanz d'Ovide* can be identified with Ovid's *Remedia Amoris*; the *art d'amors* is Ovid's *Ars amatoria* (Art of Love), and the *mors de l'espaule* is the Pelops story in the *Metamorphoses*, Book 6. These works of Chrétien have all been lost. Only the *muance de la hupe et de l'aronde et del rossignol* (the Philomela story in *Metamorphoses*, Book 6) is preserved in a version which might be his.

Chrétien also informs us here that he composed a poem *del roi Marc et d'Ysalt la blonde*. As far as we know, this was the first treatment of this famous Breton legend in French. Chrétien does not tell us whether he had written a full account of the tragic love of Tristan and Isolde, and most scholars today agree that he treated only an episode of that legend (since Mark's name, rather than Tristan's, is linked with Isolde). But we are nonetheless permitted to believe that he is in some measure responsible for the subsequent success of that story, as he was to be in large measure for that of King Arthur. Indeed, in his earliest romances, Chrétien seems obsessed with the Tristan legend, which he mentions several times in *Erec* and against which his *Cligés* (often referred to as an "anti-Tristan") is seen to react.

From such allusions it can be assumed that Chrétien received the standard preparation of a *clerc* in the flourishing church schools in Troyes, and therefore entered minor orders. He was formed in the rhetorical traditions of classical and medieval Latin literature and was well acquainted with at least Ovid and Statius. It has been conjectured from his excellent knowledge of English topography in *Cligés* that Chrétien visited England, where he might first have been introduced to the fascinating legends circulating about King Arthur and his knights. However, given the cosmopolitan court of Champagne and the great trading center of Troyes, whose two annual fairs attracted merchants and visitors from all parts of Europe, he could as easily have garnered this knowledge without leaving his hometown.

It was perhaps at the urging of Marie of Champagne, sometime after 1159, that Chrétien turned from the Latin classics and began to treat the great Breton legends. Possibly encouraged as well by a favorable reception to his Tristan material, Chrétien continued to exploit the as yet untapped Breton legends. His first work that incorporated the Arthurian material was *Erec and Enide*, a fine psychological study. This romance posed a problem familiar to courtly circles: how can a knight, once married, maintain the prowess and glory which won him his bride? That is: can a knight serve both his honor (*armes*) and his love (*amours*)? Erec, caught up in marital bliss, neglects the pursuit of his glory until reminded by

Enide, who has overheard some knights gossiping maliciously. Accompanied by her, he sets out on a series of adventures in the course of which Erec tests both his wife and himself. The mixture of psychological penetration and extraordinary adventures would become typical both of Chrétien's style and of the Arthurian romances written in imitation of his work.

Chrétien's second major work, *Cligés*, is in part set at Arthur's court, but is principally an adventure romance based on Greco-Byzantine material, which was exceedingly popular in the second half of the twelfth century. This work exalts the pure love of Fénice for Cligés, and has been seen by many critics as a counter-argument to the adulterous passion of Isolde for Tristan. Numerous textual parallels have been adduced to support this contention, but the poem is even more interesting for its use of irony, its balanced structure, and its psychological insights into the hearts of the two lovers. Here, as elsewhere, Chrétien shows the influence of Ovid, the most popular classical writer in the twelfth century.

After the success of *Erec and Enide* and *Cligés* (in neither of which there is any indication of Marie's patronage), Chrétien composed, perhaps simultaneously, his *Yvain* and his *Lancelot*. Foerster (1914, pp. 21–46) and Holmes (1970) assigned these works to the 1160's; Paris, Hofer, Fourrier (1950), and Frappier (1968) placed them in the 1170's; and, most recently, Luttrell and Hunt (1978) have argued for the 1180's. Arguments to support these varying datings are extremely complex and are based almost exclusively upon supposed allusions to historical events of the period or possible references to other literary works in Latin or Old French. The difficulties inherent in this method of dating have been cogently demonstrated by Misrahi.

The relationship between *Lancelot* and *Yvain* is complex. There are several direct references in the latter to action which occurs in the former, particularly Meleagant's abduction of Guinevere and the subsequent quest by Lancelot. Yet at the same time the characterization of Kay in the early section of *Lancelot* seems explicable only in terms of *Yvain*. Further, the blissful conjugal scene between Arthur and Guinevere at the beginning of *Yvain* seems unusual after *Lancelot*. These contradictory factors have led some recent scholars, such as Shirt (1975, 1977), Hunt (1978), and Ménard (1971), to propose that these two romances were composed simultaneously, beginning with *Yvain*, then breaking off to

Lancelot, which itself was perhaps completed in three stages. According to this theory, Chrétien wrote the first part of *Lancelot*, then turned it over to Godefroy of Leigni (Lagny) to complete. Unhappy with the contrast between the two sections, Chrétien himself then composed the tournament of Noauz section to harmonize the two parts.

Many critics consider *Yvain* to be Chrétien's most perfectly conceived and executed work. In it he reconsiders the question of the conflict of love and valor posed in *Erec*, but from the opposite point of view: Yvain neglects his bride (*amours*), rather than the pursuit of his glory (*armes*). Like Erec, Yvain must then set out upon a series of marvelous adventures to expiate his fault and rediscover himself.

Chrétien's final work, begun sometime before the death of Philip of Flanders in 1191 and never completed, was and still is his most puzzling: the *Conte du Graal* (Story of the Grail, or *Perceval*). Controversy continues today over whether or not Chrétien intended this romance to be read allegorically. Even those critics who agree that his intent was indeed allegorical argue over the proper nature and significance of the allegory. His immediate continuers, Robert de Boron and the anonymous author of the *Perlesvaus*, clearly assumed that the allegory was Christian. Unfortunately, death apparently overtook Chrétien before he could complete his masterwork and reveal the mysteries of the Grail Castle.

In addition to these narrative works, Chrétien has left us two lyric poems in the courtly manner, which make him the first identifiable North French practitioner of the courtly lyric style begun in Provence or southern France in the early years of the twelfth century. D.D.R. Owen has recently attempted to attribute to Chrétien *Le Chevalier à l'épée* (The Knight with the Sword) and *La Mule sans frein* (The Unbridled Mule), two romances found in a manuscript containing the *Perceval*, but his attributions have not been accepted.

Artistic Achievement

In the prologue to his *Erec and Enide*, Chrétien tells us that he *tret d'un conte d'avanture/ une molt bele conjointure* (creates from an adventure tale a very beautiful arrangement). This *conjointure* is variously translated "arrangement," "linking," "coherent organization," "internal unity," etc. A good discussion is that by Eugène Vinaver, who writes in *The Rise of Romance*: "The art of *composition* [is] the proper means of turning a mere tale of adventure into a romance. . . . [The] *conjointure* is merely a method of dealing with the material; it is not a substitute for the *conte*, but something a skilful poet can and must superimpose upon it" (p. 37).

No matter what one's interpretation of the matter and meaning of *Lancelot* might be, recent critics, led by Kelly (1966), Zaddy, and Lacy (1980), no longer suggest that it is the ill-composed and loosely structured conglomeration of adventures seen by Gaston Paris, Mario Roques, and other earlier critics. As in most of his romances, Chrétien has organized his plot around the motif of the quest: after an initial transgression — a hesitation of only two steps before mounting the shameful cart — Lancelot embarks upon a series of remarkable and fantastic adventures in order to expiate his sin and reestablish his right to love and serve the queen. These adventures are not haphazardly organized, as it may appear to the casual reader, but relate directly to the transgression in what Norris Lacy (1980) has aptly termed the principle of *contrapasso*, familiar to readers of Dante, by which the punishment precisely corresponds to the nature of the sin. Lancelot's "sin" against the courtly code is to have preferred for even an instant the urgings of his knightly honor to those of his amorous duty. Hence, each of his adventures will demand that he serve women unhesitatingly. The principle of the *contrapasso* is most evident in the scene of the Tournament at Noauz, wherein Guinevere requires Lancelot not only to act unhesitatingly at her request, but to shame himself publicly for having once refused for an instant to shame himself for love by climbing into the cart.

A romance such as *Lancelot* does not possess the linearity and structural unity that modern readers frequently expect in a work of fiction, but it has its own cohesiveness based on the principle of analogy. Scenes which may have no direct bearing on the development of the central intrigue nonetheless serve the meaning of the story as analogues of other actions. Shortly after the episode of the cart, Lancelot meets with a lady who offers him lodging on the condition that he sleep with her; he accepts, but again not without a certain reluctance. After dinner Lancelot retires while the lady makes ready for bed, and when he returns, he discovers that he cannot find her. He determines, however, to seek her wherever she may be until he finds her (lines 1054–55). Going into a nearby room he hears her cries for help and sees her set upon by a knight in the presence of six armed guards. At her request for immediate help, Lancelot balks, but he finally overcomes his hesitation to rescue her in what is revealed in the end to have been a staged test. Lancelot has been caught in a dilemma: if he delays in order to help the lady, then he may be perceived as delaying in his pursuit of Guinevere; on the other hand, if he refuses to serve this woman, then he may be perceived as unworthy to serve the queen. Lancelot's hesitation to help the lady in distress is analogous to his hesitation to shame himself in his pursuit of the queen. It is a first test of his determination, a test which he fails because he has not yet found within himself the proper balance of arms and love. This scene serves as a sort of gloss on the cart episode, and the thoughts which go through Lancelot's mind here (lines 1097–125) might well be the same as those which remained unexpressed in the previous scene. Since later episodes frequently clarify earlier ones, the poem requires a greater effort on the part of the reader, calling him to reread earlier passages in the light of later ones and to keep the whole poem simultaneously in mind.

The psychological development in this and other episodes is a second aspect of Chrétien's style which deserves comment. Vinaver has shown that a good writer of romance seeks to elucidate the meaning of his story. Although action and adventure are still important to the work, they are secondary to explanation. This explanation comes in Chrétien primarily in the form of interior monologues spoken by the characters in moments of distress: Guinevere's lament upon hearing the false rumor of Lancelot's death (lines 4197–244) and Lancelot's grief when he believes that Guinevere is dead (lines 4263–83 and 4318–96) are good examples. Such monologues use personification to help elucidate the conflicting forces struggling for dominance within the minds of the characters.

Chrétien's romances operate on two levels: the more important level of the *conjointure*, associated often with the *san*, and the more direct level of action and plot, associated with the *matiere*. Nor does Chrétien neglect the latter. His works glitter with descriptions and abound in realistic details. In the scene already mentioned of the lady who lodged Lancelot on the condition that he sleep with her, Chrétien provides a precise description of her castle with its drawbridge, her tiled hall, and the opulence of her dinner preparations: the dais, the tablecloth, the candles and candelabra, the jugs of wine, the basins, and the towel. These items anchor the story in reality, yet their splendor creates an otherworldly atmosphere, complete with magnificent deeds, hideous dwarfs, fair damsels, wicked giants, and the like. Other details spring directly from this fairylike atmosphere and have no real function on the psychological level: magic rings, the mysterious tomb, the vision of lions, swift-flying rumor, and the invisible boundary of the kingdom of Gorre. Chrétien could well have completed his story without such details, but their presence helps in large measure to create the unique atmosphere which he is seeking.

In considering these details one must resist the temptation to seek an allegorical or symbolic interpretation for each one. Borrowing constantly from a reserve of symbols, Chrétien, like his reader, would have been aware of the symbolic possibilities of certain terms, of certain numbers, animals, or gems. But these symbols are handled delicately and naturally, with no continuous system. Chrétien was not writing an organized allegory, such as the *Romance of the Rose* or Dante's *Divine Comedy*. Contrary to pure allegory, his symbolic mode is discontinuous and nonexclusive: it does not function in a single predictable manner in each instance, and one interpretation does not necessarily preclude another. Rosemond Tuve says of such works: "Though a horse may betoken undisciplined impulses in one context, a knight parted from a horse in the next episode may just be a knight parted from a horse" (p. 402). The symbol may change meaning freely, or include several interpretations in a single occurrence, or even disappear. Robert Guiette states accordingly: "Allegory in the Middle Ages is a science. Symbolism, an art in which imagination and sensitivity have their role" (p. 45).

Sources and Influences

In the preface to her collection of *Lais*, a near-contemporary of Chrétien, known only as Marie de France, proclaimed that since persons with God-given knowledge and talent should write for the benefit of others to come, she had sought to find "some good story to adapt from Latin into French." However, she soon concluded that too many others had already done this and determined instead to adapt new material to please and inform her listeners. This new material she chose from among the rich folk sources of Brittany and the British Isles, especially Ireland and Wales.

Many of Chrétien's tales as well, among them *Lancelot*, seem to have their roots in the soil of the British Isles. Particularly popular in Celtic mythology is the abduction story or *aithed*. Typically, a mysterious stranger claims a married woman, makes off with her through a ruse or by force, and carries her to his otherworldly home. Her husband pursues the abductor and, after triumphing over seemingly impossible odds, penetrates the mysterious kingdom and rescues his wife. Guinevere is the subject of such an abduction story in the Latin *Vita sancti Gildae* (Life of St. Gildas) by Caradoc of Llancarvan (c. 1150), which contains much Celtic mythology. She is carried off by Melwas or Maheloas, lord of the *aestiva regio* (land of summer), to the *Urbs Vitrea* (City of Glass, associated with Glastonbury in Somersetshire). From there she is rescued by King Arthur with the aid of the Abbot of Glastonbury. This Latinized and edifying version has been compared to the Celtic legend of the abduction of the fairy Winlogee, sculpted on the Arthurian portal of the Modena Cathedral in the early years of the twelfth century.

These stories differ so much from Chrétien's *Lancelot* that they cannot be cited as his direct source. Most notably, the role of Lancelot del Lac (of the Lake) is nowhere to be found there. Though his story has been largely lost, his name "implies the existence of a legend about his childhood under the care of a water-fay" (Frappier, ed. Loomis, p. 178). The magic ring given him by the fairy who raised him (*Lancelot*, lines 2345 – 47) no doubt relates to this myth. Chrétien listed Lancelot third among the knights of the Round Table in *Erec*, and he reappears in *Cligés* during the tournament near Oxford. It seems clear from such mentions that legends, now mostly lost, were already attached to his name. We would particularly like to know whether this love was imputed to him by Chrétien, perhaps at the suggestion of Marie of Champagne.

In spite of many attempts at explanation, we must still wonder how this legendary material reached France and French-speaking

England from its Celtic homelands. Numerous routes have been proposed, but none seems truly satisfactory. There is no doubt that the tales of Tristan and King Arthur were indeed circulating in France by the 1160's, but we cannot be certain under what form, nor how widely disseminated they were. William of Malmesbury asserts in his *Historia regum anglorum* (History of the English Kings, 1125) that "idle fictions" and "wild tales" were already being told by that time about the great King Arthur, whom he accepts as an historical figure. In the beginning of *Erec and Enide*, Chrétien tells us that he has incorporated into this carefully structured work materials which earlier storytellers were wont to mutilate (*depecier*) and corrupt (*corronpre*). Evidence might be deduced from these statements to support the contention that there was no fixed Arthurian tradition at this time, or one might argue conversely that there was a true tradition which Chrétien knew and wished to restore. Chrétien's listing of the knights of the Round Table in *Erec* (lines 1671–706) includes many knights never mentioned elsewhere, but omits Perceval, who would become a significant hero in Chrétien's subsequent work, as well as in the romances of others. This suggests to many critics that the canon of knights was not yet fixed, and that perhaps Chrétien had much to do with fixing it, for he was the first to write what we today know as an Arthurian romance. The reference to a garbled and mutilated tradition could well be a standard literary device to render acceptable the modifications and inventions of Chrétien himself.

Chrétien seems to have gathered together the threads of a raveled tradition to weave his beautiful fabric (*bele conjointure*: *Erec*, line 14). Where did he first hear these legends? It is doubtful that Chrétien himself understood the Celtic dialects, though he may have visited the British Isles, as we noted earlier. If so, we can imagine that he visited Glastonbury, one of the great centers in the diffusion of the Arthurian legends, for the Abbot of Glastonbury from 1125 to 1171, Henry of Blois, was the brother of the English King Stephen and the uncle of Marie of Champagne's husband, Count Henry I (the Liberal). Henry of Blois was most interested in the development of Glastonbury and no doubt favored the spread of the Arthurian materials which brought it fame. In 1191, some twenty years after Abbot Henry's death, the "body" of King Arthur was mysteriously recovered at Glastonbury.

Even had he not visited England, Chrétien could well have heard these stories and legends on the French mainland, from Henry of Blois on the occasion of one of his trips through France to Cluny or Rome, or from wandering storytellers, many of whom were of Breton origin and who, like many modern Bretons, were bilingual. At the close of *Yvain* Chrétien tells us that he is ending his tale because he had *heard* no more (6806: *n'onques plus conter n'en oï*), and in *Erec and Enide* he specifically condemns the professional storytellers (22: *cil qui de conter vivre vuelent*) who mutilated and corrupted this legend. Much similar testimony is offered by other writers to attest to the existence of these wandering storytellers in the twelfth century.

In addition to first-hand tellings of these tales and legends, Chrétien was certainly familiar with the pseudo-historical *Historia regum Britanniae* (History of the Kings of Britain) by Geoffrey of Monmouth, in which the author purports to give a history of the kings of Britain from the time of their mythical ancestor Brut to the present (1136–37). Modern scholars have shown that Geoffrey used more imagination than research, but his work was widely accepted as true, and was translated into French in 1155 by the Anglo-Norman Wace. Though Geoffrey had already given his story a courtly flavoring with his inclusion of chess games, feasts, and tourneys, Wace far surpassed his predecessor. Where Geoffrey had written of fortresses, Wace substituted castles; in his writing, senators became barons and consuls became counts. In addition, Wace first mentioned the soon to be celebrated Round Table and introduced the important figure of Merlin.

From Geoffrey and Wace, as from oral tradition, Chrétien could have taken little more than the names of characters, perhaps some rudiments of story lines or characterizations, and a general tone. It was his genius alone to assemble these various fictions into a coherent form which would guarantee them their immense success. Even critics most partial to Celtic origins recognize that the material has been extensively altered by Chrétien, and that many of the motifs may also be found elsewhere — for example, the abduction tale has been likened to the Persephone and Eurydice stories in Classical Greek and Latin mythology. Nor have critics failed to point out the striking analogies with Christian salvation history: the Messianic role of Lancelot, who humbles himself to ride in a cart and who triumphs over death in rescuing Guinevere and mankind from a Limbo-like imprisonment in the land of Gorre (see Micha, 1950, and Fowler). The most wide-reaching Messianic interpretation of *Lancelot* is that by Jacques Ribard. Thus the central motif of the cart, which was long given a Celtic explanation, can be likened to the Cross. David J. Shirt (1973) has seen in *Lancelot* the all-pervasive influence of contemporary and courtly society, and has linked the cart to twelfth-century feudal customs.

Chrétien himself tells us only that the Countess Marie of Champagne gave him the *matiere* and *san* of his work. Critics have generally agreed that the *matiere* referred to Chrétien's source story, perhaps given him orally and in a loosely connected manner by the Countess, and that the *san* was the interpretation or meaning to be given to this matter. This interpretation or meaning has been related to the concept of "courtly love," a term first coined by Gaston Paris in the 1880's in his pioneering articles on the *Lancelot*.

On the subject of courtly love or *fin'amors* (the medieval term), scholars are loosely divided into two opposing camps: the *realists*, who believe that such an institution existed in the Middle Ages and is reflected in the literature of the period; and the *idealists*, who believe that it is a critical construct and was in the Middle Ages at most a game to be taken lightly and ironically (see Wind, Newman, and Ferrante-Economou).

Love as it is seen in the *Lancelot* is an all-absorbing passion, which has an ennobling and refining effect upon the lover. Lancelot is totally submissive to every whim of his beloved, but for his efforts he hopes for and receives a frankly sexual recompense. The passion portrayed in this romance is adulterous, and Lancelot appears to substitute a religion of love for the traditional Christian ethic, even going so far as to genuflect upon leaving Guinevere's bedchamber (see lines 4652–53, 4716–18). Yet nowhere is there any direct condemnation, either by the characters or the narrator. Realists see in Lancelot the epitome of the courtly lover. For them, Marie was a leading proponent of the doctrine of *fin'amors*, which was practiced extensively at her court. To illustrate and further this concept, she commissioned Andreas Capellanus to draw up the rules for love in his *De arte honeste amandi* (Art of Loving Nobly) and her favorite poet, Chrétien, to compose a romance whose central theme (*san*) was to be that of the perfect courtly-love relationship. But Chrétien never completed his romance, an indication perhaps that he was not in sympathy with the theme proposed to him by the Countess.

Idealists agree that the subject matter of the *Lancelot* did not appeal to Chrétien, but allege different reasons. Citing the fact that adultery was harshly condemned by the medieval Church, they argue that what we today call "courtly love" would have been recognized as an idolatrous and treasonable passion. John Benton says: "Chrétien has gone out of his way to describe [in the *Lancelot*] behavior he could be sure the courtly audience would condemn. In Chrétien's story the knight who rides in a shameful cart is no casual lover, but one who betrays his lord. . . . If we find Lancelot a sympathetic figure because he was guided by love rather than reason, it is because modern attitudes differ from medieval ones in ways Chrétien could not foresee" (ed. Newman, p. 28). The idea of Lancelot lost in thoughts of love and being unceremoniously unhorsed or jousting behind his back to keep Guinevere in view could only appear ridiculous.

Most realists today will concede a degree of ironic humor in the portrayal of Lancelot, but contend that the question of morality is a moot point: as Moshé Lazar has shown, *fin'amors* (now widely preferred as a term to "courtly love") is an essentially non-Christian concept, neither moral nor immoral, but amoral. Sensitive to the attacks of the idealists, they now downplay the importance of Andreas Capellanus, whose concept of "pure love" has led many commentators astray, and stress the distinctions between periods and works. The love portrayed by Dante or in Chaucer's *Book of the Duchess* is of another period and qualitatively different from that of the troubadours or trouvères. Indeed, love in the poems of the Northern French trouvères is itself different from that of the troubadours. But the contention remains that there was a type of ennobling love which was directly associated with court life during the period. Joan Ferrante says that this love "is the product of a courtly setting and courtly behavior; it is restricted in its formative period to those who participate in court life and therefore can be properly called 'courtly'" (1980, p. 688). For some realists, *Lancelot* remains the classical portrayal of *fin'amors*; for others, it is a tongue-in-cheek critique of an institution which was very real in its day, but of which Chrétien did not approve.

The question of Chrétien and his sources remains vexed. We are not likely ever to be certain of his attitudes toward *fin'amors*, or even if there was such a thing as courtly love. Nor are we likely ever to be able to gauge with precision the extent to which he shaped his original source materials. While it seems undeniable that Celtic stories were present in Chrétien's mind and milieu, it is likewise undeniable that he was no slavish imitator. Beginning with a basic story concept furnished by Marie of Champagne, he fleshed out this tale by drawing upon the skills and background acquired in the Church schools in which he was educated; he may well have employed myths found in classical literature, Christian motifs which were predominant in the thought of his period, or a courtly love theme given him by the Countess. But Chrétien was too skilled a writer and too great an ironist to let any one concept predominate; the resulting subtleties and complexities of his romances have intrigued readers and interpreters throughout the ages.

Editorial Policy for This Text and Translation

The *Chevalier de la Charrete* (Knight of the Cart) was given its name by Chrétien himself in lines 24–25:

> Del Chevalier de la Charrete
> comance Crestïens son livre.

Likewise, Godefroy of Leigni (Lagny), who composed approximately the final thousand lines of the work, wrote at the close of his section:

> Godefroiz de Leigni, li clers,
> a parfinee la Charrete.

Most manuscript explicits also give this title, but the Guiot MS ends: *Ci faut li romans de Lancelot de la Charrete.* For this reason it has become customary to refer to the poem by the dual title, *Lancelot, le Chevalier de la Charrete.* This is unfortunate, for much of the interest of the opening section depends upon the mysterious identity of the unknown knight, and Chrétien employs considerable dramatic and poetic skill in the revelation of his name.

The Knight of the Cart exists in seven manuscripts and fragments, described by Micha (1966), no one of which contains the poem precisely as it was composed by Chrétien:

- A — Chantilly, Musée Condé, 472. Picard-Walloon, late 13th century.
- C — Paris, Bibl. Nationale, 794. Champenois, early 13th century.
- E — Madrid, Escorial, M.III.21. Northern and Western French, early 13th century.
- F — Paris, Bibl. Nationale, 1450. Picard, first half of the 13th century.
- G — Princeton University, Garrett 125. Picard, late 13th century.
- T — Paris, Bibl. Nationale, 12560. Champenois, 13th century.
- V — Rome, Bibl. Vaticana, 1725. Picard, second half of the 13th century.

Scholars are in general agreement that the version of the poem in Bibl. Nationale 794 (C), copied in the early years of the thirteenth century by the Champenois scribe Guiot, is the most reliable redaction of the *Lancelot*. It was copied shortly after the composition of Chrétien's original by a scribe who used the same dialect as the poet. The manuscripts of the *Lancelot* are described by Foerster in the introduction to his 1899 edition. Roques provides a more detailed study of C in his introduction.

Manuscript C was edited in a very conservative manner for the Classiques Français du Moyen Age series in 1958. Roques' edition was considered by many as definitive, replacing the earlier critical edition by Foerster. However, subsequent scholarship has shown that, as good as it may be on the whole, there are nonetheless a number of specific instances in which Guiot betrayed Chrétien. Additionally, in my collation of the manuscript for the present volume, I have been able to correct about a hundred minor, mostly typographical errors which slipped into Roques' text. In the first thousand lines, for example, I have noted errors at 201, 234, 434, 439, 473, 479, 481, 520, 712, 728, 755, 764, 812, 846, 851, 872, 918, 923, and 995. The present edition is based closely on Guiot, but departs from the former in a number of instances in which readings from other manuscripts allow us a better glimpse of Chrétien's purpose. While still essentially dependent upon C for spelling, word order, verb tenses, and the like, I have been considerably less conservative than Roques in emending those passages in which Guiot's version was patently less satisfactory than that of another manuscript. For the emendations I have generally found myself in agreement with the suggestions of Foerster, whose edition, while not perfect, was nonetheless based on all known manuscripts, except the recently discovered Garrett 125. Also of particular use in establishing my text were the notes to Frappier's 1962 translation, Dufournet's 1964 review of that translation, and Micha (1966). To facilitate comparisons, I have retained the line numbers of C used by Roques; lines not in C which I have felt obliged to add are indicated by small letters: 29a, 360a, etc. Major textual divisions, signaled by large capitals in the manuscript, are indicated by indentations in the text and translation. Folio numbers are bracketed and in italics in the right-hand margin.

The entire edition has been checked against a photocopy of the Guiot manuscript. I have taken the accustomed editorial liberties: resolving all abbreviations, including those for numbers; distinguishing *i* from *j* and *u* from *v*; providing punctuation and capitalization where required; supplying an accent for tonic final *e* in words of more than one syllable, and using the diaresis sparingly; dividing words according to current editorial practices rather than relying upon the varying divisions found in the manuscript.

The Textual Notes are designed to answer questions of a textual and interpretive nature and to explain medieval terms and customs which might create some misunderstanding or confusion. All words and expressions reflecting medieval institutions or customs potentially unfamiliar to the modern reader and essential to a proper understanding of the text are presented.

Lancelot was translated into English in 1914 by W.W. Comfort for Everyman's Library. Styles in translation have changed since then, and I have attempted to eliminate the many archaisms introduced by Comfort and to reproduce in verse something of the mood of the original. I have been able to eliminate as well many inconsistencies and inaccuracies introduced by Comfort. In translating, I have attempted to remain as faithful as possible to the original. However, the elliptical nature of Old French syntax, as well as its tendency to separate relative clauses from their antecedents and to use a postpositioned subject, sometimes makes it impossible to give a readable translation if there is too close an attempt to reproduce the original sentence patterns. For examples of these problems, see lines 2894–96, 3828–29 (dangling relative clauses) and 4876–77, 5096–97 (postpositioned subjects). To reduce parataxis and make the lines flow more smoothly in English, I have often omitted *et* (and) at the beginnings of lines. Like other Old French poets, Chrétien made little effort to avoid ambiguity in his use of personal pronouns. Therefore, I have frequently been obliged to provide a proper noun where the Old French has only a pronoun (e.g., at 3222, 3857, 6171, 6224). Old French poets did not couch their stories in a single narrative tense, but switched freely from present to past and back again. I have not attempted to reproduce this trait, which only seems inattentive in English, but have chosen instead to narrate the story exclusively in the past.

There is no way to reproduce in free verse the flowing versification of the octosyllabic rhymed couplet practiced by Chrétien. Particularly difficult are the complex figures of speech which seem to have delighted Chrétien and his contemporaries—such as the chiasmus at line 1402 or the annominatio of lines 4057–63. No translation can do justice to the skill and intricacy of Chrétien's style, but it is hoped that the present one will at least allow the interested reader to become more familiar with one of France's greatest writers.

I have been encouraged and helped throughout this project by many individuals. I particularly wish to acknowledge the numerous happy touches given the translation by my colleagues James I. Wimsatt and Kurth Sprague of the Department of English at the University of Texas. The onerous task of proofreading was aided by Hubert P. Heinen for the English and Jean-Louis Picherit for the Old French. Finally, many constructive suggestions were offered by the Garland General Editor, James J. Wilhelm, who read the entire volume with unusual care. Typing costs were covered in large part by a Special Research Grant from The University Research Institute of the University of Texas. Special thanks go to the Trustees of the Bibliothèque Nationale (Paris), Princeton University Library, and the Pierpont Morgan Library (New York), for permission to reproduce materials from their collections.

Melegant arrives at Arthur's court during mealtime to deliver his challenge to the knights of the Round Table (lines 43–60). From folio 34r of Garrett Manuscript 125 of the Princeton University Library.

Select Bibliography

I. Major Editions

Christian von Troyes. *Sämtliche erhaltene Werke, nach allen bekannten Handschriften herausgegeben von Wendelin Foerster.* 4 vols. Halle: Niemeyer, 1884–99. I (1884) *Cligés*; II (1887) *Der Löwenritter (Yvain)*; III (1890) *Erec und Enide*; IV (1899) *Der Karrenritter (Lancelot) und das Wilhelmsleben (Guillaume d'Angleterre)*. Critical editions based on all MSS known at the time.

Les Romans de Chrétien de Troyes. Classiques français du moyen âge, *80, 84, 86, 89*. Paris: Champion, 1952–64. I (1952) *Erec et Enide*, ed. Mario Roques; II (1957), *Cligés*, ed. Alexandre Micha; III (1958) *Le Chevalier de la Charrete*, ed. Mario Roques; IV (1960) *Le Chevalier au Lion (Yvain)*, ed. Mario Roques. Very conservative editions based on the Guiot manuscript.

Guillaume d'Angleterre. Ed. Maurice Wilmotte. Classiques français du moyen âge, *55*. Paris: Champion, 1927.

Le Roman de Perceval ou, Le Conte du Graal. Ed. William Roach. Textes littéraires français, *71*. Geneva: Droz, 1956.

Zai, Marie-Claire. *Les Chansons courtoises de Chrétien de Troyes.* Berne and Frankfurt: Lang, 1974.

II. Translations of *Lancelot*

Comfort, William W. *Arthurian Romances.* Everyman's Library, *698*. London: Dent; New York: Dutton, 1914; frequent reprints. Includes *Erec et Enide, Cligés, Yvain,* and *Lancelot*. Accurate translations, but in aging Victorian style.

Foucher, Jean-Pierre. *Romans de la Table Ronde: Le Cycle Courtois.* Livre de Poche Classique, *1998*. Paris: Gallimard, 1970. Very unprofessional translations into modern French prose of *Lancelot* and *Yvain*, as well as selections from *Erec et Enide* and *Cligés*.

Frappier, Jean. *Chrétien de Troyes, Le Chevalier de la Charrette (Lancelot): Roman traduit de l'ancien français*. Paris: Champion, 1962; 2nd rev. ed., 1969. Fine translation, with important textual notes (pp. 19–25).

III. Criticism and Study Guides

A. *Guides to Bibliography*

Kelly, Douglas. *Chrétien de Troyes: An Analytic Bibliography*. Research Bibliographies and Checklists, *17*. London: Grant & Cutler, 1976. Virtually complete bibliographic survey under 21 headings with cross-references to the *Bulletin bibliographique de la Société Internationale Arthurienne*.

Shirt, David J. "Chrétien's *Charrette* and Its Critics, 1964–1974." *Modern Language Review*, 73 (1978), 38–50. Reviews 36 books and articles devoted to the poem during the ten years covered.

B. *Full-Length Studies of Chrétien or* Lancelot

Cohen, Gustave. *Un grand romancier d'amour et d'aventure au XII⁰ siècle: Chrétien de Troyes et son oeuvre*. Paris: Boivin, 1931; new ed., 1948.

Frappier, Jean. *Chrétien de Troyes, l'homme et l'oeuvre*. Connaissance des Lettres, *50*. Paris: Hatier, 1957; new rev. ed., 1968. Covers Chrétien and his period, his originality and influence; one chapter devoted to each of the major romances.

Hofer, Stefan. *Chrétien de Troyes: Leben und Werke des altfranzösischen Epikers*. Graz-Köln: Böhlaus, 1954. Studies sources and influences; rejects Celtic influence; prefers early dating. Chapter X (pp. 126–49) covers *Lancelot*.

Holmes, Urban Tigner, Jr. *Chrétien de Troyes*. Twayne's World Authors Series, *94*. New York: Twayne, 1970. Only general introduction in English. After chapters on Chrétien's life and times, there are individual chapters devoted to each romance. Chapter 6 (pp. 87–101) treats *Lancelot*.

Kelly, Douglas. *Sens and Conjointure in the "Chevalier de la Charrette."* The Hague: Mouton, 1966. Reviews research and proposes a coherent structure for *Lancelot*. The *sens* is one of courtly love.

Lacy, Norris. *The Craft of Chrétien de Troyes: An Essay on Narrative Art.* Davis Medieval Texts and Studies, 3. Leiden, The Netherlands: E.J. Brill, 1980. Studies the quest, narrative point of view, and the use of analogy.

Ribard, Jacques. *Le Chevalier de la Charrette: Essai d'interprétation symbolique.* Paris: Nizet, 1972. Lancelot has a Messianic mission. All elements of the poem have symbolic interpretations relating to the "quest for salvation."

Zaddy, Z.P. *Chrétien Studies: Problems of Form and Meaning in "Erec," "Yvain," "Cligés," and the "Charrete."* Glasgow: University of Glasgow Press, 1973. Chapter 5 proposes a tripartite structure of *Lancelot* and emphasizes the coherence of the poem.

C. Briefer Studies of Chrétien and Lancelot

BBSIA: *Bulletin bibliographique de la Société Internationale Arthurienne.*

Brault, Gerard J. "Chrétien de Troyes' *Lancelot*: The Eye and the Heart." *BBSIA*, 24 (1972), 142–53.

Cross, Tom Peete, and William A. Nitze. *Lancelot and Guinevere: A Study on the Origins of Courtly Love.* Chicago: University of Chicago Press, 1930.

Dufournet, Jean. "Chrétien de Troyes: *Le Chevalier de la Charrette.* A propos d'un livre récent." *Le Moyen Age,* 70 (1964), 502–23. Detailed, laudatory review of Frappier's translation.

Foulon, Charles. "Les deux humiliations de Lancelot." *BBSIA,* 8 (1956), 79–90.

Fourquet, Jean. "Le rapport entre l'oeuvre et la source chez Chrétien de Troyes et le problème des sources bretonnes." *Romance Philology,* 9 (1956), 298–312. Chrétien's romances function on two levels: the courtly and the mythic.

Fourrier, Anthime. "Encore la chronologie des oeuvres de Chrétien de Troyes." *BBSIA,* 2 (1950), 69–88. Dates Chrétien's romances in the 1170's.

———. "Retour au 'terminus.'" In *Mélanges Jean Frappier.* Geneva: Droz,

1970, I, 299–311. Argues for the continued acceptance of 1164 as the date for the finalization of the marriage contract between Marie and Henry of Champagne.

Fowler, David C. "L'amour dans le *Lancelot* de Chrétien." *Romania*, *91* (1970), 378–91.

——."Love in Chrétien's *Lancelot*." *Romanic Review*, *63* (1972), 5–14. Sees a mixture of courtly and divine elements, but no clear allegorical structure.

Frappier, Jean. "Le Prologue du *Chevalier de la Charrette* et son interprétation." *Romania*, *93* (1972), 337–79. Response to Rychner's new interpretation.

Gallais, Pierre. Review of Chrétien de Troyes, *Le Chevalier de la Charrette* (*Lancelot*), trans. J. Frappier. *Cahiers de civilisation médiévale*, *6* (1963), 63–66. Proposes changes for Guiot's text in addition to those made by Frappier.

Grigsby, John. "Narrative Voices in Chrétien de Troyes: A Prolegomenon to Dissection." *Romance Philology*, *32* (1979), 261–73.

Holmes, Urban T., Jr. Review of *Chrétien de Troyes, Le Chevalier de la Charrette (Lancelot): Roman traduit de l'ancien français par Jean Frappier*. *Speculum*, *38* (1963), 334–38.

——, and Sister M. Amelia Klenke. *Chrétien, Troyes, and the Grail*. Chapel Hill: University of North Carolina Press, 1959.

Hunt, Tony. "Tradition and Originality in the Prologues of Chrestien de Troyes." *Forum for Modern Language Studies*, *8* (1972), 320–44. Prologues show the influence of Chrétien's Latin schooling, but exploit *topoi* and rhetorical precepts in a highly original manner. Agrees with Rychner in opposing traditional interpretation of lines 21–23 of the *Lancelot* prologue.

——. "Redating Chrestien de Troyes." *BBSIA, 30* (1978), 209–37. Supports a late dating, in the 1180's, following Luttrell.

Kelly, Douglas. "Two Problems in Chrétien's *Charrette*: The Boundary of Gorre and the Use of *Novele*." *Neophilologus*, *48* (1964), 115–21.

Lacy, Norris. "Thematic Structure in the *Charrette*." *L'Esprit Créateur*, *12* (1972), 13–18. Diverse scenes are related by the principle of analogy.

——. "Spatial Form in Medieval Romance." *Yale French Studies*, *51* (1974), 160–69.

Loomis, Roger Sherman. *Arthurian Tradition and Chrétien de Troyes.* New York: Columbia University Press, 1949. Strong proponent of Celtic sources.

Luttrell, Claude A. *The Creation of the First Arthurian Romance: A Quest.* London: Edward Arnold, 1974. Dates Chrétien's romances in the 1180's.

Lyons, Faith. "*Entencion* in Chrétien's *Lancelot.*" *Studies in Philology,* 51 (1954), 425–30.

Maranini, Lorenza. "Queste e amore cortese nel *Chevalier de la Charrette.*" *Rivista di letterature moderne e comparate,* N.S. 2 (1951), 204–23.

Ménard, Philippe. "Un terme de jeu dans le *Chevalier de la Charrette*: le mot *san.*" *Romania,* 91 (1970), 400–05.

———. "Note sur la date du *Chevalier de la Charrette.*" *Romania,* 92 (1971), 118–26.

Micha, Alexandre. "Sur les sources de la *Charrette.*" *Romania,* 71 (1950), 345–58.

———. *La Tradition manuscrite des romans de Chrétien de Troyes.* Geneva: Droz, 1966. Most detailed study of the MS tradition.

Mickel, Emanuel J. "The Theme of Honor in Chrétien's *Lancelot.*" *Zeitschrift für romanische Philologie,* 91 (1975), 243–72.

Misrahi, Jean. "More Light on the Chronology of Chrétien de Troyes." *BBSIA,* 11 (1959), 89–120. Reviews previous scholarship, showing how little solid evidence we have regarding dating.

Nitze, William A. "Sens et matière dans les oeuvres de Chrétien de Troyes." *Romania,* 44 (1915), 14–36.

———. "'Or est venuz qui aunera': A Medieval Dictum." *Modern Language Notes,* 56 (1941), 405-09.

Owen, D.D.R. "Two More Romances by Chrétien de Troyes?" *Romania,* 92 (1971), 246–60. Attributions of two romances proposed here are not generally accepted; see Life of the Author.

Paris, Gaston. "Etudes sur les romans de la Table Ronde: *Lancelot du Lac.*" *Romania,* 10 (1881), 465–96; and *Romania,* 12 (1883), 459–534. Pioneering studies of Chrétien and courtly love; the term *amour courtois* appears in modern scholarhip in *12,* 519.

———. Review of W. Foerster, ed., *Cligés*; rpt. in *Gaston Paris: Mélanges de littérature française du moyen âge.* Ed. Mario Roques. Paris: Champion, 1910.

Rahilly, Leonard J. "Le manuscrit Garrett 125 du *Chevalier de la Charrette* et du *Chevalier au Lion*: un nouveau manuscrit." *Romania*, 94 (1973), 407– 10. Announces discovery of a new illustrated MS.

————. "La tradition manuscrite du *Chevalier de la Charrette* et le manuscrit Garrett 125." *Romania, 95* (1974), 395– 413.

Robertson, D.W., Jr. "Some Medieval Literary Terminology with Special Reference to Chrétien de Troyes." *Studies in Philology, 48* (1951), 669– 92.

Roques, Mario. "Pour l'interprétation du *Chevalier de la Charrete* de Chrétien de Troyes." *Cahiers de Civilisation Médiévale, 1* (1958), 141– 52.

Rychner, Jean. "Le Prologue du *Chevalier de la Charrette*." *Vox Romanica*, 26 (1967), 1– 23. Proposes new interpretation of the prologue. The discussion continues in the following three articles. See also Hunt and Frappier.

————. "Le sujet et la signification du *Chevalier de la Charrette*." *Vox Romanica*, 27 (1968), 50– 76.

————. "Le Prologue du *Chevalier de la Charrette* et l'interprétation du roman." *Mélanges offerts à Rita Lejeune.* Gembloux: Duculot, 1969, II, 1121– 35.

————. "Encore le prologue du *Chevalier de la Charrette*." *Vox Romanica, 31* (1972), 263– 71.

Shirt, David J. "Chrétien de Troyes and the Cart." In *Studies in Medieval Literature and Languages in Memory of Frederick Whitehead.* Manchester University Press, 1973, pp. 279– 301.

————. "Chrétien de Troyes et une coutume anglaise." *Romania, 94* (1973), 178– 95. Gives a balanced summary of the arguments for Chrétien's having visited England; shows further that he had accurate knowledge of a peculiarly English usage of the cart.

————. "Godefroy de Lagny et la composition de la *Charrete*." *Romania, 96* (1975), 27– 52.

————. "How Much of the Lion Can We Put Before the Cart? Further Light on the Chronological Relationship of Chrétien de Troyes' *Lancelot* and *Yvain*." *French Studies, 31* (1977), 1– 17.

Southward, Elaine. "The Unity of Chrétien's *Lancelot*." *Mélanges offerts à Mario Roques*. Paris: Didier, 1953, II, 281–90.

Stone, Herbert K. "Corrections: Le *Karrenritter* de Foerster." *Romania*, 63 (1937), 389–401. Proposes emendations to Foerster's edition.

Taylor, Archer. "'Or est venuz qui aunera' and the English Proverbial Expression 'To Take his Measure.'" *Modern Language Notes*, 65 (1950), 344–45.

Vinaver, Eugène. "Les deux pas de Lancelot." *Mélanges pour Jean Fourquet*. Paris: Klincksieck, 1969, pp. 355–61. Shows that the two lines omitted by Roques in his edition of *Lancelot* are essential to the poem.

———. *A la recherche d'une poétique médiévale*. Paris: Nizet, 1970. Chapter 5 treats Chrétien and *conjointure*.

———. *The Rise of Romance*. New York and Oxford: Oxford University Press, 1971. Chapters 2 and 3 are a fine study of Chrétien's importance.

Wilmotte, Maurice. "Chrétien de Troyes et le conte de *Guillaume d'Angleterre*." *Romania*, 46 (1920), 1–38. Attributes *Guillaume d'Angleterre* to Chrétien with good arguments.

D. *Courtly Love or* Fin'Amors

Benton, John. "Clio and Venus: An Historical View of Medieval Love." In *The Meaning of Courtly Love*. Ed. F.X. Newman. Albany: State University of New York Press, 1968, pp. 19–42.

Ferrante, Joan M. "*Cortes'Amor* in Medieval Texts." *Speculum*, 55 (1980), 686–95. There is a real and essential connection between love and courtliness. "Courtly love" is a valid medieval concept, not merely a nineteenth-century construct.

———, and George D. Economou, eds. *In Pursuit of Perfection*. Port Washington, N.Y.: Kennikat Press, 1975. Well-balanced collection of articles about courtly love by important specialists.

Frappier, Jean. "Le Motif du 'don contraignant' dans la littérature du moyen âge." *Travaux de linguistique et de littérature publiés par le Centre de philologie et de littératures romanes de l'Université de Strasbourg*, 7 (1969), 7–46; rpt. in *Amour Courtois et Table Ronde*. Geneva: Droz, 1973, pp. 225–64.

Lazar, Moshé. *Amour courtois et fin'amors dans la littérature du XIIe siècle*. Paris: Klincksieck, 1964.

Newman, F.X., ed. *The Meaning of Courtly Love*. Albany: State University of New York Press, 1968. A major collection of articles which stresses the belief that "courtly love" is not a medieval concept.

Wind, Bartina. "Ce jeu subtil, l'Amour courtois." *Mélanges offerts à Rita Lejeune*. Gembloux: Duculot, 1969, II, 1257–61.

E. Works of General Interest

Anderson, William. *Castles of Europe from Charlemagne to the Renaissance*. New York: Random House, 1970.

Guiette, Robert. "Symbolisme et 'Senefiance' au moyen âge." *Romanica Gandensia*, 8 (1960), 33–49; rpt. in *Forme et sénéfiance*. Geneva: Droz, 1978, pp. 29–45.

Henry. Albert. *Le Jeu de Saint Nicolas de Jean Bodel*. Brussels: Presses Universitaires, 1962.

Holmes, Urban T., Jr. Review of *Durmart le Galois: Roman arthurien du treizième siècle*, ed. J. Gildea. *Speculum*, 44 (1969), 640–42.

Köhler, Erich. *L'aventure chevaleresque: Idéal et réalité dans le roman courtois*. Paris: Gallimard, 1974.

Koenig, V. Frederic. "'La genealogie Nostre Dame' and the Legend of the Three Mary's." *Romance Philology*, 14 (1961), 207–15.

Loomis, Roger Sherman. *Arthurian Literature in the Middle Ages: A Collaborative History*. Oxford: Clarendon Press, 1959. A general introduction to Arthurian literature stressing Celtic sources and analogues. Each chapter is contributed by an eminent specialist in the area concerned.

Ménard, Philippe. *Manuel du français du moyen âge*. 1. *Syntaxe de l'ancien français*. Bordeaux: SOBODI, 1973.

Moignet, Gérard. *Grammaire de l'ancien français*. Paris: Klincksieck, 1973.

Rychner, Jean, ed. *Les Lais de Marie de France*. Classiques français du moyen âge, 93. Paris: Champion, 1966.

Schultz, Alwin. *Das höfische Leben zur Zeit der Minnesinger*. 2 vols. Leipzig: S. Hirzel, 1889. The classic study of everyday life in the twelfth and thirteenth centuries.

Tobler, A., ed. *Li Proverbe au Vilain. Die Sprichwörter des gemeinen Mannes: altfranzösische Dichtung nach den bisher bekannten Handschriften*. Leipzig: S. Hirzel, 1895.

Tuve, Rosemond. *Allegorical Imagery*. Princeton University Press, 1966.

Lancelot
or, The Knight of the Cart
(Le Chevalier de la Charrete)

LANCELOT

LE CHEVALIER DE LA CHARRETE

Puis que ma dame de Chanpaigne   [27b]
vialt que romans a feire anpraigne,
je l'anprendrai molt volentiers,
come cil qui est suens antiers
de quanqu'il puet el monde feire,   5
sans rien de losange avant treire.
Mes tex s'an poïst antremetre
qui li volsist losenge metre;
si deïst (et jel tesmoignasse)
que ce est la dame qui passe   10
totes celes qui sont vivanz,
si con li funs passe les vanz
qui vante en mai ou en avril.
Par foi, je ne sui mie cil
qui vuelle losangier sa dame;   15
dirai je: "Tant com une jame
vaut de pelles et de sardines,*
vaut la contesse de reïnes?"*
Naie voir; je n'en dirai rien,
s'est il voirs maleoit gré mien;   20
mes tant dirai ge que mialz oevre
ses comandemanz an ceste oevre
que sans ne painne que g'i mete.
Del Chevalier de la Charrete
comance Crestïens son livre;   25
matiere et san li done et livre
la contesse, et il s'antremet
de panser si que rien n'i met
fors sa painne et s'antancïon;
des or comance sa raison.*   29a
Et dit qu'a une Acenssïon   30

17. pailes 28. p. que gueres

LANCELOT

THE KNIGHT OF THE CART

Since my lady of Champagne*
Wishes me to begin a romance,
I shall do so most willingly,
As one who is entirely at her service
In anything he can undertake in this world.   5
I say this without any flattery,
Though another might begin his story
With the desire to flatter her.
He might say (and I would agree)
That she is the lady who surpasses   10
All women who are alive,
Just as the foehn* surpasses the other winds
Which blow in May or April.
Certainly I am not one
Intent upon flattering his lady;   15
Will I say: "As the polished diamond
Eclipses the pearl and the sard,
The countess eclipses queens"?
Indeed not; I'll say nothing of the sort
Though it be true in spite of me.   20
I will say, however, that her command
Has more importance in this work
Than any thought or effort I might put into it.
Chrétien begins his book
About the Knight of the Cart;   25
The source and the meaning are furnished and given him
By the countess, and he strives
Carefully to add nothing
But his effort and diligence;*
Now he begins his story.   29a
On a certain Ascension Day   30

*Asterisks indicate that further information is provided in
the Textual Notes at the end. Asterisks in the translation
refer to explanatory matter; asterisks in the original relate
to textual problems.

3

fu venuz devers Carlĩon*   30a
li rois Artus et tenu ot
cort molt riche a Chamaalot,
si riche com a roi estut.
Aprés mangier ne se remut
li rois d'antre ses conpaignons.   35
Molt ot an la sale barons,
et si fu la reïne ansanble;
si ot avoec aus, ce me sanble,
mainte bele dame cortoise,
bien parlant an lengue françoise;   40
et Kex qui ot servi as tables   *[27c]*
manjoit avoec les conestables.
La ou Kex seoit au mangier,
atant ez vos un chevalier
qui vint a cort molt acesmez,   45
de totes ses armes armez.
Li chevaliers a tel conroi
s'an vint jusque devant le roi
la ou antre ses barons sist;
nel salua pas, einz li dist: 50
"Rois Artus, j'ai en ma prison
de ta terre et de ta meison
chevaliers, dames et puceles;
mes ne t'an di pas les noveles
por ce que jes te vuelle randre,   55
ençois te voel dire et aprandre
que tu n'as force ne avoir
par quoi tu les puisses avoir.
Et saches bien qu'ainsi morras
que ja aidier ne lor porras."   60
Li rois respont qu'il li estuet
sofrir s'amander ne le puet,
mes molt l'an poise duremant.
Lors fet li chevaliers sanblant
qu'aler s'an voelle; si s'an torne; 65
devant le roi plus ne sejorne
et vient jusqu'a l'uis de la sale;
mes les degrez mie n'avale,
einçois s'areste et dit des la:
"Rois, s'a ta cort chevalier a   70
nes un an cui tu te fïasses
que la reïne li osasses
baillier por mener an ce bois
aprés moi la ou ge m'an vois,
par un covant l'i atandrai   75
que les prisons toz te randrai
qui sont an prison an ma terre

31. Artus cort tenue ot 32. riche et bele tant con lui plot

4

King Arthur was in the region near Caerleon*
And held his court
Splendidly at Camelot,
And luxuriant as befitted a king.
After the meal, the king did not stir
From among his companions.   35
Many were the barons in the hall
And the queen was among them;
Also with them, I'm sure,
Were numerous beautiful courtly ladies,
Skillful at conversing in French;   40
And Kay, who'd overseen the feast,
Was eating with those who had served.
While Kay was still at table,
There appeared before them a knight,
Who came to court equipped   45
And fully armed for battle.
Outfitted in such a manner, the knight
Came forward to where the king
Was seated among his barons.
Instead of the customary greeting, he declared: 50
"King Arthur, I hold imprisoned
From your land and household
Knights, ladies, and maidens;
I do not tell you this
Because I intend to return them to you;   55
Rather I wish to tell and inform you
That you have neither wealth enough nor power
By which you might assure their release.
And know you well that you will die
Before you are able to aid them."   60
The king replied that he must
Accept this, if he could not remedy it,
But that it grieved him deeply.
Then the knight acted as though
He wished to leave; he turned   65
And strode from the king
Until he reached the door of the great hall;
But rather than descend the stairs,
He stopped and made this challenge from there:
"Sir, if at your court there is   70
Even one knight in whom you have faith enough
To dare entrust the queen,
To accompany her into the woods
After me where I am going,
I give my oath that I will await him there   75
And will deliver all the prisoners
Who are captive in my land--

5

se il la puet vers moi conquerre
et tant face qu'il l'an ramaint."
Ce oïrent el palés maint,   80
s'an fu la corz tote estormie.
La novele en a Kex oïe
qui avoec les sergenz manjoit;
le mangier leit, si vient tot droit
au roi, si li comance a dire   [27d]
tot autresi come par ire:
"Rois, servi t'ai molt boenemant
par boene foi et lëaumant;
or praing congié, si m'an irai
que jamés ne te servirai;   90
je n'ai volenté ne talant
de toi servir d'ore en avant."
Au roi poise de ce qu'il ot,
mes quant respondre mialz li pot,
si li a dit eneslepas: 95
"Est ce a certes ou a gas?"
Et Kex respont: "Biax sire rois,
je n'ai or mestier de gabois,
einz praing congié trestot a certes.
Je ne vos quier autres dessertes   100
n'autre loier de mon servise;
ensi m'est or volantez prise
que je m'an aille sanz respit."
"Est ce par ire ou par despit,"
fet li rois, "qu'aler an volez?   105
Seneschax, si con vos solez,
soiez a cort et sachiez bien
que je n'ai en cest monde rien
que je, por vostre demorance,
ne vos doigne sanz porloignance."   110
"Sire," fet il, "ce n'a mestier:
ne prandroie pas un setier*
chascun jor d'or fin esmeré."
Ez vos le roi molt desperé,
si est a la reïne alez.   115
"Dame," fet il, "vos ne savez
del seneschal que il me quiert?
Congié demande et dit qu'il n'iert
a ma cort plus; ne sai por coi.
Ce qu'il ne vialt feire por moi   120
fera tost por vostre proiere.
Alez a lui, ma dame chiere;
quant por moi remenoir ne daigne,
proiez li que por vos remaigne
et einz l'an cheez vos as piez,   125
que jamés ne seroie liez
se sa conpaignie perdoie."

6

If he is able to win the queen from me
And succeed in returning her to you."
Many there in the palace heard this   80
And all the court was in turmoil.
Kay, who was eating with the servants,
Heard the news as well;
He left his place, came directly
To the king, and began to say to him   85
As if in anger:
"My king, I have served you well,
In good faith and loyally;
Now I take my leave; I shall go away
And never more will serve you;   90
I have neither will nor desire
To serve you henceforth."
The king was saddened by what he heard,
But when he could reply
He said to him at once: 95
"Is this in truth or jest?"
"Fair King," replied Kay,
"I have no need to jest--
In truth I take my leave.
I ask no further recompense   100
Nor wages for my service;
I have firmly resolved
To depart without delay."
"Is it through anger or spite
That you wish to leave?" asked the king.   105
"Seneschal,* remain at court
As you have in the past, and know full well
That there's nothing I own in all this world
Which--to keep you here--
I'd not give you unhesitatingly."   110
"Sir," he said, "no need for that.
I would not take for each day's stay
A half-liter of purest gold."
In desperation King Arthur
Went to his queen and asked: 115
"My lady, have you no idea
What the seneschal wants from me?
He has asked for leave and says that he will
Quit my court. I know not why.
What he would not do for me   120
He will do at once at your request.
Go to him, my dear lady;
Though he deign not stay for my sake,
Pray him that he stay for yours
And fall at his feet if necessary,   125
For I would never again be happy
If I were to lose his company."

7

Li rois la reïne i anvoie
au seneschal, et ele i va;
avoec les autres le trova,   130
et quant ele vint devant lui,
si li dit: "Kex, a grant enui
me vient--ce sachiez a estros--
ce qu'ai oï dire de vos.
L'an m'a conté, ce poise moi,   135
que partir vos volez del roi.
Don vos vient? et de quel corage?
Ne vos an tieng or mie a sage
ne por cortois, si con ge suel.
Del remenoir proier vos vuel: 140
Kex, remenez, je vos an pri!"
"Dame," fet il, "vostre merci,
mes je ne remanroie mie."
Et la reïne ancor l'an prie
et tuit li chevalier a masse;   145
et Kex li dit qu'ele se lasse
de chose qui rien ne li valt;
et la reïne de si haut
com ele estoit, as piez li chiet.
Kex li prie qu'ele se liet,   150
mes ele dit que nel fera:
jamés ne s'an relevera
tant qu'il otroit sa volenté.
Lors li a Kex acreanté
qu'il remandra, mes que li rois   155
otroit ce qu'il voldra einçois,
et ele meïsmes l'otroit.
"Kex," fet ele, "que que ce soit
et ge et il l'otroierons.
Or an venez, si li dirons   160
que vos estes einsi remés."
Avoec la reïne an va Kes;
si sont devant le roi venu:
"Sire, je ai Keu retenu,"
fet la reïne, "a grant travail: 165
mes par un covant le vos bail
que vos feroiz ce qu'il dira."
Li rois de joie an sopira
et dit que son comandemant
fera, que que il li demant.   170
"Sire," fet il, "ce sachiez dons
que je voel et quex est li dons
don vos m'avez asseüré;
molt m'an tieng a boen eüré
quant je l'avrai, vostre merci: 175

134. dire *repeated*

The king sent the queen
To the seneschal. She went there
And found him with the others;   130
And when she had approached him,
Said: "Kay, know well that
What I have heard told of you
Comes to me as a great shock.
I have been informed, and it saddens me,   135
That you wish to leave the king's service.
What gave you this thought? What feelings compel you?
I no longer consider you wise
And courtly, as once I did.
I would pray you to remain.   140
Kay, I beg of you--stay!"
"My lady," he said, "with your leave,
But I would not stay."
The queen once again implored him,
As did all the knights together with her.   145
Kay replied that she was wasting her strength
Asking for what would not be granted;
Then the queen, in all her majesty,
Fell down at his feet.
Kay begged her to rise,   150
But she replied that she would not do so:
She would never again rise
Until he had granted her desire.
Thereupon Kay promised her
That he would remain, but the king   155
And the queen herself
Must first grant his request.
"Kay," said she, "no matter what it may be,
Both he and I will grant it.
Now come and we shall tell him   160
That on this condition you will remain."
Kay accompanied the queen,
And together they approached the king.
"My lord," said the queen,
"With great effort I have retained Kay;   165
But I bring him to you with the assurance
That you will do whatever he is about to ask."
The king was overjoyed
And promised to grant Kay's request,
No matter what he might demand.*   170
"My lord," said Kay, "know then
What I want and the nature of the gift
Which you have promised me;
I consider myself most fortunate
To gain it by your grace: 175

9

la reïne que je voi ci
m'avez otroiee a baillier,
s'irons aprés le chevalier
qui nos atant an la forest."
Au roi poise et si l'an revest,   180
car einz de rien ne se desdist;
mes iriez et dolanz le fist,
si que bien parut a son volt.
La reïne an repesa molt,
et tuit dïent par la meison   185
qu'orguel, outrage et desreison
avoit Kex demandee et quise.
Et li rois a par la main prise
la reïne, et si li a dit:
"Dame," fet il, "sanz contredit   190
estuet qu'avoec Keu en ailliez."
Et cil dit: "Or la me bailliez
et si n'an dotez ja de rien,
car je la ramanrai molt bien
tote heitiee et tote sainne."   195
Li rois li baille et cil l'an mainne.
Aprés ax deus s'an issent tuit;
n'i a un seul cui molt n'ennuit.
Et sachiez que li seneschax
fu toz armez et ses chevax   200
fu enmi la cort amenez;
uns palefroiz estoit delez,
tex com a reïne covient.
La reïne au palefroi vient,
qui n'estoit braidis ne tiranz;   205
mate et dolante et sopiranz
monte la reïne, et si dist
an bas por ce qu'an ne l'oïst:
"Ha! Amis, se le seüssiez,*
ja ce croi ne l'otroiesiez   210
que Kex me menast un seul pas."
(Molt le cuida avoir dit bas,
mes li cuens Guinables l'oï
qui au monter fu pres de li.)
Au departir si grant duel firent   215
tuit cil et celes qui le virent
con s'ele geüst morte an biere;   [28a]
ne cuident qu'el reveigne arriere
jamés an tretost son aage.
Li seneschax par son outrage   220
l'an mainne la ou cil l'atant;
mes a nelui n'an pesa tant
que del sivre s'antremeïst,

209. Ha rois se vos ce s.   216. loirent

10

You have agreed to entrust to me
The queen whom I see here before me,
And we shall go after the knight
Who awaits us in the forest."
Though it saddened the king, he entrusted her to Kay,   180
For never was he known to break his pledge.
But his anger and pain
Were written clearly on his face.
The queen was likewise saddened
And all those in the household insisted   185
That what Kay had requested and sought
Was proud, rash, and mad.
Arthur took by the hand
His queen and said to her:
"My lady, there is no way   190
To prevent your going with Kay."
"Now trust her to me," said Kay,
"And have no fear of anything,
For I shall easily bring her back
Quite happy and healthy."   195
The king handed her over to Kay, who led her away.
The members of the court followed after the two of them;
There was not a soul who remained unmoved.
You must know that the seneschal
Was fully armed; his horse   200
Was led to the middle of the yard;
Beside it was a palfrey,
As befitted a queen.
The queen approached the palfrey,
Which was neither restive nor high-spirited;   205
Weak, sad, and sighing,
The queen mounted, then said
Beneath her breath for fear she might be heard:
"Ah! My friend, if you knew,
I think you would never permit   210
Kay to lead me even a single step away."
(She thought she had spoken in a low tone,
But she was overheard by Count Guinable,
Who was near her as she mounted.)
At their departure all at court   215
--Man and woman alike--who saw this lamented
As if she were lying dead in a bier;
No one thought that she would return
Ever again in her lifetime.
The seneschal Kay in his rashness   220
Led her to where the knight was waiting;
Yet no one was inspired by his grief
To attempt to follow him,

11

tant que messire Gauvains dist
au roi son oncle en audïence: 225
"Sire," fet il, "molt grant anfance
avez feite et molt m'an mervoil;
mes, se vos creez mon consoil,
tant com il sont ancor si pres
je et vos irïens aprés,   230
et cil qui i voldront venir.
Je ne m'an porroie tenir
qu'aprés n'alasse isnelemant.
Ce ne seroit pas avenant
que nos aprés ax n'alessiens   235
au moins tant que nos seüssiens
que la reïne devandra
et comant Kex s'an contandra."
"Alons i, biax niés," fet li rois.
"Molt avez or dit que cortois;   240
et des qu'anpris avez l'afeire,
comandez les chevax fors treire
et metre frains et anseler,
qu'il n'i ait mes que del monter."
Ja sont li cheval amené,   245
apareillié et anselé;
li rois monte toz primerains,
puis monta messire Gauvains
et tuit li autre qui ainz ainz;
chascuns an volt estre conpainz,   250
si va chascuns si con lui plot:
armé furent de tex i ot,
s'an i ot sanz armes asez.
Messire Gauvains fu armez
et si fist a deus escuiers   255
mener an destre deus destriers.
Et einsi com il aprochoient
vers la forest issir an voient
le cheval Kex, sel reconurent
et virent que les regnes furent   260
del frain ronpues anbedeus.   *[28b]*
Li chevax venoit trestoz seus,
s'ot de sanc tainte l'estriviere
et de la sele fu derriere
li arçons frez et peçoiez.   265
N'i a nul qui n'an soit iriez;
et li uns l'autre an cingne et bote.
Bien loing devant tote la rote
messire Gauvains chevalchoit;
ne tarda gaires quant il voit   270
venir un chevalier le pas
sor un cheval duillant et las,
apantoisant et tressüé.

Until my lord Gawain said
Loudly to his uncle the king: 225
"My lord, it surprises me
That you have done such a foolish thing.
However, if you will accept my advice,
While they are yet so near
You and I should hurry after them,   230
With any others who might wish to come.
I cannot restrain myself
From setting out at once in pursuit.
It would be unseemly
Should we not follow them   235
At least until we know
What will become of the queen
And how well Kay will acquit himself."
"Let us be off, fair nephew," said the king.
"Your words are nobly spoken.   240
Since it is you who have suggested this course,
Order our horses to be brought,
Bridled and saddled
So they will be ready to mount."
The horses were immediately led forth,   245
Well turned out and saddled;
The king mounted first,
My lord Gawain after him,
Then the others as quickly as they could;
Everyone sought to be among the party,   250
And each went as it pleased him:
Some with arms
And many unarmed.
My lord Gawain was armed
And had two squires beside him   255
Leading in hand two destriers.
As they were approaching
The forest, they recognized
Kay's horse coming out
And saw that the reins were   260
Both broken from the bit.
The horse was riderless,
Its stirrup-leathers stained with blood;
The cantle of its saddle
Was broken and in pieces.   265
Everyone was angered;
They nudged one another and exchanged comprehending glances.
My lord Gawain was riding
Well in advance of the others;
It was not long before he saw   270
A knight approaching slowly
On a horse which was sore and tired,
Breathing hard and lathered in sweat.

Li chevaliers a salüé
monseignor Gauvain primerains,   275
et puis lui messire Gauvains.
Et li chevaliers s'arestut,
qui monseignor Gauvain conut,
si dist: "Sire, don ne veez
con mes chevax est tressüez   280
et tex qu'il n'a mes nul mestier?
Et je cuit que cist dui destrier
sont vostre. Or si vos prieroie,
par covant que je vos randroie
le servise et le guerredon,   285
que vos ou a prest ou a don
le quel que soit me baillessiez."
Et cil li dit: "Or choisissiez
des deus le quel que il vos plest."
Mes cil, cui granz besoigne en est,   290
n'ala pas querant le meillor
ne le plus bel ne le graignor,
einz monta tantost sor celui
que il trova plus pres de lui,
si l'a maintenant eslessié.   295
Et cil chiet morz qu'il a lessié,
car molt l'avoit le jor pené
et traveillié et sormené.
Li chevaliers sanz nul arest
s'an vet poignant par la forest,   300
et messire Gauvains aprés
lo siut et chace com angrés
tant qu'il ot un tertre avalé . . .
Et quant il ot grant piece alé,
si retrova mort le destrier   [28c]
qu'il ot doné au chevalier,
et vit molt grant defoleïz
de chevax et grant froisseïz
d'escuz et de lances antor.
Bien resanbla que grant estor   310
de plusors chevaliers i ot;
se li pesa molt et desplot
ce que il n'i avoit esté.
N'i a pas granmant aresté,
einz passe outre grant aleüre   315
tant qu'il revit par avanture
le chevalier tot seul a pié,
tot armé, le hiaume lacié,
l'escu au col, l'espee ceinte.
Si ot une charrete atainte.   320
De ce servoit charrete lores

290. besoigne nest 300. vet armez

14

The knight greeted
My lord Gawain first,   275
And my lord Gawain then returned his greeting.
The knight, who recognized
My lord Gawain, stopped
And said: "My lord, do you not see
How my horse is bathed in sweat   280
And in such state that he is no longer of use?
I believe that these two war-horses
Are yours. Now I would pray you,
With the promise to return you
The service and the favor,   285
Give me one or the other at your choice,
Either as a loan or gift."
Gawain replied: "Choose
Whichever of the two you please."
But the unknown knight, who was in desperate need,   290
Did not take time to choose the better
Nor the more handsome nor the larger;
Rather, he leapt upon that one
Which he found nearest him,
Thus affirming his choice.   295
And that horse he left fell dead,
For that day it had been over-ridden,
Hardspent, and had suffered much.
The knight galloped straightway
Back into the forest,   300
And my lord Gawain followed after
And pursued him vehemently
Until he reached the bottom of a hill . . .*
After he had ridden a great distance
Gawain came upon the war-horse   305
Which he had given the knight. It was dead now.
Gawain saw that the ground had been trampled
By many horses and was strewn
With the fragments of many shields and lances.
It clearly seemed that a pitched battle   310
Had been waged there between many knights;
Gawain was bitterly disappointed
Not to have been present.
He did not tarry long
But passed quickly beyond   315
Until by chance he again caught sight of
That same knight, now alone on foot
Though still fully armed, with helmet laced,
Shield at his neck and sword girded.
He had overtaken a cart.   320
In those days carts were used

don li pilori servent ores;
et en chascune boene vile
ou or en a plus de trois mile
n'en avoit a cel tans que une;   325
et cele estoit a ces comune,
ausi con li pilori sont,
qui traïson ou murtre font,*
et a ces qui sont chanp cheü,
et as larrons qui ont eü   330
autrui avoir par larrecin
ou tolu par force an chemin.
Qui a forfet estoit repris,
s'estoit sor la charrete mis
et menez par totes les rues;   335
s'avoit totes enors perdues,
ne puis n'estoit a cort oïz
ne enorez ne conjoïz.
Por ce qu'a cel tens furent tex
les charretes et si cruex,   340
fu premiers dit: "Quant tu verras
charrete et tu l'ancontreras,
fei croiz sor toi et te sovaigne
de Deu, que max ne t'an avaigne."
Li chevaliers a pié, sanz lance,   345
aprés la charrete s'avance
et voit un nain sor les limons
qui tenoit come charretons
une longue verge an sa main.   [28d]
Et li chevaliers dit au nain: 350
"Nains," fet il, "por Deu, car me di
se tu as veü par ici
passer ma dame la reïne?"
Li nains cuiverz de pute orine
ne l'en vost noveles conter,   355
einz li dist: "Se tu viax monter
sor la charrete que je main,
savoir porras jusqu'a demain
que la reïne est devenue."
Tantost a sa voie tenue   360
qu'il ne l'atant ne pas ne ore;   360a
tant solemant deus pas demore*   360b
li chevaliers que il n'y monte.
Mar le fist et mar en ot honte
que maintenant sus ne sailli,
qu'il s'an tendra por mal bailli.
Mes Reisons, qui d'Amors se part,   365
li dit que del monter se gart;
si le chastie et si l'anseigne

328. A ces qui murtre et larron sont

16

As are pillories now;
Each large town where now there are
More than three thousand carts
In those times had but one.   325
Like our pillories,
It was for all criminals alike,
For all traitors and murderers,
For all those who had lost trials by combat,
And for all those who had stolen   330
Another's possessions by larceny
Or snatched them by force on the highways.
The guilty person was taken
And made to mount in the cart
And led through every street;   335
He thus lost his feudal rights
And was never again heard at court,
Nor invited nor honored there.
Since in those days
Carts were so dreadful,   340
The saying first arose: "Whenever you see
A cart and come upon its path,
Cross yourself and think
Of God, so that evil will not befall you."
The knight, on foot and without his lance,   345
Hurried after the cart
And saw, sitting on its shaft, a dwarf
Who held, as would a driver,
A long switch in his hand.
The knight said to the dwarf: 350
"Dwarf, for God's sake, tell me
If you have seen
My lady the queen pass by this way?"
The uncouth, low-born dwarf
Would give him no information;   355
He said instead: "If you want to get into
This cart I'm driving,
By tomorrow you'll know
What has become of the queen."
The dwarf continued on his way   360
Without slowing down even an instant for the knight,   360a
Who waited but two steps   360b
Before climbing in.
He would regret this moment of hesitation
And be accursed and shamed for it;
Later he would consider himself ill-fortuned.
But Reason, which does not follow Love's command,   365
Told him not to get in,
And chastised and counseled him

17

que rien ne face ne anpreigne
dom il ait honte ne reproche.
N'est pas el cuer, mes an la boche, 370
Reisons qui ce dire li ose;
mes Amors est el cuer anclose
qui li comande et semont
que tost an la charrete mont.
Amors le vialt et il i saut-- 375
que de la honte ne li chaut
puis qu'Amors le comande et vialt.
Et messire Gauvains s'aquialt
aprés la charrete poignant,
et quant il i trueve seant 380
le chevalier, si s'an mervoille.
Puis li dit: "Nains, car me consoille
de la reïne, se tu sez."
Li nains dit: "Se tu tant te hez
con cist chevaliers qui ci siet, 385
monte avoec lui se il te siet,
et je te manrai avoec li."
Quant messire Gauvains l'oï,
si le tint a molt grant folie
et dit qu'il n'i montera mie, 390
car trop vilain change feroit
se charrete a cheval chanjoit.   [28e]
"Mes va quel part que tu voldras
et g'irai la ou tu iras."
    Atant a la voie se metent-- 395
cil chevalche, cil dui charretent,
et ansanble une voie tindrent.
De bas vespre a un chastel vindrent,
et ce sachiez que li chastiax
estoit molt riches et molt biax. 400
Tuit trois antrent par une porte.
Del chevalier que cil aporte
sor la charrete se mervoillent
les genz, mes mie nel consoillent;
einz le huient petit et grant 405
et li veillart et li anfant
parmi les rues a grant hui;
s'ot molt li chevaliers de lui
vilenies et despit dire.
Tuit demandent: "A quel martire 410
sera cist chevaliers randuz?
Iert il escorchiez ou panduz,
noiez ou ars an feu d'espines?

386. *after this line someone has lightly barred through*
Quant messire G. loi   394. voldras

18

Not to do or undertake anything
For which he might gather shame or reproach.
Reason, who dared tell him this,   370
Spoke from the lips, not from the heart;
But Love, which held sway within his heart,
Urged and commanded him
To climb into the cart at once.
Love wished it and he jumped in--   375
The shame mattered not to him
Since Love ruled his action.
My lord Gawain quickly
Spurred on after the cart
And was astonished   380
To find the knight seated in it.
Then he said: "Dwarf, tell me
About the queen, if you know anything."
The dwarf said: "If you think so little of yourself
As this knight sitting here,   385
Then get in beside him if you like
And I'll drive you along with him."
When my lord Gawain heard this,
He thought it was madness
And said that he would not get in,   390
For it would be a poor bargain
To trade a horse for a cart.
"But go wherever you will
And I shall follow after."
    So they set off on their way--   395
The one on horseback, the two others in the cart,
All on the same path.
About nightfall they came to a fortified town
Which, I assure you,
Was exceedingly strong and beautiful.   400
All three entered through a gate.
The people wondered
At the knight in the dwarf's cart,
But did not hide their feelings--
Great and small, old and young,   405
All mocked him loudly
As he was borne through the streets;
The knight heard many a vile
And scornful word at his expense.
Everyone questioned: "To what death   410
Will this knight be put?
Will he be flayed or hanged,
Drowned or burned upon a fire of thorns?

Di, nains, di--tu qui le traïnes--
a quel forfet fu il trovez?   415
Est il de larrecin provez?
Est il murtriers? ou chanp cheüz?"
Et li nains s'est adés teüz
qu'il ne respont ne un ne el.
Le chevalier mainne a l'ostel,   420
et Gauvains siut adés le nain
vers une tor qui ert a plain,
qui delez la vile seoit.
D'autre part praerie avoit
et d'autre part estoit assise   425
la torz sor une roche bise,
haute et tranchiee contre val.
Aprés la charrete, a cheval
entre Gauvains dedanz la tor.
An la sale ont de bel ator   430
une dameisele ancontree,
n'avoit si bele an la contree;
et voient venir deus puceles
avoeques li, gentes et beles.
Tot maintenant que eles virent   435
monseignor Gauvain, si li firent   [28f]
grant joie et si le salüerent
et del chevalier demanderent:
"Nains, qu'a cist chevaliers mesfet
que tu mainnes come contret?"   440
Cil ne lor an vialt reison rendre;
einz fet le chevalier descendre
de la charrete, si s'an va;
ne sorent ou il s'an ala.
Et messire Gauvains descent;   445
atant vienent vaslet avant
qui anbedeus les desarmerent.
Deus mantiax veirs qu'il afublerent
fist la dameisele aporter.
Quant il fu ore de soper,   450
li mangiers fu bien atornez.
La dameisele sist delez
monseignor Gauvain au mangier.
Por neant volsissent changier
lor ostel por querre meillor,   455
car molt lor i fist grant enor
et conpeignie boene et bele
tote la nuit la dameisele.
    Qant il orent assez mangié,
dui lit furent apareillié   460
anmi la sale haut et lonc;*

461. En une s.

20

Say, dwarf, tell us--you're driving him--
Of what is he guilty?   415
Is he convicted of theft?
Is he a murderer? Did he lose in single combat?"
The dwarf held his silence
And answered none of them.
Followed constantly by Gawain,   420
The dwarf led the knight to his lodgings,
A tower keep which was straight ahead
And on the opposite side of the town.
Meadows stretched out
Beyond where the keep stood   425
On a high granite cliff
Which fell sharply off into the valley.
Gawain, on horseback,
Followed the cart into the keep.
In the great hall they met   430
A richly dressed girl,
The fairest in all the land.
Accompanying her they saw
Two comely and beautiful maidens.
As soon as the maidens saw   435
My lord Gawain,
They greeted him warmly
And inquired about the other knight:
"Dwarf, what ill has this knight done
Whom you drive like a cripple?"   440
Not deigning to answer,
He made the knight get down
From the cart, then left;
No one knew where he went.
My lord Gawain dismounted,   445
Then several valets came forward
To relieve both knights of their armor.
The girl had two miniver-lined cloaks
Brought forward for them to wear.
When the hour for supper came,   450
The food was splendidly arrayed.
The girl sat at table
Beside my lord Gawain.
Nothing would have made them wish to change
Their lodging to seek better,   455
For the girl did them great honor
And gave them fair and pleasant company
All through that evening.*
    After they had eaten their fill,
Two long, high beds   460
Were prepared in the hall;

21

et s'en ot un autre selonc,
plus bel des autres et plus riche,
car--si con li contes afiche--
il i avoit tot le delit   465
qu'an seüst deviser an lit.
Quant del couchier fu tans et leus,
la dameisele prist andeus
ses ostes qu'ele ot ostelez;
deus liz molt biax et lons et lez   470
lor mostre, et dit: "A oés voz cors
sont fet cist dui lit ça defors;
mes an cest lit qui est deça
ne gist qui desservi ne l'a.
Ne fu pas fez cist a voz cors."   475
Li chevaliers li respont lors
(cil qui sor la charrete vint)
qu'a desdaing et a despit tint
la desfanse a la dameisele.
"Dites moi," fet il, "la querele   [29a]
por coi cist liz est an desfanse."
Cele respondi, pas ne panse,
qui en ere apansee bien:
"A vos," fet ele, "ne tient rien
del demander ne de l'anquerre.   485
Honiz est chevaliers an terre
puis qu'il a esté an charrete;
si n'est pas droiz qu'il s'antremete
de ce don vos m'avez requise,
entesmes ce que il i gise,   490
qu'il le porroit tost conparer.
Ne ge ne l'ai pas fet parer
si richemant por vos colchier.
Vos le conparriez molt chier
se il vos venoit nes an pans."   495
"Ce verroiz vos," fet il, "par tans."
"Jel verrai?"--"Voire."--"Or i parra!"
"Je ne sai qui le conparra,"
fet li chevaliers," par mon chief.
Cui qu'il enuit ne cui soit grief,   500
an cestui lit voel ge jesir
et reposer tot a leisir."
    Maintenant qu'il fu deschauciez,
el lit, qui fu lons et hauciez
plus des autres deus demie aune,   505
se couche soz un samit jaune,
un covertor d'or estelé.*
N'estoit mie de veir pelé
la forreüre, ainz ert de sables;

484. taint 500. t *of* soit *added above line* 506. sor

Alongside these was a third bed,
More resplendent and richer than the others,
For--as the tale affirms--
It had all the perfections   465
One could devise for a bed.
When the hour came to retire,
The girl took both
Of the guests to whom she had given lodging;
She showed them the two spacious, comfortable beds,   470
Saying: "These two beds out here
Are made up for you;
But in this third bed nearest us
Only the one who has earned the right may sleep.
It was not prepared for you."   475
The knight (he who had arrived in the cart)
Replied thereupon
That he was disdainful and cared not at all
For the girl's command.
"Tell me," he said, "why   480
This bed is forbidden."
The girl, having anticipated this question,
Replied without hesitation:
"It is not," she said, "for you
To ask or inquire.   485
A knight who has ridden in a cart
Is shamed throughout the land;
He has not the right to be concerned
With what you have asked about,
And especially has no right to lie herein,   490
For he might soon regret it.
Nor did I have it arrayed
So splendidly for you to lie upon.
You would pay very dearly
If you were even to think of such."   495
"You will see about that," he said, "in due time."
"Will I?"--"Yes."--"Then let us see."
"By my head, I do not know
Who will pay dearly," said the knight.
"Whether you like it or not,   500
Here in this bed I intend to lie
And repose at my ease."
    As soon as he had removed his armor
He got into bed, which was half an ell* longer
And higher than the other two,   505
And lay down beneath a gold-starred
Coverlet of yellow silk.
The fur which lined it
Was not skinned miniver, but sable;

23

bien fust a oés un roi metables   510
li covertors qu'il ot sor lui.
Li liz ne fu mie de glui
ne de paille ne de viez nates.
A mie nuit de vers les lates
vint une lance come foudre,   515
le fer desoz, et cuida coudre
le chevalier parmi les flans
au covertor et as dras blans
et au lit la ou il gisoit.
En la lance un panon avoit   520
qui estoit toz de feu espris;
el covertor est li feus pris
et es dras et el lit a masse.
Et li fers de la lance passe   [29b]
au chevalier lez le costé,   525
si qu'il li a del cuir osté
un po, mes n'est mie bleciez.
Et li chevaliers s'est dreciez,
s'estaint le feu et prant la lance;
enmi la sale la balance.   530
Ne por ce son lit ne guerpi,
einz se recoucha et dormi
tot autresi seüremant
com il ot fet premieremant.
    L'andemain par matin, au jor,   535
la dameisele de la tor
lor ot fet messe apareillier,
ses fist lever et esveillier.
Quant an lor ot messe chantee,
as fenestres devers la pree   540
s'an vint li chevaliers pansis
(cil qui sor la charrete ot sis)
et esgardoit aval les prez.
A l'autre fenestre delez
estoit la pucele venue,   545
si l'i ot a consoil tenue
messire Gauvains an requoi
une piece. Ne sai de quoi;
ne sai don les paroles furent.
Mes tant sor la fenestre jurent   550
qu'aval les prez lez la riviere
an virent porter une biere;
s'avoit dedanz un chevalier,
et delez ot duel grant et fier
que trois dameiseles feisoient.   555
Aprés la biere venir voient
une rote, et devant venoit
uns granz chevaliers qui menoit
une bele dame a senestre.

The coverlet he had over him 510
Was suited for a king.
The mattress was not thatch,
Nor straw, nor old matting.
Just at midnight from the rafters
Came a lance like a lightning bolt 515
Point first, and nearly pinned
The knight through his flanks
To the coverlet, to the white sheets,
And to the bed where he was lying.
On the lance was a pennon 520
That was all ablaze;
It set afire the coverlet,
The sheets, and the whole bed.
The iron tip of the lance grazed
The knight's side; 525
It removed a little skin,
But he was not actually wounded.
The knight sat up,
Put out the flame, then grabbed the lance
And hurled it to the middle of the hall. 530
For all this he did not leave the bed;
Instead he lay back down and slept
Just as soundly
As he had been sleeping before.
   The next morning at daybreak 535
The girl of the keep
Had preparations made for Mass,
Then awoke the knights and bade them rise.
When Mass had been celebrated for them,
The knight (he who had been seated in the cart) 540
Came to the window which overlooked the meadow
And gazed worriedly
Out across the fields below.
The girl had come
To the window nearby 545
Where my lord Gawain
Spoke with her a while in private.
I assure you that I
Do not know what was said.
But while they were leaning on the window ledge 550
They saw a bier being carried
Alongside the river in the fields below;
A knight was lying in it,
And beside it three girls
Were weeping bitterly. 555
Behind the bier they saw coming
A crowd, at the head of which rode
A tall knight escorting
A beautiful lady riding on his left.

25

Li chevaliers de la fenestre   560
conut que c'estoit la reïne;
de l'esgarder onques ne fine,
molt antentis et molt li plot,
au plus longuemant que il pot.
Et quant plus ne la pot veoir,   565
si se vost jus lessier cheoir
et trebuchier aval son cors;
et ja estoit demis defors   [29c]
quant messire Gauvains le vit;
sel trait arrieres, se li dit: 570
"Merci, sire, soiez an pes!
Por Deu nel vos pansez jamés
que vos faciez tel desverie;
a grant tort haez vostre vie."
"Mes a droit," fet la dameisele.   575
"Don n'iert seüe la novele
par tot de la maleürté
qu'il a en la charrete esté?
Bien doit voloir qu'il fust ocis,
que mialz valdroit il morz que vis.   580
Sa vie est desormés honteuse
et despite et maleüreuse."
Atant lor armes demanderent
li chevalier, et si s'armerent.
Et lors corteisie et proesce   585
fist la dameisele et largesce;
que, quant ele ot asez gabé
le chevalier et ranponé,
si li dona cheval et lance
par amor et par acordance.   590
Li chevalier congié ont pris
come cortois et bien apris
a la dameisele, et si l'ont
salüee; puis si s'an vont
si con la rote aler an virent;   595
mes si fors del chastel issirent
c'onques nus nes i aparla.
Isnelemant s'an vont par la
ou la reïne orent veüe;
n'ont pas la rote aconseüe,   600
qu'il s'an aloient eslessié.
Des prez antrent an un plessié
et truevent un chemin ferré.
S'ont tant par la forest erré
qu'il pot estre prime de jor,   605
et lors ont en un quarrefor
une dameisele trovee.

565. quant il ne 595. route

26

The knight at the other window   560
Recognized that it was the queen;
As long as she was in view
He gazed attentively
And with pleasure at her.
When he was no longer able to see her   565
He would gladly have cast himself
Down to shatter his body below.
He was already half out the window
When my lord Gawain saw him and,
After dragging him back, said to him: 570
"For pity's sake, sir, be calm!
For the love of God never think
Such foolish thoughts again;
It is very wrong to despise your life."
"No, it is right he should," said the girl,   575
"For will not the news
Of his disgrace in the cart
Be known by all?
He should certainly want to be killed,
For he is better off dead than living.   580
Henceforth his life is shamed,
Scorned, and wretched."
Thereupon the knights asked
For their armor, which they donned.
The girl acted properly toward them,   585
With courtesy and generosity.
Now that she had mocked the knight
And ridiculed him enough,
She gave him a horse and lance
As token of her esteem and sympathy.   590
With proper courtesy
The knights took leave
Of the girl. Having first
Thanked her, they then set off
In the direction they had seen the crowd taking   595
And were able to pass through the castle yard
Without anyone speaking to them.
As quickly as possible they rode
To where they had seen the queen;
But they were unable to overtake the crowd,   600
For it was moving along at a rapid pace.
Beyond the fields they entered into an enclosed area
And found a beaten path.
They rode along in the forest
Until near prime,   605
When at a crossroads
They came upon a girl.

Si l'ont anbedui salüee,
et chascuns li requiert et prie,
s'ele le set, qu'ele lor die   610
ou la reïne an est menee.
Cele respont come senee,   [29d]
et dit: "Bien vos savroie metre,
tant me porrïez vos prometre,
el droit chemin et an la voie,   615
et la terre vos nomeroie
et le chevalier qui l'en mainne.
Mes molt i covendroit grant painne
qui an la terre antrer voldroit!
Einz qu'il i fust molt se doldroit."   620
Et messire Gauvains li dist;
"Dameisele, se Dex m'aïst,
je vos an promet a devise
que je mete an vostre servise
quant vos pleira tot mon pooir,   625
mes que vos m'an dites le voir."
Et cil qui fu sor la charrete
ne dit pas que il l'an promete
tot son pooir, einçois afiche
(come cil cui Amors fet riche   630
et puissant et hardi par tot)
que, sanz arest et sanz redot,
quanqu'ele voldra li promet
et toz an son voloir se met.
"Donc le vos dirai ge," fet ele.   635
Lors lor conte la dameisele:
"Par foi, seignor, Meleaganz,
uns chevaliers molt forz et granz,
filz le roi de Gorre, l'a prise
et si l'a el rëaume mise   640
don nus estranges ne retorne,
mes par force el païs sejorne
an servitune et an essil."
Et lors li redemande cil:
"Dameisele, ou est cele terre?   645
Ou porrons nos la voie querre?"
Cele respont: "Bien le savroiz,
mes--ce sachiez--molt i avroiz
anconbriers et felons trespas,
que de legier n'i antre an pas   650
se par le congié le roi non:
li rois Bademaguz a non.
Si puet l'en antrer totevoies
par deus molt perilleuses voies
et par deus molt felons passages.   [29e]

611. *repeated at top of [29d]*   650. an *added above line*

28

Both greeted her
And each implored and prayed her
To tell them, if she knew,   610
Where the queen had been taken.
She replied fittingly,
Saying: "If you are able
To promise me enough I can put you
On the road and in the right direction   615
And can name for you the land where she is going
And the knight who is taking her.
But whoever would wish to enter into that land
Must undergo great tribulations.
He will suffer much before arriving there."   620
Said my lord Gawain to her:
"So help me God, Miss,
I pledge my word
That if it should please you
I shall put all my strength into your service,   625
If only you will tell me the truth."
The knight who had ridden in the cart
Did not say that he pledged her
All his strength, but rather swore
(Like one whom Love has made powerful   630
And strong and bold for any endeavor)
To do, without hesitation or fear,
Anything she might wish
And to be entirely at her command in everything.
"Then I shall tell you," said she.   635
The girl spoke to them as follows:
"By my faith, lords, Meleagant,
A huge and mighty knight,
Son of the King of Gorre,* has carried her off
And taken her into the kingdom   640
From whence no foreigner returns,
But is forced to remain in that land
In servitude and exile."
Then the knight asked further:
"Miss, where is this land?   645
Where can we find the road which leads there?"
"You will be told," she replied,
"But you may be sure that you will encounter
Difficulties and treacherous passes,
For it is no easy matter to enter   650
Without permission of the king
Who is called Bademagu.
Nonetheless, one can enter therein
By two extremely perilous ways
And by two exceptionally treacherous passes.   655

29

Li uns a non: li Ponz Evages,
por ce que soz eve est li ponz,
et s'a des le pont jusqu'au fonz
autant desoz come desus,
ne de ça moins ne de la plus,   660
einz est li ponz tot droit en mi;
et si n'a que pié et demi
de lé et autretant d'espés.
Bien fet a refuser cist mes,
et s'est ce li moins perilleus;   665
mes il a assez antre deus
avantures don je me tes.
Li autre ponz est plus malvés
et est plus perilleus assez
qu'ainz par home ne fu passez,   670
qu'il est com espee tranchanz;
et por ce trestotes les genz
l'apelent: le Pont de l'Espee.
La verité vos ai contee
de tant con dire vos an puis."   675
Et cil li redemande puis:
"Dameisele, se vos daigniez,
ces deus voies nos anseigniez."
Et la dameisele respont:
"Vez ci la droite voie au Pont   680
desoz Eve, et cele de la
droit au Pont de l'Espee an va."
Et lors a dit li chevaliers,
cil qui ot esté charretiers;
"Sire, je vos part sanz rancune: 685
prenez de ces deus voies l'une,
et l'autre quite me clamez;
prenez celi que mialz amez."
"Par foi," fet messire Gauvains,
"molt est perilleus et grevains   690
li uns et li autres passages.
Del prandre ne puis estre sages,
je ne sai preu le quel je praigne;
mes n'est pas droiz qu'an moi remaingne
quant parti m'an avez le geu: 695
au Pont desoz Eve me veu."
"Donc est il droiz que je m'an voise
au Pont de l'Espee sanz noise,"
fet l'autres, "et je m'i otroi."   [29f]
Atant se departent tuit troi,   700
s'a li uns l'autre comandé
molt deboneiremant a Dé.
Et quant ele aler les an voit,

686. deus *missing in MS*

30

One is named: The Underwater Bridge,
Because the bridge is below the water,
With as much running below
The bridge as above,
Neither more nor less,   660
For the bridge is precisely in the middle;
And it is but a foot and a half
In width and of equal thickness.
This choice is certainly to be shunned,
Yet it is the less dangerous;   665
And there are many perils besides
About which I say nothing.
The other bridge is more difficult
And so much more dangerous
That it has never been crossed by man,   670
For it is like a trenchant sword;
Therefore everyone
Calls it: The Sword Bridge.
I have told you the truth
As far as I can give it to you."   675
Then he bid her further:
"Miss, would you please deign
To show us these two ways?"
And the girl replied:
"This is the direct way to the   680
Underwater Bridge, and that way
Goes straight to the Sword Bridge."
Thereupon the knight
Who had been driven in the cart said:
"Sir, I willingly share with you: 685
Choose one of these two ways
And leave me the other;
Take whichever you prefer."
"In faith," said my lord Gawain,
"Both passages are   690
Exceedingly perilous and difficult.
I cannot choose wisely
And hardly know which to take;
But it is not right that I should delay
When you have offered me the choice: 695
I take the Underwater Bridge."
"Then it is right that I go
To the Sword Bridge without complaint,"
Said the other, "which I agree to do."
The three then parted,   700
Commending one another
Gently to God's care.
When the girl saw them riding off

31

si dit: "Chascuns de vos me doit
un guerredon a mon gré randre   705
quele ore que jel voldrai prandre;
gardez, ne l'obliez vos mie."
"Nel ferons nos, voir, dolce amie,"
font li chevalier anbedui;
atant s'an va chascuns par lui.   710
Et cil de la charrete panse
con cil qui force ne desfanse
n'a vers Amors qui le justise;
et ses pansers est de tel guise
que lui meïsmes en oblie;   715
ne set s'il est, ou s'il n'est mie;
ne ne li manbre de son non;
ne set s'il est armez ou non,
ne set ou va, ne set don vient.
De rien nule ne li sovient   720
fors d'une seule, et por celi
a mis les autres en obli;
a cele seule panse tant
qu'il n'ot ne voit ne rien n'antant.
Et ses chevax molt tost l'en porte,   725
que ne vet mie voie torte,
mes la meillor et la plus droite;
et tant par avanture esploite
qu'an une lande l'a porté.
An cele lande avoit un gué   730
et d'autre part armez estoit
uns chevaliers qui le gardoit;
s'ert une dameisele o soi
venue sor un palefroi.
Ja estoit prés de none basse,   735
n'ancor ne se remuet ne lasse
li chevaliers de son panser.
Li chevax voit et bel et cler
le gué, qui molt grant soif avoit;
vers l'eve cort quant il la voit.   740
Et cil qui fu de l'autre part
s'escrie: "Chevaliers, ge gart
le gué, si le vos contredi!"   [30a]
Cil ne l'antant ne ne l'oï,
car ses pansers ne li leissa;   745
et totesvoies s'esleissa
li chevax vers l'eve molt tost.
Cil li escrie que il l'ost:
"Lai le gué, si feras que sages,
que la n'est mie li passages!"   750
Et jure le cuer de son vantre
qu'il le ferra se il i antre.*
Mes li chevaliers ne l'ot mie,   752a

32

She said: "Each of you must grant me
A favor at my choosing,   705
Whenever I request it;
Take care not to forget that."
"In truth, we'll not forget, fair friend,"
The two knights replied.
They then went their separate ways;   710
The Knight of the Cart was lost in thought,
A man with no strength or defense
Against Love, who torments him;
His meditation was so deep
That he forgot his own identity;   715
He was uncertain whether he truly existed or not;
He was unable to recall his own name;
He did not know if he were armed or not,
Nor where he went nor whence he came.
He remembered nothing at all   720
Save one creature, for whom
He forgot all others;
He was so intent upon her alone
That he did not hear, or see, or attend to anything.
His horse carried him quickly along,   725
Following not the crooked way,
But taking the better and more direct path;
Thus unguided it bore him
Onto a heath.
In this heath was a ford,   730
And beyond the ford was an armed
Knight who guarded it;
With him was a girl
Who had come on a palfrey.
Though by this time it was mid-afternoon,   735
Our knight had not grown weary
Of his unceasing reflections.
His horse, by now quite thirsty,
Saw the clear good water
And galloped toward the ford.   740
From the other side the guardian
Cried out: "Knight, I guard
The ford and forbid you to cross it!"
Still deep in thought,
Our knight did not hear or pay attention;   745
And all the while his horse
Was hastening toward the water.
The guard cried out loudly enough to be heard:
"You will do wisely not to take the ford,
For that is not the way to cross!"   750
And he swore by the heart within his breast
That he would strike him if he entered the ford.
Yet the knight heard him not,   752a

et cil tierce foiz li escrie:
"Chevalier, n'antrez mie el gué
sor ma desfense et sor mon gré,
que par mon chief je vos ferrai
si tost come el gué vos verrai!" 752f
Cil panse tant qu'il ne l'ot pas;
et li chevax eneslepas
saut an l'eve et del chanp se soivre, 755
par grant talant comance a boivre.
Et cil dit qu'il le conparra,
ja li escuz ne l'an garra
ne li haubers qu'il a el dos.
Lors met le cheval es galos 760
et des galoz el cors l'anbat,
et fiert celui si qu'il l'abat
enmi le gué tot estandu
que il li avoit desfandu.
Si li cheï tot a un vol 765
la lance et li escuz del col.
Quant cil sant l'eve, si tressaut;
toz estormiz an estant saut
ausi come cil qui s'esvoille;
s'ot et si voit et se mervoille 770
qui puet estre qui l'a feru.
Lors a le chevalier veü,
si li cria: "Vasax, por coi
m'avez feru--dites le moi--
quant devant moi ne vos savoie 775
ne rien mesfet ne vos avoie?"
"Par foi, si aviez," fet cil.
"Don ne m'eüstes vos molt vil
quant je le gué vos contredis
trois foiees et si vos dis 780
au plus haut que je poi crier?
Bien vos oïstes desfïer
au moins, fet cil, deus foiz ou trois,
et si antrastes sor mon pois,
et bien dis que je vos ferroie 785
tantost qu'an l'eve vos verroie."
Li chevaliers respont adonques: [30b]
"Dahez ait qui vos oï onques
ne vit onques mes, qui je soie!
Bien puet estre--mes je pansoie-- 790
que le gué me contredeïstes.
Bien sachiez que mar le feïstes
se ge au frain une des mains
vos pooie tenir au mains."
Et cil respont: "Qu'an avandroit 795

792. mar me feristes

34

So he shouted to him a third time:
"Knight, do not enter the ford
Against my order and my desire,
Or by my head I'll strike you
The moment I see you there!"   752f
The knight, still lost in his meditations, heard nothing.
His horse jumped quickly
Into the water, freed himself from the bit,   755
And began to drink thirstily.
The guard swore that the knight would pay for this
And that neither his shield
Nor the hauberk* on his back would ever save him.
He urged his horse to a gallop   760
And from the gallop to a run,
And struck the knight from his mount
Flat into the ford that
He had forbidden him to cross.
The knight's lance fell into the stream   765
And his shield flew from round his neck.*
The cold water awakened him with a shock;
He leapt startled to his feet
Like a dreamer from his sleep.
He regained his sight and hearing and wondered   770
Who could have struck him.
He then saw the guard,
And shouted to him: "Varlet, tell me
Why you struck me
When I was unaware of your presence   775
And had done you no wrong."
"In faith, you have indeed," he answered.
"Did you not scorn me
When I forbade you three times to cross
The ford and shouted this   780
As loudly as I could?
You certainly heard me warn you
At least two or three times,
Yet you entered in spite of me,
And I said that I would strike you   785
As soon as I saw you in the water."
Upon that the knight replied:
"May I be damned if ever
I heard you or if ever before I saw you!
It's quite possible--but I was deep in thought--   790
That you did warn me not to cross the ford.
Be assured that you will regret it
If I can get but one hand
On your reins."
He replied: "What good would that bring you?   795

Tenir me porras orandroit
au frain, se tu m'i oses prandre.
Je ne pris pas plain poing de cendre
ta menace ne ton orguel!"
Et cil respont: "Je mialz ne vuel: 800
que qu'il an deüst avenir,
je t'i voldroie ja tenir."
Lors vient li chevaliers avant
enmi le gué; et cil le prant
par la resne a la main senestre   805
et par la cuisse a la main destre.
Sel sache et tire et si l'estraint
si durement que cil se plaint,
qu'il li sanble que tote fors
li traie la cuisse del cors.   810
Se li prie que il le lest,
et dit: "Chevaliers, se toi plest
a moi conbatre par igal,
pran ton escu et ton cheval
et ta lance, si joste a moi."   815
Cil respont: "Non ferai, par foi,
que je cuit que tu t'an fuiroies
tantost qu'eschapez me seroies."
Quant cil l'oï, s'en ot grant honte,
si li ra dit: "Chevaliers, monte   820
sor ton cheval seüremant,
et je te creant lëaumant
que je ne ganchisse ne fuie,
Honte m'as dite, si m'enuie."
Et cil li respont autre foiz: 825
"Einz m'an iert plevie la foiz:
se vuel que tu le me plevisses
que tu ne fuies ne ganchisses,
et que tu ne me tocheras
ne vers moi ne t'aprocheras   830
tant que tu me verras monté.   [30c]
Si t'avrai fet molt grant bonté
quant je te tieng, se ge te les."
Cil li plevist, qu'il n'an puet mes.
Et quant il en ot la fïance,   835
si prant son escu et sa lance
qui par le gué flotant aloient
et totesvoies s'avaloient,
s'estoient ja molt loing aval.
Puis revet prendre son cheval;   840
quant il l'ot pris et montez fu,
par les enarmes prant l'escu
et met la lance sor lo fautre;
puis point li uns ancontre l'autre
tant con cheval lor poent randre.   845

36

Go ahead and grab
My reins if you dare.
I don't give a fistful of ashes
For your haughty threats!"
He replied: "I'd like nothing better   800
Than to seize you now,
No matter what may come of it."
Then the guardian advanced
To the middle of the ford. The unknown knight grabbed
The reins with his left hand   805
And a leg with the right.
He tugged and dragged and pulled him so
That the guard cried out,
For it seemed to him that his leg
Was being pulled from his body.   810
He implored him to cease,
Saying: "Knight, if it pleases you
To fight me on equal terms,
Take your shield, your horse,
And your lance, and joust with me."   815
"I'll not do it, upon my word,
For I think you will try to run away
As soon as you are loose from my grip."
When the other heard this, he was greatly shamed
And answered: "Sir knight, mount   820
Your horse and have no fear,
For I pledge you loyally
That I shall neither flinch nor flee.
What you have said is shameful and offends me."
The unknown knight replied: 825
"First you will pledge your word:
I want you to swear to me
That you will neither flinch nor flee,
And that you will not touch
Or approach me   830
Until you see me upon my horse.
Indeed I shall have been extremely generous toward you
If I set you free, since now I have you."
The guardian of the ford could do nothing but give his oath.
When the knight heard his pledge,   835
He went after his shield and lance
Which had been floating in the ford,
Going along with the current,
And were by now a good distance downstream.
Then he returned to get his horse;   840
When he had overtaken it and remounted,
He took the shield by the straps*
And braced the lance against the saddletree;
Then the two spurred toward each other
As fast as their steeds could carry them.   845

37

Et cil qui le gué dut desfandre
l'autre premieremant requiert
et si tres duremant le fiert
que sa lance a estros peçoie.
Et cil fiert lui si qu'il l'envoie   850
el gué tot plat desoz le flot,
si que l'eve sor lui reclot.
Puis se trest arriers et descent,
car il an cuidoit bien tex cent
devant lui mener et chacier.   855
Del fuerre treit le brant d'acier
et cil saut sus, si treit le suen
qu'il avoit flanbeant et buen.
Si s'antrevienent cors a cors;
les escuz ou reluist li ors   860
traient avant et si s'an cuevrent;
les espees bien i aoevrent,
qu'eles ne finent ne reposent;
molt granz cos antredoner s'osent
tant que la bataille a ce monte   865
qu'an son cuer en a molt grant honte
li chevaliers de la charrete,
et dit que mal randra la dete
de la voie qu'il a enprise
quant il si longue piece a mise   870
a conquerre un seul chevalier.
S'il an trovast en un val hier
tex sen, ne croit il pas ne panse
qu'il eüssent vers lui desfanse,
s'an est molt dolanz et iriez   [30d]
quant il est ja si anpiriez
qu'il pert ses cos et le jor gaste.
Lors li cort sore et si le haste
tant que cil li ganchist et fuit;
le gué, mes que bien li enuit,   880
et le passage li otroie.
Et cil le chace totevoie
tant que il chiet a paumetons;
lors li vient sus li charretons,
si jure quanqu'il puet veoir   885
que mar le fist el gué cheoir
et son panser mar li toli.
La dameisele que o li
li chevaliers amenee ot
les menaces antant et ot;   890
s'a grant peor et se li prie
que por li lest qu'il ne l'ocie.
Et il dit que si fera voir;

859. antrevient

38

The knight who had to guard the ford
Reached the other first
And struck him so hard
That he completely splintered his lance.
The other dealt him a blow that sent him   850
Tumbling flat beneath the water,
Which closed completely over him.
Then the Knight of the Cart withdrew and dismounted,
Sure that he could drive away
A hundred such before him.   855
He drew his steelblade sword from its scabbard
And the other knight sprang up and drew
His fine, flashing blade.
Again they clashed in hand-to-hand struggle,
Protected behind their shields   860
Which gleamed with gold.
Their swords struck
Repeated and unceasing blows.
They struck such fierce blows
And the battle was so lengthy   865
That the Knight of the Cart
Was ashamed in his heart
And said that he would be unable to meet the trials
Of the way he had taken,
Since he needed so long   870
To defeat a single knight.
Had he met yesterday in a valley
A hundred such, he was certain
There would have been no defense against him,
And he was exceedingly sad and angry   875
To be so weak today
That his blows were wasted and his day spent.
Thereat he ran upon the guard and rushed him
Until he gave way and fled;
Though he was loath to do so,   880
He left the ford's passage free.
Our knight pursued him
Until he fell forward onto his hands;
Then the rider of the cart came up to him
And swore by all he could see   885
That he would rue having knocked him into the ford
And having disturbed his meditation.
The girl whom the guardian of the ford
Had brought with him,
Upon hearing the threats,   890
Was most fearful and begged our knight
For her sake not to kill the other.
But he said that in truth he must;

ne puet por li merci avoir
que trop li a grant honte feite.   895
Lors li vient sus, l'espee treite;
et cil dit qui fu esmaiez:
"Por Deu et por moi l'en aiez
la merci que je vos demant."
Et cil respont: "Se Dex m'amant,   900
onques nus tant ne me mesfist
se por Deu merci me requist
que por Deu, si com il est droiz,
merci n'an eüsse une foiz.
Et ausi avrai ge de toi,   905
car refuser ne la te doi
des que demandee la m'as;
mes ençois me fïanceras
a tenir la ou ge voldrai
prison quant je t'an semondrai."   910
Cil li plevi cui molt est grief.
La demeisele derechief
dit: "Chevaliers, par ta franchise,
des que il t'a merci requise
et tu otroiee li as,   915
se onques prison deslïas
deslie moi cestui prison.
Clainme moi quite sa prison,
par covant que quant leus sera   [30e]
tel guerredon con toi pleira   920
t'an randrai selonc ma puissance."
Et lors i ot cil conuissance
par la parole qu'ele ot dite:
si li rant le prison tot quite.
Et cele en a honte et angoisse   925
qu'ele cuida qu'il la conoisse,
car ele ne le volsist pas.
Et cil s'an part eneslepas;
et cil et cele le comandent
a Deu et congié li demandent.   930
Il lor done, puis si s'an va
tant que de bas vespre trova
une dameisele venant,
molt tres bele et molt avenant,
bien acesmee et bien vestue.   935
La dameisele le salue
come sage et bien afeitiee,
et cil respont: "Sainne et heitiee,
dameisele, vos face Dex."
Puis il dit: "Sire, mes ostex   940
vos est ci pres apareilliez,

923. Por

40

He could not show the mercy she asked
Since the other had done such a shameful thing.   895
Then he came up to him, sword drawn;
The guard, frightened, said:
"For God's sake and mine, show me
The mercy I ask of you."
"As God is my witness," replied the Knight of the Cart,   900
"No person has ever treated me so vilely
That, should he beg me for mercy in God's name,
I would not show it to him once
For God's sake, as is right.
Therefore, I will show you mercy   905
Since I would do wrong to refuse
What you have asked in His name;
But first you will swear
To be my prisoner wherever
And whenever I summon you."   910
With heavy heart he swore this to the knight.
Thereupon the girl
Said: "Sir knight, since by your goodness
You have granted him
The mercy he requested,   915
If ever you have released a captive,
Release this one to me.
Free him for me,
And when the time comes I swear
To repay you whatever you would be pleased   920
To request that is within my power to grant."
And then the knight understood,
By the words she had spoken, who she was
And released his prisoner to her.
She was troubled and upset,   925
For she feared he had recognized her,
Which she did not wish.
But he was eager to be off,
So the girl and her knight commended him
To God and asked his leave.   930
He granted this and went his way
Until near nightfall when he beheld
Coming toward him a girl,
Most comely and attractive,
Handsomely dressed and attired.   935
The girl greeted him
Properly and graciously,
And he replied: "May God
Keep you well and happy."
"Sir," she then said, "my house   940
Is ready nearby to welcome you

se del prandre estes conseilliez.
Mes par itel herbergeroiz
que avoec moi vos coucheroiz--
einsi le vos ofre et presant."   945
Plusor sont qui de ce presant
li randissent cinc cenz merciz,
et il an fu trestoz nerciz
et li a respondu tot el:
"Dameisele, de vostre ostel   950
vos merci ge, si l'ai molt chier;
mes, se vos pleisoit, del couchier
me soferroie je molt bien."
"Je n'an feroie autremant rien,"
fet la pucele, "par mes ialz.   955
Et cil, des que il ne puet mialz,
l'otroie si com ele vialt;
de l'otroier li cuers li dialt.
Quant itant seulemant le blesce,
molt avra au couchier tristesce;   960
molt i avra travail et painne
la dameisele qui l'an mainne.
Espoir tant le puet ele amer,   [30 f]
ne l'en voldra quite clamer.
Puis qu'il li ot acreanté   965
son voloir et sa volenté,
si l'en mainne jusqu'an un baile--
n'avoit plus bel jusqu'an Thessaile,
qu'il estoit clos a la reonde
de hauz murs et d'eve parfonde;   970
et la dedanz home n'avoit
fors celui que ele atandoit.*
    Cele i ot fet por son repeire
asez de beles chanbres feire,
et sale molt grant et pleniere.   975
Chevauchant lez une riviere
s'an vindrent jusqu'au herberjage,
et an lor ot por le passage
un pont torneïz avalé.
Par sor le pont sont anz alé;   980
s'ont trovee la sale overte,
qui de tiules estoit coverte.
Par l'uis qu'il ont trové overt
antrent anz et voient covert
un dois d'un tablier grant et lé;   985
et sus estoient aporté
li mes et les chandoiles mises
es chandeliers totes esprises,
et li henap d'argent doré,

961· orguel et p.

                        42

If you will accept my hospitality.
But you may lodge there
Only if you agree to sleep with me--
On this condition I make my offer."   945
Many there are who, for such a gift,
Would have thanked her five hundred times,
But he became quite doleful
And answered her very differently:
"I thank you most sincerely   950
For your kind offer of hospitality;
But, if you please,
I would prefer not to sleep with you."
"By my eyes," said the girl,
"On no other condition will I lodge you."   955
The knight, when he saw he could not do otherwise,
Granted her what she wished,
Though it distressed his heart to do so.
Yet if it wounded him now,
How much more would it pain him at bedtime!   960
The girl, too, who accompanied him
Would suffer disappointment and sorrow.
Perhaps she would love him so much
That she would not want to let him go.
After he had granted her   965
Her wish and her desire,
She led him to a bailey--*
The fairest from there to Thessaly.
It was enclosed round about
By high walls and a deep moat.   970
There was no one within,
Save him whom she has been awaiting.
    For her residence she had had
A number of fine rooms outfitted,
As well as a large and spacious hall.   975
Riding along a riverbank,
They came to the lodging,
And a drawbridge was lowered
To let them pass.
They crossed over the bridge   980
And found the tile-roofed hall
Open before them.
They entered through the opened door
And saw a table covered
With a long, wide cloth;   985
Upon it the meal was set out.
There were lighted candles
Placed in candelabra,
And gilded silver goblets,

et dui pot, l'uns plains de moré   990
et li autres de fort vin blanc.
Delez le dois, au chief d'un banc,
troverent deus bacins toz plains
d'eve chaude a laver lor mains;
et de l'autre part ont trovee   995
une toaille bien ovree,
bele et blanche, as mains essuier.
Vaslet ne sergent n'escuier
n'ont trové leanz ne veü.
De son col oste son escu   1000
li chevaliers et si le pant
a un croc, et sa lance prant
et met sor un hantier an haut.
Tantost de son cheval jus saut
et la dameisele del suen.   1005
Au chevalier fu bel et buen
quant ele tant nel vost atendre   [31a]
que il li eidast a descendre.
Tantost qu'ele fu descendue,
Sanz demore et sanz atandue   1010
tresqu'a une chanbre s'an cort;
un mantel d'escarlate cort
li aporte, si l'en afuble.
La sale ne fu mie enuble,
si luisoient ja les estoiles;   1015
mes tant avoit leanz chandoiles
tortices, grosses et ardanz,
que la clartez estoit molt granz.
Quant cele li ot au col mis
le mantel, si li dit: "Amis,   1020
veez ci l'aigue et la toaille;
nus ne la vos ofre ne baille,
car ceanz fors moi ne veez.
Lavez voz mains, si asseez
quant vos pleira et boen vos iert;   1025
l'ore et li mangiers le requiert,
si con vos le poez veoir.
Car lavez, s'alez asseoir."
"Molt volantiers." Et cil s'asiet
et cele lez lui cui molt siet,   1030
et mangierent ansanble et burent
tant que del mangier lever durent.
    Quant levé furent del mangier,
dist la pucele au chevalier:
"Sire, alez vos la fors deduire,   1035
mes que il ne vos doie nuire;
et seulemant tant i seroiz,
se vos plest, que vos panseroiz

44

And two pots, one filled with red wine   990
And the other with a heady white wine.
Beside the table, on the end of a bench,
They found two basins brimming
With hot water to wash their hands.
On the other end they saw   995
A finely embroidered
White towel to dry them.
They neither saw nor found
Valet, servant, or squire therein.
The knight lifted his shield   1000
From his neck and hung it
On a hook; he took his lance
And laid it upon a rack.
Then he jumped down from his horse
And the girl from hers.   1005
The knight was pleased
That she did not wish to wait
For his help to dismount.
As soon as she had dismounted,
Without hesitation or delay   1010
She hastened to a room
From which she brought forth a short mantle
Of rich material to place upon him.
The hall was not at all dark
Though the stars were already shining;   1015
A great light from the many large,
Twisted wax candles banished
All darkness from the hall.
After placing over his shoulders
The mantle, she said: "My friend,   1020
Here is the water and the towel.
No one else offers or gives them to you,
For here you see no one but myself.
Wash your hands and be seated
When it pleases you to do so;   1025
The hour and the food require it,
As you can see.
Now wash, then take your place."
"Most willingly."--Then he sat down
With her beside him, which pleased him.   1030
They ate and drank together
Until it was time to leave the table.
When they had risen from eating,
The girl said to the knight:
"Sir, go out and entertain yourself a while,   1035
If you do not object;
But only remain without,
If you please, until you think

45

que je porrai estre couchiee.
Ne vos enuit ne ne dessiee, 1040
que lors porroiz a tans venir
se covant me volez tenir."
Et cil respont: "Je vos tendrai
vostre covant, si revandrai
quant je cuiderai qu'il soit ore." 1045
Lors s'an ist fors et si demore
une grant piece enmi la cort,
tant qu'il estuet qu'il s'an retort--
car covant tenir li covient.
Arriere an la sale revient, 1050
mes cele qui se fet s'amie [31b]
ne trueve, qu'el n'i estoit mie.
Quant il ne la trueve ne voit,
si dit: "An quel leu qu'ele soit
je la querrai tant que je l'aie." 1055
Del querre plus ne se delaie
por le covant que il li ot.
En une chanbre antre, si ot
an haut crier une pucele;
et ce estoit meïsmes cele 1060
avoec cui couchier se devoit.
Atant d'une autre chanbre voit
l'uis overt et vient cele part
et voit tot enmi son esgart
c'uns chevaliers l'ot anversee, 1065
si la tenoit antraversee
sor le lit, tote descoverte;
cele, qui cuidoit estre certe
que il li venist en aïe,
crioit an haut: "Aïe! aïe! 1070
chevaliers--tu qui es mes ostes--
se de sor moi cestui ne m'ostes,
ne troverai qui le m'an ost; 1072a
et se tu ne me secors tost* 1072b
il me honira veant toi!
Ja te doiz tu couchier o moi,
si con tu m'as acreanté! 1075
Fera donc cist sa volenté
de moi, veant tes ialz, a force?
Gentix chevaliers, car t'esforce,
si me secor isnelemant!"
Cil voit que molt vileinnemant 1080
tenoit la dameisele cil
descoverte jusqu'au nonbril,
s'en a grant honte et molt l'en poise
quant a nu a li adoise.
Si n'en ert mie talentos, 1085
ne tant ne quant n'an ert jalos.*

46

That I am in bed.
Do not be displeased or troubled,   1040
For then you may come to me at once
If you will keep the promise you have made."
He replied: "I will keep
My promise to you and return
When I believe the time is come."   1045
Then he went out and tarried
A long while in the courtyard,
Until he had to return--
For he could not break his promise.
He came back into the hall   1050
But could not find his would-be love,
For she was not there.
Unable to see or discover her,
He said: "Wherever she might be
I'll seek until I have her."   1055
He set off at once to find her
On account of the promise he had given.
Upon entering the first room, he heard
A girl scream out loudly:
It was that very one   1060
With whom he was to lie.
Then he saw before him the open door
Of another room; he came in that direction
And right before his eyes he saw
That a knight had attacked her   1065
And was holding her
Quite naked across the bed.
The girl, who thought surely
That he would help her,
Screamed out: "Help! Help!   1070
Sir knight--you who are my guest--
If you do not pull this other knight from off me,
I'll not find anyone to pull him away;   1072a
And if you do not help me at once   1072b
He will shame me before your eyes!
You are the one to share my bed,
As you have sworn to me!   1075
Will this man forcibly have his will
With me before your eyes?
Gentle knight, take strength
And aid me quickly!"
He saw that the other villainously   1080
Held down the girl
Uncovered to the waist,
And he was embarrassed and troubled
To see that naked body touching hers.
Yet this sight evoked no desire in our knight,   1085
And he felt not the least bit of jealousy.

47

Mes a l'entree avoit portiers
trestoz armez: deus chevaliers
qui 'espees nues tenoient;
aprés quatre sergent estoient,   1090
si tenoit chascuns une hache
tel don l'en poïst une vache
tranchier outre parmi l'eschine,
tot autresi con la racine
d'un genoivre ou d'une geneste.   [31c]
Li chevaliers a l'uis s'areste
et dit: "Dex, que porrai ge feire?
Meüz sui por si grant afeire
con por la reïne Guenievre.
Ne doi mie avoir cuer de lievre   1100
quant por li sui an ceste queste.
Se Malvestiez son cuer me preste
et je son comandemant faz,
n'ateindrai pas ce que je chaz.
Honiz sui se je ci remaing.   1105
Molt me vient or a grant desdaing,
quant j'ai parlé del remenoir--
molt en ai le cuer triste et noir.
Or en ai honte, or en ai duel
tel que je morroie, mon vuel,   1110
quant je ai tant demoré ci.
Ne ja Dex n'ait de moi merci
se jel di mie por orguel
et s'asez mialz morir ne vuel
a enor que a honte vivre.   1115
Se la voie m'estoit delivre,
quele enor i avroie gié
se cil me donoient congié
de passer oltre sanz chalonge?
Donc i passeroit, sanz mançonge,   1120
ausi li pires hom qui vive;
et je oi que ceste chestive
me prie merci molt sovant
et si m'apele de covant
et molt vilmant le me reproche."   1125
Maintenant jusqu'a l'uis s'aproche
et bote anz le col et la teste;
si regarde amont vers la feste,
si voit les espees venir;*
adonc se prist a retenir.   1130
Li chevalier lor cos ne porent
detenir, qu'esmeüz les orent:
an terre les espees fierent
si qu'anbedeus les peçoierent.

1128. Et garde amont par la fenestre

Furthermore, doormen guarded the entrance:
Two well-armed knights
With drawn swords;
Behind them four men-at-arms,   1090
Each holding an axe--
The kind with which one could split
A cow's spine
As easily as a root
Of juniper or broom.   1095
The knight stopped at the doorway
And said: "My God, what can I do?
I am engaged in pursuit
Of no one less than the queen, Guinevere.
I must not have a hare's heart   1100
Since I am in quest of her.
If Cowardice lends me its heart
And I follow its command,
I'll never attain what I pursue.
I am disgraced if I remain here.   1105
Indeed, I am greatly shamed
Even to have considered holding back--
My heart is black with sadness.
I am so shamed and filled with despair
That I feel I should die   1110
For having delayed here so long.
May God never have mercy on me
If there is a word of pride in all I say
And if I would not rather die
Honorably than live shamed.   1115
If the way to her were clear,
What honor would there be
Were these enemies to give me leave
To cross unchallenged?
In truth, the basest man alive   1120
Could save her then;
Yet still I hear this poor victim
Who beseeches my aid constantly,
Reminding me of my promise
And reproaching me most bitterly!"   1125
He came at once to the doorway
And thrust his head and neck through;
Looking up toward the gable
He saw swords flashing toward him
And swiftly drew back.   1130
The knights could not
Check their strokes
And both swords shattered
As they struck the ground.

Quant eles furent peçoiees,   1135
moins en a les haches prisiees
et moins les an crient et redote.
Puis saut entr'ax, et fiert del cote
un sergent et un autre aprés.   [31d]
Les deus que il trova plus pres   1140
hurte des codes et des braz
si qu'andeus les abat toz plaz;
et li tierz a a lui failli,
et li quarz qui l'a asailli
fiert si que le mantel li tranche   1145
et la chemise et la char blanche
li ront anprés l'espaule tote,
si que li sans jus an degote.
Et cil qui rien ne se delaie
ne se plaint mie de sa plaie,   1150
einz vet et fet ses pas plus emples
tant qu'il aert parmi les temples
celui qui esforçoit s'ostesse.
(Randre li porra la promesse
et son covant einz qu'il s'an aut.)   1155
Volsist ou non, le dresce an haut;
et cil qui a lui failli ot
vient aprés lui plus tost qu'il pot
et lieve son cop derechief--
sel cuide bien parmi le chief   1160
jusqu'es danz de la hache fandre.
Et cil qui bien s'an sot desfandre
li tant le chevalier ancontre
et cil de la hache l'ancontre
la ou l'espaule au col se joint,   1165
si que l'un de l'autre desjoint.
Et li chevaliers prant la hache,
des poinz isnelemant li sache
et leisse cel que il tenoit,
car desfandre le covenoit,   1170
que li chevalier sus li vienent,
et cil qui les trois haches tienent
si l'asaillent molt crüelmant.
Et cil saut molt delivremant
antre le lit et la paroi   1175
et dit: "Or ça, trestuit a moi!
que s'or estïez vint et set,
des que ge ai tant de recet
si avroiz vos bataille assez.
Ja n'en serai par vos lassez!"   1180
Et la pucele qui l'esgarde
dit: "Par mes ialz, vos n'avez garde

1151. u *deleted after* fet

50

After they were shattered, 1135
He was less concerned about the axes,
And feared and dreaded them less.
He leapt among them and jabbed one man down
With his elbows and another after him.
The two he found nearest 1140
He struck with his elbows and forearms
And beat them both to the ground;
The third missed his stroke,
But the fourth, attacking,
Struck him a blow which ripped his mantle 1145
And his chemise and tore open
The white flesh of his shoulder,
Causing blood to flow from the wound.
Yet he took no respite,
And without complaining of his hurt 1150
He went and redoubled his efforts
Until he had grabbed the head
Of the one who was raping his hostess.
(Before he leaves, our knight
Will be able to keep his pledge and promise to her.) 1155
He stood him up in spite of his resistance.
But the man who had missed his blow
Came after him as fast as he could
And prepared to strike another--
He meant to hack the knight's skull 1160
Through to the teeth with his axe.
Yet our knight, skilled in defense,
Held the other knight in front of himself
And the axeman's blow struck him
Where the shoulder joins the neck, 1165
Splitting the two asunder.
The knight seized the axe
And wrested it free from his grip.
He dropped the man he'd been holding
To look once more to his own defense, 1170
For the two knights were upon him,
And the three remaining axemen
Were again most cruelly assailing him.
He leapt to safety
Between the bed and the wall 1175
And challenged them: "Come on all of you!
Even if there were twenty-seven of you,
You would find your match
As long as I hold this position.
You will never have the better of me!" 1180
The girl, who was watching him,
Said: "By my eyes, you need not worry

51

d'or en avant la ou ge soie."   [31e]
Tot maintenant arriere anvoie
les chevaliers et les sergenz;   1185
lors s'an vont tuit cil de laienz
sanz arest et sanz contredit;
et la dameisele redit:
"Sire, bien m'avez desresniee
ancontre tote ma mesniee.   1190
Or an venez, je vos an main."
An la sale an vont main a main;
et celui mie n'abeli,
qu'il se soffrist molt bien de li.
    Un lit ot fet enmi la sale,   1195
don li drap n'erent mie sale,
mes blanc et lé et delïé.
N'estoit pas de fuerre esmïé
la couche, ne de coutes aspres;
un covertor de deus dïaspres   1200
ot estandu desor la couche.
Et la dameisele s'i couche,
mes n'oste mie sa chemise.
Et cil a molt grant poinne mise
au deschaucier et desnüer: 1205
d'angoisse le covint süer;
totevoies parmi l'angoisse
covanz le vaint et si le froisse.
Donc est ce force? Autant se vaut;
par force covient que il s'aut   1210
couchier avoec la dameisele.
Covanz l'en semont et apele.
Et il se couche tot a tret,
mes sa chemise pas ne tret,
ne plus qu'ele ot la soe feite.   1215
De tochier a li molt se gueite,
einz s'an esloingne et gist anvers;
ne ne dit mot ne c'uns convert
cui li parlers est desfanduz
quant an son lit gist estanduz.   1220
N'onques ne torne son esgart
ne devers li ne d'autre part.
Bel sanblant feire ne li puet.
Por coi? Car del cuer ne li muet,
qu'aillors a mis del tot s'antante--   1225
mes ne pleist mie n'atalante
quanqu'est bel et gent a chascun.   [31f]
Li chevaliers n'a cuer que un,
et cil n'est mie ancor a lui;
einz est comandez a autrui   1230
si qu'il nel puet aillors prester.
Tot le fet an un leu ester

From now on, as long as I am with you."
She immediately dismissed
The knights and men-at-arms,   1185
And they all left their presence
At once without objection.
Then the girl continued:
"You have defended me well, sir,
Against my entire household.   1190
Now come along with me."
Hand in hand they entered the hall;
Yet he was not pleased,
For he would gladly have been free of her.
    A bed had been set up in the middle of the hall. 1195
Nothing had soiled
Its fine broad, white sheets.
The bedding was neither of cut straw
Nor rough-quilted padding.
A covering of two silk cloths of floral design   1200
Was stretched over the mattress.
The girl lay down,
But without removing her chemise.*
The knight was at great pain
To remove his leggings and take off his clothes.   1205
He was sweating from the effort,
But in the midst of his sufferings
His promise overpowered him and urged him on.
Is this duress? As good as such,
For because of it he had to go   1210
To lie with the girl.
His promise summoned and beckoned to him.
He lay down hesitatingly;
Like her, he did not
Remove his chemise.   1215
He carefully kept from touching her,
Moving away and turning his back.
Nor did he say any more than would a lay brother
To whom speech was forbidden
When lying in bed.   1220
Not once did he look toward her,
Nor anywhere but straight before him.
He could show her no favor.
But why? Because his heart felt nothing for her
Since it was focused on another--   1225
Not everyone desires or is pleased
By what is beautiful and fair.
The knight had but one heart,
And it no longer belonged to him.
Rather, it was promised to another,   1230
So he could not bestow it elsewhere.
His heart was kept fixed on a single object

53

Amors, qui toz les cuers justise.
Toz? Nel fet, fors cez qu'ele prise.
Et cil s'an redoit plus prisier   1235
cui ele daigne justisier.
Amors le cuer celui prisoit
si que sor toz le justisoit
et li donoit si grant orguel
que de rien blasmer ne le vuel   1240
s'il lait ce qu'Amors li desfant
et la ou ele vialt antant.
La pucele voit bien et set
que cil sa conpaignie het
et volentiers s'an sofferroit,   1245
ne ja plus ne li requerroit,
qu'il ne quiert a li adeser.
Et dit: "S'il ne vos doit peser,
sire, de ci me partirai;
en ma chanbre couchier m'irai   1250
et vos an seroiz plus a eise.
Ne cuit mie que molt vos pleise
mes solaz ne ma conpaignie.
Nel tenez pas a vilenie
se je vos di ce que je cuit.   1255
Or vos reposez mes enuit,
que vos m'avez randu si bien
mon covant que nes une rien
par droit ne vos puis demander.
Or vos voel a Deu comander,   1260
si m'an irai." Lors si se lieve.
Au chevalier mie ne grieve,
einz l'an leisse aler volentiers
con cil qui est amis antiers
autrui que li. Bien l'aparçoit   1265
la dameisele et bien le voit;
si est an sa chanbre venue
et si se couche tote nue,
et lors a dit a li meïsmes:
"Des lores que je conui primes   1270
chevalier, un seul n'an conui   [32a]
que je prisasse fors cestui
la tierce part d'un angevin.
Car si con ge pans et devin,
il vialt a si grant chose antendre   1275
q'ainz chevaliers n'osa enprendre
si perilleuse ne si grief;
et Dex doint qu'il an veigne a chief!"
Atant s'andormi et si jut
tant que li jorz clers aparut.   1280

1247. a *of* adeser *added above line* 1260. Si

54

By Love, which rules all hearts.
All hearts? Not really, only those it esteems.
And whomever Love deigns to rule   1235
Should esteem himself the more.
Love esteemed this knight's heart
And ruled it more than any other
And gave it such sovereign pride
That I would not wish to find fault with him   1240
For refusing what Love forbids him
And for setting his purpose by Love's commands.
The girl saw clearly and understood
That he disliked her company
And would gladly be rid of her,   1245
And that he would never seek her favors,
For he had no wish to touch her.
Said she: "If it does not displease you,
Sir, I will depart from here
And go to bed in my own room   1250
So you might be more at ease.
I hardly think that the comfort
Of my presence is pleasing to you.
Do not think me ill-bred
For telling you what I believe.   1255
Now rest well this night,
For you have kept so faithfully
Your promise that I have no right
To ask even the least thing more of you.
Now I wish to commend you to God,   1260
Then I'll leave."--With these words she arose.
This did not upset the knight;
On the contrary he willingly let her go,
For his heart was wholly given
To another. Having perceived   1265
This clearly, the girl
Went into her room,
Disrobed completely, and lay in bed
Saying to herself:
"Of all the knights I have ever known,   1270
There is not one except this knight
That I would esteem
The third part of an angevin.*
For as I surmise and believe,
He is intent upon a quest   1275
More dangerous and painful
Than any ever undertaken by a knight.
May God grant that he succeed in it!"
Thereupon she fell asleep and lay abed
Until the light of day appeared.   1280

    Tot maintenant que l'aube crieve
isnelemant et tost se lieve.
Et li chevaliers si resvoille,
si s'atorne et si s'aparoille
et s'arme que nelui n'atant.   1285
La dameisele vient atant,
si voit qu'il est ja atornez.
"Boens jorz vos soit hui ajornez,"
fet ele quant ele le voit.
"Et vos, dameisele, si soit,"   1290
fet li chevaliers d'autre part.
Et cil dit que molt li est tart
qu'an li ait son cheval fors tret.
La pucele amener li fet
et dit: "Sire, je m'an iroie   1295
o vos grant piece an ceste voie,
se vos mener m'an osïez
et conduire m'i devïez
par les us et par les costumes
qui furent ainz que nos ne fumes   1300
el reaume de Logres mises."
Les costumes et les franchises
estoient tex a cel termine
que dameisele ne meschine,
se chevaliers la trovast sole,   1305
ne plus qu'il se tranchast la gole
ne feïst se tote enor non,
s'estre volsist de boen renon.
Et s'il l'esforçast, a toz jorz
an fust honiz an totes corz.   1310
Mes se ele conduit eüst
uns autres, se tant li pleüst
qu'a celui bataille an feïst
et par armes la conqueïst,
sa volenté an poïst faire   [32b]
sanz honte et sanz blasme retraire.
Por ce la pucele li dist
que, se il l'osast ne volsist
par ceste costume conduire
que autres ne li poïst nuire,   1320
qu'ele s'an alast avoec lui.
Et cil li dit: "Ja nus enui
ne vos fera, ce vos otroi,
que premiers ne le face moi."
"Dons i voel ge," fet ele, "aler."   1325
Son palefroi fet anseler;
tost fu ses comandemanz fez;
li palefroiz li fu fors trez
et li chevax au chevalier.
Andui montent sanz escuier,   1330

                        56

Just as the dawn broke
She got quickly out of bed.
The knight awoke,
Arose, then dressed
And armed himself without waiting for anyone.   1285
The girl arrived at this moment
And saw that he was already dressed.
"I hope a good day has dawned for you,"
She said, when she saw him.
"The same to you, dear lady,"   1290
Replied the knight.
And he remarked that he was impatient
For someone to bring his horse.
The girl had it brought to him
And said: "Sir, I will accompany   1295
You some distance along your way,
If you dare to escort me
And can conduct me
According to the customs and usages
Which have been observed in the Kingdom of Logres*   1300
Since long before our days."
The customs and practices
Were such at this time
That if a knight found a girl alone--
Be she a lady or a maid-servant--   1305
He would as soon cut his own throat
As treat her dishonorably,
If he prized his good name.
And should he assault her, forever
Would he be disgraced at every court.   1310
But if she were being escorted
By another and the knight chose
To do battle with her defender
And defeated him in arms,
Then he might do with her as he pleased   1315
Without incurring dishonor or disgrace.
These were the reasons for which the girl told him
That, if he dared and wished
To escort her according to this custom
And protect her from those who might do her ill,   1320
Then she would accompany him.
"I assure you," he replied,
"That no one will ever harm you
If he has not first harmed me."
"Then," said she, "I wish to go with you."   1325
Her palfrey was saddled
As quickly as she commanded it,
And was brought forth
Along with the knight's horse.
Both mounted without the help of a squire   1330

57

si s'an vont molt grant aleüre.
Cele l'aresne et il n'a cure
de quanque ele l'aparole,
einçois refuse sa parole:
pansers li plest, parlers li grieve.   1335
Amors molt sovant li escrieve
la plaie que feite li a;
onques anplastre n'i lïa
por garison ne por santé,
qu'il n'a talant ne volanté,   1340
d'emplastre querre ne de mire,
se sa plaie ne li anpire;
mes celi queroit volantiers . . .*
Tant tindrent voies et santiers
si con li droiz chemins les mainne   1345
qu'il vienent pres d'une fontainne.*
La fontainne est enmi uns prez
et s'avoit un perron delez.
Sor le perron qui ert iqui
avoit oblïé ne sai qui   1350
un peigne d'ivoire doré.
Onques des le tens Ysoré
ne vit si bel sages ne fos.
Es danz del peigne ot des chevos
celi qui s'an estoit peigniee   1355
remés bien demie poigniee.
    Qant la dameisele parçoit
la fontainne et le perron voit,
se ne volt pas que cil la voie,   [32c]
einz se mist en une autre voie.   1360
Et cil, qui se delite et pest
de son panser qui molt li plest,
ne s'aparçoit mie si tost
que ele fors sa voie l'ost;
mes quant il s'est aparceüz,   1365
si crient qu'il ne soit deceüz,
qu'il cuide que ele ganchisse
et que fors de son chemin isse
por eschiver aucun peril.
"Ostez, dameisele," fet il.   1370
"N'alez pas bien; venez deça.
Onques ce cuit ne s'adreça
qui fors de cest chemin issi."
"Sire, nos irons mialz par ci,"
fet la pucele, "bien le sai."   1375
Et cil li respont: "Je ne sai,
dameisele, que vos pansez;
mes ce poez veoir asez

1346. Que il voient une

58

And rode off rapidly.
She talked to him, but he paid
No heed to what she said
And refused to speak himself:
To reflect was pleasing, to speak was pain.   1335
Love frequently reopened
The wound it had dealt him;
Yet he never wrapped it
To let it heal or recover,
For he had no desire or thought   1340
To find a doctor or to bandage it,
Unless the wound grew deeper.
But willingly would he seek that certain one . . .
They held to the tracks and trails
As the main road led them   1345
Until they approached a spring*
In the middle of a meadow.
Beside it was a flat rock
On which someone--
I know not whom--   1350
Had left a comb of gilded ivory.
Not since the time of the giant Ysoré*
Had anyone, wise man or fool, seen so fine a comb.
In the teeth of the comb
She who had used it had left   1355
Fully half a handful of hair.
    When the girl noticed
The spring and the flat rock
She took another path,
Since she did not want the knight to see them.   1360
And he, delighting in and feasting on
His pleasant meditations,
Did not at once perceive
That she had left the main path;
But when he did notice   1365
He was afraid that she was deceiving him,
For he believed that she had turned aside
And had left the main road
To flee some danger.
"Stop, Miss!" he said.   1370
"You have gone astray; come back!
I do not think anyone ever found the right way
By leaving this road."
"Sir," the girl said, "I am certain
We shall do better to go this way."   1375
And he replied: "I don't know
What you're thinking, Miss,
But you can plainly see

que c'est li droiz chemins batuz.
Des que ge m'i sui anbatuz,   1380
je ne tornerai autre san;
mes, s'il vos plest, venez vos an,
que g'irai ceste voie adés."
Lors s'an vont tant qu'il vienent pres
del perron et voient le peigne.   1385
"Onques certes don moi soveigne,"
fet li chevaliers, "mes ne vi
tant bel peigne con je voi ci."
"Donez le moi," fet la pucele.
"Volentiers," dit il, "dameisele."   1390
Et lors s'abeisse et si le prant.
Quant il le tint, molt longuemant
l'esgarde et les chevox remire;
et cele an comança a rire.
Et quant il la voit, se li prie   1395
por qu'ele a ris qu'ele li die;
et cele dit: "Teisiez vos an;
ne vos an dirai rien oan."
"Por coi?" fet il. "Car je n'ai cure."
Et quant cil l'ot, si li conjure   1400
come cil qui ne cuidoit mie
qu'amie ami, n'amis amie
doient parjurer a nul fuer: [32d]
"Se vos rien nule amez de cuer,
dameisele, de par celi   1405
vos conjur et requier et pri
que vos plus ne le me celez."
"Trop a certes m'an apelez,"
fet ele, "si le vos dirai.
De rien nule n'an mantirai: 1410
cist peignes, se j'onques soi rien,
fut la reïne--jel sai bien.
Et d'une chose me creez
que les chevox que vos veez,
si biax, si clers et si luisanz,   1415
qui sont remés antre les danz,
que del chief la reïne furent.
Onques en autre pré ne crurent."
Et li chevaliers dit: "Par foi,
assez sont reïnes et roi--   1420
mes de la quel volez vos dire?"
Et cele dit: "Par ma foi, sire,
de la fame le roi Artu."
Quant cil l'ot, n'a tant de vertu
que tot nel coveigne ploier;   1425
par force l'estut apoier
devant a l'arçon de la sele.
Et quant ce vit la dameisele,

That this is the beaten path.
Since I have started along this road, 1380
I'll take no other.
If it pleases you, accompany me,
For I plan to continue along this way."
Then they rode on until they neared
The stone and saw the comb. 1385
"Never, as long as I can remember,"
Said the knight, "have I ever seen
A finer comb than this."
"Give it to me," the girl said.
"Most willingly, Miss," he answered. 1390
Then he bent down and picked it up.
As he held it, he gazed steadfastly
And contemplated the hair
Until the girl began to laugh.
When he saw her laughing, he asked her 1395
To tell him the reason,
And she replied: "Don't be so curious;
I'll tell you nothing for the moment."
"Why?" he asked.--"Because I don't want to."
Hearing this reply, he begged her 1400
Like one who felt
That lovers should never
Betray each other in any way:
"If you love anyone in your heart,
By his name, Miss, 1405
I beg and request and pray you
Not to hide your thoughts from me."
"Your appeal is too strong,"
She said: "I'll tell you,
I'll hide nothing from you: 1410
I am as sure as I have ever been that this comb
Belonged to the queen--I know it.
Believe me when I assure you
That the beautiful, light,
Shining hair which you see 1415
Entangled in its teeth
Has come from the queen's own head.
No other meadow grows so fair."
The knight replied: "In faith,
There are many kings and queens-- 1420
Which one do you mean?"
She said: "Upon my word, sir,
The wife of King Arthur."
On hearing this, the knight had not strength enough
To keep from falling forward 1425
And was forced to catch himself
Upon the saddle-bow before him.
When the girl saw this

si s'an mervoille et esbaïst,
qu'ele cuida que il cheïst.   1430
S'ele ot peor ne l'en blasmez,
qu'ele cuida qu'il fust pasmez.
Si ert il, autant se valoit;
molt po de chose s'an failloit
qu'il avoit au cuer tel dolor   1435
que la parole et la color
ot une grant piece perdue.
Et la pucele est descendue
et si cort quanqu'ele pot corre
por lui retenir et secorre,   1440
qu'ele ne le volsist veoir
por rien nule a terre cheoir.
Quant il la vit, s'en ot vergoigne,
si li a dit: "Por quel besoigne
venistes vos ci devant moi?"   1445
Ne cuidiez pas que le porcoi
la dameisele l'an conoisse,   [32e]
qu'il an eüst honte et angoisse
et si li grevast et neüst
se le voir l'en reconeüst.   1450
Si s'est de voir dire gueitiee,
einz dit come bien afeitiee:
"Sire, je ving cest peigne querre,
por ce sui descendue a terre--
que de l'avoir oi tel espans,   1455
ja nel cuidai tenir a tans."
Et cil, qui vialt que le peigne ait,
li done et les chevox an trait
si soëf que nul n'an deront.
Jamés oel d'ome ne verront   1460
nule chose tant enorer,
qu'il les comance a aorer
et bien cent mile foiz les toche
et a ses ialz et a sa boche,
et a son front et a sa face.   1465
N'est joie nule qu'il n'an face:
molt s'an fet liez, molt s'an fet riche.
An son sain pres del cuer les fiche,
entre sa chemise et sa char.
N'en preïst pas chargié un char   1470
d'esmeraudes ne d'escharboncles;
ne cuidoit mie que reoncles
ne autres max jamés le praingne;
dïamargareton desdaigne
et pleüriche et tirïasque,   1475
neïs saint Martin et saint Jasque!

1468. soing

62

She was amazed and terrified,
Thinking he would fall.   1430
Do not reproach her for this fear,
Because she thought that he had fainted.
Indeed he had come
Quite near fainting,
For the pain he felt in his heart   1435
Had driven away his speech
And the color from his face.
The girl dismounted
And ran as quickly as she could
To support and aid him,   1440
Because not for anything
Did she wish to see him fall.
When he saw her he was ashamed
And said to her: "For what reason
Have you come here before me?"   1445
Do not suppose that the girl
Would reveal the true reason;
For he would be ashamed and troubled,
And it would pain and wound him
If she were to reveal the truth.   1450
Therefore she hid the truth
And said with utmost tact:
"Sir, I came to pick up this comb,
That is why I dismounted--
I wanted it so much   1455
I could no longer wait."
He was willing for her to have the comb
But removed the hair first,
Careful not to break a single strand.
Never will the eye of man see   1460
Anything so highly honored
As those strands, which he began to adore,
Touching them a hundred thousand times
To his eyes, his mouth,
His forehead, and his cheeks.   1465
He showed his joy in every way
And felt himself most happy and rewarded.
He placed them on his breast near his heart,
Between his chemise and his skin.
He would not trade them for a cart loaded   1470
With emeralds and carbuncles;
Nor did he fear that ulcers
Or any other disease would afflict him;
He had no use for magic potions mixed with pearls,
For drugs to combat pleurisy, for theriaca* . . .   1475
No use for prayers to St. Martin and St. James!

Car an ces chevox tant se fie
qu'il n'a mestier de lor aïe.
Mes quel estoient li chevol?
Et por mançongier et por fol   1480
m'an tanra l'en, se voir an di:
quant la foire iert plainne au Lendi
et il i avra plus avoir,
nel volsist mie tot avoir
li chevaliers--c'est voirs provez--   1485
si n'eüst ces chevox trovez.
Et se le voir m'an requerez,
ors cent mile foiz esmerez
et puis autantes foiz recuiz
fust plus oscurs que n'est la nuiz   1490
contre le plus bel jor d'esté
qui ait an tot cest an esté,   [32f]
qui l'or et les chevols veïst,
si que l'un lez l'autre meïst.
Et que feroie ge lonc conte?   1495
La pucele molt tost remonte
atot le peigne qu'ele an porte;
et cil se delite et deporte
es chevox qu'il a en son saing.
Une forest aprés le plaing   1500
truevent et vont par une adresce
tant que la voie lor estresce,
s'estut l'un aprés l'autre aler,
qu'an n'i poïst mie mener
deus chevax por rien coste a coste.   1505
La pucele devant son oste
s'an vet molt tost la voie droite.
La ou la voie ert plus estroite
voient un chevalier venant.
La dameisele maintenant,   1510
de si loing com ele le vit,
l'a coneü et si a dit:
"Sire chevaliers, veez vos
celui qui vient ancontre nos
toz armez et prez de bataille?   1515
Il m'an cuide mener sanz faille
avoec lui sanz nule desfanse;
ce sai ge bien que il le panse,
qu'il m'ainme et ne fet pas que sages,
et par lui et par ses messages   1520
m'a proiee molt a lonc tans.
Mes m'amors li est an desfans,
que por rien amer nel porroie--
si m'aïst Dex, einz me morroie

1484. *Line omitted, added later next to 1483* 1514. vos

64

He placed so much faith in these strands of hair
That he had no need of any other aid.*
But what were these strands like?
I would be taken for a liar and a fool   1480
Were I to describe them truthfully:
When the Lendi fair was at its height*
And all the finest goods were gathered there,
This knight would not have accepted it all
--it's the proven truth--   1485
Should it prevent his finding this hair.
Do you still demand the truth?
If you took gold which had been refined a hundred thousand times
And melted down as many,
And if you put it beside these strands of hair,   1490
The gold would appear to one who saw them both
As dull as the darkest night compared
To the brightest summer day
Of all this year.
But why should I lengthen my story?   1495
The girl remounted at once,
Still holding the comb;
And the knight rejoiced and delighted
In the strands which he held to his breast.
Beyond the plain they found a forest   1500
And took a short cut
Until the path narrowed,
Such that they were forced to continue one behind the other,
Since it was impossible to ride
Two horses abreast.   1505
The girl preceded her escort
Along the main path.
Just at the narrowest place along the path
They saw a knight coming toward them.
Immediately the girl,   1510
From the moment she saw him,
Recognized him, and said to her escort:
"Sir knight, do you see
That knight coming toward us
Fully armed and ready to do battle?   1515
He certainly intends to carry me off
With him without meeting resistance;
I know he thinks this,
Because he loves me (though in vain)
And for a long time has implored me,   1520
Both in person and by messenger.
But my love is not for him;
There is no way I could love him--
God help me, I'd rather die

65

que je l'amasse an nul androit!   1525
Je sai bien qu'il a orandroit
si grant joie et tant se delite
con s'il m'avoit ja tote quite.
Mes or verrai que vos feroiz!
Or i parra se preuz seroiz,   1530
or le verrai, or i parra
se vostre conduiz me garra.
Se vos me poëz garantir,
donques dirai ge sanz mantir
que preuz estes et molt valez."   1535
et il li dit: "Alez, alez."   [33a]
Et ceste parole autant vaut
con se il deïst: "Po m'an chaut,
que por neant vos esmaiez
de chose que dite m'aiez."   1540
    Que que il vont ensi parlant,
ne vint mie cele part lant
li chevaliers qui venoit seus
les granz galoz ancontre aus deus.
Et por ce li plest a haster   1545
qu'il ne cuide mie gaster
et por boens eürez se clainme
quant la rien voit que il plus ainme.
Tot maintenant que il l'aproche,
de cuer la salue et de boche   1550
et dit: "La riens que je plus vuel,
don moins ai joie et plus me duel,
soit bien veignanz don qu'ele veingne."
N'est mie droiz que cele teingne
vers lui sa parole si chiere   1555
que ele ne li rande arriere,
au moins de boche, son salu.
Molt a au chevalier valu
quant la pucele le salue,
qui sa boche pas n'en palue   1560
ne ne li a neant costé.
Et s'il eüst tres bien josté
cele ore a un tornoiemant
ne s'an prisast il mie tant,
ne ne cuidast avoir conquis   1565
ne tant d'enor ne tant de pris.
Por ce que mialz s'an ainme et prise
l'a par la resne del frain prise,
et dit: "Or vos an manrai gié--
molt ai hui bien et droit nagié,   1570
qu'a molt boen port sui arivez.
Or sui ge toz descheitivez:

1535. *repeated at top of [33a]*

66

Than ever love him at all! 1525
I know that he is now
Very happy and rejoicing
As if he had already won me.
So let us see what you will do!
We shall learn if you are bold; 1530
We shall see if your escort
Can bring me safely through.
If you can protect me,
Then I shall be able to say without lying
That you are bold and very worthy." 1535
He answered only: "Go on, go on."
Which was as much
As to say: "I'm not worried
By anything you have told me.
You've no reason to be frightened." 1540
While they went along conversing thus,
The single knight
Was rapidly coming in that direction
At full gallop toward them.
He hastened so because 1545
He was confident of success
And considered himself fortunate
To see the one he most loved.
As soon as he drew near her,
He greeted her with words of his heart on his tongue, 1550
Saying: "May the one whom I most desire,
From whom I have the least joy and the greatest pain,
Be well come from wherever she is coming."
It was fitting that she
Not be so stingy with her words 1555
As to refuse to return his greeting,
From her tongue, if not from her heart.
The knight was elated
By the girl's greetings,
Though it cost her little effort 1560
And was not allowed to stain her lips.*
And had he fought brilliantly
That day at a tournament
He would not have esteemed himself so much
Nor felt that he had won 1565
As much honor or renown.
Out of pride and vanity
He reached for her bridle rein
And said: "Now I'll take you away--
Today's fine sailing 1570
Has brought my ship to a good port.
Now my troubles are ended:

67

de peril sui venuz a port,
de grant enui a grant deport,
de grant dolor a grant santé.   1575
Or ai tote ma volanté,
qant en tel meniere vos truis
qu'avoec moi mener vos an puis
orandroit, que n'i avrai honte."   [33b]
Et cele dit: "Rien ne vos monte,   1580
que cist chevaliers me conduit."
"Certes, ci a malvés conduit,"
fet il, "qu'adés vos en maing gié.
Un mui de sel avroit mangié
cist chevaliers, si con je croi,   1585
einçois qu'il vos desraist vers moi.
Ne cuit c'onques home veïsse
vers cui je ne vos conqueïsse.
Et quant je vos truis ci an eise,
mes que bien li poist et despleise,   1590
vos an manrai veant ses ialz,
et s'an face trestot son mialz."
Li autres de rien ne s'aïre
de tot l'orguel qu'il li ot dire,
mes sanz ranpone et sanz vantance   1595
a chalongier la li comance,
et dist: "Sire, ne vos hastez
ne voz paroles ne gastez,
mes parlez un po par mesure.
Ja ne vos iert vostre droiture   1600
tolue, quant vos l'i avroiz.
Par mon conduit, bien le savroiz,
est ci la pucele venue.
Lessiez la; trop l'avez tenue,
qu'ancor n'a ele de vos garde."   1605
Et cil otroie que an l'arde
s'il ne l'an mainne maugré suen.
Cil dit: "Ce ne seroit pas buen
se mener la vos an lessoie;
sachiez, einçois m'en combatroie.   1610
Mes se nos bien nos voliens
conbatre, nos ne porriens
an cest chemin por nule painne.
Mes alons desqu'a voie plainne,
ou jusqu'a pree ou jusqu'a lande."   1615
Cil dit que ja mialz ne demande,
et dist: "Certes bien m'i acort:
de ce n'avez vos mie tort
que cist chemins est trop estroiz--
ja iert mes chevax si destroiz   1620

1589. truis an

68

After shipwreck, I have reached port;
After trial, happiness;
After pain, health.   1575
My wishes are now fulfilled
Since I have found you in this manner
And can take you away
Presently without incurring dishonor."
"Don't be overconfident," said she.   1580
"I am being escorted by this knight."
"Then you have poor protection indeed!"
Said he. "I intend to take you at once.
This knight would eat a full hogshead
Of salt, so I believe,   1585
Before he'd dare try to wrest you from me.
I don't think I've ever seen the man
Whom I could not defeat to have you.
Since I have you here so opportunely,
Though it may upset or displease him,   1590
I intend to lead you off before his very eyes,
In spite of all he might do to prevent it."
The other did not become angered
By all the boasting he had heard;
Rather, without impudence or pride   1595
He began to challenge him,
Saying: "Sir, don't be too hasty
And don't waste your words.
Speak more reasonably.
Your rights will not be taken   1600
From you, when once you have won them.
Just remember that the girl
Has come here under my safekeeping.
Now let her be; you have detained her much too long
And she has no reason to fear you."   1605
The other granted that he would rather be burned alive
Than fail to carry her off in spite of her knight.
He said: "It would be cowardice
To let you take her from me.
Consider it settled: I must fight.   1610
But if we wish to do combat
Properly, we cannot
By any means do it here on this path.
Let us rather go to a main road,
Or to a meadow or heath."   1615
The other replied that this suited him perfectly,
Saying: "Indeed I grant your wish,
For you are quite right
That this path is too narrow--
My horse would be so hampered here,   1620

einçois que ge torner le puisse,
que je crien qu'il se brit la cuisse."
Lors se torne a molt grant destresce,
mes son cheval mie ne blesce
ne de rien n'i est anpiriez;   1625
et dit: "Certes molt sui iriez
quant antre ancontré ne nos somes
an place lee et devant homes,
que bel me fust que l'en veïst
li quex de nos mialz le feïst.   1630
Mes or venez, se l'irons querre;
nos troverons pres de ci terre
tote delivre et grant et lee."
Lors s'an vont jusqu'a une pree;
an cele pree avoit puceles   1635
et chevaliers et dameiseles,
qui jooient a plusors jeus
por ce que biax estoit li leus.
Ne jooient pas tuit a gas,
mes as tables et as eschas,   1640
li un as dez, li autre au san,
a la mine i rejooit l'an.
A ces jeus li plusors jooient;
li autre qui iluec estoient
redemenoient lor anfances,   1645
baules et queroles et dances,
et chantent et tunbent et saillent,
et au luitier se retravaillent.
      Uns chevaliers auques d'ahé
estoit de l'autre part del pré   1650
sor un cheval d'Espaigne sor;
s'avoit lorain et sele d'or
et s'estoit de chienes meslez.
Une main a l'un de ses lez
avoit par contenance mise;   1655
por le bel tans ert an chemise,
s'esgardoit les geus et les baules;
un mantel ot par ses espaules
d'escarlate et de veir antier.
De l'autre part, lez un santier,   1660
en avoit jusqu'a vint et trois
armez sor boens chevax irois.
Tantost con li troi lor sorvienent,
tuit de joie feire se tienent
et crïent tuit parmi les prez: 1665
"Veez le chevalier, veez,
qui fu menez sor la charrete!
N'i ait mes nul qui s'antremete
de joër, tant con il i ert.
Dahez ait qui joër i quiert   1670

I fear I'd break his leg
Before I could turn him about."
Then with very great effort
And attentive not to hurt his steed,
He managed to change directions.   1625
"I am very upset," he said,
"That we have not met
In an open place before other men,
For I wish it could be witnessed
Which of us fights the better.   1630
But come now, let us begin our search;
Nearby we'll find a clearing,
Both long and wide."
They rode until they reached a meadow.
In this meadow were ladies-in-waiting   1635
And knights and ladies
Playing at many games,
For the place was pleasant.
They were not all occupied in idle sport.
Some were playing backgammon and chess,   1640
And others were occupied in
Various games of dice.*
Most were engaged in these diversions,
Though others there were who
Played at childhood games--   1645
Rounds and dances and reels,
Singing, tumbling, and leaping.
A few were struggling in wrestling matches.
    A knight, advanced in years,
Was across the meadow from the others,   1650
And was mounted on a Spanish sorrel.
His saddle and trappings were of gold,
And his armor was of grey mesh.
One hand was placed smartly
On one of his hips   1655
As he watched the games and dances.
Because of the fair weather, he was dressed in his chemise,*
And a rich mantle trimmed in vair
Was thrown over his shoulders.
Opposite him, beside a path,   1660
Were as many as twenty-three
Armed knights on fine Irish steeds.
As the three riders neared them,
They abandoned their sport
And their shouts were heard throughout the meadows: 1665
"Look at that knight, look!
It's the one who was driven in the cart.
Let no one dare continue
His play while he is among us.
Damned be anyone who seeks to amuse himself   1670

71

et dahez ait qui daingnera
joër tant con il i sera."
Et antretant ez vos venu
le fil au chevalier chenu,
celui qui la pucele amoit   1675
et por soe ja la tenoit;
si dist: "Sire, molt ai grant joie--
et qui le vialt oïr si l'oie--
que Dex m'a la chose donee
que j'ai toz jorz plus desirree.   1680
N'il ne m'aüst pas tant doné
s'il m'eüst fet roi coroné,
ne si boen gré ne l'en seüsse
ne tant gahaignié n'i eüsse--
car cist gaainz est biax et buens."   1685
"Ne sai encor se il est tuens,"
fet li chevaliers a son fil.
Tot maintenant li respont cil:
"Nel savez? Nel veez vos donques?
Por Deu, sire, n'an dotez onques   1690
quant vos veez que je la tieng!
An cele forest don je vieng
l'ancontrai ore ou el venoit;
je cuit que Dex la m'amenoit,
si l'ai prise come la moie."   1695
"Ne sai ancor se cil l'otroie
que je voi venir aprés toi.
Chalongier la te vient, ce croi."
Antre ces diz et ces paroles
furent remeses les queroles   1700
por le chevalier que il virent,
ne jeu ne joie plus ne firent
por mal de lui et por despit.
Et li chevaliers sanz respit
vint molt tost aprés la pucele.   1705
"Lessiez," fet il, "la dameisele,
chevaliers, que n'i avez droit.
Se vos osez, tot orandroit
la desfandrai vers vostre cors."
Et li chevaliers vialz dist lors: 1710
"Don ne le savoie je bien?   *[33e]*
Biax filz, ja plus ne la retien,
la pucele, mes leisse l'i."
A celui mie n'abeli,
einz jure qu'il n'en randra point,   1715
et dit: "Ja Dex puis ne me doint
joie que je la li randrai.
Je la tieng et si la tendrai

1715. Quil

And damned be anyone who deigns
To play as long as he is here!"
While they were thus speaking,
The old knight's son
(The one who loved the girl   1675
And already considered her his)
Approached his father and said: "Sir, I am overjoyed--
Let him who wishes to hear harken to this:
God has granted me the one thing
I have always most desired.   1680
He would not have rewarded me as much
If He had had me crowned king,
Nor would I have been so grateful,
Nor would I have profited so--
For what I have gained is fair and good."   1685
"I am not yet sure she is yours,"
The old knight said to his son.
The answer was swift in coming:
"Are you not sure? Can't you see, then?
By God, sir, how can you have any doubts   1690
When you see that she is with me?
I met her just now as she was riding
Along in the forest from which I have just come.
I think God was leading her my way,
So I took her as my own."   1695
"I'm not certain if that knight
I see following you will agree to this.
I believe he is coming to challenge you for her."
While these words were being spoken
The others abandoned their dancing;   1700
They ceased their games and their sport
Out of spite and hatred
For the knight they saw approaching.
And the knight unhesitatingly
Followed swiftly after the girl.   1705
"Knight," he said, "give up this girl,
For you have no right to her.
If you dare, I will forthwith
Defend her against you."
Then the old knight said: 1710
"Was I not right?
My son, keep the girl no longer;
Return her to her escort."
The son was not at all pleased
And swore he would never give her up,   1715
Saying: "May God never again grant me
Joy if I release her to him.
I have her and intend to keep her

come la moie chose lige.*
Einz iert de mon escu la guige   1720
ronpue et totes les enarmes,
ne an mon cors ne an mes armes
n'avrai je puis nule fïance,
ne an m'espee n'en ma lance,
quant je li lesserai m'amie."   1725
Et cil dit: "Ne te leirai mie
conbatre por rien que tu dies.
An ta proesce trop te fies;
mes fai ce que je te comant."
Cil par orguel respont itant: 1730
"Sui j'anfes a espoanter?
De ce me puis je bien vanter:
qu'il n'a tant con la mers aceint
chevalier, ou il en a meint,
nul si boen cui je la leissasse   1735
et cui ge feire n'an cuidasse
an molt po d'ore recreant."
Li peres dit: "Je t'acreant,
biax filz, ensi le cuides tu,
tant te fïes an ta vertu;   1740
mes ne voel ne ne voldrai hui
que tu t'essaies a cestui."
Et cil respont: "Honte feroie
se je vostre consoil creoie.
Maudahez ait qui le cresra   1745
et qui por vos se recresra,
que fieremant ne me conbate!
Voirs est que privez mal achate;
mialz poïsse aillors barguignier,
que vos me volez angingnier.   1750
Bien sai qu'an un estrange leu
poïsse mialz feire mon preu;
ja nus qui ne me coneüst
de mon voloir ne me meüst,
et vos m'an grevez et nuisiez.   [33f]
Tant an sui je plus angoissiez
por ce que blasmé m'an avez;
car qui blasme--bien le savez--
son voloir a home n'a fame,
plus en art et plus en anflame.   1760
Mes se je rien por vos an les,
ja Dex joie ne me doint mes;
einz me conbatrai mau gré vostre!"
"Foi que doi saint Pere l'apostre,"
fet li peres, "or voi ge bien   1765
que proiere n'i valdroit rien.
Tot pert quanque je te chasti;
mes je t'avrai molt tost basti

74

As something of my own.*
I will break my shield   1720
Strap and all its armlets;
I will have lost confidence
In my strength and my weapons,
In my sword and in my lance,
Before I abandon her to him!"   1725
"I'll not let you fight," replied his father,
"No matter what you say.
You are overconfident of your own prowess.
So do now as I order."
He answered proudly: 1730
"Am I a child to be cowed?
Of this I can boast:
Though there are many knights in this wide world,
Not one for as far as the sea stretches
Is powerful enough that I would abandon her to him.   1735
I am sure I can quickly bring
Any one of them to submission."
The father said: "I do not doubt,
Fair son, that you believe this,
So greatly do you trust in your own strength;   1740
But I do not consent, nor will I consent this day,
That you test yourself against this man."
His son replied: "I would be shamed
If I followed your advice.
May he be damned who would take it   1745
And abandon the field
Without fighting bravely!*
It's true that it's bad business to deal with friends;
It is better to trade elsewhere,
For you intend to cheat me.   1750
I can see that I could better test my courage
In some far-off place,
Where no one would know me
And attempt to dissuade me from my intention,
As you seek to bring me low.   1755
I am all the more upset
Because you have found fault with me.
As you well know, if one reproaches
A man's or woman's intent,
This sparks and inflames him the more.   1760
Should I once hesitate because of you,
May God never again grant me joy.
No, in spite of your wishes I will fight!"
"By the faith I owe the holy apostle Peter,"
His father said, "I can clearly see   1765
That pleading is to no avail.
I am wasting time reproaching you;
But ere long I shall devise a way

tel plet que maleoit gré tuen
t'estovra feire tot mon buen,
car tu an seras au desoz."
Tot maintenant apele toz
les chevaliers, qui a lui viegnent;
si lor comande qu'il li tiegnent
son fil qu'il ne puet chastïer,
et dit: "Jel feroie lïer
einz que conbatre le lessasse.
Vos estes tuit mi home a masse,
si me devez amor et foi--
sor quanque vos tenez de moi
le vos comant et pri ansanble.
Grant folie fet, ce me sanble,
et molt li vient de grant orguel,
quant il desdit ce que je vuel."
Et cil dïent qu'il le panront,
ne ja puis que il le tanront
de conbatre ne li prendra
talanz, et si li covendra
mau gré suen la pucele randre.
Lors le vont tuit seisir et prandre
et par les braz et par le col.
"Dons ne te tiens tu or por fol?"
fet li peres. "Or conuis voir:
or n'as tu force ne pooir
de conbatre ne de joster
que que il te doie coster,
que qu'il t'enuit ne qu'il te griet.
Ce qu'il me plest et qui me siet
otroie, si feras que sages.
Et sez tu quiex est mes corages?
Por ce que mandres soit tes diax,
siudrons moi et toi, se tu viax,
le chevalier hui et demain
et par le bois et par le plain,
chascuns sor son cheval anblant.
De tel estre et de tel sanblant
le porrïens nos tost trover
que je t'i leiroie esprover
et conbatre a ta volanté."
Lors li a cil acreanté
mau gré suen, quant feire l'estuet.
Et cil qui amander nel puet
dist qu'il s'an sosferroit por lui,
mes qu'il le siudront amedui.
Et quant ceste avanture voient
les genz qui par le pré estoient,

1770

1775

1780

1785

1790

1795

[34a]
1800

1805

1810

1815

1773. second two letters of viegnent are obliterated on MS

76

To force you to do my will,
Whether or not you want to,   1770
For I shall have you in my power."
Thereupon he called all
His knights about him
And ordered them to seize
His son, who would pay no attention to him,   1775
Saying: "I'll have him bound
Before I'll let him fight.
You're all my liegemen
And owe me esteem and loyalty--
By whatever you hold from me   1780
I order and pray you all.
He has acted madly, it seems to me,
And with unbridled pride
In contradicting my desires."
They said that they would seize him.   1785
Nor would he ever want to fight
As long as they held him,
And they would compel him,
Despite his wishes, to release the girl.
Then they all seized him, grabbing him   1790
By the arms and around the neck.
"Do you not think you look foolish now?"
Said his father. "Admit the truth:
Now you do not have the strength or power
To fight or to joust,   1795
And no matter how much it upsets you
Your feelings will do you no good now.
Grant what I want and what suits me;
You'll act well to follow my advice.
And do you know what I am thinking?   1800
In order to lessen your disappointment,
You and I, if you want, will follow
This knight today and tomorrow,
Through the forest and across the plain,
Each of us on his ambling steed.   1805
We might soon find him to be
Of such character and bearing
That I would let you test him
And fight him as you want."
Then the son agreed   1810
Against his will, for he had no choice.
The other knight, seeing no other solution,
Reluctantly accepted this proposal
Provided they both follow him.
When the people who were gathered   1815
In the meadow saw this,

si dïent tuit: "Avez veü?
Cil qui sor la charrete fu
a hui conquise tel enor
que l'amie au fil mon seignor   1820
en mainne et sel suefre mes sire.
Por verité poomes dire
que aucun bien cuide qu'il ait
an lui, quant il mener li lait.
Et cent dahez ait qui meshui   1825
lessera a joer por lui.
Ralons joer!" Lors recomancent
lor jeus, si querolent et dancent.
   Tantost li chevaliers s'an torne,
en la pree plus ne sejorne;   1830
mes aprés lui pas ne remaint
la pucele qu'il ne l'en maint.
Andui s'an vont a grant besoing.
Li filz et li peres de loing
les sivent. Par un pré fauchié   1835
s'ont jusqu'a none chevalchié,
et truevent en un leu molt bel
un mostier et, lez le chancel,
un cemetire de murs clos.
Ne fist que vilains ne que fos   1840
li chevaliers qui el mostier
entra a pié por Deu proier.
Et la dameisele li tint   [34b]
son cheval tant que il revint.
Quant il ot feite sa proiere   1845
et il s'an revenoit arriere,
si li vient uns moinnes molt vialz
a l'encontre devant ses ialz.
Quant il l'encontre, se li prie
molt dolcemant que il li die   1850
que par dedanz ces murs avoit,
et cil respont qu'il i avoit
un cemetire. Et cil li dist:
"Menez m'i, se Dex vos aïst."
"Volentiers, sire." Lors l'en mainne;   1855
el cemetire aprés le mainne*
antre les tres plus beles tonbes
qu'an poïst trover jusqu'a Donbes,
ne de la jusqu'a Panpelune.
Et s'avoit letres sor chascune   1860
qui les nons de ces devisoient
qui dedanz les tonbes girroient.
Et il meïsmes tot a tire
comança lors les nons a lire

1821. mainne sel siudra

78

They all said: "Did you see that?
The man who was in the cart
Has won such honor today
That he is leading away my lord's son's   1820
Mistress, and my lord permits it.
We may truthfully say
That he thinks there is some merit
In the man to let him lead her off.
A hundred curses on anyone   1825
Who stops his play on his account.
Let's return to our games!"--Then they resumed
Their games and danced their rounds.
    The knight turned
And rode out of the meadow at once.   1830
The girl had no desire
To remain behind without him.
Both set off with dispatch.
The son and the father followed
At a distance. Through a mowed field   1835
They rode until mid-afternoon,
When in a most pleasant spot they found
A church with a walled cemetery
Alongside the chancel.
Showing himself neither boor nor fool,   1840
The knight entered the church
On foot to pray to God.
The girl looked after
His horse until his return.
When he had offered his prayer   1845
And was returning,
He saw an elderly monk
Coming directly toward him.
When the knight met him, he asked him
With becoming courtesy to explain   1850
What was within these walls.
The monk replied that there was
A cemetery. And the knight said:
"As God may help you, take me in there."
"Willingly, sir."--Then he led him   1855
Into the cemetery
Among the most beautiful tombs
That could be found from there to Dombes,*
Or even to Pamplona.
Upon each were carved letters   1860
Forming the names of those
Who were to be buried in them.
The knight himself began to read
Through the names

79

et trova: "Ci girra Gauvains, 1865
ci Looys,* et ci Yvains."
Aprés ces trois i a mainz liz
des nons as chevaliers esliz,
des plus prisiez et des meillors
et de cele terre et d'aillors. 1870
Antre les autres une an trueve
de marbre, et sanble estre de l'ueve
sor totes les autres plus bele.
Li chevaliers le moinne apele
et dit: "Ces tonbes qui ci sont, 1875
de coi servent?" Et cil respont:
"Vos avez les letres veües;
se vos les avez antendues,
don savez vos bien qu'eles dïent
et que les tonbes senefïent. 1880
"Et de cele plus grant me dites
de qu'ele sert." Et li hermites
respont: "Jel vos dirai assez:
c'est uns veissiax qui a passez
toz ces qui onques furent fet. 1885
Si riche ne si bien portret
ne vit onques ne ge ne nus; [34c]
biax est defors et dedanz plus;*
mes ce metez en nonchaloir,
que rien ne vos porroit valoir, 1890
que ja ne la verroiz dedanz;
car set homes molt forz et granz
i covandroit au descovrir,
qui la tonbe voldroit ovrir,
qu'ele est d'une lame coverte. 1895
Et sachiez que c'est chose certe
qu'au lever covandroit set homes
plus forz que moi et vos ne somes.
Et letres escrites i a
qui dïent: 'Cil qui levera 1900
cele lanme seus par son cors
gitera ces et celes fors
qui sont an la terre an prison,
don n'ist ne clers ne gentix hon*
des l'ore qu'il i est antrez, 1905
n'ancor n'en est nus retornez.
Les estranges prisons retienent,
et cil del païs vont et vienent
et anz et fors a lor pleisir.'"
Tantost vet la lame seisir 1910
li chevaliers, et si la lieve
si que de neant ne s'i grieve,

1871. les autre   1872. *final e of* ueve *added above* v
1888. dedanz et deforz

And discovered: "Here will lie Gawain, 1865
Here Lionel, and here Yvain."
After these three there were many resting places
Bearing the names of many fine knights,
The most esteemed and greatest
Of this land or any other. 1870
Among the tombs he found one
Of marble which seemed to be more finely
Worked than all the others.
The knight called the monk
And said: "What is the purpose 1875
Of all these tombs here?" And he replied:
"You have seen the letters;
If you have studied them attentively,
Then you well know what they say
And what is the meaning of the tombs." 1880
"Tell me what that largest
One is for." The hermit
Replied: "I'll tell you all there is to know:
This sarcophagus surpasses
All others which have ever been made. 1885
Never have I nor anyone seen
A more elaborate or finely carved tomb;
It is beautiful without and even more so within.
But do not be concerned about that,
For it can never do you any good, 1890
And never will you see inside;
For if anyone were to wish to open the tomb
He would need, to uncover it,
Seven very large and strong men,
For it is covered by a heavy stone slab. 1895
And you can be certain that to lift it
Would require seven men
Stronger than either you or I.
On it are carved letters
Which say: 'He who will lift 1900
This slab by his unaided strength
Will free all the men and women
Who are imprisoned in the land.
Since first they were imprisoned
Not a clerk or nobleman has been freed, 1905
Nor has anyone returned home,
Foreigners are kept prisoners,
While those of this land come and go
Back and forth as they please.'"
The knight went at once and seized hold 1910
Of the slab and lifted it
Without the least difficulty,

mialz que dis home ne feïssent
se tot lor pooir i meïssent.
Et li moinnes s'an esbahi,   1915
si que bien pres qu'il ne chaï
quant veü ot ceste mervoille,
car il ne cuidoit la paroille
veoir an trestote sa vie.
Si dit: "Sire, or ai grant envie   1920
que je seüsse vostre non;
direiez le me vos?"--"Je, non,"
fet li chevaliers, "par ma foi."
"Certes," fet il, "ce poise moi;
mes se vos le me diseiez   1925
grant corteisie fereiez,
si porreiez avoir grant preu.
Qui estes vos? et de quel leu?"
"Uns chevaliers sui, ce veez,
del rëaume de Logres nez--   1930
atant an voldroie estre quites.   *[34d]*
Et vos, s'il vos plest, me redites
an cele tonbe qui girra?"
"Sire, cil qui delivrera
toz ces qui sont pris a la trape   1935
el rëaume don nus n'eschape."
Et quant il li ot tot conté,
li chevaliers l'a comandé
a Deu et a trestoz ses sainz;
et lors est, c'onques ne pot ainz,   1940
a la dameisele venuz.
Et li vialz moinnes, li chenuz,
fors de l'eglise le convoie;
atant vienent enmi la voie
et que que la pucele monte,   1945
li moinnes trestot li reconte
quanque cil leanz fet avoit,
et son non, s'ele le savoit,
li pria qu'ele li deïst,
tant que cele li regeïst   1950
qu'ele nel set, mes une chose
seürement dire li ose:
qu'il n'a tel chevalier vivant
tant con vantent les quatre vant.

    Tantost la pucele le leisse,   1955
aprés le chevalier s'esleisse.
Maintenant cil qui les sivoient
vienent et si truevent et voient
le moinne seul devant l'eglise.
Li vialz chevaliers an chemise   1960

1928. Dom

More easily than ten men could have done
By putting all their strength to the task.
The monk was so astounded   1915
That he nearly fainted
When he saw this miracle,
For he never thought to see the like
Of it in all his life.
He said: "Sir, now I am most anxious   1920
To know your name.
Will you tell me?"--"I will not,"
Answered the knight, "upon my word."
"Indeed," said the other, "this weighs heavy on me.
But if you were to tell me   1925
You would be acting nobly
And might be rewarded well.
Who are you? Where are you from?"
"I am a knight, as you see,
Born in the Kingdom of Logres--   1930
I think that that is sufficient.
And now, if you please, it is your turn to tell me
Who will lie in this tomb."
"Sir, he who will free
All those held captive   1935
In the kingdom from which none escape."
When the monk had told him all there was to know,
The knight commended him
To God and to all his saints,
Then returned to the girl   1940
As rapidly as he could.
The old, gray-haired monk
Accompanied him from the church
Till they reached the road.
While the girl was mounting,   1945
The monk told her all
That the knight had done while inside
And begged her to tell him
His name if she knew it.
She assured him   1950
That she did not know it, but there was
One certain thing she dared say:
There was not a living knight to equal him
As far as the four winds blow.
    The girl then left the monk   1955
And hurried after the knight.
Those who were following them came
Immediately and found and saw
The monk alone before the church.
The old knight in chemise   1960

83

li dist: "Sire, veïstes vos
un chevalier--dites le nos--
qui une dameisele mainne?"
Et cil respont: "Ja ne m'iert painne
que tot le voir ne vos an cont,   1965
car orandroit de ci s'an vont.
Et li chevaliers fu leanz,
si a fet mervoilles si granz
que toz seus la lame leva,
c'onques de rien ne s'i greva,   1970
de sor la grant tonbe marbrine.
Il vet secorre la reïne,
et il la secorra sanz dote
et avoec li l'autre gent tote.
Vos meïsmes bien le savez,   [34e]
qui sovant leües avez
les letres qui sont sor la lame.
Onques voir d'ome ne de fame
ne nasquié n'en sele ne sist
chevaliers qui cestui vausist."   1980
Et lors dit li pere a son fil:
"Filz, que te sanble? Don n'est il
molt preuz qui a fet tel esforz?
Or sez tu bien cui fu li torz;
bien sez se il fu tuens ou miens.   1985
Je ne voldroie por Amiens
qu'a lui te fusses conbatuz;
si t'an ies tu molt debatuz
einçois qu'an t'an poïst torner.
Or nos an poons retorner,   1990
car grant folie feriens
s'avant de ci les suïens."
Et cil respont: "Je l'otroi bien;
li siudres ne nos valdroit rien.
Des qu'il vos plest, ralons nos an."   1995
Del retorner a fet grant san.
Et la pucele totevoie
le chevalier de pres costoie,
si le vialt feire a li antendre
et son non vialt de lui aprendre.   2000
Ele li requiert qu'il li die;
une foiz et autre li prie
tant que il li dit par enui:
"Ne vos ai ge dit que je sui
del rëaume le roi Artu?   2005
Foi que doi Deu et sa vertu,
de mon non ne savroiz vos point."
Lors li dit cele qu'il li doint
congié, si s'an ira arriere;
et il li done a bele chiere.   2010

84

Said: "Sir, tell us
If you have seen a knight
Escorting a girl."
The monk answered: "It will be no trouble
To tell you all I know,   1965
Because they have just this moment left here.
While the knight was inside,
Alone and with no effort at all
He did a most marvelous thing
By lifting the stone   1970
From the huge marble tomb.
He is going to rescue the queen
And no doubt will--and will rescue
All the other people along with her.
You who have often read   1975
The letters on the stone slab
Know well that this is so.
Truly, never was a knight of man and woman
Born, nor ever sat in a saddle,
Who was as worthy as he."   1980
Then the father said to his son:
"My son, what do you think? Is he not
Most bold to have performed such a deed?
Now you can clearly see who was in the wrong;
You know if it was you or I.   1985
For all the town of Amiens, I would not have wanted
You to fight with him;
Yet you struggled hard
Before you could be swayed from your purpose.
Now we can return,   1990
For it would be madness
To follow them beyond this spot."
Replied the son: "I agree with that;
We're wasting our time following him.
Let us return as soon as you are ready."   1995
He was very wise to turn back.
And the girl continued
Close beside the knight,
Wanting him to pay attention to her.
She wished to learn his name   2000
And asked him to tell her;
Time and again she begged him
Until in his annoyance he spoke to her:
"Did I not tell you I am
From the Kingdom of Arthur?   2005
I swear to God and to His Power
That you'll not learn my name."
Then she asked him for
Leave to turn back,
Which he gladly granted her.   2010

85

Atant la pucele s'an part
et cil, tant que il fu molt tart,
a chevalchié sanz conpaignie.
Aprés vespres, androit conplie,
si com il son chemin tenoit   2015
vit un chevalier qui venoit
del bois ou il avoit chacié.
Cil venoit le hiaume lacié
et a sa venison trossee,   [34f]
tel con Dex li avoit donee,   2020
sor un grant chaceor ferrant.
Li vavasors molt tost errant
vient ancontre le chevalier,
si le prie de herbergier.
"Sire," fet il, "nuiz iert par tans: 2025
de herbergier est hui mes tans,
sel devez feire par reison;
et j'ai une moie meison
ci pres ou ge vos manrai ja.
Einz nus mialz ne vos herberja   2030
lonc mon pooir que je ferai,
s'il vos plest, et liez an serai."
"Et g'en resui molt liez," fet cil.
Avant en anvoie son fil
li vavasors tot maintenant   2035
por feire l'ostel avenant
et por la cuisine haster.
Et li vaslez sanz arester
fist tantost son comandemant
molt volantiers et lëaumant,   2040
si s'an vet molt grant aleüre.
Et cil qui del haster n'ont cure
ont aprés lor chemin tenu,
tant qu'il sont a l'ostel venu.
Li vavasors avoit a fame   2045
une bien afeitiee dame,
et cinc filz qu'il avoit molt chiers
(trois vaslez et deus chevaliers),
et deus filles gentes et beles
qui ancor estoient puceles.   2050
N'estoient pas del païs né,
mes il estoient anserré
et prison tenu i avoient
molt longuemant, et si estoient
del rëaume de Logres né.   2055
Li vavasors a amené
le chevalier dedanz sa cort,
et la dame a l'encontre cort,
et si fil et ses filles saillent.
Por lui servir trestuit se baillent,   2060

86

Thereupon the girl left
And the knight rode on alone
Until it was very late.
After vespers, about complin,
As he was going along his way   2015
He saw a knight coming out
Of the woods from hunting.
He had his helmet strapped on
And had the venison
Which God had permitted him to take   2020
Tied over the back of his iron-grey hunter.
This vavasor* quickly rode
Forward to meet the knight
And offered to lodge him.
"Sir," said he, "it will soon be night   2025
And is already the time
When it is wise to think of lodging.
One of my manor houses is
Nearby to which I now will take you.
No one has ever lodged you better   2030
Than I shall do, to the best of my means.
If you accept I shall be quite happy."
"For my part, I am happy to accept," said he.
The vavasor immediately
Sent his son ahead   2035
To make ready the house
And hasten the supper preparations.
Without delay the youth
Willingly and loyally
Followed his command,   2040
Riding off rapidly.
The others, in no hurry,
Continued their easy pace
Until they reached the house.
The vavasor had married   2045
A very accomplished lady
And had five beloved sons
(Three mere youths and two already knighted),
As well as two beautiful and charming
Daughters, who were still unmarried.   2050
They were not natives of this land
But were held captive there,
Having been imprisoned   .
For a long while away from
Their homeland of Logres.   2055
When the vavasor led
The knight into his courtyard,
His wife ran forward to meet him,
And his sons and daughters all hastened out
And vied with one another to serve him.   2060

87

si le salüent et descendent;
a lor seignor gaires n'antendent
ne les serors ne li cinc frere,
car bien savoient que lor pere
voloit que ensi le feïssent.   2065
Molt l'enorent et conjoïssent;
et quant il l'orent desarmé,
son mantel li a afublé
l'une des deus filles son oste,
au col li met et del suen l'oste.   2070
S'il fu bien serviz au soper,
de ce ne quier je ja parler;
mes quant ce vint aprés mangier,
onques n'i ot puis fet dongier
de parler d'afeires plusors.   2075
Premieremant li vavasors
comança son oste a enquerre
qui il estoit et de quel terre;
mes son non ne li anquist pas.
Et il respont eneslepas: 2080
"Del rëaume de Logres sui,
einz mes an cest païs ne fui."
Et quant li vavasors l'entant,
si s'an mervoille duremant
et sa fame et si anfant tuit;   2085
n'i a un seul cui molt n'enuit,
si li ancomancent a dire:
"Tant mar i fustes, biax dolz sire,
tant est granz domages de vos:
c'or seroiz ausi come nos   2090
en servitume et an essil."
"Et dom estes vos donc?" fet il.
"Sire, de vostre terre somes.
An cest païs a mainz prodomes
de vostre terre an servitume.   2095
Maleoite soit tex costume
et cil avoec qui la maintienent,
que nul estrange ça ne vienent
qu'a remenoir ne lor covaingne
et que la terre nes detaigne.   2100
Car qui se vialt antrer i puet,
mes a remenoir li estuet.
De vos meïsmes est or pes:
vos n'en istroiz, ce cuit, jamés."
"Si ferai," fet il, "se je puis."   2105
Li vavasors li redit puis:
"Comant? Cuidiez an vos issir?"
"Oïl, se Deu vient a pleisir;

2091. Et en servage

They greeted the knight and helped him dismount.
The sisters and five brothers
Almost ignored their father,
For they knew that he
Would want it so.   2065
They made the stranger welcome and honored him;
When they had relieved him of his armor,
One of his host's two daughters
Took her own mantle from off her shoulders
And threw it about his neck.   2070
I do not intend to give you any details
About the fine dinner he was served,
But after the meal
They showed no reluctance
To converse about many topics.   2075
First, the vavasor
Began to ask his guest
Who he was and from what land,
But did not inquire his name.
Our knight answered at once: 2080
"I am from the Kingdom of Logres
And have never before been in this land."
When the vavasor heard this,
He and his wife and all his children
Were greatly astonished.   2085
They were all most upset
And began to say to him:
"Woe that you were ever there, fair sir,
For you will only be sorry for it.
Like us, you will be reduced   2090
To servitude and exile."
"And where then are you from?" the knight queried.
"Sir, we are from your land.
Many good men from your land
Are held in servitude here.   2095
Cursed be the custom,
And those who promote it, which dictates
That any foreigner
Who enters here must stay,
Detained in this land.   2100
Anyone who wishes may come in,
But once here he must remain.
Even for you there is no more hope:
I do not believe you'll ever leave."
"I will indeed," he said, "if I am able."   2105
The vavasor said to him further:
"What? Do you believe you can escape?"
"Yes, if God is willing,

et g'en ferai mon pooir tot."
"Donc an istroient sanz redot
trestuit li autre quitemant,
car puis que li uns lëaumant
istra fors de ceste prison
tuit li autre, sanz mesprison,
an porront issir sanz desfanse."
Atant li vavasors s'apanse
qu'an li avoit dit et conté
c'uns chevaliers de grant bonté
el païs a force venoit
por la reïne que tenoit
Meleaganz, li filz le roi.
Et dit: "Certes, je pans et croi
que ce soit il; dirai li donques."
Lors li dist: "Ne me celez onques,
sire, rien de vostre besoigne
par un covant que je vos doigne
consoil au mialz que je savrai.
Je meïsmes preu i avrai
se vos bien feire le poëz.
La verité m'an desnoëz
por vostre preu et por le mien.
An cest païs, ce cuit je bien,
estes venuz por la reïne
antre ceste gent sarradine,
qui peïor que Sarrazin sont."
Et li chevaliers li respont:
"Onques n'i ving por autre chose.
Ne sai ou ma dame est anclose,
mes a li rescorre tesoil
et s'ai grant mestier de consoil.
Conseilliez moi, se vos savez."
Et cil dit: "Sire, vos avez
anprise voie molt grevainne.
La voie ou vos estes vos mainne
au Pont de l'Espee tot droit.
Consoil croire vos covendroit;
se vos croire me voliez,
au Pont de l'Espee iriez
par une plus seüre voie,
et je mener vos i feroie."
Et cil qui la menor covoite
li demande: "Est ele ausi droite
come ceste voie de ça?"
"Nenil," fet il, "einçois i a
plus longue voie et plus seüre."
Et cil dit: "De ce n'ai ge cure.
Mes an cesti me conseilliez,
car je i sui apareilliez."

2110

2115

2120

2125

2130

2135

2140

2145

2150
[35c]

2155

And I will do everything in my power."
"Then all the others 2110
Can leave without fear,
For when one person is able to escape
This imprisonment without trickery,
All the others, I assure you,
Will be able to leave unchallenged." 2115
The vavasor remembered then
That he had been told and advised
That a knight of great goodness
Was coming boldly into the land
To seek the queen who was being held 2120
By Meleagant, the king's son.
He said [to himself]: "Indeed, I think and feel
That this is he; I shall tell him so."
Then he spoke: "Sir, do not hide
Any of your purpose from me, 2125
And I promise to give you
The best counsel that I know.
I myself stand to gain
By any success you might have.
Reveal the truth to me 2130
For your profit and mine.
I am convinced that you came
Into this land to seek the queen
Among this heathen people,
Who are worse than Sarracens." 2135
And the knight answered him:
"I came for no other reason.
I do not know where my lady is imprisoned,
But I am intent upon rescuing her
And thus am in great need of counsel. 2140
Advise me if you can."
"Sir," said he, "you have
Chosen a most difficult path.
The one on which you are presently engaged
Will lead you directly to the Sword Bridge. 2145
You must heed my advice;
If you will believe me,
I'll have you led
To the Sword Bridge
By a safer route." 2150
Anxious to take the shortest route,
He asked: "Is that path as direct
As the one before me?"
"Not at all,"said his host. "It is
Longer, but safer." 2155
He replied: "Then I have no use for it.
Tell me about this one,
For I am ready to take it."

"Sire, voir, ja n'i avroiz preu.
Se vos alez par autre leu,   2160
demain venroiz a un passage
ou tost porroiz avoir domage;
s'a non li Passages des Pierres.
Volez que je vos die gierres
del passage com il est max?   2165
N'i puet passer c'uns seus chevax;
lez a lez n'i iroient pas
dui home, et si est li trespas
bien gardez et bien desfanduz.
Ne vos sera mie randuz   2170
maintenant que vos i vandroiz;
d'espee et de lance i prandroiz
maint cop et s'an randroiz assez
einz que soiez outre passez."
Et quant il li ot tot retret,   2175
uns chevaliers avant se tret
qui estoit filz au vavasor,
et dit: "Sire, avoec cest seignor
m'an irai, se il ne vos grieve."
Atant uns des vaslez se lieve   2180
et dit: "Ausins i irai gié."
Et li pere an done congié
molt volentiers a enbedeus.
Or ne s'an ira mie seus
li chevaliers, ses an mercie,   2185
qui molt amoit la conpaignie.
     Atant les paroles remainnent,
le chevalier couchier an mainnent;
si dormi se talant en ot.
Tantost con le jor veoir pot   2190
se lieve sus, et cil le voient
qui avoec lui aler devoient;
si sont tot maintenant levé.
Li chevalier se sont armé,
si s'an vont, et ont congié pris;   [35d]
et li vaslez s'est devant mis.
Et tant lor voie ansanble tienent
qu'au Passage des Pierres vienent
a ore de prime tot droit.
Une bretesche enmi avoit,   2200
ou il avoit un home adés.
Einçois que il venissent pres,
cil qui sor la bretesche fu
les voit et crie a grant vertu:
"Cist vient por mal! Cist vient por mal!"   2205
Atant ez vos sor un cheval
un chevalier sor la bretesche,
armé d'une armeüre fresche,

92

"Indeed, sir, it will never profit you.
If you take the path I advise against,   2160
You will come tomorrow to a pass
Where you may be easily harmed;
It is called the Stone Passage.
Do you want me to give you some idea
Of how bad a pass it is?   2165
Only one horse can go through there at a time;
Two men could not go abreast
Through it, and the pass is
Well guarded and defended.
Do not expect it to be surrendered to you   2170
When first you get there;
You'll have to take many a sword's and lance's
Blow and return full measure
Before you can pass through."
When he had told him everything,   2175
One of the knighted sons
Of the vavasor came forward
And said: "Sir, I will go
With this knight, if it is not displeasing to you."
Thereupon one of the young boys got up   2180
And said: "And I'll go too."
Their father gave leave
Willingly to both.
Now the knight would not be obliged
To travel alone, and he thanked them,   2185
Being most pleased with the escort.
    Then they ceased their conversation
And showed the knight to his bed
So he might sleep if he so desired.
As soon as he could see the day   2190
He arose, and those
Who were to accompany him saw this
And immediately got up.
The knights put on their armor,
Took their leave, and rode off   2195
With the youth in front.
They travelled on together until
They came to the Stone Passage
Right at the hour of prime.
In the middle of the pass was a battlement   2200
In which a man was always on guard.
As soon as they neared,
The man in the tower
Saw them and shouted loudly:
"Enemy approaching! Enemy approaching!"   2205
Then immediately a mounted knight
Appeared upon the battlement,
Armed in unsullied armor

et de chascune part sergenz
qui tenoient haches tranchanz.   2210
Et quant il au passage aproche,
cil qui l'esgarde li reproche
la charrete molt laidemant,
et dit: "Vasax, grant hardemant
as fet et molt es fos naïs,   2215
quant antrez ies an cest païs.
Ja hom ça venir ne deüst
qui sor charrete esté eüst,
et ja Dex joïr ne t'an doint!"
Atant li uns vers l'autre point   2220
quanque cheval porent aler;
et cil qui doit le pas garder
peçoie sa lance a estros
et lesse andeus cheoir les tros.
Et cil an la gorge l'asanne   2225
trestot droit par desus la panne*
de l'escu, si le giete anvers
desus les pierres an travers.
Et li sergent as haches saillent,
mes a esciant a lui faillent,   2230
qu'il n'ont talant de feire mal
ne a lui ne a son cheval.
Et li chevaliers parçoit bien
qu'il nel voelent grever de rien
ne n'ont talant de lui mal feire;   2235
si n'a soing de s'espee treire,
einz s'an passe oltre sanz tançon
et aprés lui si conpaignon.
Et li uns d'ax a l'autre dit: [35e]
"Nus si buen chevalier ne vit,   2240
ne nus a lui ne s'aparoille.*
Dont n'a il feite grant mervoille
qui par ci est passez a force?"
"Biax frere, por Deu, car t'esforce,"
fet li chevaliers a son frere,   2245
"tant que tu vaignes a mon pere,
si li conte ceste avanture."
Et li vaslez afiche et jure
que ja dire ne li ira,
ne jamés ne s'an partira   2250
de ce chevalier tant qu'il l'ait
adobé et chevalier fait.
Mes il aut feire le message,
se il en a si grant corage.
Atant s'an vont tuit troi a masse,   2255
tant qu'il pot estre none basse.

2226. desoz   2240. Conques tel ch.

94

And surrounded by men-at-arms
Carrying sharp battle-axes.   2210
As the knight neared the pass,
The one who was watching him reproached him
Bitterly for having ridden in the cart,
Saying: "Vassal, you acted boldly,
But like a naïve fool,   2215
In coming into this land.
A man who has ridden in a cart
Should never enter here.
May God never reward you for it!"
Thereupon the two spurred toward one another   2220
As fast as their horses could go.
The knight whose duty it was to guard the pass
Split his lance with the first blow
And let both pieces fall.
The other took aim at his throat   2225
Just above the upper edge
Of his shield, and tossed him backwards
Flat upon the stones.
The men-at-arms leapt to their axes
But deliberately avoided striking him,   2230
For they had no desire to hurt
Either him or his horse.
The knight saw clearly
That they did not want to wound him in any way
And harbored no desire to hurt him,   2235
So without drawing his sword
He passed through unchallenged,
With his companions after him.
And the one remarked to his brother:
"Never have I seen such a good knight,   2240
Nor could there be any to equal him.
Has he not performed an amazing feat
By forcing passage through here?"
"Fair brother," the knight replied,
"Now hurry for God's sake   2245
Until you reach my father,
And tell him of this adventure."
The youth swore and affirmed
That he would never go tell him,
Nor would he ever leave   2250
This knight, until he had been
Dubbed and knighted by him.
Let his brother deliver the message
If he is so set upon it.
The three then rode on together   2255
Until about mid-afternoon,

Vers none un home trové ont
qui lor demande qui il sont;
et il dïent: "Chevalier somes
qui an noz afeires alomes." 2260
Et li hom dit au chevalier:
"Sire, or voldroie herbergier
vos et voz conpaignons ansanble."
A celui le dit qui li sanble
que des autres soit sire et mestre, 2265
et il li dit: "Ne porroit estre
que je herberjasse a ceste ore,
car malvés est qui se demore
ne qui a eise se repose
puis qu'il a enprise tel chose; 2270
et je ai tel afeire anpris
qu'a piece n'iert mes ostex pris."
Et li hom li redit aprés:
"Mes ostex n'est mie ci pres,
einz est grant piece ça avant. 2275
Venir i poëz par covant
que a droite ore ostel prendroiz,
que tart iert quant vos i vendroiz."
"Et je," fet il, "i irai donques."
A la voie se met adonques 2280
li hom devant qui les an mainne,
et cil aprés la voie plainne.
Et quant il ont grant piece alé, [35f]
s'ont un escuier ancontré
qui venoit trestot le chemin 2285
les granz galoz sor un roncin
gras et reont com une pome.
Et li escuiers dit a l'ome:
"Sire, sire, venez plus tost,
car cil de Logres sont a ost 2290
venu sor ces de ceste terre,
s'ont ja comanciee la guerre
et la tançon et la meslee!
Et dïent qu'an ceste contree
s'est uns chevaliers anbatuz 2295
qui an mainz leus s'est conbatus,
n'en ne li puet contretenir
passage ou il vuelle venir,
que il n'i past cui qu'il enuit.
Ce dïent an cest païs tuit 2300
que il les deliverra toz
et metra les noz au desoz.
Or si vos hastez, par mon los!"
Lors se met li hom es galos,

2290. son

96

When they encountered a man
Who asked them who they were.
They answered: "We are knights
Going about our business."   2260
And the man said to the knight:
"Sir, now I would like to offer lodging
To you and to your companions as well."
He addressed this to the one he thought
To be the lord and master of the others,   2265
Who answered him: "It is impossible
For me to take lodging at this hour.
Only cowardice makes one tarry
Or relax at one's leisure
When he has undertaken anything;   2270
And I am engaged in such a task
That I will not take lodging for a long while yet."
Upon hearing this, the man replied:
"My house is not at all nearby,
But is a long distance ahead.   2275
I promise that you will be able
To lodge there at a suitable hour,
For it will be late when you arrive."
"In that case, I will go there," said the stranger.
The man who was their guide   2280
Then set off before them along the way,
And the others followed after him.
When they had gone a great distance,
They encountered a squire
Who was galloping full speed   2285
Toward them on a nag
Which was as fat and round as an apple.
The squire called out to the man:
"Sir, sir, come quickly!
The men of Logres have raised an army   2290
Against the people of this land
And the war and skirmishes
And fighting have already begun.
They say that a knight
Who has fought in many places   2295
Has invaded this land,
And they cannot keep him
From going anywhere he wishes,
Whether they like it or not.
All the people in this land say   2300
That he will soon free them
And defeat our people.
Now take my advice and hurry!"
The man quickened his pace to a gallop.

et cil an sont molt esjoï 2305
qui autresi l'orent oï,
car il voldront eidier as lor.
Et dit li filz au vavasor:
"Sire, oez que dit cist sergenz!
Alons, si eidons a noz genz 2310
qui sont meslé a ces de la!"
Et li hom tot adés s'an va
qu'il nes atant, ençois s'adrece
molt tost vers une forterece
qui sor un tertre estoit fermee; 2315
et cort tant qu'il vient a l'entree,
et cil aprés a esperon.
Li bailes estoit anviron
clos de haut mur et de fossé.
Tantost qu'il furent anz antré, 2320
si lor lessierent avaler,
qu'il ne s'an poïssent raler,
une porte aprés les talons.
Et cil dient: "Alons! alons!
Que ci n'aresterons nos pas!" 2325
Aprés l'ome plus que le pas
vont tant qu'il vienent a l'issue [36a]
qui ne lor fu pas desfandue;
mes maintenant que cil fu fors
li lessierent aprés le cors 2330
cheoir une porte colant.*
Et cil an furent molt dolant
quant dedanz anfermé se voient,
car il cuident qu'anchanté soient.
Mes cil don plus dire vos doi 2335
avoit un anel an son doi
don la pierre tel force avoit
qu'anchantemanz ne le pooit
tenir, puis qu'il l'avoit veüe.
L'anel met devant sa veüe, 2340
s'esgarde la pierre, et si dit:
"Dame, dame, se Dex m'aït,
or avroie je grant mestier
que vos me poïssiez eidier."
     Cele dame une fee estoit 2345
qui l'anel doné li avoit,
et si le norri an s'anfance;
s'avoit an li molt grant fiance
que ele an quel leu que il fust
secorre et eidier li deüst. 2350
Mes il voit bien a son apel

2327. Tant que il   2329. quil furent fors   2330. lor l.
apres les cors

98

The others, who had also heard it,   2305
Were filled with joy
Because they wished to help their countrymen.
The vavasor's son exclaimed:
"Sir, listen to what this servant has said!
Let's go help our people   2310
Who are fighting their enemies!"
Their guide hurried off
Without waiting for them and made his way
Straight toward a fortress
Which stood strongly on a hill.   2315
He rode until he reached the gate,
With the others spurring after him.
The bailey was surrounded
By a high wall and moat.
As soon as they had entered,   2320
A gate was lowered
Upon their heels
So they could not get out again.
"Let's go! Let's go!" they shouted.
"Let's not stop here!"   2325
They hastened after the man
Until they reached a passage
Which was not closed to them;
But as soon as the man
They were following had gone through it   2330
A gate slid shut behind him.
They were most upset
To find themselves trapped within,
For they thought they must be bewitched.
But the one I must speak most about   2335
Had a ring on his finger
Whose stone had the power
To break any spell
After he gazed at it.
He placed the ring before his eyes,   2340
Looked at the stone, and said:
"Lady, lady, by the grace of God,
I greatly need you
To come now to my aid."
   This lady was a fairy   2345
Who had given him the ring
And had cared for him in his infancy;
So he was certain
That she would come to succor and aid him
Wherever he might be.   2350
But he could tell from his appeal

et a la pierre de l'anel
qu'il n'i a point d'anchantemant,
et set trestot certainnemant
qu'il sont anclos et anserré.   2355
Lors vienent a un huis barré
d'une posterne estroite et basse.
Les espees traient a masse,
si fiert tant chascuns de s'espee
qu'il orent la barre colpee.   2360
Quant il furent defors la tor,
si voient comancié l'estor*
aval les prez molt grant et fier,
et furent bien mil chevalier
que d'une part que d'autre au mains   2365
estre la jaude des vilains.
Quant il vindrent aval les prez,
come sages et atremprez
li filz au vavasor parla:
"Sire, einz que nos vaigniemes la   2370
feriemes, ce cuit, savoir   [36b]
qui iroit anquerre et savoir
de quel part les noz genz se tienent.
Je ne sai de quel part il vienent,
mes g'i irai se vos volez."   2375
"Jel voel," fet il. "Tost i alez
et tost revenir vos covient."
Il i va tost et tost revient,
et dit: "Molt nos est bien cheü,
que j'ai certainnemant veü   2380
que ce sont li nostre de ça."
Et li chevaliers s'adreça
vers la meslee maintenant.
S'ancontre un chevalier venant
et joste a lui, sel fiert si fort   2385
parmi l'uel que il l'abat mort.
Et li vaslez a pié descent,
le cheval au chevalier prent
et les armes que il avoit,
si s'an arme bel et adroit.   2390
Quant armez fu, sanz demorance
monte et prant l'escu et la lance
qui estoit granz et roide et peinte;
au costé ot l'espee ceinte,
tranchant et flanbeant et clere.   2395
An l'estor est aprés son frere
et aprés son seignor venuz,
qui molt bien s'i est maintenuz
an la meslee une grant piece--

2362. Et comancie voient

100

And from the stone in the ring
That there was no spell cast here,
And he knew perfectly well
That they were locked in and confined.   2355
They came now to the barred door
Of a low and narrow postern gate.
All three drew their swords
And struck so many blows
That they hacked through the bar.   2360
Once they were out of the tower
They saw the battle raging
Great and fierce down in the meadows,
With a full thousand knights
At least on either side,   2365
Not counting the mass of peasants.
When they came down into the meadows,
The vavasor's son spoke
Wisely and calmly:
"Sir, before entering the fray   2370
We would do well, I believe,
To have one of us go inquire to learn
On which side are our countrymen.
I do not know from which side they come,
But I will go if you want."   2375
"I wish you would go quickly," he said,
"And return as quickly to us."
He went quickly and returned quickly.
"It has turned out well for us," he said.
"I've seen with certainty   2380
That our men are on this near side."
Then the knight rode
At once into the battle.
He jousted with a knight he met
Coming toward him and hit him such a blow   2385
In the eye that he struck him dead.
The vavasor's younger son dismounted,
Took the dead knight's horse
And the armor he was wearing,
And armed himself properly and skillfully.   2390
When he was armed he remounted
Without delay and took up the shield
And the long, straight,and painted lance;
At his side hung the sharp,
Gleaming, and bright sword.   2395
Into battle he followed his brother
And their lord,
Who had been defending himself
Fiercely throughout the combat--

qu'il ront et fant et si depiece   2400
escuz et hiaumes et haubers.
Nes garantist ne fuz ne fers
cui il ataint, qu'il ne l'afolt
ou morz jus del cheval ne volt.
Il seus si tres bien le feisoit   2405
que trestoz les desconfisoit,
et cil molt bien le refeisoient
qui avoec lui venu estoient.
Mes cil de Logres s'en mervoillent,
qu'il nel conuissent, et consoillent   2410
de lui au fil au vavasor;
tant an demandent li plusor
qu'an lor dist: "Seignor, ce est cil
qui nos gitera toz d'essil
et de la grant maleürté   [36c]
ou nos avons lonc tans esté.
Se li devons grant enor feire
quant, por nos fors de prison treire,
a tant perilleus leus passez
et passera ancor assez.   2420
Molt a a feire et molt a fait."
N'i a celui joie n'en ait*
quant la novele est tant alee
que ele fu a toz contee;
tuit l'oïrent et tuit le sorent.   2425
De la joie que il en orent
lors croist force et s'an esvertüent
tant que mainz des autres an tüent;
et plus les mainnent leidemant
por le bien feire seulemant   2430
d'un seul chevalier, ce me sanble,
que por toz les autres ansanble.
Et s'il ne fust si pres de nuit,
desconfit s'an alassent tuit;
mes la nuiz si oscure vint   2435
que departir les an covint.
    Au departir, tuit li cheitif
autresi come par estrif
environ le chevalier vindrent;
de totes parz au frain le pristrent,   2440
si li ancomancent a dire:
"Bien veignanz soiez vos, biax sire!"
Et dit chascuns: "Sire, par foi,
vos vos herbergeroiz o moi!
Sire, por Deu et por son non,   2445
ne herbergiez se o moi non!"
Tuit dïent ce que dit li uns,

2401. Escuz et lances

102

Breaking, cleaving, and splitting   2400
Shields, helmets, and hauberks.
Neither wood nor iron served as defense
To those he attacked, as he knocked them
Dead or wounded from their steeds.
With unaided prowess   2405
He routed all he met,
And those who had come with him
Did their share as well.
The men of Logres marvelled
At the deeds of this unknown knight;   2410
And asked the vavasor's son about him.
They persisted in their questioning
Until they were told: "Lords, this is he
Who will lead us out of exile
And free us from the great misery   2415
We have been in for so long.
We should honor him highly
Since, to set us free,
He has crossed many a treacherous pass
And will cross more to come.   2420
He has much yet to do, and has already done much."
When the news had spread
Throughout the crowd, there was no one
Who was not filled with joy;
All heard, and all understood.   2425
From the elation they felt
Sprang the strength that enabled them
To slay many of their enemies.
Yet it seems to me
That the enemy was defeated more   2430
By the effort of a single knight
Than by that of all the others combined.
Were it not so near nightfall
The enemy would have been fully routed;
But the night grew so dark   2435
That they were obliged to separate.
    At the parting, all the prisoners
From Logres pressed excitedly
About the knight,
Grabbing his reins from every side   2440
And saying to him:
"Fair sir, you are indeed welcome!"
To which each added: "Sir, in faith,
You will take your lodging with me!
Sir, by God and by his Holy Name,   2445
Do not lodge anywhere but at my house!"
Everyone echoed these words,

que herbergier le vialt chascuns
ausi li juenes con li vialz;
et dit chascuns: "Vos seroiz mialz   2450
el mien ostel que an l'autrui."
Ce dit chascuns androit de lui
et li uns a l'autre le tost,
si con chascuns avoir le vost,
et par po qu'il ne s'an conbatent.   2455
Et il lor dit qu'il se debatent
de grant oiseuse et de folie.
"Lessiez," fet il, "ceste anreidie,
qu'il n'a mestier n'a moi n'a vos.   [36d]
Noise n'est pas boene antre nos,   2460
einz devroit li uns l'autre eidier.
Ne vos covient mie pleidier
de moi herbergier par tançon,
einz devez estre an cusançon
de moi herbergier an tel leu   2465
por ce que tuit i aiez preu,
que je soie an ma droite voie."
Ancor dit chascuns totevoie:
"C'est a mon ostel."--Mes au mien."
"Ne dites mie ancore bien,"   2470
fet li chevaliers. "A mon los,
li plus sages de vos est fos
de ce don ge vos oi tancier.
Vos me devrïez avancier,
et vos me volez feire tordre.   2475
Se vos m'avïez tuit en ordre
li uns aprés l'autre a devise
fet tant d'enor et de servise
con an porroit feire a un home,
par toz les sainz qu'an prie a Rome   2480
ja plus boen gré ne l'en savroie,
quant la bonté prise en avroie,
que je faz de la volanté.
Se Dex me doint joie et santé,
la volantez autant me haite   2485
con se chascuns m'avoit ja faite
molt grant enor et grant bonté;
si soit an leu de fet conté!"
Ensi les vaint toz et apeise.
Chiés un chevalier molt a eise   2490
el chemin a ostel l'en mainnent,
et de lui servir tuit se painnent.
Trestuit l'enorent et servirent
et molt tres grant joie li firent
tote la nuit jusqu'au couchier,   2495
car il l'avoient tuit molt chier.
Le main quant vint au dessevrer

104

For young and old alike
Wanted him to lodge with them,
Saying: "You will be better   2450
Provided for at my house than elsewhere."
Everyone there about him was saying this
And was trying to pull him away from the others,
Because each wanted to have him,
Until they nearly came to blows.   2455
He told them that it was
Idle and foolish to quarrel so.
"Stop this bickering," he said,
"For it will profit neither me nor you.
Rather than quarrel among ourselves,   2460
We should help one another.
You should not argue
Over who will lodge me,
But should be intent
Upon lodging me in such a place   2465
That will bring honor to all
And will help me along my way."
Yet each kept saying:
"At my house."--"No, at mine."
"You're all talking foolishly still,"   2470
Said the knight. "To my mind
The wisest of you is a fool
For arguing this way.
You should help me along,
But all you want to do is divert me.   2475
By all the saints invoked at Rome,
I am as grateful now
For your good intentions,
As I would have been
If all of you,   2480
One after another,
Had provided me as much honor and service
As one can give a man.
As surely as God gives me happiness and health,
Your good intentions please me as much   2485
As if each one of you had already shown me
Great honor and kindness.
So may the intention be counted for the deed!"
Thus he persuaded and appeased them all.
They took him along the road to the house   2490
Of a very well-to-do knight,
And everyone made a great effort to serve him.
They all honored and served him
And showed their joy at his presence;
Out of respect for him   2495
They entertained him until bedtime.
In the morning when it was time to depart,

vost chascuns avoec lui aler;
chascuns se poroffre et presante.
Mes lui ne plest ne n'atalante   2500
que nus hom s'an voist avoec lui,
fors que tant solemant li dui
que il avoit la amenez;   [36e]
ces, sanz plus, en avoit menez.
Cel jor ont des la matinee   2505
chevalchié tresqu'a la vespree
qu'il ne troverent aventure.
Chevalchant molt grant aleüre
d'une forest molt tart issirent;
a l'issir une meison virent   2510
a un chevalier; et sa fame,
qui sanbloit estre boene dame,
virent a la porte seoir.
Tantost qu'ele les pot veoir
s'est contre aus an estant dreciee;   2515
a chiere molt joiant et liee
les salue, et dit: "Bien vaingniez!
Mon ostel voel que vos praigniez.
Herbergiez estes, descendez."
"Dame, quant vos le comandez,   2520
vostre merci, nos descendrons;
vostre ostel enuit mes prendrons."
Il descendent; et au descendre
la dame fet les chevax prendre,
qu'ele avoit mesniee molt bele.   2525
Ses filz et ses filles apele,
et il vindrent tot maintenant:
vaslet cortois et avenant,
et chevalier et filles beles.
As uns comande oster les seles   2530
des chevax et bien conreer.
N'i a celui qui l'ost veher,
einz le firent molt volentiers.
Desarmer fet les chevaliers;
au desarmer les filles saillent;   2535
desarmé sont, puis si lor baillent
a afubler trois corz mantiax.
A l'ostel qui molt estoit biax
les an mainnent eneslepas.
Mes li sires n'i estoit pas,   2540
einz ert en bois, et avoec lui
estoient de ses filz li dui.
Mes il vint lués, et sa mesniee
qui molt estoit bien anresniee
saut contre lui defors la porte.   2545

2537. .ij. corz

106

Everyone wanted to go with him
And offered his services.
But it was not his pleasure or will   2500
That anyone should accompany him
Except the two alone
Whom he had brought there with him.
He took these two, and no more.
They rode that day   2505
From early morning until dusk
Without encountering adventure.
In the evening late they came riding
Rapidly out of a forest
And saw the manor house   2510
Of a knight. His wife,
Who seemed to be a gentle lady,
They saw seated in the doorway.
As soon as she could see them,
She rose up to meet them;   2515
With a broad, happy smile
She greeted them, saying: "Welcome!
I want you to stay in my house.
Dismount and take your lodging here."
"My lady, since you order it,   2520
By your leave we'll dismount
And stay here this night."
When they had dismounted,
The lady had their horses cared for
By the excellent members of her household.   2525
She called her sons and daughters,
Who came at once:
Youths, who were courteous and proper,
Knights and beautiful daughters.
Some she asked to unsaddle   2530
And groom the horses,
Which they willingly did
Without a word of argument.
At her request
The girls hastened to disarm the knights,   2535
And when they were disarmed, they were given
Three short mantles to wear.
Then they were led straightway
To their well-appointed lodgings.
The lord of the manor was not there,   2540
For he had been in the woods
Hunting with his two sons.
But he soon returned and his household,
With proper manners,
Hastened to meet him at the gate.   2545

La veneison que il aporte
destrossent molt tost et deslïent   [36f]
et si li recontent et dïent:
"Sire, sire, vos ne savez:
trois ostes chevaliers avez."   2550
"Dex an soit aorez!" fet il.
Li chevaliers et si dui fil
font de lor oste molt grant joie;
et la mesniee n'est pas coie,
que toz li mandre s'aprestoit   2555
de feire ce qu'a feire estoit.
Cil corent le mangier haster;
cil les chandoiles alumer,
si les alument et espranent;
la toaille et les bacins pranent,   2560
si donent l'eve as mains laver
(de ce ne sont il mie aver).
Tuit levent, si vont asseoir.
Riens qu'an poïst leanz veoir
n'estoit charjable ne pesanz.   2565
Au premier mes vint uns presanz
d'un chevalier a l'uis defors,
plus orguelleus que n'est uns tors--
que c'est molt orguilleuse beste!
Cil des les piez jusqu'a la teste   2570
sist toz armez sor son destrier.
De l'une janbe an son estrier
fu afichiez, et l'autre ot mise
par contenance et par cointise
sor le col del destrier crenu.   2575
Estes le vos ensi venu
c'onques nus garde ne s'an prist,
tant qu'il vint devant aus et dist:
"Li quex est ce--savoir le vuel--
qui tant a folie et orguel   2580
et de cervel la teste vuide,
qu'an cest païs vient et si cuide
au Pont de l'Espee passer?
Por neant s'est venuz lasser;
por neant a ses pas perduz."   2585
Et cil, qui ne fu esperduz,
molt seüremant li respont:
"Je sui qui vuel passer au Pont."
"Tu? Tu! Comant l'osas panser?
Einz te deüsses apanser,   2590
que tu anpreïsses tel chose,   [37a]
a quel fin et a quel parclose
tu an porroies parvenir,

2550. ij. ostes 2555. li miaudres

They unpacked and untied
The venison he was carrying,
And said as they met him:
"Sir, sir, you don't know,
But you're entertaining three knights."   2550
"May God be praised!" he replied.
The knight and his two sons
Were very pleased to have this company,
And even the least member of the household
Did his best to carry out   2555
What had to be done.
Some hastened to prepare the meal,
Others to light the tapers;
They lit them and set them glowing.
Still others fetched the towel and basins   2560
And brought water (of which they were not
At all sparing) for washing their hands.
When they had all washed they took their seats.
Nothing to be found therein
Was unpleasant or objectionable.   2565
During the first course there came before them*
At the outside door a knight,
Who was prouder than a bull--
Which is a very proud beast!
Armed from his feet to his head,   2570
He sat upon his charger,
With one foot fixed
In his stirrup and his other leg,
For style, thrown jauntily
Over his steed's flowing mane.   2575
He had advanced in this fashion
Without being noticed,
Until he was just before them, and said:
"I want to know which one of you it is
Who is so proud and foolish,   2580
And so brainless,
As to come into this land and believe
That he can cross the Sword Bridge?
He's wasting his strength;
He's wasting his steps."   2585
Our knight, unruffled,
Answered him with confidence:
"I am he who wishes to cross the Bridge."
"You? you! How did you even dare presume?
Before undertaking such a thing   2590
You should contemplate
What end and what issue
You might come to;

109

si te deüst resovenir
de la charrete ou tu montas.   2595
Ce ne sai ge se tu honte as
de ce que tu i fus montez,
mes ja nus qui fust bien senez
n'eüst si grant afaire anpris
s'il de cest blasme fust repris."   2600
A ce que cil dire li ot
ne li daigne respondre un mot,
mes li sires de la meison
et tuit li autre par reison
s'an mervoillent a desmesure: 2605
"Ha, Dex! con grant mesavanture!"
fet chascuns d'ax a lui meïsmes.
"L'ore que charrete fu primes
pansee et feite soit maudite,
car molt est vix chose et despite.   2610
Ha, Dex! de coi fu il retez?
Et por coi fu il charretez?
Por quel pechié? Por quel forfet?
Ce li ert mes toz jorz retret.
S'il fust de cest reproche mondes,   2615
an tant con dure toz li mondes
ne fust uns chevaliers trovez
tant soit de proesce esprovez,
qui cest chevalier resanblast;
et qui trestoz les assanblast   2620
si bel ne si gent n'i veïst,
por ce que le voir an deïst."
Ce disoient comunemant.
Et cil molt orguilleusemant
sa parole recomança,   2625
et dist: "Chevaliers, antant ça,
qui au Pont de l'Espee an vas:
se tu viax, l'eve passeras
molt legieremant et soëf.
Je te ferai an une nef   2630
molt tost oltre l'eve nagier.
Mes se je te vuel paagier
quant de l'autre part te tandrai,
se je vuel, la teste an prandrai;
ou ce non, an ma merci iert."   [37b]
Et cil respont que il ne quiert
avoir mie desavanture:
ja sa teste an ceste avanture
n'iert mise por nes un meschief.
Et cil li respont derechief: 2640
"Des que tu ce feire ne viax,
cui soit la honte ne li diax
venir te covendra ça fors

110

You ought to reflect
Upon the cart in which you rode.   2595
I do not know if you feel shame
For having ridden in it,
But anyone with any sense
Would never have undertaken such a feat
If he were so blameworthy."   2600
To what had been said
He did not deign to reply a single word,
But the lord of the manor
And all the others were rightfully
Astounded beyond measure at this.   2605
"Oh, God! What a misfortune!"
Said each to himself.
"Damned be the hour when a cart
Was first conceived of and built,
For it is a vile and despicable thing.   2610
Oh God! What was he accused of?
Why was he driven in the cart?
For what sin? For what crime?
He will be reproached forever for it.
If he were clear of this curse,   2615
As far as the world extends
No knight could be found,
No matter how bold he proves himself,
Who would match this knight;
And should all knights be assembled in one spot,   2620
You'd not see a more genteel or handsome one,
If the truth be told."
Upon this they all agreed.
The intruder began
To speak haughtily again,   2625
Saying: "Knight, hear this,
You who are going to the Sword Bridge:
If you wish you can cross the water
Very easily and safely.
I will have you taken   2630
Across quickly in a boat.
However, if I decide to make you pay the passage
When I have gotten you across,
Then I'll have your head if I wish;
Or, if not, it will be at my mercy."   2635
Our knight replied that he was not
Seeking to have any trouble
And would never risk his head this way,
No matter what the consequences.
Upon which the intruder continued: 2640
"Since you do not want to accept my aid,
You must come outside here
To face me in single combat,

111

a moi conbatre cors a cors."
Et cil dit por lui amuser: 2645
"Se jel pooie refuser,
molt volantiers m'an sosferoie;
mes ainçois voir me conbatroie
que noauz feire m'esteüst."
Einçois que il se remeüst   2650
de la table ou il se seoient,
dist as vaslez qui le servoient
que sa sele tost li meïssent
sor son cheval, et si preïssent
ses armes, ses li aportassent.   2655
Et cil del tost feire se lassent.
Li un de lui armer se painnent,
li autre son cheval amainnent;
et, sachiez, ne resanbloit pas,
si com il s'an aloit le pas   2660
armez de trestotes ses armes
et tint l'escu par les enarmes
et fu sor son cheval montez,
qu'il deüst estre mescontez
n'antre les biax n'antre les buens.   2665
Bien sanble qu'il doie estre suens
li chevax, tant li avenoit,
et li escuz que il tenoit
par les enarmes anbracié.
Si ot un hiaume el chief lacié   2670
qui tant i estoit bien assis
que il ne vos fust mie avis
qu'anprunté n'acreü l'eüst;
einz deïssiez, tant vos pleüst,
qu'il fu ensi nez et creüz.   2675
De ce voldroie estre creüz.
    Fors de la porte, an une lande,
est cil qui la joste demande,
ou la bataille estre devoit.*   [37c]
Tantost con li uns l'autre voit,   2680
point li uns vers l'autre a bandon,
si s'antrevienent de randon
et des lances tex cos se donent
que eles ploient et arçonent
et anbedeus an pieces volent.   2685
As espees les escuz dolent
et les hiaumes et les haubers;
tranchent les fuz, ronpent les fers
si que an plusors leus se plaient.
Par ire tex cos s'antrepaient   2690
con s'il fussent fet a covant.

2682. a bandon

112

Which will be to the shame and grief of one of us."
To show his ease, the knight answered: 2645
"If I could refuse,
I'd gladly pass it by;
But, indeed, I'd prefer to fight
Than to have something worse befall me."
Before arising 2650
From where he was seated at table,
He told the youths who were serving him
To saddle his horse
At once and to fetch
His armor and bring it to him. 2655
They hurried to obey.
Some took pains to arm him;
Others brought forward his horse.
And you can be sure that it seemed,
When he was riding off 2660
Fully armed,
Mounted on his horse
And holding his shield by its armstraps,
That he could only be counted
Among the fair and the good. 2665
The horse could not be anything
But his own, so well did it suit him--
As did the shield he held
By the armstraps.
He had a helmet laced on his head 2670
Which fit so perfectly
You would never have thought
He had borrowed it or wore it on credit.
Rather you would say, so pleasing was the sight of him,
That he had been born and raised to it. 2675
All this I would have you believe on my word.
    Beyond the gate, on a heath
Where the battle was to be held,
The challenger waited.
As soon as the one saw the other, 2680
They spurred full speed to the attack
And met with a clash,
Striking such mighty thrusts with their lances
That they bent like bows
Before flying into splinters. 2685
They dented their shields, helmets,
And hauberks with sword blows;
They split the wood and broke the chain links
And were each wounded in several places.
Every blow was in payment for another, 2690
As if they were settling a debt in their fury.

113

Mes les espees molt sovant
jusqu'as cropes des chevax colent;
del sanc s'aboivrent et saolent
que jusque es flans les anbatent, 2695
si que andeus morz les abatent.
Et quant il sont cheü a terre,
li uns vet l'autre a pié requerre;
et s'il de mort s'antrehaïssent,
ja por voir ne s'antranvaïssent 2700
as espees plus cruelmant.
Plus se fierent menüemant
que cil qui met deniers an mine,
qui de joer onques ne fine
a totes failles deus et deus. 2705
Mes molt estoit autres cist jeus--
que il n'i avoit nule faille,
mes cos et molt fiere bataille,
molt felenesse et molt cruel.
Tuit furent issu de l'ostel: 2710
sires, dame, filles et fil,
qu'il n'i remest cele ne cil
(ne li privé ne li estrange),
ainçois estoient tuit an range
venu por veoir la meslee 2715
an la lande qui molt fu lee.
Li chevaliers a la charrete
de malvestié se blasme et rete
quant son oste voit qui l'esgarde:
et des autres se reprant garde 2720
qui l'esgardoient tuit ansanble;
d'ire trestoz li cors li tranble,
qu'il deüst--ce li est avis-- [37d]
avoir molt grant pieç'a conquis
celui qui a lui se conbat. 2725
Lors le fiert, si qu'il li anbat
l'espee molt pres de la teste;
si l'anvaïst come tanpeste,
car il l'anchauce, si l'argüe
tant que place li a tolue. 2730
Se li tost terre et si le mainne
tant que bien pres li faut l'alainne,
s'a an lui molt po de desfanse.
Et lors li chevaliers s'apanse
que il li avoit molt vilmant 2735
la charrete mise devant.
Si li passe et tel le conroie
qu'il n'i remaint laz ne corroie
qu'il ne ronpe antor le coler;
si li fet le hiaume voler 2740
del chief et cheoir la vantaille.

Often their sword blows
Struck through to their horses's croups;
They were so drunk in their thirst for blood
That their blows fell even on the horses's flanks   2695
Till both fell dead.
When their steeds had fallen,
They pursued each other on foot;
Had they hated one another with mortal passion,
In truth they could not have struck   2700
More mightily with their swords.
Their payment fell more swiftly
Than the coins of the gambler
Who doubles the wager
With each toss of the dice.   2705
But this game was different--
There were no dice cast,
Only blows and fearful combat,
Treacherous and savage.
Everyone had come out of the house: 2710
Lords, ladies, daughters, and sons;
Not a person remained within--woman or man,
Member of the household or not;
All had assembled
To watch the battle   2715
On the broad heath.
The Knight of the Cart
Blamed and accused himself of faintheartedness
When he saw that his host was watching him.
Then, as he saw the others   2720
Together there observing him,
His whole body shook with anger,
For he was certain that he should
Long since have beaten
His adversary.   2725
With his sword he struck him
A blow near his head,
Then stormed him,
Pushing him relentlessly backwards
Until he had driven him from his position.   2730
He drove him and forced him to retreat
Until the man had almost lost his breath
And was nearly defenseless.
Then our knight remembered
That he had reproached him most basely   2735
For having ridden in the cart.
He struck and assailed him
Until no lacing or strap remained
Unbroken around his neck-band. *
He knocked the helmet   2740
From his head, and the ventail flew off.

115

Tant le painne et tant le travaille
que a merci venir l'estuet.
Come l'aloe qui ne puet
devant l'esmerillon durer   2745
ne ne s'a ou aseürer
puis que il la passe et sormonte,
ausi cil a tote sa honte
li vet requerre et demander
merci, qu'il nel puet amander.   2750
Et quant il ot que cil requiert
merci, si nel toche ne fiert,
einz dit: "Viax tu merci avoir?"
"Molt avez or dit grant savoir,"
fet cil, "ce devroit dire fos!   2755
Onques rien nule tant ne vos
con je faz merci orandroit."
Et cil dit: "Il te covandroit
sor une charrete monter.
A neant porroies conter   2760
quanque tu dire me savroies,
s'an la charrete ne montoies
por ce que tant fole boche as
que vilmant la me reprochas."
Et li chevaliers li respont: 2765
"Ja Deu ne place que g'i mont!"
"Non?" fet cil, "et vos i morroiz."   [37e]
"Sire, bien feire le porroiz.
Mes, por Deu, vos quier et demant
merci, fors que tant seulemant   2770
qu'an charrete monter ne doive.
Nus plez n'est que je n'an reçoive
fors cestui, tant soit griés ne forz.
Mialz voldroie estre, je cuit, morz
que fet eüsse cest meschief.   2775
Ja nule autre chose si grief
ne me diroiz, que je ne face
por merci et por vostre grace."
    Que que cil merci li demande,
atant ez vos parmi la lande   2780
une pucele l'anbleüre
venir sor une fauve mure,
desafublee et desliee;
et si tenoit une corgiee
don la mule feroit grant cos,   2785
et nus chevax les granz galos,
por verité, si tost n'alast
que la mule plus tost n'anblast.
Au chevalier de la charrete
dist la pucele: "Dex te mete,   2790
chevaliers, joie el cuer parfite

He pressed him and belabored him so
That he was compelled to beg mercy.
Like the lark which is
Unable to find cover   2745
And is powerless before the merlin,
Which flies more swiftly and attacks it from above,
The man, to his great shame,
Had to ask and plead for
Mercy, for he could not better him.   2750
When the victor heard his foe pleading
For mercy, he did not strike or touch him,
But said: "Do you want me to spare you?"
"You have asked a smart question,"
Said he, "such as even a fool might ask!   2755
Never had I wanted anything
As much as I now want mercy."
And he said: "Then you shall have
To ride in a cart.
You can say anything you wish;   2760
Nothing will have any effect on me
Unless you mount the cart
For having reproached me so basely
With your foolish tongue."
And the proud knight answered him: 2765
"May it never please God that I ride in a cart!"
"No?" he said. "Then you will die!"
"Sir, you have my life in your hands.
But for God's sake, I beg and ask
Your mercy, only don't have me   2770
Climb up into a cart.
There is nothing I wouldn't do
Except this, no matter how difficult or painful.
I would rather be dead, I am sure,
Than to have done this dishonor.   2775
No matter what else you could ask of me,
However difficult, I would do it
To have your mercy and pardon."
    As he was asking him for mercy,
There came a girl riding   2780
Across the heath
On a tawny mule,
With her mantle unpinned and hair dishevelled.
She had a whip
With which she was striking her mule,   2785
And no horse at full gallop,
In truth, could have gone
Faster than that mule was running.
To the Knight of the Cart
The girl spoke: "May God fill   2790
Your heart with perfect happiness

117

de la rien qui plus te delite."
Cil qui volantiers l'ot oïe
li respont: "Dex vos beneïe,
pucele, et doint joie et santé!"
Lors dist cele sa volanté:
"Chevaliers," fet ele, "de loing
sui ça venue a grant besoing
a toi por demander un don,
en merite et an guerredon
si grant con ge te porrai feire.
Et tu avras encor afeire
de m'aïde, si con je croi."
Et cil li respont: "Dites moi
que vos volez, et se je l'ai,
avoir le porroiz sanz delai,
mes que ne soit chose trop griés."
Et cele dit: "Ce est li chiés
de cest chevalier que tu as
conquis; et voir, einz ne trovas
si felon ne si desleal.
Ja ne feras pechié ne mal,
einçois feras aumosne et bien,
que c'est la plus desleax rien
qui onques fust ne jamés soit."
Et quant cil qui vaincuz estoit
ot qu'ele vialt que il l'ocie,
si li dist: "Ne la creez mie,
qu'ele me het. Mes je vos pri
que vos aiez de moi merci
por ce Deu qui est filz et pere,
et qui de celi fist sa mere
qui estoit sa fille et s'ancele."
"Ha! chevaliers!" fet la pucele,
"ne croire pas ce traïtor.
Que Dex te doint joie et enor
si grant con tu puez covoitier,
et si te doint bien esploitier
de ce que tu as entrepris!"
Or est li chevaliers si pris
qu'el panser demore et areste:
savoir s'il an donra la teste
celi qui la rueve tranchier,
ou s'il avra celui tant chier
qu'il li praigne pitiez de lui.
Et a cesti et a celui
viaut feire ce qu'il li demandent:
Largece et Pitiez li comandent
que lor boen face a enbedeus

2795

2800

2805

2810
[37 f]

2815

2820

2825

2830

2835

2798. besoig

118

And grant your every wish."
He, who was delighted to hear this greeting,
Replied: "May God bless you
And grant you joy and good health!"   2795
Then she announced her purpose:
"Knight," said she, "I have come
From afar in great distress
To ask a favor of you,
For which you will deserve   2800
The greatest reward I can offer.
A time will come when you will need
My assistance, I believe."
"Tell me," he answered her,
"What you desire, and if I have it,   2805
You will receive it at once,
If it be not something extravagant."
She said: "I ask for the head
Of this knight you have just
Defeated; in truth, you have never encountered   2810
A more base and faithless knight.
You will commit no sin nor evil,
But will instead do a good and charitable act,
For he is the most faithless being
Who ever was or ever will be."   2815
When the defeated knight
Heard that she wanted him killed,
He said to the other: "Do not believe a word she says,
For she hates me. Rather, I pray you,
Have mercy on me   2820
By this God who is both Father and Son,
And who made His daughter
And handmaiden to be His mother."
"Ah, Knight!" said the girl,
"Don't believe this traitor.   2825
May God give you joy and honor
As much as you desire,
And may he give you success
In what you have undertaken!"
Now the victorious knight hesitated   2830
And reflected upon his decision:
Should he give the head to this girl
Who has asked him to cut it off,
Or should he be touched by pity
For the fallen knight?   2835
He wishes to content
Both the one and the other:
Generosity and Compassion demand
That he satisfy them both,

119

qu'il estoit larges et piteus.   2840
Mes se cele la teste an porte,
donc iert Pitiez vaincue et morte;
et s'ele ne l'an porte quite,
donc iert Largece desconfite.
An tel prison, an tel destrece   2845
le tienent Pitiez et Largece,
que chascune l'angoisse et point.
La teste vialt que il li doint
la pucele qui li demande;
et d'autre part li recomande   2850
sor pitié et sor sa franchise.*
Et des que il li a requise
merci, donc ne l'avra il donques?
Oïl, ce ne li avint onques
que nus, tant fust ses anemis,   [38a]
des que il l'ot au desoz mis
et merci crïer li covint,
onques ancor ne li avint
c'une foiz merci li veast--
mes au sorplus ja ne baast.*   2860
Donc ne la vehera il mie
cestui qui li requiert et prie,
des que ensi feire le sialt.*
Et cele qui la teste vialt,
avra la ele? Oïl, s'il puet.   2865
"Chevaliers," fet il, "il t'estuet
conbatre derechief a moi,
et tel merci avrai de toi,
se tu viax ta teste desfandre,
que je te lesserai reprendre   2870
ton hiaume et armer derechief
a leisir ton cors et ton chief
a tot le mialz que tu porras.
Mes saches que tu i morras
se je autre foiz te conquier."   2875
Et cil respont: "Ja mialz ne quier,
n'autre merci ne te demant."
"Et ancor assez t'i amant,"
fet cil, "que je me conbatrai
a toi que ja ne me movrai   2880
d'ensi con ge sui ci elués."
Cil s'atorne et revienent lués
a la bataille com angrés,
mes plus le reconquist aprés
li chevaliers delivremant   2885
qu'il n'avoit fet premieremant.
Et la pucele eneslepas

2863. vialt

For he is equally generous and merciful.   2840
Yet if the girl carries off the head,
Compassion will be vanquished and put to death;
And if she must leave without it,
Generosity will be defeated.
Compassion and Generosity hold   2845
Him doubly imprisoned, with each in turn
Spurring him on and causing him anguish.
One wishes him to give the head
To the girl who asked for it;
The other urges   2850
Pity and Kindness.
But since the man has begged
For mercy, will he not have it?
Indeed, for no matter
How much he hates a knight,   2855
He has never refused to grant mercy once--
But only one time--
If that knight has been
Defeated and forced to plead
With him for his life.   2860
So he will not refuse it
To this man who begs and implores him,
Since thus is his wont.
And she who desires the head,
Will she have it? Yes, if possible.   2865
"Knight," he said, "you must
Fight with me again
If you wish to defend your head.
I will show such mercy to you
That I shall allow you to take up   2870
Your helmet and to arm anew
Your body and head
As best you are able.
But know that you will die
If I defeat you again."   2875
The knight replied: "I could wish no better
And ask no other mercy."
"I shall give you this advantage,"
The Knight of the Cart said, "that I will fight
You without moving   2880
From this spot I have claimed."
The other knight made ready, and they returned
Eagerly to the fight,
But he was defeated now
With more ease   2885
Than he had been the first time.
Immediately the girl

crie: "Ne l'espargnier tu pas,
chevaliers, por rien qu'il te die,
certes qu'il ne t'espargnast mie   2890
s'il t'eüst conquis une foiz!
Bien saches tu: se tu le croiz
il t'angignera derechief.
Tranche au plus desleal le chief
de l'empire et de la corone,   2895
frans chevaliers, si le me done.
Por ce le me doiz bien doner
que jel te cuit guerredoner
molt bien ancor tex jorz sera.   [38b]
S'il puet, il te rangignera   2900
de sa parole autre foiee."
Cil qui voit sa mort aprochiee
li crie merci molt an haut,
mes ses criers rien ne li vaut,
ne chose que dire li sache;   2905
que cil par le hiaume le sache,
si que trestoz les laz an tranche:
la vantaille et la coiffe blanche
li abat de la teste jus.
Et cil se haste, ne puet plus: 2910
"Merci, por Deu! Merci, vassax!"
Cil respont: "Se je soie sax,
james de toi n'avrai pitié,
puis c'une foiz t'ai respitié."
"Ha!" fet il, "pechié feriez   2915
se m'anemie creïez
de moi an tel meniere ocirre."
Et cele qui sa mort desirre
de l'autre part li amoneste
qu'isnelemant li trant la teste,   2920
ne plus ne croie sa parole.
Cil fiert et la teste li vole
enmi la lande, et li cors chiet.
A la pucele plaist et siet.
Li chevaliers la teste prant   2925
par les chevox et si la tant
a celi qui grant joie an fait,
et dit: "Tes cuers si grant joie ait
de la rien que il plus voldroit,
con li miens cuers a orandroit   2930
de la rien que je plus haoie.
De nule rien ne me doloie
fors de ce que il vivoit tant.
Uns guerredons de moi t'atant
qui molt te vanra an boen leu;   2935
an cest servise avras grant preu
que tu m'as fet, ce t'acreant.

122

Shouted: "Do not spare him,
Knight, no matter what he says,
For certainly he would not have spared you   2890
Had he defeated you even once!
If you accept his pleas, you know
He will trick you again.
Cut off the head of this most faithless man
In the empire and kingdom,   2895
Fair knight, and give it to me.
You should let me have it,
For that good day will come
When I intend to reward you for it.
If he could, he would deceive you   2900
Again with his promises."
The knight, seeing his death at hand,
Cried out loudly for mercy,
But his cries and all the arguments
He could muster were of no avail to him.   2905
The other grabbed him by the helmet,
Tearing off all the fastenings:
The ventail and the white coif
He struck from off his head.
The knight struggled till he could no more: 2910
"Mercy, for the love of God! Mercy, noble vassal!"
He answered: "Even were it to assure my salvation,
I'd never again show you pity
After having once let you free."
"Ah!" said he, "you would sin   2915
If you believed my enemy
And slayed me thus!"
She, desirous of his death,
Was urging the knight
To behead him quickly   2920
And not to believe his words.
His blow sent the head flying
Out onto the heath; the body crumpled.
This pleased and suited the girl.
The knight grasped the head   2925
By the hair and presented it
To her who, taking great joy in it,
Said: "May your heart have great joy
In whatever it most desires,
As my heart now has   2930
In what I most hated.
I had only one grief in life:
That he lived so long.
I have a recompense awaiting you
Which will come when you most need it;   2935
Be assured that you will be greatly rewarded
For this service you have done me.

123

Or m'an irai, si te comant
a Deu, qui d'anconbrier te gart."
Tantost la pucele s'an part, 2940
et li uns l'autre a Deu comande.
Mes a toz ces qui an la lande
orent la bataille veüe [38c]
an est molt grant joie creüe.
Si desarment tot maintenant 2945
le chevalier, joie menant,
si l'enorent de quanqu'il sevent.
Tot maintenant lor mains relevent,
qu'al mangier asseoir voloient;
or sont plus lié qu'il ne soloient, 2950
si manjüent molt lieemant.
Quant mangié orent longuemant,
li vavasors dist a son oste
qui delez lui seoit an coste:
"Sire, nos venimes pieç'a 2955
del rëaume de Logres ça.
Né an somes, si voudrïens
qu'annors vos venist et granz biens
et joie an cest païs, que nos
i avrïens preu avoec vos, 2960
et a maint autre preuz seroit
s'enors et biens vos avenoit
an cest païs, an ceste voie."
Et cil respont: "Dex vos en oie."
   Quant li vavasors ot lessiee 2965
sa parole et l'ot abessiee,
si l'a uns de ses filz reprise,
et dist: "Sire, an vostre servise
devrïens toz noz pooirs metre
et doner einçois que promete. 2970
Se mestier aviez del prendre,
nos ne devrïens mie atendre
tant que vos le demandesiez.
Sire, ja ne vos esmaiez
de vostre cheval s'il est morz, 2975
car ceanz a chevax bien forz.
Tant voel que vos aiez del nostre:
tot le meillor an leu del vostre
en manroiz, bien vos est mestiers."
Et cil respont: "Molt volantiers." 2980
Atant font les liz atorner,
si se couchent. A l'anjorner
lievent matin et si s'atornent.
Atorné sont, puis si s'an tornent.
Au departir rien ne mesprant: 2985

2961. Et au moins autrui 2971. Boen mestier avriez

124

In leaving now I commend you
To God, that He might keep you from harm.
Thereupon the girl took her leave   2940
And each commended the other to God.
Great joy spread through
All those who had seen
The battle in the heath.
All now joyfully   2945
Removed the victor's armor
And honored him as best they knew how.
They then rewashed their hands,
As they were anxious to return to their meal;
Now they were much happier than usual   2950
And the meal passed amid high spirits.
When they had been eating for some time,
The vavasor remarked to his guest,
Who was seated beside him:
"Sir, we came here long ago   2955
From the Kingdom of Logres,
Where we were born. We want
You to receive great honor and fortune
And happiness in this land, for we ourselves
And many others as well   2960
Would have great profit
If honor and fortune were to come to you
In this land, in this undertaking."
"May God hear your prayer," he replied.
   When the vavasor had lowered   2965
His voice and broken off his speech,
One of his sons continued it,
Saying: "Sir, in your service
We should put all our resources
And give more than just promises.   2970
If you have need of our help,
We should not delay giving it
Until you request it.
Sir, do not be upset
If your horse is slain,   2975
For there are more strong horses here.
I want you to have all you need that we possess:
Our best horse will be brought forth
To replace yours, for you have need of it."
"I accept willingly," answered the knight.   2980
Thereupon they had the beds prepared
And went to sleep. They arose early
The next morning and outfitted themselves.
They departed as soon as they had dressed,
Without forgetting any politeness: 2985

a la dame et au seignor prant,
et a toz les autres, congié.
Mes une chose vos cont gié
por ce que rien ne vos trespas:
que li chevaliers ne volt pas   2990
monter sor le cheval presté
qu'an li ot a l'uis presanté;
einz i fist (ce vos voel conter)
un des deus chevaliers monter
qui venu erent avoec lui,   2995
et il sor le cheval celui
monte, qu'ainsi li plot et sist.
Quant chascuns sor son cheval sist,
si s'acheminerent tuit troi
par le congié et par l'otroi   3000
lor oste, qui serviz les ot
et enorez de quanqu'il pot.
Le droit chemin vont cheminant
tant que li jorz vet declinant,
et vienent au Pont de l'Espee   3005
aprés none vers la vespree.
Au pié del pont qui molt est max
sont descendu de lor chevax
et voient l'eve felenesse,
noire et bruiant, roide et espesse,   3010
tant leide et tant espoantable
con se fust li fluns au deable,
et tant perilleuse et parfonde
qu'il n'est riens nule an tot le monde,
s'ele i cheoit, ne fust alee   3015
ausi com an la mer betee.*
Et li ponz qui est an travers
estoit de toz autres divers,
qu'ainz tex ne fu ne jamés n'iert.
Einz ne fu, qui voir m'an requiert,   3020
si max ponz ne si male planche:
d'une espee forbie et blanche
estoit li ponz sor l'eve froide,
mes l'espee estoit forz et roide
et avoit deus lances de lonc.   3025
De chasque part ot un grant tronc
ou l'espee estoit closfichiee.
Ja nus ne dot que il i chiee
por ce que ele brist ne ploit,
que tant i avoit il d'esploit   3030
qu'ele pooit grant fes porter.
Ce feisoit molt desconforter
les deus chevaliers qui estoient

3030. si ne sanble il pas qui la voit   3031. puisse

They took leave of the lady and of the lord,
And of all the others.
But I must tell you one thing
So that nothing will be omitted:
Our knight did not wish   2990
To mount upon the borrowed horse
Which had been presented him at the gate.
Instead (I would have you to know) he had
One of the two knights
Who had come with him mount it,   2995
And he mounted that knight's horse,
Since thus it pleased and suited him.
When each was seated on his horse,
The three of them rode off
With the leave and permission   3000
Of their host, who had served
And honored them as best he could.
They rode straight on
Until night started to fall,
And reached the Sword Bridge   3005
In the late afternoon, about vespers.
At the foot of that very dangerous bridge
They got down from their horses
And saw the treacherous water,
Black and gurgling, dark and thick,   3010
As horrid and as frightening
As if it were the Devil's river,
And so perilous and deep
That there is nothing in the whole world which,
If it were to fall into it, would not be lost   3015
As surely as if it had fallen into the frozen sea.
The bridge across it
Was unlike any other;
There never was, nor ever will be another like it.
If you ask me the truth, there was never   3020
Such a treacherous bridge or planking:
The bridge across the cold water
Was a sharp gleaming sword,
But the sword was strong and stiff
And as long as two lances.   3025
On either side were large stumps
Into which the sword was fixed.
No one need have fear of falling
Because of the sword's breaking or bending,
For it was so well made   3030
That it could support a heavy weight.
What caused the two knights who accompanied
The third to be most discomfited,

avoec le tierz, que il cuidoient
que dui lÿon ou dui liepart   3035
au chief del pont de l'autre part
fussent lÏé a un perron.
L'eve et li ponz et li lÿon
les metent an itel freor
que il tranblent tuit de peor,   3040
et dÏent: "Sire, car creez
consoil de ce que vos veez,
qu'il vos est mestiers et besoinz.
Malveisemant est fez et joinz
cist ponz, et mal fu charpantez.   3045
S'atant ne vos an retornez,
au repantir vanroiz a tart.
Il covient feire par esgart
de tex choses i a assez.
Or soit c'outre soiez passez--   3050
ne por rien ne puet avenir,
ne que les vanz poez tenir
ne desfandre qu'il ne vantassent,
et as oisiax qu'il ne chantassent
si qu'il n'osassent mes chanter,   3055
ne que li hom porroit antrer
el vantre sa mere et renestre;
mes ce seroit qui ne puet estre
ne qu'an porroit la mer voidier--
poez vos savoir et cuidier   3060
que cil dui lÿon forsené
qui de la sont anchaené,
que il ne vos tüent et sucent
le sanc des voinnes, et manjucent
la char et puis rungent les os?   3065
Molt sui hardiz quant je les os
veoir et quant je les esgart!
Se de vos ne prenez regart,
il vos ocirront, ce sachiez:
molt tost ronpuz et arachiez   3070
les manbres del cors vos avront,
que merci avoir n'an savront.
Mes or aiez pitié de vos,
si remenez ansanble nos.
De vos meïsmes avroiz tort   [38 f]
s'an si certain peril de mort
vos meteiez a escïant."
Et cil lor respont an rïant:
"Seignor," fet il, "granz grez aiez
quant por moi si vos esmaiez--   3080
d'amor vos vient et de franchise.

3055. Ne

However, was that they thought
There were two lions or two leopards   3035
Tied to a large stone
At the other end of the bridge.
The water and the bridge and the lions
Put them in such a fright
That they trembled in fear,   3040
Saying: "Sir, take heed
Of what you see before you;
You must rightfully show caution.
This bridge is vilely constructed
And joined together, and vilely built.   3045
If you do not turn back at once,
Repentance will come too late.
There are many such things which should
Only be undertaken with great foresight.
Suppose that you do get across--   3050
But that could never happen,
No more than you could contain the winds
Or forbid them to blow,
Or prevent the birds from singing
Such that they stop their song;   3055
No more than a man could reenter
His mother's womb and be born again;
All this could not be,
Any more than one could empty the sea--
If you do get across, could you believe and be sure   3060
That those two wild lions,
Which are chained over there,
Would not kill you and suck
The blood from your veins and eat
Your flesh and then gnaw upon your bones?   3065
I am exceedingly bold if I even dare
See and look at them!
If you do not take care,
I assure you, they will slay you:
They will break and tear   3070
The members from your body
And show no mercy.
But take pity on yourself
And stay here with us.
You would do wrong   3075
To put yourself knowingly
In such certain danger of death."
With a laugh he reassured them:
"My lords, receive my thanks
For being so concerned about me--   3080
It comes from love and kindness.

Bien sai que vos an nule guise
ne voldrïez ma mescheance;
mes j'ai tel foi et tel creance
an Deu qu'il me garra par tot.   3085
Cest pont ne ceste eve ne dot
ne plus que ceste terre dure,
einz me voel metre en aventure
de passer outre et atorner.
Mialz voel morir que retorner!"   3090
Cil ne li sevent plus que dire;
mes de pitié plore et sopire
li uns et li autres molt fort.
Et cil de trespasser le gort
au mialz que il set s'aparoille,   3095
et fet molt estrange mervoille
que ses piez desarme et ses mains--
n'iert mie toz antiers ne sains
quant de l'autre part iert venuz!
Bien s'iert sor l'espee tenuz,   3100
qui plus estoit tranchanz que fauz,
as mains nues et si deschauz,
que il ne s'est lessiez an pié
souler ne chauce n'avanpié.*
De ce gueres ne s'esmaioit   3105
s'es mains et es piez se plaioit;
mialz se voloit il mahaignier
que cheoir del pont et baignier
an l'eve don jamés n'issist.
A la grant dolor c'on li fist   3110
s'an passe outre et a grant destrece--
mains et genolz et piez se blece;
mes tot le rasoage et sainne
Amors qui le conduist et mainne,
si li estoit a sofrir dolz.   3115
A mains, a piez et a genolz
fet tant que de l'autre part vient.
Lors li remanbre et resovient
des deus lÿons qu'il i cuidoit   [39a]
avoir veüz quant il estoit   3120
de l'autre part. Lors s'i esgarde:
n'i avoit nes une leisarde
ne rien nule qui mal li face.
Il met sa main devant sa face,
s'esgarde son anel et prueve.   3125
(Quant nul des deus lÿons n'i trueve
qu'il i cuidoit avoir veüz,
si cuida estre deceüz;
mes il n'i avoit rien qui vive.)

3097. desire   3108. cheoir el pont

130

I know that you would never
Wish me to fall into any misfortune,
But so strong is my faith and belief
In God, that He will protect me always.   3085
I do not fear this bridge and this water
Any more than I do this solid earth.
No, I intend to prepare myself
To undertake a crossing.
I would rather die than turn back!"   3090
They did not know what more to say to him;
Both the one and the other wept
And sighed deeply with compassion.
The knight prepared himself as best
He could to cross the chasm   3095
And surprised them exceedingly
By removing the armor from his feet and hands--
He would not be whole and uninjured
When he reached the other side!
He would support himself on the sword,   3100
Which was sharper than a scythe,
On his bare hands and feet.
He left nothing on his feet:
Neither shoes, mail leggings, nor socklets.
It scarcely mattered to him   3105
If he would wound his hands and feet;
He would rather maim himself
Than fall from the bridge and bathe
In the water from which there was no escape.
In the extreme pain it caused him   3110
And in great distress he crossed,
Wounding his hands, knees, and feet.
But Love, which led and guided him,
Comforted and healed him at once
And made his suffering a pleasure.   3115
On hands, feet, and knees
He advanced until he reached the other side.
Then he recalled and remembered
The two lions which he thought
He had seen when he was   3120
Still on the other side. He looked,
But there was not so much as a lizard
To do him harm.
He raised his hand before his face,
Gazed at his ring, then looked again.*   3125
(Since he had found neither of the lions
Which he had thought to have seen,
He believed there was some enchantment;
Yet there was no living thing there.)

131

Et cil qui sont a l'autre rive,   3130
de ce qu'ainsi passé le voient
font tel joie com il devoient;
mes ne sevent pas son mehaing.
Et cil le tint a grant guehaing
quant il n'i a plus mal soffert;   3135
le sanc jus de ses plaies tert
a sa chemise tot antor.
Et voit devant lui une tor
si fort c'onques de sa veüe
n'avoit nule si fort veüe--   3140
la torz miaudre ne pooit estre.
Apoiez a une fenestre
s'estoit li rois Bademaguz,
qui molt ert soutix et aguz
a tote enor et a tot bien,   3145
et lëauté sor tote rien
voloit par tot garder et faire.
Et ses filz, qui tot le contraire
a son pooir toz jorz feisoit,
car deslëautez li pleisoit,   3150
n'onques de feire vilenie
et traïson et felenie
ne fu lassez ne enuiez,
s'estoit delez lui apoiez.
S'orent veü des la amont   3155
le chevalier passer le pont
a grant poinne et a grant dolor.
D'ire et de mautalant color
en a Meleaganz changiee;
bien set c'or li ert chalongiee   3160
la reïne. Mes il estoit
tex chevaliers qu'il ne dotoit
nul home, tant fust forz ne fiers.   [39b]
Nus ne fust miaudres chevaliers,
se fel et deslëaus ne fust;   3165
mes il avoit un cuer de fust
tot sanz dolçor et sanz pitié.
Ce fet le roi joiant et lié
don ses filz molt grant duel avoit.
Li rois certeinnemant savoit   3170
que cil qui ert au pont passez
estoit miaudres que nus assez,
que ja nus passer n'i osast
a cui dedanz soi reposast
Malvestiez, qui fet honte as suens   3175
plus que Proesce enor as suens.
Donc ne puet mie tant Proesce
con fet Malvestiez et Peresce,
car voirs est--n'an dotez de rien--

Those on the other side,   3130
Seeing that he had passed over,
Rejoiced, as well they should;
But they were unaware of his injuries.
He considered himself most fortunate
Not to have been more seriously wounded;   3135
He was able to staunch the flow of blood
From his wounds by wrapping them with his chemise.
Before him he perceived a tower
So mighty that never with his eyes
Had he seen one so mighty--   3140
In no way could it have been more perfect.
Leaning on a window ledge
Was King Bademagu,
Who was most scrupulous and keen
In every matter of honor and right,   3145
And who esteemed and practiced
Loyalty above all other virtues.
And his son, who strove
Constantly to do the opposite,
For disloyalty pleased him   3150
And he was never bored
Nor wearied of baseness,
Treason, and felony,
Was resting there beside him.
From their vantage point they had seen   3155
The knight cross the bridge
Amid great pain and hardship.
Meleagant's face reddened
With anger and wrath;
He knew well that now he would be challenged   3160
For the queen. But he was
Such a knight that he feared
No man, no matter how strong or brave.
There would have been no finer knight
Had he not been treasonous and disloyal;   3165
But his wooden heart
Was devoid of kindness and compassion.
What caused the son to suffer so
Made the king pleased and happy.
The king recognized with certainty   3170
That he who had crossed the bridge
Was far better than any other man,
For no one would dare cross
Who harbored within himself
Cowardice, which shames him who has it   3175
More than Nobility could honor him.
Nobility cannot do as much
As Cowardice and Sloth,
For the truth is--and never doubt it--

133

qu'an puet plus feire mal que bien.   3180
    De ces deus choses vos deïsse
molt, se demore n'i feïsse;
mes a autre chose m'ator,
qu'a ma matiere m'an retor,
s'orroiz comant tient a escole   3185
li rois son fil qu'il aparole.
"Filz," fet il, "avanture fu
quant ci venimes gié et tu
a ceste fenestre apoier,
s'an avons eü tel loier   3190
que nos avons apertemant
veü le plus grant hardemant
qui onques fust mes nes pansez.
Or me di se boen gré ne sez
celui qui tel mervoille a feite.   3195
Car t'acorde a lui et afeite,
si li rant quite la reïne;
ja n'avras preu an l'ateïne,
einz i puez avoir grant domage.
Car te fai or tenir por sage   3200
et por cortois, si li anvoie
la reïne einçois qu'il te voie.
Fei lui tel enor an ta terre,
que ce que il est venuz querre
li done ainz qu'il le te demant--   3205
car tu sez bien certainnemant
qu'il quiert la reïne Ganievre.   [39c]
Ne te fai tenir por anrievre
ne por fol ne por orguilleus.
Se cist est an ta terre seus,   3210
se li doiz conpaignie feire,
que prodom doit prodome atreire
et enorer et losangier;
nel doit pas de lui estrangier.
Qui fet enor, l'anors est soe: 3215
bien saches que l'enors iert toe
se tu fez enor et servise
a cestui qui est a devise
li miaudres chevaliers del monde."
Cil respont: "Que Dex me confonde,   3220
s'ausins boen ou meillor n'i a."
Mal fist quant lui i oblia,
qu'il ne se prise mie mains,
et dit: "Joinz piez et jointes mains,
volez, espoir, que je devaigne   3225
ses hom et de lui terre taigne?
Si m'aïst Dex, ainz devandroie *

3203. Fei li   3220. Dex le c.

134

That evil is easier done than good.   3180
    I could tell you many things about
These qualities if we could linger here,
But I must turn toward something else
And return to my matter,
And you will hear how the king   3185
Spoke and instructed his son.
"Son," said he, "it was by chance
That you and I came here
To lean upon this windowledge,
And we have been repaid   3190
By witnessing with our own eyes
The very boldest deed
That ever was conceived.
Now tell me if you do not esteem
The knight who did such a wondrous feat.   3195
Go make peace with him,
And surrender the queen.
You will never gain by fighting with him,
But are likely to suffer greatly for it.
So let yourself be known as wise   3200
And noble, and send him
The queen before he encounters you.
Honor him in your land
By giving him what he came
To seek before he asks it of you--   3205
For you know quite well
That he is seeking Queen Guinevere.
Don't let yourself be thought obstinate
Or foolish or proud.
If he has entered alone into your land,   3210
You must keep company with him,
For a gentleman must welcome,
Honor, and praise another gentleman,
And should not snub him.
He who does honor is honored by it: 3215
Know you well that honor will be yours
If you honor and serve
Him who is beyond doubt
The best knight in the world."
The son replied: "May I be damned   3220
If there is no other as good or better than he!"
(The king had unwisely neglected Meleagant,
Who esteemed himself no little bit!)
"Perhaps you want me to kneel before him
With folded hands and become   3225
His liege man and hold my lands from him?
So help me God, I'd rather be

ses hom que je ne li randroie!
Ja certes n'iert par moi randue,
mes contredite et desfandue   3230
vers toz ces qui si fol seront
que venir querre l'oseront."
Lors derechief li dit li rois:
"Filz, molt feroies que cortois
se ceste anreidie lessoies.   3235
Je te lo et pri qu'an pes soies.
Ce sez tu bien que hontes iert
au chevalier s'il ne conquiert
vers toi la reïne an bataille.
Il la doit mialz avoir, sanz faille,   3240
par bataille que par bonté,
por ce qu'a pris li ert conté.
Mien esciant, il n'anquiert point
por ce que l'an an pes li doint,
einz la vialt par bataille avoir.   3245
Por ce feroies tu savoir
se la bataille li toloies.
Molt me poise quant tu foloies:*
mes se tu mon consoil despis,
moins m'an sera, s'il t'an est pis;   3250
et granz max avenir t'an puet,   [39d]
que rien au chevalier n'estuet
doter fors que seulemant toi.
De toz mes homes et de moi
li doing trives et seürté.   3255
Onques ne fis deslëauté
ne traïson ne felenie,
ne je nel comancerai mie
por toi ne que por un estrange.
Ja ne t'an quier dire losange,   3260
einz promet bien au chevalier
qu'il n'avra ja de rien mestier--
d'armes ne de cheval--qu'il n'ait,
des qu'il tel hardemant a fait
que il est jusque ci venuz.   3265
Bien iert gardez et maintenuz
vers trestoz homes sauvemant
fors que vers toi tot seulemant;
et ce te voel je bien aprandre,
que s'il vers toi se puet desfandre   3270
il nel covient d'autrui doter."
"Assez me loist ore escoter,"
fet Meleaganz, "et teisir
et vos diroiz vostre pleisir,

3248. Je te lo et pri quan pes soies 3249. Et
3273-74. *reversed in* C

136

His liege than return Guinevere to him!
She'll certainly not be handed over by me,
But held and defended   3230
Against all who are fool enough
To dare to come seek her."
Then the king answered him:
"Son, you would be acting most nobly
In abandoning this obstinacy.   3235
I beg and advise you to hold your peace.
You know that it would be a dishonor
To this knight should he not win
The queen from you in battle.
There can be no doubt that he would rather gain her   3240
Through battle than through generosity,
For this would enhance his fame.
I think he is not seeking her
So that she may be given to him peaceably,
But because he wishes to win her in battle.   3245
So you would act wisely
In keeping him from battle.
It hurts me to see you play the fool:
But if you ignore my counsel,
I will care little if you are defeated;   3250
And you stand to suffer greatly for your refusal,
Since the knight need fear
No one here but yourself.
I offer him peace and protection
On behalf of all my men and myself.   3255
I have never acted deceitfully
Nor practiced treason or felony,
And I will no more do such
For your sake than for a complete stranger's.
I have no intention of lying to you: 3260
Rather, I shall promise the knight
That he will need nothing--
Neither arms nor horses--which will not be given him,
Since he has shown such courage
In coming this far.   3265
He will be guarded and protected
And kept safe from all men,
Except yourself alone;
And I want you to know
That if he can defend himself against you   3270
He need fear no other."
"For the moment I am content to listen,"
replied Meleagant, "and keep silent.
And you may say what you will,

mes po m'est de quanque vos dites.   3275
Je ne sui mie si hermites,
si prodon* ne si charitables,
ne tant ne voel estre enorables
que la rien que plus aim li doingne.
N'iert mie feite sa besoigne   3280
si tost ne si delivremant,
einçois ira tot autremant
qu'antre vos et lui ne cuidiez.
Ja se contre moi li aidiez,
por ce nel vos consantiromes;   3285
se de voz et de toz voz homes
a pes et trives, moi que chaut?
Onques por ce cuers ne me faut,
einz me plest molt, se Dex me gart,
que il n'ait fors de moi regart.   3290
Ne je ne vos quier por moi feire
rien nule, ou l'an puise retreire
deslëauté ne traïson.
Tant con vos plest soiez prodon,
et moi lessiez estre cruel!"   [39e]
"Comant? N'an feroies tu el?"
"Nenil," fet cil.--"Et je m'an tes.
Or fei ton mialz, que je te les,
s'irai au chevalier parler.
Offrir li voel et presanter   3300
m'aïde et mon consoil del tot,
car je me tieng a lui de bot."
    Lors descendi li rois aval
et fet anseler son cheval.
L'an li amainne un grant destrier,   3305
et il i monte par l'estrier
et mainne avoec lui de ses genz--
trois chevaliers et deus sergenz,
sanz plus, fet avoec lui aler.
Einz ne finerent d'avaler   3310
tant que il vindrent vers la planche
et voient celui qui estanche
ses plaies et le sanc en oste.
Lonc tans le cuide avoir a oste
li rois por ses plaies garir,   3315
mes a la mer feire tarir
porroit autresi bien antendre.
Li rois se haste del descendre;
et cil qui molt estoit plaiez
s'est lors ancontre lui dreciez,   3320
non pas por ce qu'il le conoisse;
ne ne fet sanblant de l'angoisse

3316. garnir

138

But little do I care for all I've heard.   3275
I do not have the faint heart of a monk
Or do-gooder or almsgiver,
Nor do I care to have that honor
Which requires that I give him what I most love.
His task will not be accomplished   3280
So quickly and easily,
But will turn out quite differently
Than you and he think.
If you aid him against me,
We will not make peace on this account;   3285
If you and all your men
Offer him peace, what do I care?
My courage is not lacking for all this--
In fact, it pleases me greatly, so help me God,
That he has none to fear but myself.   3290
Nor do I ask you to do a thing
For me that might be interpreted
As disloyalty or treason.
Be a gentleman as long as you please,
And let me be villainous!"   3295
"What? Will you not do otherwise?"
"Not at all," he replied. -- "Then I am silent.
Do your best. I leave you to it;
I shall go speak to the knight.
I want to offer and grant him   3300
My aid and counsel in every matter,
For I am entirely on his side."
    Then the king went down
And had his horse saddled.
A huge destrier was brought to him,   3305
Which he mounted by the stirrup.
He took with him some of his men,
Ordering three knights and two men-at-arms,
No more, to accompany him.
They rode down from the castle heights   3310
Until they neared the bridge
And saw the knight, who was tending
His wounds and wiping the blood from them.
The king thought to have him as his guest
For a long time before his wounds were healed,   3315
But he might as well have expected
To drain the sea.
King Bademagu dismounted at once,
And the knight, though he was seriously wounded
And did not know him,   3320
Rose to greet him.
He gave no more evidence of the pain

qu'il avoit es piez et es mains
ne plus que se il fust toz sains.
Li rois le vit esvertüer,   3325
si le cort molt tost salüer
et dit: "Sire, molt m'esbaïs
de ce que vos an cest païs
vos estes anbatuz sor nos.
Mes bien veignanz i soiez vos,   3330
que jamés nus ce n'anprendra,
ne mes n'avint ne n'avandra
que nus tel hardemant feïst
que an tel peril se meïst.
Et sachiez, molt vos en aim plus,   3335
quant vos avez ce fet que nus
n'osast panser antemes feire.
Molt me troveroiz deboneire
vers vos et leal et cortois.   [39f]
Je sui de ceste terre rois,   3340
si vos offre tot a devise
tot mon consoil et mon servise;
et je vois molt bien esperant
quel chose vos alez querant:
la reïne, ce croi, querez."   3345
"Sire, fet il, bien esperez--
autres besoinz ça ne m'amainne."
"Amis, il i covendroit painne,"
fet li rois, "ainz que vos l'aiez,
et vos estes formant plaiez: 3350
je voi les plaies et le sanc.
Ne troveroiz mie si franc
celui qui ça l'a amenee
qu'il la vos rande sanz meslee,
mes il vos covient sejorner   3355
et voz plaies feire sener
tant qu'eles soient bien garies.
De l'oignemant as trois Maries
et de meillor, s'an le trovoit,
vos donrai ge, car molt covoit   3360
vostre aise et vostre garison.
La reïne a boene prison
que nus de char a li n'adoise,
neïs mes filz (cui molt an poise)
qui avoec lui ça l'amena.   3365
Onques hom si ne forssena
com il s'an forssene et anrage.
Et j'ai vers vos molt boen corage,
si vos donrai, se Dex me saut,
molt volantiers quanqu'il vos faut.   3370

3330. bien *added above line*

140

He had in his feet and hands
Than if he had been completely well.
The king saw his effort   3325
And hastened to greet him,
Saying: "Sir, I am very amazed
That you have penetrated
Into this land among us.
But be welcome here,   3330
For no one will undertake this feat again,
Nor has it happened, nor will it happen again
That anyone will have the daring
To face such danger.
And know that I esteem you the more   3335
For having done this deed which no one
Before dared to conceive.
You will find me most pleasant,
Loyal, and courteous toward you.
I am king of this land   3340
And willingly offer you
My counsel and my aid.
I believe I know quite well
What you are seeking here:
You seek, I presume, the queen."   3345
"Sir," the wounded knight replied, "you presume correctly--
No other duty brings me here."
"My friend, you will have to suffer,"
Said the king, "before you have her,
And you are grievously hurt: 3350
I see the wounds and the blood.
You will not find
The one who brought her here so generous
That he will return her without battle,
So you must rest   3355
And have your wounds treated
Until they are well healed.
I shall give you the ointment of the Three Marys*
And better, if such be found,
Because I am most eager   3360
For your comfort and recovery.
The queen is securely confined,
Safe from the lusts of men,
Even that of my son (much to his chagrin),
Who brought her here with him.   3365
No one has ever become
So crazy and mad as he.
My heart goes out to you
And, if God be with me, I will give you
Most willingly anything you need.   3370

Ja si boenes armes n'avra
mes filz, qui mal gré m'an savra,
qu'altresi boenes ne vos doigne,
et cheval tel con vos besoigne.
Et si vos praing, cui qu'il enuit,   3375
vers trestoz homes an conduit;
ja mar doteroiz de nelui
fors que seulemant de celui
qui la reïne amena ça.
Onques hom si ne menaça   3380
autre con ge l'ai menacié,
et par po je ne l'ai chacié
de ma terre par mautalant   [40a]
por ce que il ne la vos rant.
S'est il mes filz, mes ne vos chaille: 3385
se il ne vos vaint an bataille,
ja ne vos porra sor mon pois
d'enui faire vaillant un pois."
"Sire," fet il, "vostre merci!
Mes je gast trop le tans ici   3390
que perdre ne gaster ne vuel.
De nule chose ne me duel,
ne je n'ai plaie qui me nuise.
Menez moi tant que je le truise,
car a tex armes con je port   3395
sui   prez c'orandroit me deport
a cos doner et a reprandre."
"Amis, mialz vos valdroit atandre
ou quinze jorz ou trois semainnes,
tant que voz plaies fussent sainnes.   3400
Car boens vos seroit li sejorz
tot au moins jusqu'a quinze jorz,
que je por rien ne sosferroie
ne esgarder ne le porroie
qu'a tex armes n'a tel conroi   3405
vos conbatessiez devant moi."
Et cil respont: "S'il vos pleüst,
ja autres armes n'i eüst,
que volantiers a ces feïsse
la bataille; ne ne queïsse   3410
qu'il i eüst, ne pas ne ore,
respit ne terme ne demore.
Mes por vos ore tant ferai
que jusqu'a demain atendrai;
et ja mar an parleroit nus,   3415
que je ne l'atandroie plus!"
Lors a li rois acreanté
qu'il iert tot a sa volanté,
puis le fet a ostel mener;
et prie et comande pener   3420

142

Though my son will be angry with me,
He will never have such good arms
That I'll not give you just as good,
And a horse too, which you will need.
I shall protect you against everyone,   3375
No matter whom it might offend;
You need fear no one
Except him alone
Who brought the queen here.
Never has anyone threatened   3380
Another as I threatened him
And all but chased him
From my land in anger
Because he did not return her to you.
He is my son, but do not worry,   3385
For unless he defeats you in battle,
He can never, against my will,
Do you the least harm."
"Sir," said he, "I thank you!
But I am losing too much time here,   3390
Which I do not wish to waste.
Nothing has hurt me,
Nor do I have any wound which causes me pain.
Take me to where I can find him,
For in such armor as I'm wearing   3395
I am prepared now
To strike or receive blows."
"My friend, it is better that you wait
Two or three weeks
Until your wounds heal.   3400
A delay of at least a fortnight
Would do you good,
For I would never permit
Nor could I countenance
Your fighting before me   3405
With such arms and equipment."
"If it pleases you," he replied,
"I would have no arms but these,
For with them I shall gladly do
Battle; nor would I seek   3410
Even the slightest
Respite, postponement, or delay.
However, at your request
I shall wait until tomorrow;
But no matter what might be said,   3415
I shall not wait any longer!"
Thereupon the king swore
That all would be as the knight wished,
And had him shown his lodging.
He prayed and ordered those   3420

143

de lui servir ces qui l'en mainnent,
et il del tot an tot s'an painnent.
Et li rois, qui la pes queïst
molt volantiers, se il poïst,
s'an vint derechief a son fil,   3425
si l'aparole come cil
qui volsist la pes et l'acorde;   [40b]
si li dit: "Biax filz, car t'acorde
a cest chevalier sanz conbatre.
N'est pas ça venuz por esbatre   3430
ne por berser ne por chacier,
einz vient por s'enor porchacier
et son pris croistre et aloser;
s'eüst mestier de reposer
molt grant, si con je l'ai veü.   3435
Se mon consoil eüst creü,
de cest mois ne de l'autre aprés
ne fust de la bataille angrés
dom il est ja molt desirranz.
Se tu la reïne li ranz,   3440
criens an tu avoir desenor?
De ce n'aies tu ja peor,
qu'il ne t'an puet blasmes venir;
einz est pechiez del retenir
chose ou an n'a reison ne droit.   3445
La bataille tot orandroit
eüst feite molt volantiers,
si n'a il mains ne piez antiers,
einz les a fanduz et plaiez."
"De folie vos esmaiez,"   3450
fet Meleaganz a son pere.
"Ja par la foi que doi saint Pere
ne vos cresrai de cest afeire;
certes, l'an me devroit detreire
a chevax, se je vos creoie!   3455
S'il quiert s'anor, et je la moie;
s'il quiert son pris, et je le mien;
et s'il vialt la bataille bien,
ancor la voel je plus cent tanz!"
"Bien voi qu'a la folie antanz,"   3460
fet li rois, "si la troveras.
Demain ta force esproveras
au chevalier, quant tu le viax."
"Ja ne me vaigne plus granz diax,"
fet Meleaganz, "de cestui!   3465
Mialz volsisse qu'ele fust hui
assez que je ne faz demain.
Veez or con ge m'an demain

3432. Einz est venuz por p.

144

Who escorted the knight to strive to serve him,
And they saw to his every need.
The king, who would promote peace
Actively if he were able,
Returned meanwhile to his son   3425
And spoke to him in accordance
With his desire for peace and harmony;
He told him: "Fair son, be reconciled
With this knight without a fight.
He has not come here to amuse himself   3430
Nor to hunt or chase,
But rather he has come to seek his honor
And to further and increase his renown.
I have seen that he
Is in great need of rest.   3435
Had he taken my advice,
Neither this month nor the following
Would he seek the battle
Which he already so desires.
Are you afraid of incurring dishonor   3440
By returning the queen to him?
Do not fear this,
For blame cannot come to you from it;
Rather, it is a sin to retain
Something to which one has no right.   3445
He would gladly have done
Battle here without delay,
Though his hands and feet are not sound,
But gashed and wounded."
"You are foolish to be concerned,"   3450
Said Meleagant to his father.
"By the faith I owe St. Peter, I'll not
Follow your advice in this matter;
Indeed, I should be torn apart
By horses if I did as you say!   3455
If he seeks his honor, so do I;
If he seeks his renown, so do I;
If he is eager for battle,
I am a hundred times more so!"
"I plainly see that you are pursuing madness,"   3460
Said the king, "and you will attain it.
Since you wish, you shall try your strength
Against the knight tomorrow."
"May no greater trial ever come to me
Than this!" said Meleagant.   3465
"I would much rather it were
For today than tomorrow.
See how I am acting

plus matemant que ge ne suel:
molt m'an sont or troblé li oel, 3470
et molt en ai la chiere mate. [40c]
Jamés tant que ge me conbate
n'avrai joie ne bien ne eise,
ne m'avendra rien qui me pleise."
    Li rois ot qu'an nule meniere 3475
n'i valt rien consauz ne proiere,
si l'a lessié tot maugré suen;
et prant cheval molt fort et buen
et beles armes, ses anvoie
celui an cui bien les anploie. 3480
Iluec fu uns hom anciens
qui molt estoit boen crestïens--
el monde plus leal n'avoit--
et de plaies garir savoit
plus que tuit cil de Monpellier. 3485
Cil fist la nuit au chevalier
tant de bien con feire li sot,
car li rois comandé li ot.
Et ja savoient les noveles
li chevalier et les puceles 3490
et les dames et li baron
de tot le païs anviron.
Si vindrent d'une grant jornee
tot anviron, de la contree
et li estrange et li privé; 3495
tuit chevalchoient abrivé
tote la nuit anjusqu'au jor.
D'uns et d'autres devant la tor
ot si grant presse a l'enjorner
qu'an n'i poïst son pié torner. 3500
Et li rois par matin se lieve,
cui de la bataille molt grieve;
si vient a son fil derechief,
qui ja avoit le hiaume el chief
lacié, qui fu fez a Peitiers. 3505
N'i puet estre li respitiers
ne n'i puet estre la pes mise;
se l'a li rois molt bien requise,
mes ne puet estre qu'il la face.
Devant la tor enmi la place 3510
ou tote la genz se fu treite,
la sera la bataille feite,
que li rois le vialt et comande.
Le chevalier estrange mande
li rois molt tost, et l'an li mainne [40d]
an la place qui estoit plainne
des genz del rëaume de Logres.
Ausi con por oïr les ogres

146

More downcast than usual:
My eyes are very troubled 3470
And my face is very pale.
Until I do battle I'll not
Feel happy or at ease,
Nor will anything pleasing to me come to pass."
    The king understood that no amount 3475
Of advice or pleading would avail,
So reluctantly he left his son.
He selected a strapping fine horse
And good weapons, which he sent
To the one who needed them. 3480
In that land lived an aged man,
An excellent Christian--
The finest in all the world--
Who was better at healing wounds
Than all the doctors of Montpellier .* 3485
That evening he cared for the knight
As best he knew how,
For such was the King's command.
Already the news had spread
To the knights and maidens, 3490
To the ladies and barons
From the whole land round about.
They all rode rapidly
Through the night until daybreak,
Both strangers and friends, 3495
And came from every direction
As far away as a hard day's travel.
By daybreak there were so many
Crowded before the tower
That there was no room to move. 3500
The king arose that morning,
Disturbed about the battle;
He came directly to his son,
Who had already laced upon his head
His Poitevin helmet.* 3505
No delay was possible,
Nor could peace be established;
Though the king sought it,
He could achieve nothing.
In accordance with the king's wish and order, 3510
The battle was to occur
Before the keep in the square,
Where all the people were gathered.
The king sent at once
For the foreign knight, who was then led 3515
Into the square, which was filled
With people from the Kingdom of Logres.
Just as people are wont

vont au mostier a feste anel
a Pantecoste ou a Noël   3520
les genz acostumeemant,
tot autresi comunemant
estoient la tuit aüné.
Trois jorz avoient geüné
et alé nuz piez et an lenges   3525
totes les puceles estrenges
del rëaume le roi Artu,
por ce que Dex force et vertu
donast contre son aversaire
au chevalier qui devoit faire   3530
la bataille por les cheitis.
Et autresi cil del païs
reprioient por lor seignor,
que Dex la victoire et l'enor
de la bataille li donast.   3535
Bien main ainz que prime sonast
les ot an endeus amenez
enmi la place toz armez
sor deus chevax de fer coverz.
Molt estoit genz et bien aperz   3540
Meliaganz, et bien tailliez
de braz, de janbes, et de piez;
et li hiaumes et li escuz
qui li estoit au col panduz
trop bien et bel li avenoient.   3545
Mes a l'autre tuit se tenoient--
nes cil qui volsissent sa honte--
et dïent tuit que rien ne monte
de Meliagant avers lui.
Maintenant qu'il furent andui   3550
enmi la place, et li rois vient
qui tant con il puet les detient,
si se painne de la peis feire,
mes il n'i puet son fil atreire.
Et il lor dit: "Tenez voz frains   3555
et voz chevax atot le mains
tant qu'an la tor soie montez.
Ce n'iert mie trop granz bontez
se por moi tant vos delaiez."   [40e]
Lors se part d'ax molt esmaiez   3560
et vient droit la ou il savoit
la reïne, qui li avoit
la nuit proié qu'il la meïst
an tel leu que ele veïst
la bataille tot a bandon.   3565
Et il l'en otrea le don,
si l'ala querre et amener,
car il se voloit molt pener

148

To go to hear the organs
At churches on the great annual feasts 3520
Of Pentecost or Christmas,
So in like manner had they
All assembled here.
All the foreign maidens
From the kingdom of King Arthur 3525
Had fasted three days
And gone barefoot in hairshirts
So that God might give strength
And courage to the knight
Who was to do battle 3530
Against his enemy on behalf of the captives.
In like manner, the natives of this land
Prayed for their lord,
That God might give him victory
And honor in the battle. 3535
Early in the morning, before prime had sounded,
The two of them were led
Fully armed to the center of the square
On two iron-clad horses.
Meleagant was exceedingly handsome 3540
And alert; his arms,
Legs, and feet were muscular,
And his helmet and the shield
Which was hanging from his neck
Complemented him perfectly. 3545
But all were intent upon the other--
Even those who wished to see him shamed--
And all agreed that Meleagant
Was nothing in comparison with him.
As soon as both were 3550
In the center of the square, the king came
And did his best to delay them
And strove to establish peace,
But he was again unable to dissuade his son.
He said to them: "Rein in 3555
And restrain your horses at least
Until I have climbed the tower.
It will not be too much
To delay that long for me."
Downcast, he left them 3560
And went straight to where he knew
The queen to be, who had
Begged him the night before to put her
Somewhere where she might
Have a clear view of the battle. 3565
He granted her request
And went to find and escort her,
For he was ever striving

149

de s'anor et de son servise.
A une fenestre l'a mise   3570
et il fu delez li a destre
couchiez sor une autre fenestre.
Si ot avoec aus deus assez
et d'uns et d'autres amassez
chevaliers et dames senees,   3575
et puceles del païs nees.
Et molt i avoit des cheitives
qui molt estoient antantives
en orisons et an proieres;
li prison et les prisonieres   3580
trestuit por lor seignor prioient,
qu'an Deu et an lui se fioient
de secors et de delivrance.
Et cil font lors sanz demorance
arriere treire les genz totes;   3585
et hurtent les escuz des cotes,
s'ont les enarmes anbraciees
et poignent si que deus braciees
parmi les escuz s'antranbatent
des lances, si qu'eles esclatent   3590
et esmïent come brandon.
Et li cheval tot de randon
s'antrevienent que front a front
et piz a piz hurté se sont;
et li escu hurtent ansanble   3595
et li hiaume, si qu'il resanble
de l'escrois que il ont doné
que il eüst molt fort toné,
qu'il n'i remest peitrax ne cengle,
estriés ne resne ne varengle   3600
a ronpre, et des seles peçoient
li arçon qui molt fort estoient.
Ne n'i ont pas grant honte eü   [40 f]
se il sont a terre cheü
des que trestot ce lor failli;   3605
tost refurent an piez sailli,
si s'antrevienent sanz jengler
plus fieremant que dui sengler,
et se fierent sanz menacier
granz cos des espees d'acier,   3610
come cil qui molt s'antreheent.
Sovant si aspremant se reent
les hiaumes et les haubers blans
qu'aprés le fer an saut li sans.
La bataille molt bien fornissent,   3615
qu'il s'estoutoient et leidissent
des pesanz cos et des felons.
Mainz estors fiers et durs et lons

150

To do her honor and service.
He placed her before a window, 3570
While he reclined at another,
Beside and to the right of her.
Together with the two of them
There were both many knights,
And many courtly ladies, 3575
And maidens native to this land.
There were also many captive maidens,
Who were very intent upon
Their petitions and prayers,
And prisoners, both men and women, 3580
All praying for their lord,
For to God and him they had entrusted
Their help and deliverance.
With no more delay, the two contestants
Had all the people fall back. 3585
Then they seized the shields from their sides
And thrust their arms through the straps.
They now spurred forward until their lances
Pierced fully two arm's lengths
Through the other's shield, which broke 3590
And splintered like flying sparks.
Their horses quickly
Squared off head to head
And met breast to breast.
Shields clashed together, 3595
And helmets, until it seemed
That their roars were
Mighty claps of thunder.
Not a breast-strap, girth,
Stirrup, rein, nor flap 3600
Remained unbroken; even the strong
Saddle-bows split.
Nor was it any shame
To fall to the ground
When all this gave way beneath them. 3605
They leapt at once to their feet
And without mincing words rushed together
More fiercely than two wild boars.
What good were threats?
They struck mighty strokes with their steel swords 3610
Like hated enemies.
They savagely slashed
Helmets and gleaming hauberks,
Causing blood to gush from beneath the torn metal.
They fought a mighty battle, 3615
Stunning and wounding one another
With strong, treacherous blows.
They sustained many fierce, hard, long

151

s'antredonerent par igal,
c'onques ne del bien ne del mal
ne s'an sorent auquel tenir.   3620
Mes ne pooit pas avenir
que cil qui ert au pont passez
ne fust afebloiez assez
des mains que il avoit plaiees.   3625
Molt an sont les genz esmaiees,
celes qui a lui se tenoient,
car ses cos afebloier voient,
si crient qu'il ne l'an soit pis;
et il lor estoit ja avis   3630
que il en avoit le peior
et Meliaganz le meillor;
si an parloient tot antor.
Mes as fenestres de la tor
ot une pucele molt sage,   3635
qui panse et dit an son corage
que li chevaliers n'avoit mie
por li la bataille arramie,
ne por cele autre gent menue
qui an la place estoit venue--   3640
ne ja enprise ne l'eüst
se por la reïne ne fust.
Et panse se il la savoit
a la fenestre ou ele estoit,
qu'ele l'esgardast ne veïst,   3645
force et hardemant an preïst.
Et s'ele son non bien seüst,   [41a]
molt volantiers dit li eüst
qu'il se regardast un petit.
Lors vint a la reïne et dit: 3650
"Dame, por Deu et por le vostre
preu vos requier, et por le nostre,
que le non a ce chevalier
(por ce que il li doie eidier)
me dites, se vos le savez."   3655
"Tel chose requise m'avez,
dameisele," fet la reïne,
"ou ge n'antant nule haïne
ne felenie, se bien non.
Lanceloz del Lac a a non   3660
li chevaliers, mien esciant."
"Dex! Com en ai lié et riant
le cuer, et sain!" fet la pucele.
Lors saut avant et si l'apele,
si haut que toz li pueples l'ot,   3665
a molt haute voiz: "Lancelot!
Trestorne toi et si esgarde
qui est qui de toi se prant garde!"

Bouts with equal valor,
Such that it was never possible   3620
To determine who was in the right.
Yet it was inevitable
That the one who had crossed the bridge
Would start to lose strength
In his wounded hands.   3625
Those who sided with him
Were most concerned,
For they saw his blows weaken
And feared he would be defeated;
And they were already certain   3630
That he was getting the worst of it,
And Meleagant the better;
They were all discussing it,
But in the windows of the tower
Was an astute maiden,   3635
Who thought and said within her heart
That the knight had not
Undertaken the battle for her sake,
Nor for that of the common people
Assembled in the square--   3640
He would never have agreed to it
Had it not been for the queen.
She thought that if he knew
The queen was at the window,
Watching and seeing him,   3645
He would take on new strength and courage.
Had the girl known his name,
She would surely have told him
To look about himself a little.
So she came to the queen and said: 3650
"My lady, for God's sake and your own,
As well as ours, I beg you
To tell me the name
Of this knight if you know it,
For it may be of help to him."   3655
"In what you have requested,
Wise maiden," replied the queen,
"I see no hatred
Or evil, only good.
I believe the knight   3660
Is called Lancelot of the Lake."
"God knows how happy and joyful
I am at heart!" exclaimed the girl.
Then she rushed forward and called to him,
Shouting for all to hear   3665
In a very loud voice: "Lancelot!
Turn around and behold
Who it is who is watching you!"

153

Qant Lanceloz s'oï nomer,
ne mist gaires a lui torner;   3670
trestorne soi et voit amont
la chose de trestot le mont
que plus desirroit a veoir,
as loges de la tor seoir.*
Ne puis l'ore qu'il l'aparçut   3675
ne se torna ne ne se mut
de vers li ses ialz ne sa chiere,
einz se desfandoit par derriere.
Et Meleaganz l'enchauçoit
totesvoies plus qu'il pooit,   3680
si est molt liez con cil qui panse
c'or n'ait james vers lui desfanse.
S'an sont cil del païs molt lié,
et li estrange si irié
qu'il ne se pueent sostenir,   3685
einz an i estut mainz venir
jusqu'a terre toz esperduz,
ou as genolz ou estanduz.
Ensi molt joie et duel i a.
Et lors derechief s'escria   3690
la pucele des la fenestre: [41b]
"Ha! Lancelot! Ce que puet estre
que si folemant te contiens?
Ja soloit estre toz li biens
et tote la proesce an toi,   3695
ne je ne pans mie ne croi
c'onques Dex feïst chevalier
qui se poïst apareillier
a ta valor ne a ton pris!
Or te veons si antrepris   3700
qu'arriere main gietes tes cos,   3700a
si te conbaz derrier ton dos.*   3700b
Torne toi si que de ça soies
et que adés ceste tor voies,
que boen veoir et bel la fet."
Ce tient a honte et a grant let
Lanceloz, tant que il s'an het,   3705
c'une grant piece a--bien le set--
le pis de la bataille eü;
se l'ont tuit et totes seü.
Lors saut arriere et fet son tor,
et met antre lui et la tor   3710
Meleagant trestot a force;
et Meleaganz molt s'esforce
que de l'autre part se retort.
Et Lanceloz sore li cort,

3675. saparcut

154

When Lancelot heard his name,
He turned about at once   3670
And saw above him,
Sitting in one of the tower loges,
That one whom he desired to see
More than any other in the whole world.
From the moment he beheld her,   3675
He did not turn or divert
His face and eyes from her,
But defended himself from behind.
Meleagant pursued him
Unceasingly, as best he could,   3680
Elated to think
That now he had him defenseless.
The men of that kingdom were likewise elated,
But the foreigners were so distraught
That they could scarcely stand,   3685
And many could not help
But sink to their knees
Or fall prostrate to the ground.
Thus were both joy and sorrow extreme.
Then the girl called   3690
Again from the window:
"Ah, Lancelot! What could it be
That makes you act so foolishly?
Once all goodness
And all prowess were in you,   3695
And I cannot conceive or believe
That God ever made a knight
Who could compare with
Your valor and worth!
Yet now you seem so distracted   3700
That you're striking blows behind you,   3700a
And fighting with your back turned.   3700b
Turn around so you'll be over here
Where you can keep this tower in sight,
For seeing it will bring you succor."
Lancelot was most ashamed
And vexed and hated himself,   3705
Since he knew that for a long while now
He had been getting the worst of the battle,
And that everyone realized it.
He maneuvered around behind his enemy,
Forcing Meleagant to fight   3710
Between himself and the tower;
And Meleagant struggled mightily
To regain his position.
Lancelot carried the fight to him,

155

sel hurte de si grant vertu   3715
de tot le cors atot l'escu,
quant d'autre part se vialt torner,
que il le fet tot chanceler
deus foiz ou plus, mes bien li poist.
Et force et hardemanz li croist,   3720
qu'Amors li fet molt grant aïe
et ce que il n'avoit haïe
rien nule tant come celui
qui se conbat ancontre lui.
Amors et Haïne mortex,   3725
si granz qu'ainz ne fu encor tex,
le font si fier et corageus
que de neant nel tient a geus
Meliaganz, ainz le crient molt,
c'onques chevalier si estolt   3730
n'acointa mes ne ne conut,
ne tant ne li greva ne nut
nus chevaliers mes con cil fet.
Volantiers loing de lui se tret,
se li ganchist et se reüse,   [41c]
que ses cos het et ses refuse.
Et Lanceloz pas nel menace,
mes ferant vers la tor le chace,
ou la reïne ert apoiee--
sovant l'a servie et loiee--*   3740
de tant que si pres l'i menoit
qu'a remenoir le covenoit
por ce qu'il ne la veïst pas
se il alast avant un pas.
Ensi Lanceloz molt sovant   3745
le menoit arriers et avant
par tot la ou boen li estoit,
et totevoies s'arestoit
devant la reïne sa dame,
qui li a mis el cors la flame   3750
por qu'il la va si regardant.
Et cele flame si ardant
vers Meleagant le feisoit,
que par tot la ou li pleisoit
le pooit mener et chacier.   3755
Come avugle et come eschacier
le mainne, maugré an ait il.
Li rois voit si ataint son fil
qu'il ne s'aïde ne desfant;
si l'an poise et pitiez l'en prant.   3760
S'i metra consoil se il puet;
mes la reïne l'an estuet

3734. loing *added above line*

156

Shoving him so hard 3715
With his full weight behind his shield
When he tried to get to the other side,
That he caused him to stagger
Twice or more in spite of himself.
Lancelot's strength and courage grew 3720
Because Love aided him,
And because he had never before hated
Anything so much
As this adversary.
Love and mortal Hatred, 3725
The greatest ever conceived,
Made him so bold and courageous
That Meleagant realized this was
No game and began to fear him exceedingly,
For never had he known or faced 3730
Such a bold knight,
Nor had any knight ever harmed
Or injured him as had this one.
He withdrew willingly
And kept his distance, 3735
Dodging and avoiding his hated blows.
And Lancelot did not threaten him,
But pursued him with his sword toward the tower
Where the queen was leaning--
He often served and did homage to her-- 3740
Until he drove him so close
That he had to desist,
For he could not have seen her
If he had advanced a step farther.
Thus Lancelot repeatedly 3745
Drove him back and forth
Wherever he would,
Stopping each time
Before his lady the queen,
Who had so enflamed him 3750
That he was constantly gazing at her.
And this flame so stirred him
Against Meleagant
That he could drive and pursue him
Anywhere he pleased. 3755
Meleagant was driven mercilessly,
Like a man blinded or lame.
The king, seeing his son so pressed
That he could neither help nor defend himself,
Felt sorry and took pity on him. 3760
He intended to intervene if possible;
But to act in proper fashion he must

proier, se il le vialt bien feire.
Lors li comança a retreire:
"Dame, je vos ai molt amee   3765
et molt servie et enoree
puis qu'an ma baillie vos oi.
Onques chose feire ne soi
que volantiers ne la feïsse,
mes que vostre enor i veïsse.   3770
Or m'an randez le guerredon;
mes demander vos voel un don
que doner ne me devrïez
se par amor nel feïsiez:
bien voi que de ceste bataille   3775
a mes filz le poior sanz faille;
ne por ce ne vos an pri mie
qu'il m'an poist, mes que ne l'ocie
Lanceloz, qui en a pooir.   [41d]
Ne vos nel devez pas voloir--   3780
non pas por ce que il ne l'ait
bien vers vos et vers lui mesfait!
Mes por moi, la vostre merci,
li dites--car je vos an pri--
qu'il se taigne de lui ferir.   3785
Ensi me porrïez merir
mon servise, se boen vos iere."
"Biax sire, por vostre proiere
le voel ge bien," fet la reïne.
"Se j'avoie mortel haïne   3790
vers vostre fil, cui ge n'aim mie,
se m'avez vos si bien servie,
que por ce que a gré vos vaigne
voel ge molt bien que il se taigne."
Ceste parole ne fu mie   3795
dite a consoil, ainz l'ont oïe
Lanceloz et Meleaganz.
Molt est qui ainme obeïssanz,
et molt fet tost et volentiers
la ou il est amis antiers   3800
ce qu'a s'amie doie plaire.
Donc le dut bien Lanceloz faire,
qui plus ama que Piramus,
s'onques nus hom pot amer plus.
La parole oï Lanceloz;   3805
Ne puis que li darrïens moz
de la boche li fu colez,
puis qu'ele ot dit: "Quant vos volez
que il se taigne, jel voel bien,"
puis Lanceloz por nule rien   3810
nel tochast ne ne se meüst,
se il ocirre le deüst.

First ask the queen,
So he began by saying to her:
"My lady, I have ever loved,   3765
Served, and honored you
While you have been in my care.
I was always prompt
To do anything which I saw
Might be to your honor.   3770
Now I wish to be repaid;
But I wish to ask for a favor
Which you should not grant me
Except through true affection:
I clearly see that my son   3775
Is getting the worst of this battle;
I do not beg you because I am sorry
To see him defeated, but so that Lancelot,
Who has the power to do so, not kill him.
Nor should you want him killed--   3780
Though it is true that he deserves death
For having so wronged both you and Lancelot!
But on my behalf, I beg you
In your mercy to ask Lancelot
To refrain from slaying him.   3785
Thus might you repay
My service, if you see fit."
"Fair sir, because it is your request,
I wish it so," replied the queen.
"Even had I a mortal hatred   3790
For your son, whom I do not love,
Yet you have served me well,
And because it pleases you
I wish Lancelot to restrain himself."
These words, which had not been   3795
Spoken in a whisper, were overheard by
Lancelot and Meleagant.
One who loves totally
Is ever obedient,
And willingly and completely does   3800
Whatever might please his love.
Thus Lancelot, who loved more
Than Pyramus* (if ever a man could love
More deeply) must do her bidding.
Lancelot heard what was spoken.   3805
No sooner had the last words
Flowed from her mouth--
No sooner had she said, "Because it pleases you,
I wish Lancelot to restrain himself"--
Than nothing could have made Lancelot   3810
Touch Meleagant or make any movement,
Even had the other attempted to slay him.

159

Il nel toche ne ne se muet;
et cil fiert lui tant con il puet,
d'ire et de honte forssenez   3815
quant ot qu'il est a ce menez
que il covient por lui proier.
Et li rois por lui chastïer
est jus de la tor avalez;
an la bataille an est alez   3820
et dist a son fil maintenant:
"Comant? Est or ce avenant
qu'il ne te toche et tu le fiers?   [41e]
Trop par es or cruex et fiers,
trop es or preuz a mal eür!   3825
Et nos savons tot de seür
qu'il est au desore de toi."
Lors dit Melïaganz au roi,
qui de honte fu desjuglez:
"Espoir vos estes avuglez!   3830
Mien escïant, n'i veez gote!
Avuglez est qui de ce dote
que au desor de lui ne soie!"
"Or quier," fet li rois, "qui te croie!
Que bien sevent totes ces genz   3835
se tu diz voir ou se tu manz.
La verité bien an savons."
Lors dit li rois a ses barons
que son fil arriere li traient.
Et cil de rien ne se delaient;   3840
tost ont son comandemant fet:
Melïagant ont arriers tret.
Mes a Lancelot arriers treire
n'estut il pas grant force feire,
car molt li poïst grant enui   3845
cil feire ainçois qu'il tochast lui.
Et lors dist li rois a son fil:
"Si m'aïst Dex, or t'estuet il
pes feire et randre la reïne!
Tote la querele anterine   3850
t'estuet lessier et clamer quite."
"Molt grant oiseuse avez or dite!
Molt vos oi de neant debatre!
Fuiez! Si nos lessiez conbatre
et si ne vos an merlez ja!"   3855
Et li rois dit que si fera,
que bien set que cist l'ocirroit
qui conbatre les lesseroit.*
"Il m'ocirroit? Einz ocirroie

3836. tu repeated   3857. bien sai q.c. tocirroit
3858. vos l.

160

He did not touch him or move;
But Meleagant, shamed and enraged
Out of his mind to hear that he had sunk so low   3815
That his father had had to intervene,
Struck Lancelot repeatedly.
The king went down
From the tower to reproach him;
He stepped into the fray   3820
And spoke to his son at once:
"What? Is it proper
That you strike him when he does not touch you?
You are unspeakably cruel and savage,
And your rashness condemns you!   3825
We all know for certain
That he has vanquished you."
Beside himself with shame,
Meleagant then spoke to the king:
"Perhaps you're blind!   3830
I don't think you can see a thing!
A person would have to be blind
To doubt that I have conquered him!"
"Then find someone who believes you!" replied the king;
"All these people know quite well   3835
Whether you speak truly or lie.
We know the truth."
Then the king told his barons
To hold back his son.
Without any delay   3840
They did his bidding immediately,
And Meleagant was pulled back.
But no great force was needed
To restrain Lancelot,
For Meleagant could have done him   3845
Great harm before he would have touched him.
Then the king said to his son:
"So help me God, now you must
Make peace and hand over the queen!
You must give up and call an end   3850
To this whole dispute."
"You've just spoken like an old fool!
I hear you talking nonsense!
Go on! Keep out of our way
And let us fight!"   3855
The King said he must intervene,
For he well knew that Lancelot would kill Meleagant
If he were to let them continue fighting.
"Him, kill me? Hardly!

161

je lui molt tost et conquerroie,   3860
se vos ne nos destorbeiez
et conbatre nos lesseiez."
Lors dit li rois: "Se Dex me saut,
quanque tu diz rien ne te vaut."
"Por coi?" fet il--"Car je ne vuel.   3865
Ta folie ne ton orguel
ne cresrai pas por toi ocirre.   [41f]
Molt est fos qui sa mort desirre,
si con tu fez, et tu nel sez.
Et je sai bien que tu m'an hez   3870
por ce que je t'an voel garder.
Ta mort veoir ne esgarder
ne me leira ja Dex, mon vuel,
car trop en avroie grant duel."
Tant li dit et tant le chastie   3875
que pes et acorde ont bastie.
La pes est tex que cil li rant
la reïne, par tel covant
que Lanceloz sanz nule aloigne
quele ore que cil l'an semoigne   3880
des le jor que semont l'avra
au chief de l'an se conbatra
a Meliagant derechief.
Ce n'est mie Lancelot grief.
A la pes toz li pueples cort   3885
et devisent que a la cort
le roi Artus iert la bataille,
qui tient Bretaigne et Cornoaille;
la devisent que ele soit,
s'estuet la reïne l'otroit   3890
et que Lanceloz l'acreant
que, se cil le fet recreant,
qu'ele avoec lui s'an revanra
ne ja nus ne la detanra.
La reïne ensi le creante,   3895
et Lancelot vient a creante.
Si les ont ensi acordez
et departiz et desarmez.
    Tel costume el païs avoit
que, puis que li uns s'an issoit   3900
que tuit li autre s'an issoient.
Lancelot tuit beneïssoient,
et ce poez vos bien savoir
que lors i dut grant joie avoir,
et si ot il sanz nule dote.   3905
La genz estrange asanble tote,
qui de Lancelot font grant joie
et dïent tuit por ce qu'il l'oie:
"Sire, voir, molt nos esjoïsmes

162

I'd kill him at once, and win,   3860
If you don't bother us
And let us fight."
"By God," said the king,
"All that you say will avail you nothing!"
"Why?" he asked.--"Because I am opposed.   3865
I will not trust in your folly
And pride, which would kill you.
Only a fool seeks his own death,
As you do, without knowing it.
And I am well aware that you hate me   3870
For wishing to save you.
I believe God will never let me
See or consent to your death,
Because I would be too grief-stricken."
He reasoned with his son and reproved him   3875
Until a truce was established.
This accord affirmed that Meleagant would hand over
The queen on the condition
That Lancelot would agree
To fight him again   3880
One year and no more
From that day on which
He should be challenged.
This did not disturb Lancelot.
With the truce all the people hastened up   3885
And decided that the battle
Would take place at the court of King Arthur,
Who held Britain and Cornwall;
There they decided it would be.
And the queen had to consent   3890
And Lancelot to promise
That if Meleagant were to defeat him
No one would prevent
Her returning with him.
The queen confirmed this,   3895
And Lancelot agreed.
In this manner the knights were reconciled,
Separated, and disarmed.
    It was the custom of this land
That, when one person left,   3900
All the others could leave.
They all blessed Lancelot,
And you can be sure
That great joy was felt then,
As well it should be.   3905
All the foreigners came together,
Greatly praising Lancelot,
And saying, so that he might hear:
"Sir, in truth, we were very elated

163

tantost con nomer vos oïsmes,   3910
que seür fumes a delivre   [42a]
c'or serïons nos tuit delivre."
A cele joie ot molt grant presse,
que chascuns se painne et angresse
comant il puisse a lui tochier.   3915
Cil qui plus s'an puet aprochier
an fu plus liez que ne pot dire.
Assez ot la et joie et ire:
que cil qui sont desprisoné
sont tuit a joie abandoné,   3920
mes Melïaganz et li suen
n'ont nule chose de lor buen,
einz sont pansif et mat et morne.
Li rois de la place s'an torne;
ne Lancelot n'i lesse mie,   3925
ençois l'an mainne; et cil li prie
que a la reïne le maint.
"En moi," fet li rois, "ne remaint,
que bien a feire me resanble.
Et Quex le seneschal ansanble   3930
vos mosterrai ge, s'il vos siet."
A po que as piez ne l'an chiet
Lanceloz, si grant joie en a.
Li rois maintenant l'an mena
en la sale, ou venue estoit   3935
la reïne qui l'atandoit.
    Quant la reïne voit le roi,
qui tient Lancelot par le doi,
si s'est contre le roi dreciee
et fet sanblant de correciee,   3940
si s'anbruncha et ne dist mot.
"Dame, veez ci Lancelot,"
fet li rois, "qui vos vient veoir.
Ce vos doit molt pleire et seoir.
"Moi? Sire, moi ne puet il plaire;   3945
de son veoir n'ai ge que faire."
"Avoi! dame," ce dit li rois
qui molt estoit frans et cortois,
"ou avez vos or cest cuer pris?
Certes vos avez trop mespris   3950
d'ome qui tant vos a servie,
qu'an ceste oirre a sovant sa vie
por vos mise an mortel peril,
et de Melïagant mon fil   [42b]
vos a resqueusse et desfandue,
qui molt iriez vos a randue."
"Sire, voir, mal l'a enploié;

3913. gr. feste

164

As soon as we heard your name,   3910
For we were quite certain
That we would all soon be freed."
A great crowd was celebrating there,
With everyone pushing and striving
Eagerly to find some way to touch Lancelot.   3915
Those who were able to get nearest
Were happy beyond words.
There was great joy, but anger too:
Those who were freed
Were given over to happiness;   3920
But Meleagant and his followers
Shared none of their joy;
Rather, they were sad, downcast, and taciturn.
The king turned away from the square;
He did not leave Lancelot behind,   3925
But led him away; and he begged
To be taken to the queen.
"I am not opposed," said the king,
"For it seems to me a good thing to do.
If you wish, I'll show you   3930
The seneschal Kay as well."
Lancelot was so overjoyed
That he almost fell at his feet.
The king led him forthwith
Into the hall where the queen   3935
Had come to await him.
    When the queen saw the king
Leading Lancelot by the hand,
She stood up before the king
And acted as if she were angered.   3940
She lowered her head and said not a word.
"My lady, this is Lancelot,"
Said the king, "who has come to see you.
That should please and suit you."
"Me? Sir, he cannot please me.   3945
I have no interest in seeing him."
"My word, lady," said the king,
Who was very noble and courtly,
"Where did you get this feeling?
Indeed you are too disdainful   3950
Of one who has served you so well,
And who on this journey
Often risked his life for you,
And who rescued and defended you
From my son Meleagant,   3955
Who was most reluctant to give you over."
"Sir, in truth, he has wasted his effort;

ja par moi ne sera noié
que je ne l'an sai point de gré."
Ez vos Lancelot trespansé,   3960
se li respont molt belemant
a meniere de fin amant:
"Dame, certes, ce poise moi,
ne je n'os demander por coi."
    Lanceloz molt se demantast   3965
se la reïne l'escoutast;
mes por lui grever et confondre
ne li vialt un seul mot respondre,
einz est an une chanbre antree.
Et Lanceloz jusqu'a l'antree   3970
des ialz et del cuer la convoie;
mes as ialz fu corte la voie,
que trop estoit la chanbre pres;
et il fussent antré aprés
molt volantiers, s'il poïst estre.   3975
Li cuers, qui plus est sire et mestre
et de plus grant pooir assez,
s'an est oltre aprés li passez,
et li oil sont remés defors,
plain de lermes, avoec le cors.   3980
Et li rois a privé consoil
dist: "Lancelot, molt me mervoil
que ce puet estre et don ce muet,
que la reïne ne vos puet
veoir, n'aresnier ne vos vialt.   3985
S'ele onques a vos parler sialt,
n'an deüst or feire dangier
ne voz paroles estrangier,
a ce que por li fet avez.
Or me dites, se vos savez,   3990
por quel chose, por quel mesfet,
ele vos a tel sanblant fet."
"Sire, orandroit ne m'an gardoie.
Mes ne li plest qu'ele me voie
ne qu'ele ma parole escolt;   3995
il m'an enuie et poise molt."
"Certes," fet li rois, "ele a tort,
que vos vos estes jusqu'a mort
por li en avanture mis.   [42c]
Or an venez, biax dolz amis,   4000
s'iroiz au seneschal parler."
"La voel je molt," fet il, "aler."
Au seneschal an vont andui.
Quant Lanceloz vint devant lui,
se li dist au premerain mot   4005
li seneschax a Lancelot:
"Con m'as honi!"--"Et je de quoi?"

166

I shall always deny
That I feel any gratitude toward him."
You could see Lancelot's confusion,   3960
But he answered her politely
And like a perfect lover:
"My lady, indeed this grieves me;
Yet I dare not ask your reasons."
    Lancelot would have poured out his woe   3965
If the queen had listened,
But to pain and embarrass him further
She refused to answer him a single word
And passed into another room instead.
Lancelot's eyes and heart   3970
Accompanied her to the entrance;
His eyes' journey was short,
For the room was near at hand,
Yet they would have entered after her
Gladly, if that had been possible.   3975
His heart, its own lord and master
And more powerful by far,
Was able to follow after her,
While his eyes, full of tears,
Remained outside with his body.   3980
The king whispered to him,
Saying: "Lancelot, I am amazed
That this has happened, and wonder what it means
When the queen refuses to see
You and is so unwilling to speak with you.   3985
If ever she cared to speak with you,
She should not now be reticent
Nor refuse to listen to you,
Because of all you have done for her.
So tell me, if you know,   3990
For what reason, or for what failing of yours,
She has treated you this way."
"Sir, I never expected this sort of welcome.
But she certainly does not care to see me
Or listen to what I have to say,   3995
And this disturbs and grieves me deeply."
"Of course," said the king, "she is mistaken,
For you have risked
Death on her account.
Well, come now, my fair friend,   4000
And go speak with the seneschal Kay."
"I am very eager to do so," said he.
They both went to the seneschal.
When Lancelot came before him,
The seneschal spoke first   4005
To Lancelot, as follows:
"How you have shamed me!--"How could I?"

fet Lanceloz, "dites le moi:
quel honte vos ai ge donc feite?"
"Molt grant, que tu as a chief treite   4010
la chose que ge n'i poi treire,
s'as fet ce que ge ne poi feire."
    Atant li rois les lesse andeus;
de la chanbre s'an ist toz seus.
Et Lanceloz au seneschal   4015
anquiert s'il a eü grant mal.
"Oïl," fet il, "et ai encor.
Onques n'oi plus mal que j'ai or,
et je fusse morz grant piece a
ne fust li rois qui de ci va,   4020
qui m'a mostré par sa pitié
tant de dolçor et d'amistié
c'onques, la ou il le seüst,
rien nule qui mestier m'eüst,
ne me failli nule foiee,   4025
qui ne me fust apareilliee
maintenant que il le savoit.
Ancontre un bien qu'il me feisoit,
Meliaganz de l'autre part, *
ses filz qui plains est de mal art,   4030
par traïson a lui mandoit
les mires, si lor comandoit
que sor mes plaies me meïssent
tex oignemanz qui m'oceïssent.
Ensi pere avoie et parrastre: 4035
que quant li rois un boen anplastre
me feisoit sor mes plaies metre,
qui molt se volsist antremetre
que j'eüsse tost garison,
et ses filz par sa traïson   4040
le m'an feisoit tost remüer,
por ce qu'il me voloit tüer,
et metre un malvés oignemant.   [42d]
Mes je sai bien certainnemant
que li rois ne le savoit mie: 4045
tel murtre ne tel felenie
ne sofrist il an nule guise.
Mes ne savez pas la franchise
que il a ma dame faite:
onques ne fu par nule gaite   4050
si bien gardee torz an marche
des le tans que Noex fist l'arche,
que il mialz gardee ne l'ait,
que neïs veoir ne la lait
son fil, qui molt an est dolanz,   4055

4029. Et M. d'autre part

Answered Lancelot. "Tell me:
What shame have I done you?"
"An immense shame, because you have completed   4010
What I was unable to complete
And have done what I was unable to do."
      Thereupon the king left the two of them
And went alone out of the room;
And Lancelot asked the seneschal   4015
If he had suffered greatly.
"Yes," he answered, "and I still do.
I have never been worse off than I am now,
And I would have been dead long ago
Had it not been for the king who just left here,   4020
Because in his compassion he has shown me
So much kindness and friendship.
Whenever he was aware
That I needed anything,
He never failed to arrange   4025
To have it prepared for me
As soon as he was aware of my need.
Each time he tried to help me,
His son Meleagant,
Who is full of evil intentions,   4030
Deceitfully sent for
His own physicians and ordered them
To dress my wounds
With ointments which would kill me.
Thus I had both a father and a stepfather: 4035
For whenever the king,
Who was very desirous to see
That I was quickly healed,
Had good medicine put on my wounds,
His son, in his treachery   4040
And his desire to kill me,
Had it removed straightway
And had some harmful ointment substituted.
I am absolutely certain
That the king did not know this,   4045
For he would in no way tolerate
Such murder or treachery.
But you do not know how kindly
He treated my lady:
Never since Noah built his ark   4050
Has a tower in the march
Been guarded as carefully
As he has had her kept.
Though it upset his son,
He never let even Meleagant see her   4055

fors devant le comun des gens
ou devant le suen cors demainne.
A si grant enor la demainne
et a demené jusque ci
li frans rois, la soe merci,   4060
com ele deviser le sot.
Onques deviseor n'i ot
fors li qu'ainsi le devisa;
et li rois molt plus l'an prisa
por la lëauté qu'an li vit.   4065
Mes est ce voirs que l'an m'a dit,
qu'ele a vers vos si grant corroz
qu'ele sa parole oiant toz
vos a vehee et escondite?"
"Verité vos en a l'an dite,"   4070
fet Lanceloz, "tot a estros.
Mes por Deu, savriez me vos
dire por coi ele me het?"
Cil respont que il ne le set,
einz s'an mervoille estrangemant.   4075
"Or soit a son comandemant,"
fet Lanceloz, qui mialz ne puet;
et dit: "Congié prandre m'estuet,
s'irai monseignor Gauvain querre,
qui est antrez an ceste terre   4080
et covant m'ot que il vandroit
au Pont desoz Eve tot droit."
Atant est de la chanbre issuz;
devant le roi an est venuz
et prant congié de cele voie.   4085
Li rois volantiers li otroie;   [42e]
mes cil qu'il avoit delivrez
et de prison desprisonez
li demandent que il feront.
Et il dit: "Avoec moi vandront   4090
tuit cil qui i voldront venir;
et cil qui se voldront tenir
lez la reïne, si s'i taignent.
N'est pas droiz que avoec moi vaingnent."
Avoec lui vont tuit cil qui voelent,   4095
lié et joiant plus qu'il ne suelent.
Avoec la reïne remainnent
puceles qui joie demainnent
et dames et chevalier maint;
mes uns toz seus n'en i remaint   4100
qui mialz n'amast a retorner
an son païs que sejorner.
Mes la reïne les retient

4058. *repeated*

Except in his own presence
Or with a crowd of people.
The king in his kindness gives her,
And has always given her,
All the security   4060
For which she has asked.
No one but herself has overseen
Her confinement, and she arranged it so,
And the king esteemed her the more
Because he recognized her loyalty.   4065
But is it true, as I have been told,
That she is so upset with you
That she has publicly refused
To speak a word with you?"
"You have been told the truth,"   4070
Said Lancelot, "the whole truth.
But for God's sake, can you
Tell me why she hates me?"
He replied that he did not know,
And was extremely amazed by her action.   4075
"Then let it be as she orders,"
Said Lancelot, who could not do otherwise.
"I must take my leave," he said,
"And go seek my lord Gawain,
Who has come into this land   4080
And has sworn to me that he would go
Directly to the Underwater Bridge."
He left the room at once,
Came before the king,
And asked his leave to go there.   4085
The king willingly consented,
But those Lancelot had freed
And delivered from imprisonment
Asked him what they were to do.
Lancelot answered: "With me will come   4090
All who wish to accompany me;
And those who wish to stay
With the queen may do so.
Nothing compels them to come with me."
All who so wished accompanied him,   4095
More happy and joyful than ever.
There remained with the queen
Many maidens given over to rejoicing,
And ladies and knights as well;
But all of those remaining   4100
Would have preferred to return
To their own country rather than stay behind.
The queen only retained them

por monseignor Gauvain qui vient,
et dit qu'ele ne se movra 4105
tant que noveles an savra.
    Par tot est la novele dite
que tote est la reïne quite
et delivré tuit li prison,
si s'an iront sanz mesprison 4110
quant ax pleira et boen lor iert.
Li uns l'autre le voir an quiert,
onques parole autre ne tindrent
les genz quant tuit ansanble vindrent.
Et de ce ne sont pas irié 4115
que li mal pas sont depecié;
se va et vient qui onques vialt--
n'est pas ensi com estre sialt.
Quant les genz del païs le sorent
qui a la bataille esté n'orent 4120
comant Lanceloz l'avoit fet,
si se sont tuit cele part tret
ou il sorent que il aloit,
car il cuident qu'au roi bel soit
se pris et mené li avoient 4125
Lancelot. Et li suen estoient
tuit de lor armes desgarni,
et por ce furent escherni
que cil del païs armé vindrent.
Ne fu pas mervoille s'il prindrent [42f]
Lancelot qui desarmez iere.
Tot pris le ramainnent arriere,
les piez liez soz son cheval.
Et cil dïent: "Vos feites mal,
seignor, car li rois nos conduit. 4135
Nos somes an sa garde tuit."
Et cil dïent: "Nos nel savons,
mes ensi con pris vos avons
vos covandra venir a cort."
Novele qui tost vole et cort 4140
vient au roi que ses genz ont pris
Lancelot et si l'ont ocis.
Quant li rois l'ot, molt l'an est grief,
et jure assez plus que son chief
que cil qui l'ont mort an morront; 4145
ja desfandre ne s'an porront
et, s'il les puet tenir ou prandre
ja n'i avra mes que del pandre
ou del ardoir ou del noier.
Et se il le voelent noier, 4150
ja nes an cresra a nul fuer,
que trop li ont mis an son cuer
grant duel et si grant honte faite,

172

Because of the imminent arrival of my lord Gawain,
Saying that she would not leave   4105
Until she had heard from him.
    The word spread everywhere
That the queen was freed,
That all the captives were released,
And that they would be able to leave without question   4110
Whenever it might suit and please them.
When all the people of the land came together,
They asked one another about the truth [of this rumor]
And spoke of nothing else.
They were not at all upset   4115
That the treacherous passes had been destroyed.
Now people could come and go at will --
This was not as it had been!
When the local people
Who had not been present at the battle   4120
Learned how Lancelot had fared,
They all went to where
They knew he was to pass,
For they thought that the king would be pleased
If they captured and returned Lancelot   4125
To him. Lancelot's men had
All removed their arms
And were therefore bewildered
To see these armed men approaching.
It is no wonder that they succeeded in taking   4130
Lancelot, who was unarmed.
They returned with him captive,
His feet tied beneath his horse.
"Lords, you act unwisely," said the men of Logres.
"We travel with the king's safe-conduct.   4135
We are all under his protection."
"We are unaware of this," the others replied,
"But captive as you are
You must come to the court."
Swift-flying rumor   4140
Reached the king, saying that his people had captured
Lancelot and had killed him.
Upon hearing this he was greatly disturbed
And swore by more than his head
That those who had killed him would die for it;   4145
Never would they be able to justify themselves
And, if he should be able to capture and hold them,
They would be forthwith hanged,
Burned, or drowned.
And if they should try to deny their deed,   4150
He would not believe them at all,
For they had put in his heart
Such grief and such shame

qui li devroit estre retraite
s'il n'an estoit prise vangence;   4155
mes il l'an panra sanz dotance.
    Ceste novele par tot vait;
a la reïne fu retrait
qui au mangier estoit assise.
A po qu'ele ne s'est ocise   4160
maintenant que de Lancelot
la mançonge et la novele ot.
Mes ele la cuide veraie
et tant duremant s'an esmaie
qu'a po la parole n'an pert;   4165
mes por les genz dit en apert:
"Molt me poise, voir, de sa mort;
et s'il m'an poise n'ai pas tort,
qu'il vint an cest païs por moi;
por ce pesance avoir an doi."   4170
Puis dit a li meïsme an bas,
por ce que l'en ne l'oïst pas,
que de boivre ne de mangier
ne la covient jamés proier   [43a]
se ce est voirs que cil morz soit   4175
por la cui vie ele vivoit.
Tantost se lieve molt dolante
de la table, si se demante
si que nus ne l'ot ne escoute.
De li ocirre est si estoute   4180
que sovant se prant a la gole;
mes ainz se confesse a li sole,
si se repant et bat sa colpe,
et molt se blasme et molt s'ancolpe
del pechié qu'ele fet avoit   4185
vers celui don ele savoit
qui suens avoit esté toz dis,
et fust ancor se il fust vis.
Tel duel a de sa crualté
que molt an pert de sa biauté.   4190
Sa crualté, sa felenie
la fet molt tainte et molt nercie,
et ce qu'ele voille et geüne.
Toz ses mesfez ansanble aüne
et tuit li revienent devant;   4195
toz les recorde et dit sovant:
"Ha! lasse! De coi me sovint
quant mes amis devant moi vint
que je nel deignai conjoïr,
ne ne le vos onques oïr!   4200
Quant mon esgart et ma parole
li veai, ne fis je que fole?
Que fole? Ainz fis, si m'aïst Dex,

174

That he himself would be reproached for it
Unless he took vengeance--   4155
And without a doubt he would.
    The rumor spread everywhere;
It was even told to the queen,
Who was seated at dinner.
She almost killed herself   4160
When she heard the lying rumor
Of Lancelot's death.
She thought it was true
And was so greatly upset
That she was scarcely able to talk,   4165
But she said aloud for those present to hear:
"Indeed, his death pains me,
And I am not wrong to let it,
For he came into this land on my account,
And therefore I should be grieved."   4170
Then she said to herself in a low voice,
So she would not be heard,
That it would not be right to ask her
To drink or eat again,
If it were true that he   4175
For whom she lives were dead.
She arose from the table at once
So she could vent her grief
And not be heard.
She was so crazed with the thought of killing herself   4180
That she repeatedly grabbed her throat;
But then she confessed in conscience,
Repented, and asked God's pardon.
She accused and blamed herself
For the sin which she had committed   4185
Against the one whom she knew
Had always been hers,
And who would still be, were he alive.
Anguish caused by her own lack of compassion
Destroyed much of her beauty.   4190
Her lack of compassion, the betrayal of her love,
Combined with ceaseless vigils and fasting,
Marred and withered her.
She counted each of her unkindnesses,
And recalled them all to mind;   4195
She noted every one, and repeated often:
"Oh misery! What was I thinking
When my lover came before me
And I did not deign to welcome him,
Nor even care to listen!   4200
When I refused him a tender glance
And words, was I not a fool?
A fool? No, so help me God,

175

que felenesse et que cruex!
Et sel cuidai ge feire a gas,   4205
mes ensi nel cuida il pas,
se nel m'a mie pardoné.
Nus fors moi ne li a doné
le mortel cop, mien esciant.
Quant il vint devant moi riant   4210
et cuida que je li feïsse
grant joie, et que je le veïsse,
et onques veoir ne le vos--
ne li fu ce donc mortex cos?
Quant ma parole li veai   4215
tantost, ce cuit, le dessevrai
del cuer et de la vie ansanble.
Cil dui cop l'ont mort, ce me sanble;   [43b]
ne l'ont mort autre Breibançon.
Et Dex! Avrai ge reançon   4220
de cest murtre, de cest pechié?
Nenil voir, ainz seront sechié
tuit li flueve et la mers tarie!
Ha! lasse! Con fusse garie
et con me fust granz reconforz   4225
se une foiz, ainz qu'il fust morz,
l'eüsse antre mes bras tenu.
Comant? Certes, tot nu a nu,
por ce que plus an fusse a eise.
Quant il est morz, molt sui malveise   4230
que je ne faz tant que je muire.
Don ne me doit ma vie nuire,
se je sui vive aprés sa mort,
quant je a rien ne me deport
s'es max non que je trai por lui?   4235
Quant aprés sa mort m'i dedui
certes molt fust dolz a sa vie
li max don j'ai or grant anvie.
Malveise est qui mialz vialt morir
que mal por son ami sofrir.   4240
Mes certes, il m'est molt pleisant
que j'en aille lonc duel feisant;
mialz voel vivre et sofrir les cos
que morir et estre an repos."
La reïne an tel duel estut   4245
deus jorz, que ne manja ne but,
tant qu'an cuida qu'ele fust morte.
Assez est qui noveles porte,
einçois la leide que la bele;
a Lancelot vient la novele   4250
que morte est sa dame et s'amie.
Molt l'en pesa, n'en dotez mie;
bien pueent savoir totes genz

176

Cruel and deceitful!
I intended it as a joke,   4205
But he didn't realize this
And never forgave me for it.
It was I alone who struck
The mortal blow, I know.
When he came before me smiling,   4210
Expecting me to be happy
To have him, and I shunned him
And would never look at him--
Was that not a mortal blow?
At that moment when I refused   4215
To speak, it seems I severed
Both his heart and his life.
These two blows killed him, I feel,
And not any Brabançons.*
"Ah God! Will I be forgiven   4220
This murder, this sin?
No, in truth--all the rivers
And the sea will dry up first!
Oh misery! How it would have healed
And how it would have comforted me   4225
If once, before he died,
I had held him in my arms.
How? Yes, quite naked next to him,
In order to enjoy him fully.
If he is dead, I am wicked   4230
If I do not kill myself!
Could my life bring me anything but sorrow
Were I to live on after his death,
When I take pleasure in nothing
Except the woe I bear on his account?   4235
The sole pleasure of my life after his death--
This suffering I now court--
Would please him, were he alive.
Only a wicked woman would prefer to die
Than to endure pain for her love.   4240
Indeed, it pleases me
To mourn him for a long while;
I prefer to live and suffer life's blows
Than to die and be at rest."
The queen mourned thus   4245
For two days, without eating or drinking,
Until it was thought she was dead.
Many there are who would prefer
To carry bad news than good;
The rumor reached Lancelot   4250
That his lady and love had succumbed.
You need not doubt that he was overcome with grief,
And everyone could see

qu'il fu molt iriez et dolanz.
Por voir, il fu si adolez   4255
(s'oïr et savoir le volez)
que sa vie en ot an despit:
ocirre se volt sanz respit,
mes ainçois fist une conplainte.
D'une ceinture qu'il ot ceinte   4260
noe un des chiés au laz corrant,
et dit a lui seul an plorant: [43c]
"Ha! Morz! Con m'as or agueitié
que tot sain me fez desheitié!
Desheitiez sui, ne mal ne sant   4265
fors del duel qu'au cuer me descent:
cist diax est max, voire mortex.
Ce voel je bien que il soit tex
et, se Deu plest, je an morrai.
Comant? N'autremant ne porrai   4270
morir, se Damedeu ne plest?
Si ferai, mes que il me lest
cest laz antor ma gole estraindre,
ensi cuit bien la mort destraindre
tant que malgré suen m'ocirra.   4275
Morz, qui onques ne desirra*
se cez non qui de li n'ont cure,
ne vialt venir, mes ma ceinture
la m'amanra trestote prise,
et des qu'ele iert an ma justise   4280
donc fera ele mon talant.
Voire, mes trop vanra a lant,
tant sui desirranz que je l'aie!"
Lors ne demore ne delaie,
einz met le laz antor sa teste   4285
tant qu'antor le col li areste;
et por ce que il mal se face,
le chief de la ceinture lace
a l'arçon de sa sele estroit,
ensi que nus ne l'aparçoit.   4290
Puis se let vers terre cliner,
si se vost feire traïner
a son cheval tant qu'il estaigne--
une ore plus vivre ne daigne.
Quant a terre cheü le voient   4295
cil qui avoec lui chevalchoient,
si cuident que pasmez se soit,
que nus del laz ne s'aparçoit
qu'antor son col avoit lacié.
Tot maintenant l'ont redrecié,   4300
sel relievent antre lor braz

4275. ocirrai   4276. Comant nautremant nen porrai (cf. 4270)

That he was vexed and downcast.
He was so saddened (if you care   4255
To hear and know the truth)
That he disdained his very life:
He intended to kill himself at once
After making his lament.
He tied a sliding loop in one end   4260
Of the cord he wore around his waist
And wept to himself, saying:
"Ah! Death! How you have sought me out
And caught me in the prime of life!
I am saddened, but the only pain I feel   4265
Is the grief in my heart--
An evil, even mortal grief.
Would that it were mortal
And, if it please God, I shall die of it.
What? Could I not die   4270
In another way if the Lord God chooses?
And I shall, if He lets me
Loop this cord about my neck;
For thus, I am sure, I can force Death
To take me even against Her will.   4275
This Death, which seeks out
Only those who do not fear Her,
Does not want to come to me, but my belt
Will bring Her within my power,
And when I control Her,   4280
She will do my bidding.
Yet She will be too slow to come
Because of my eagerness to have Her!"
Then, without hesitation or delay,
He put the loop over his head   4285
Until it was taut around his neck;
And to be sure of death,*
He tied the other end of the belt
Tightly to his saddle horn,
Without attracting anyone's attention.   4290
Then he let himself slip to the ground,
Intending to be dragged
By his horse to his death--
He did not care to live another hour.
When those who were riding with him   4295
Saw him fallen to the ground,
They thought he had fainted,
For no one noticed the loop
Which he had tied around his neck.
They lifted him back up at once   4300
Into their arms

et si ont lors trové le laz
dont il estoit ses anemis,
qu'anviron son col avoit mis.
Sel tranchent molt isnelemant,   [43d]
mes la gorge si duremant
li laz justisiee li ot,
que de piece parler ne pot;
qu'a po ne sont les voinnes rotes
del col et de la gorge totes.   4310
Ne puis, se il le volsist bien,
ne se pot mal feire de rien.
Ce pesoit lui qu'an le gardoit;
a po que de duel n'en ardoit,
que molt volantiers s'oceïst   4315
se nus garde ne s'an preïst.
Et quant il mal ne se puet faire,
se dit: "Ha! Vix Morz deputaire,
Morz, por Deu, don n'avoies tu
tant de pooir et de vertu   4320
qu'ainz que ma dame m'oceïsses?
Espoir, por ce que bien feïsses,
ne volsis feire ne daignas.
Par felenie le lessas
que ja ne t'iert a el conté.   4325
Ha! quel servise et quel bonté!
Con l'as or an boen leu assise!
Dahez ait qui de cest servise
te mercie ne gré t'an set.
Je ne sai li quex plus me het: 4330
ou la Vie qui me desirre,
ou Morz qui ne me vialt ocirre.
Ensi l'une et l'autre m'ocit;
mes c'est a droit, se Dex m'aït,
que maleoit gré mien sui vis--   4335
que je me deüsse estre ocis
des que ma dame la reïne
me mostra sanblant de haïne,
ne ne le fist pas sanz reison,
einz i ot molt boene acheson,   4340
mes je ne sai quex ele fu.
Mes se ge l'eüsse seü,
einz que s'ame alast devant Dé
je le li eüsse amandé
si richemant con li pleüst,   4345
mes que de moi merci eüst.
Dex, cist forfez, quex estre pot?
Bien cuit que espoir ele sot
que je montai sor la charrete.   [43e]
Ne sai quel blasme ele me mete   4350
se cestui non. Cist m'a traï.

And found the noose,
Which had made him his own enemy
When he had placed it around his neck.
They cut it at once,   4305
But it had tightened
So around his throat that,
For a moment, he could not speak;
The veins of his neck
And throat were nearly severed.   4310
Even had he wanted,
He could no longer harm himself.
He was so distraught at being stopped
That he was aflame with anger,
And would have killed himself   4315
Had he not been watched.
When he could not harm himself,
He said: "Ah! vile, whoring Death!
For God's sake, Death, why did you not have
Enough power and strength   4320
To slay me before my lady's death?
I suppose it was because you would not
Deign or wish to do a good turn.
You did it out of treachery,
And never will you be anything but traitorous.   4325
Ah! what kindness, what goodness!
How virtuous you have been with me!
May anyone who thanks you
For this kindness, or welcomes it, be damned!
I know not which hates me more: 4330
Life, who wants me,
Or Death, who refuses to take me!
Thus they both slay me;
But it serves me right, by God,
That I be alive despite myself--   4335
For I should have killed myself
As soon as my lady the queen
Made known her hatred.
She did not show it without reason--
There was certainly a good cause,   4340
Though I do not know what it was.
Yet had I known,
I would have reconciled myself to her
In any way she wished, so that,
Before her soul went to God,   4345
She might forgive me.
My God, this crime, what could it have been?
I think that perhaps she realized
That I had mounted into the cart.
I know not what she held against me   4350
If not this. This alone was my undoing.

181

S'ele por cestui m'a haï--
Dex, cist forfez, por coi me nut?
Onques Amors bien ne conut
qui ce me torna a reproche;   4355
qu'an ne porroit dire de boche
riens qui de par Amors venist,
qui a reproche apartenist;
einz est amors et corteisie
quanqu'an puet feire por s'amie.   4360
Por m'amie nel fis je pas.
Ne sai comant je die, las!
Ne sai se die amie ou non;
ne li os metre cest sornon.
Mes tant cuit je d'Amor savoir,   4365
que ne me deüst mie avoir
por ce plus vil, s'ele m'amast,
mes ami verai me clamast,
quant por li me sanbloit enors
a feire quanque vialt Amors,   4370
nes sor la charrete monter.
Ce deüst ele Amor conter,
et c'est la provance veraie;
Amors ensi les suens essaie,
ensi conuist ele les suens.   4375
Mes ma dame ne fu pas buens
cist servises; bien le provai
au sanblant que an li trovai.
Et totevoie ses amis
fist ce don maint li ont amis   4380
por li honte et reproche et blasme;
s'ai fet ce geu don an me blasme
et de ma dolçor m'anertume,
par foi, car tex est la costume
a cez qui d'Amor rien ne sevent   4385
et qui enor en honte levent;
mes qui enor an honte moille
ne la leve pas, einz la soille.
Or sont cil d'Amors nonsachant
qui ensi les vont despisant,   4390
et molt ansus d'Amors se botent
qui son comandemant ne dotent.
Car, sanz faille, molt en amande   [43f]
qui fet ce qu'Amors li comande,
et tot est pardonable chose;   4395
s'est failliz qui feire ne l'ose."
    Ensi Lanceloz se demante;
et sa genz est lez lui dolante
qui le gardent et qui le tienent.
Et antretant noveles vienent   4400
que la reïne n'est pas morte.

182

If she hated me for this--
O God! This crime, how could it have damned me?
One who would hold this against me
Never truly knew Love;   4355
For there is nothing one could mention
Which, if prompted by Love,
Should be contemptible;
Rather, anything that one can do for his lady-love
Should be considered an act of love and courtliness.   4360
Yet I did not do it for my lady-love.
Ah, me, I know not what to call her!
Whether I dare name her
My 'lady-love,' I do not know.
But I think I know this much of Love: 4365
If she had loved me, she would not
Have esteemed me the less for this,
But would have called me her true-love,
Since it seemed to me honorable
To do anything for her that Love required,   4370
Even to mounting into the cart.
She should have ascribed this to Love,*
Its true source;
Thus does Love test her own,
And thus know her own.   4375
But by the manner of her welcome
I knew that this service
Did not please my lady.
Yet for her did her lover
Do this action for which he has oft been   4380
Shamed and reproached and accused;
Thus have I done that of which I am accused
And from sweetness I grow bitter,
In faith, for she acted
Like those who know nothing of Love   4385
And dip honor into shame;
But those who dampen honor with shame
Do not wash it, but soil it.
Those who condemn lovers
Know nothing of Love,   4390
And those who fear not His commands
Esteem themselves above Love.
There is no doubt that he
Who obeys Love's command is uplifted,
And all should be forgiven him;   4395
He who dares not follow Love's command errs greatly."
    Thus Lancelot lamented,
And those beside him who watched over
And protected him were saddened.
Meanwhile, word reached them   4400
That the queen was not dead.

183

Tantost Lanceloz se conforte;
et s'il avoit fet de sa mort,
devant, grant duel et fier et fort,
encor fu bien cent mile tanz   4405
la joie de sa vie granz.
Et quant il vindrent del recet
pres a sis liues ou a set
ou li rois Bademaguz iere,
novele que il ot molt chiere   4410
li fu de Lancelot contee--
se l'a volantiers escotee-
qu'il vit et vient sains et heitiez.
Molt an fist que bien afeitiez,
que la reïne l'ala dire.   4415
Et ele li respont: "Biax sire,
quant vos le dites, bien le croi;
mes s'il fust morz, bien vos otroi
que je ne fusse jamés liee.
Trop me fust ma joie estrangiee   4420
s'uns chevaliers an mon servise
eüst mort receüe et prise."
    Atant li rois de li se part,
et molt est la reïne tart
que sa joie et ses amis veingne;   4425
n'a mes talant que ele teigne
atahine de nule chose.
Mes novele, qui ne repose,
einz cort toz jorz qu'ele ne fine,
derechief vient a la reïne   4430
que Lanceloz ocis se fust
por li, se feire li leüst.
Ele an est liee et sel croit bien,
mes nel volsist por nule rien,
que trop li fust mesavenu.   4435
Et antretant ez vos venu
Lancelot qui molt se hastoit;   [44a]
maintenant que li rois le voit,
sel cort beisier et acoler;
vis li est qu'il doie voler,   4440
tant le fet sa joie legier.
Mes la joie font abregier
cil qui le lïerent et prindrent:
li rois lor dist que mar i vindrent,
que tuit sont mort et confondu.   4445
Et il li ont tant respondu
qu'il cuidoient qu'il vos volsist.
"Moi desplest il, mes il vos sist,"
fet li rois, "n'a lui rien ne monte--

4443. pristrent

184

Lancelot took comfort immediately
And, if earlier he had felt
Deep and passionate grief at her death,
Now his joy in her being alive   4405
Was a hundred thousand times greater.
When they came within six or seven
Leagues of the castle
Where King Bademagu was,
News which was pleasing   4410
Came to him of Lancelot--
News which he was glad to hear--
That Lancelot was alive and was coming hale and hearty.
He acted most nobly
By informing the queen.   4415
"Fair sir," she told him,
"I believe it on your word;
But were he dead, I assure you
That I would never find happiness again.
My joy would leave me altogether   4420
If Death were to claim and take
A knight in my service."
   Thereupon the king left her,
And the queen was most eager
For the arrival of her lover and her joy;   4425
She had no further desire
To quarrel with him over anything.
Rumor, which never rests,
But runs unceasingly all the while,
Returned soon to the queen with news   4430
That Lancelot would have killed himself
For her, had he not been restrained.
She was happy and believed it with all her heart,
Yet never would she have wished him ill,
For it would have been too much to bear.*   4435
Meanwhile there was Lancelot
Who was arriving in haste,
And who, upon seeing the king,
Ran to kiss and embrace him,
And his joy so lightened him   4440
That he felt as if he had wings.
But this joy was cut short
When he saw those who had taken and tied Lancelot:
The king cursed the hour in which they had come
And said they would all die and be damned.   4445
They all replied to him
That they had thought he would want Lancelot.
"It displeases me if you think you have acted wisely,"
Replied the king. "Worry not for Lancelot--

lui n'avez vos fet nule honte,   4450
se moi non qui le conduisoie;
comant qu'il soit, la honte est moie.
Mes ja ne vos an gaberoiz
quant vos de moi eschaperoiz."
    Qant Lanceloz l'ot correcier,   4455
de la pes feire et adrecier
au plus qu'il onques puet se painne
tant qu'il l'a feite. Lors l'en mainne
li rois la reïne veoir.
Lors ne lessa mie cheoir   4460
la reïne ses ialz vers terre,
einz l'ala lieemant requerre,
si l'enora de son pooir
et sel fist lez li aseoir.
Puis parlerent a grant leisir   4465
de quanque lor vint a pleisir;
ne matiere ne lor failloit,
qu'Amors assez lor an bailloit.
Et quant Lanceloz voit son eise,
qu'il ne dit rien que molt ne pleise   4470
la reïne, lors a consoil
a dit: "Dame, molt me mervoil
por coi tel sanblant me feïstes
avant hier, quant vos me veïstes,
n'onques un mot ne me sonastes: 4475
a po la mort ne m'an donastes,
ne je n'oi tant de hardemant
que tant com or vos an demant
vos en osasse demander.
Dame, or sui prez de l'amander,   4480
mes que le forfet dit m'aiez   *[44b]*
dom j'ai esté molt esmaiez."
Et la reïne li reconte:
"Comant? Don n'eüstes vos honte
de la charrete, et si dotastes?   4485
Molt a grant enviz i montastes
quant vos demorastes deus pas.
Por ce, voir, ne vos vos je pas
ne aresnier ne esgarder."
"Autre foiz me doint Dex garder,"   4490
fet Lanceloz, "de tel mesfet;
et ja Dex de moi merci n'et
se vos n'eüstes molt grant droit.
Dame, por Deu, tot orandroit
de moi l'amande an recevez;   4495
et se vos ja le me devez
pardoner, por Deu sel me dites."

4465. a lor pleisir

186

You have brought him no shame.   4450
No, but I, who promised him safe-conduct, am dishonored.
However it is, the shame is mine.
You will find it no light matter
If you try to escape me."
    When Lancelot heard his anger,   4455
He did his very best
To make and establish peace,
Until he did so. Then the king
Led him to see the queen.
This time the queen did not   4460
Let her eyes lower toward the ground
But went happily toward him
And had him sit beside her,
Honoring him with her kindest attentions.
Then they spoke at length   4465
Of everything that came into their minds;
They never lacked for subject matter,
Which Love supplied them in abundance.
When Lancelot saw how well he was received,
And that anything he said pleased   4470
The queen, he asked her
In confidence: "My lady, I wonder
Why you acted as you did
When you saw me the day before yesterday
And would not say a single word to me;   4475
You nearly caused my death,
And then I had not confidence enough
To dare to ask you
As now I am asking you.
If you would tell me, my lady,   4480
What crime has caused me such distress,
I am prepared to atone for it at once."
And the queen told him:
"What? Were you not ashamed
And fearful of the cart?   4485
By delaying for two steps you showed
Your great unwillingness to mount.
In truth, it was for this that I did not wish
To see you or converse with you."
"In the future, may God preserve me,"   4490
Said Lancelot, "from such a crime;
And may He have no mercy on me
If you are not completely in the right.
My lady, for God's sake,
Receive my penance at once;   4495
And if ever you will be able to
Forgive me, for God's sake tell me so!"

"Amis, toz an soiez vos quites,"
fet la reïne, "oltreemant:
jel vos pardoing molt boenemant."   4500
"Dame," fet il, "vostre merci;
mes je ne vos puis mie ci
tot dire quanque ge voldroie;
volantiers a vos parleroie
plus a leisir, s'il pooit estre."   4505
Et la reïne une fenestre
li mostre a l'uel, non mie au doi,
et dit: "Venez parler a moi
a cele fenestre anquenuit
quant par ceanz dormiront tuit,   4510
et si vanroiz par cel vergier.
Ceanz antrer ne herbergier
ne porroiz mie vostre cors;
je serai anz et vos defors,
que ceanz ne porroiz venir.   4515
Ne je ne porrai avenir
a vos, fors de boche ou de main;
mes, s'il vos plest, jusqu'a demain
i serai por amor de vos.
Asanbler ne porrïens nos,   4520
qu'an ma chanbre devant moi gist
Kex li seneschax, qui lenguist
des plaies dom il est coverz.
Et li huis ne rest mie overz,
einz est bien fers et bien gardez.   [44c]
Quant vos vandroiz, si vos gardez
que nule espie ne vos truisse."
"Dame," fet il, "la ou je puisse
ne me verra ja nule espie
qui mal i pant ne mal an die."   4530
Ensi ont pris lor parlemant,
si departent molt lieemant.

    Lanceloz ist fors de la chanbre,
si liez que il ne li remanbre
de nul de trestoz ses enuiz.   4535
Mes trop li demore la nuiz;
et li jorz li a plus duré,
a ce qu'il i a enduré,
que cent autre ou c'uns anz entiers.
Au parlemant molt volentiers   4540
s'an alast s'il fust anuitié.
Tant a au jor vaintre luitié
que la nuiz molt noire et oscure
l'ot mis desoz sa coverture
et desoz sa chape afublé.   4545

4518. Et

188

"Dear friend, may you be completely
Forgiven," said the queen.
"I absolve you most willingly."   4500
"My lady," said he, "I thank you;
But I cannot tell you here
All that I would.
Willingly would I speak with you
At greater length, were it possible."   4505
The queen indicated a window
To him with a glance, not by pointing.
"Come through this orchard
When all within are asleep,"
She said, "to speak with me   4510
At this window tonight.
You cannot get in
Or stay here;
I shall be inside and you without,
Since you cannot pass within.   4515
Nor shall I be able to approach
You, except by words or with my hand;
But for love of you I will stay there
Until the morrow, if you choose.
We cannot come together   4520
Because Kay the seneschal, suffering
From the wounds that cover him,
Sleeps facing me in my room.*
Moreover, the door is never left open,
But is always locked and guarded.   4525
When you come, be careful
Lest some spy see you."
"My lady," said he, "I will do all I can
So that no one will ever observe my coming
Who might consider it evil or speak badly of us."   4530
Having set their tryst,
They separated joyfully.
     On leaving the room, Lancelot was
So full of bliss that he did not remember
A single one of his many cares.   4535
But night was slow in coming;
And this day seemed longer to him,
For all that he had to put up with,
Than a hundred others or even a whole year.
He ached to be at the tryst,   4540
If night would only come.
At last dark and somber night
Conquered day's light,
Wrapped it in her covering
And hid it beneath her cloak.   4545

189

Quant il vit le jor enublé,
si se fet las et traveillié
et dit que molt avoit veillié,
s'avoit mestier de reposer.
Bien poez antendre et gloser   4550
(vos qui avez fet autretel)
que por la gent de son ostel
se fet las et se fet couchier;
mes n'ot mie son lit tant chier,
que por rien il n'i reposast--   4555
n'il ne poïst ne il n'osast
ne il ne volsist pas avoir
le hardemant ne le pooir.
Molt tost et soëf s'an leva;
ne ce mie ne li greva   4560
qu'il ne luisoit lune n'estoile,
n'an la meison n'avoit chandoile
ne lanpe ne lanterne ardant.
Ensi s'an ala regardant
c'onques nus garde ne s'an prist,   4565
einz cuidoient qu'il se dormist
an son lit trestote la nuit.
Sanz conpaignie et sanz conduit
molt tost vers le vergier s'an va   [44d]
que conpaignie n'i trova.   4570
Et de ce li est bien cheü
c'une piece del mur cheü
ot el vergier novelemant.
Par cele fraite isnelemant
s'an passe et vet tant que il vient   4575
a la fenestre; et la se tient
si coiz qu'il n'i tost n'esternue,
tant que la reïne est venue
en une molt blanche chemise;
n'ot sus bliaut ne cote mise,   4580
mes un cort mantel ot desus
d'escarlate et de cisemus.
Quant Lanceloz voit la reïne
qui a la fenestre s'acline,
qui de gros fers estoit ferree,   4585
d'un dolz salu l'a saluee.
Et ele un autre tost li rant,
que molt estoient desirrant
il de li et ele de lui.
De vilenie ne d'enui   4590
ne tienent parlemant ne plet.
Li uns pres de l'autre se tret
et andui main a main se tienent.
De ce que ansanble ne vienent
lor poise molt a desmesure,   4595

190

When Lancelot saw the day darkened,
He feigned fatigue and weariness,
Saying that he had been awake
A long while and needed repose.
You will be able to understand and interpret   4550
(You who have done likewise)
That he feigned weariness and went to bed
Because there were others in the house;
For he did not hold his bed so dear,
Because for nothing would he rest there--   4555
Nor could he, nor did he dare,
Nor did he wish to have
Such daring or such courage.
He crept out of bed as soon as possible;
And it bothered him not at all   4560
That there was no moon or star shining outside,
Nor any candle, lamp,
Or lantern burning in the house.
He moved about slowly,
Careful that no one should notice him;   4565
Rather, they all thought him to be asleep
In his bed for the whole night.
Alone, with no companion to accompany him,
He went straight to the orchard
Without encountering anyone.   4570
He had the good fortune to find
That a part of the wall
To the orchard had recently fallen.
Through this breach he quickly passed
And continued until he reached   4575
The window, where he stood
Absolutely silent, careful not to cough or sneeze,
Until the queen came up
In a spotless white gown;
She had no tunic or coat over it,   4580
Only a short mantle
Of rich cloth and marmot fur.
When Lancelot saw the queen
Leaning toward him behind the window
With its thick iron bars,   4585
He greeted her softly.
She returned his greeting at once,
Since great was his desire
For her, and hers for him.
They did not converse or speak   4590
About base or tiresome matters.
They drew near to one another
And held each other's hand.
They were immeasurably hurt
That they were unable to be together,   4595

191

qu'il an blasment la ferreüre.
Mes de ce Lanceloz se vante
que, s'a la reïne atalante,
avoec li leanz anterra--
ja por les fers ne remanra.   4600
Et la reïne li respont:
"Ne veez vos con cist fer sont
roide a ploier et fort a fraindre?
Ja tant ne les porroiz destraindre
ne tirer a vos ne sachier   4605
que les poïssiez arachier."
"Dame," fet il, "or ne vos chaille!
Ja ne cuit que fers rien i vaille--
rien fors vos ne me puet tenir
que bien ne puisse a vos venir.   4610
Se vostre congiez le m'otroie,
tote m'est delivre la voie;
mes se il bien ne vos agree,   [44e]
donc m'est ele si anconbree
que n'i passeroie por rien."   4615
"Certes," fet ele, "jel voel bien;
mes voloirs pas ne vos detient.
Mes tant atandre vos covient
que an mon lit soie couchiee,
que de noise ne vos meschiee;   4620
qu'il n'i avroit geu ne deport
se li seneschax qui ci dort
s'esveilloit ja por nostre noise.
Por c'est bien droiz que je m'an voise,
qu'il n'i porroit nul bien noter   4625
se il me veoit ci ester."
"Dame," fet il, "or alez donques,
mes de ce ne dotez vos onques
que je i doie noise faire.
Si soëf an cuit les fers traire   4630
que ja ne m'an traveillerai
ne nelui n'an esveillerai."
    Atant la reïne s'an torne,
et cil s'aparoille et atorne
de la fenestre desconfire.   4635
As fers se prant et sache et tire,
si que trestoz ploier les fet
et que fors de lor leus les tret.
Mes si estoit tranchanz li fers
que del doi mame jusqu'as ners   4640
la premiere once s'an creva,
et de l'autre doi se trancha
la premerainne jointe tote;

4641. p. ongle san crena

192

And cursed the iron bars.
But Lancelot boasted that,
If the queen wished it,
He could come in with her--
The bars would never keep him out.   4600
The queen responded:
"Can't you see that this iron is
Stiff to bend and hard to break?
You could never twist
Nor pull nor tear   4605
One of them enough to loosen it."
"My lady," he said, "don't worry!
I don't believe that iron will ever stop me--
Nothing but you yourself could keep me
From coming in to you.   4610
If you grant me your permission,
The way will soon be free;
But if you are not willing,
Then there are so many obstacles
That I shall never be able to pass."   4615
"Of course I want you with me," she replied.
"My wishes will never restrain you.
But you must wait until
I am lying in my bed,
So that you would not be endangered by any noise,   4620
For it would be a serious matter
If the seneschal sleeping here
Were to be awakened by us.
So I must go now,
For he would find no good in it   4625
Were he to see me standing here."
"My lady," said Lancelot, "go then,
But don't worry
About my making any sound.
I plan to separate the bars   4630
So smoothly and effortlessly
That no one will be awakened."
    Thereupon the queen turned away,
And Lancelot prepared and readied himself
To loosen the window.   4635
He grasped the bars, strained, and pulled,
Until he bent them all
And was able to free them from their fittings.
But the iron was so sharp
That he cut the end   4640
Of his little finger to the quick
And severed the whole
First joint of the next finger;

193

et del sanc qui jus an degote
ne des plaies nule ne sant   4645
cil qui a autre chose antant.
La fenestre n'est mie basse,
neporquant Lanceloz i passe
molt tost et molt delivremant.
An son lit trueve Kex dormant.   4650
Et puis vint au lit la reïne,
si l'aore et se li ancline,
car an nul cors saint ne croit tant.
Et la reïne li estant
ses braz ancontre, si l'anbrace;   4655
estroit pres de son piz le lace,
si l'a lez li an son lit tret;   [44f]
et le plus bel sanblant li fet
que ele onques feire li puet,
que d'Amors et del cuer li muet.   4660
D'Amors vient qu'ele le conjot;
et s'ele a lui grant amor ot
et il cent mile tanz a li,
car a toz autres cuers failli
Amors avers qu'au suen ne fist.   4665
Mes an son cuer tote reprist
Amors et fu si anterine
qu'an toz autres cuers fu frarine.
Or a Lanceloz quanqu'il vialt,
qant la reïne an gré requialt   4670
sa conpaignie et son solaz,
qant il la tient antre ses braz
et ele lui antre les suens.
Tant li est ses jeus dolz et buens,
et del beisier et del santir,   4675
que il lor avint sanz mantir
une joie et une mervoille
tel c'onques ancor sa paroille
ne fu oïe ne seüe.
Mes toz jorz iert par moi teüe,   4680
qu'an conte ne doit estre dite:
des joies fu la plus eslite
et la plus delitable cele
que li contes nos test et cele.
Molt ot de joie et de deduit   4685
Lanceloz tote cele nuit;
mes li jorz vient qui molt li grieve,
quant de lez s'amie se lieve.
Au lever fu il droiz martirs,
tant li fu griés li departirs,   4690
car il i suefre grant martire:

Yet his mind was so intent on other things
That he felt neither the wounds   4645
Nor the blood flowing from them.
Although the window was quite high up,
Lancelot passed
Quickly and easily through it.
He found Kay asleep in his bed.   4650
He came next to that of the queen;
Lancelot bowed and worshiped before her,
For he did not have this much faith in any saint.
The queen stretched out
Her arms toward him, embraced him,   4655
Hugged him to her breast
And drew him into the bed beside her,
Gazing as gently at him
As she knew how to gaze,
For her love and her heart were his.   4660
She welcomed him out of love;
But if she had strong love for him,
He felt a hundred thousand times more for her.
For love in other hearts was as nothing
Compared to the love he felt in his.   4665
Love took root in his heart,
And was so entirely there
That little was left for other hearts.
Now Lancelot had his every wish:
The queen willingly   4670
Sought his company and comfort,
As he held her in his arms,
And she held him in hers.
Her love-play seemed so gentle and good to him,
Both her kisses and caresses,   4675
That in truth the two of them felt
A joy and wonder,
The equal of which had never
Yet been heard or known.
But I shall ever keep it secret,   4680
Since it should not be written of:
The most delightful
And choicest pleasure is that
Which is hinted, but never told.
Lancelot had great joy   4685
And pleasure all that night,
But the day's coming sorrowed him deeply,
When he had to leave his love's side.
Rising was a true martyrdom,
So deep was the pain of parting;   4690
Indeed, he suffered a martyr's agony:

195

ses cuers adés cele part tire
ou la reïne se remaint.
N'a pooir que il l'an remaint,
que la reïne tant li plest   4695
qu'il n'a talant que il la lest:
li cors s'an vet, li cuers sejorne.
Droit vers la fenestre s'an torne;
mes de son cors tant i remaint*
que li drap sont tachié et taint   4700
del sanc qui cheï de ses doiz.   [45a]
Molt s'an part Lanceloz destroiz,
plains de sopirs et plains de lermes.
Del rasanbler n'est pas pris termes;
ce poise lui, mes ne puet estre.   4705
A enviz passe a la fenestre,
s'i antra il molt volantiers.
N'avoit mie les doiz antiers,
que molt fort s'i estoit bleciez;
et s'a il les fers redreciez   4710
et remis an lor leus arriere,
si que ne devant ne derriere
n'an l'un ne an l'autre costé
ne pert qu'an an eüst osté
nus des fers ne tret ne ploié.   4715
Au departir a soploié
a la chanbre et fet tot autel
con s'il fust devant un autel;
puis s'an part a molt grant angoisse.
N'ancontre home qui le conoisse,   4720
tant qu'an son ostel est venuz.
An son lit se couche toz nuz
si c'onques nelui n'i esvoille.
Et lors a primes se mervoille
de ses doiz qu'il trueve plaiez;   4725
mes de rien n'an est esmaiez,
por ce qu'il set tot de seür
que au traire les fers del mur
de la fenestre se bleça.
Por ce pas ne s'an correça: 4730
car il se volsist mialz del cors
andeus les braz avoir traiz fors
que il ne fust oltre passez;
mes s'il se fust aillors quassez
et si laidemant anpiriez,   4735
molt an fust dolanz et iriez.
    La reïne la matinee,
dedanz sa chanbre ancortinee,
se fu molt soëf andormie.
De ses dras ne se gardoit mie   4740
que il fussent tachié de sanc,

4699. son sanc

196

His heart repeatedly turned
To where the queen remained behind.
Nor was he able to take it with him,
For it so loved the queen   4695
That it had no desire to quit her:
His body left, but his heart stayed.
Lancelot returned straightway to the window,
But of his body he left enough behind
To stain and spot the sheets   4700
With the blood that dripped from his fingers.
Lancelot went away distraught,
Full of sighs and full of tears.
It grieved him that no second tryst
Had been arranged, but such was impossible.   4705
Regretfully he went out the window
Through which he had entered most willingly.
His fingers were not whole,
But deeply wounded;
He straightened the bars   4710
And replaced them in their fittings,
So that from neither front nor back,
Nor to one side nor the other
Did it appear that anyone had bent
Or pulled or removed any of the bars.   4715
On parting he bowed low
Before the room and behaved as though
He were before an altar;
Then in great anguish he left.
On the way to his lodging   4720
He encountered no one who might recognize him.
He lay down naked in his bed
Without awakening anyone.
And then at dawn, to his surprise,
He noticed his wounded fingers;   4725
But he was not at all upset,
For he knew without doubt
That he had cut himself pulling
The iron bars from the window casing.
Therefore he did not grow angry with himself,   4730
Since he would rather have
His two arms pulled from his body
Than not to have entered through the window;
Yet, if he had wounded
And so vilely injured himself in any other manner,   4735
He would have been most angry and distressed.
    In the morning the queen
Was gently sleeping
In her curtained room.*
She did not notice that her sheets   4740
Were stained with blood,

197

einz cuidoit qu'il fussent molt blanc
et molt bel et molt avenant.
Et Meliaganz, maintenant
qu'il fu vestuz et atornez,   [45b]
s'an est vers la chanbre tornez
ou la reïne se gisoit.
Veillant la trueve et les dras voit
del fres sanc tachiez et gotez;
s'en a ses conpaignons botez,   4750
et com aparcevanz de mal,
vers le lit Kex le seneschal
esgarde, et voit les dras tachiez
de sanc (que la nuit, ce sachiez,
furent ses plaies escrevees).   4755
Et dit: "Dame, or ai ge trovees
tex anseignes con je voloie!
Bien est voirs que molt se foloie
qui de fame garder se painne--
son travail i pert et sa painne;   4760
qu'ainz la pert cil qui plus la garde
que cil qui ne s'an done garde.
Molt a or bele garde feite   4762a
mes pere qui por moi vos gueite!*   4762b
De moi vos a il bien gardee,
mes enuit vos a regardee
Kex li seneschax malgré suen,   4765
s'a de vos eü tot son buen,
et il sera molt bien prové."
"Comant?" fet ele.--"J'ai trové
sanc an vos dras qui le tesmoingne,
puis qu'a dire le me besoigne.   4770
Par ce le sai, par ce le pruis,
que an voz dras et es suens truis
le sanc qui cheï de ses plaies.
Ce sont ansaignes bien veraies!"
Lors primes la reïne vit   4775
et an l'un et an l'autre lit
les dras sanglanz; si s'an mervoille,
honte en ot, si devint vermoille
et dist: "Se Damedex me gart,
ce sanc que an mes dras regart,   4780
onques ne l'i aporta Ques,
einz m'a enuit senié li nes;
de mon nes fu, au mien espoir."
Et ele cuide dire voir.
"Par mon chief," fet Meleaganz,   4785
"quanque vos dites est neanz!
N'i a mestier parole fainte,
que provee estes et atainte
et bien sera li voirs provez."   [45c]

198

But thought them still to be pure white
And fair and proper.
Meleagant, as soon as
He was dressed and ready,   4745
Came toward the room
Where the queen was lying.
He found her awake now and saw the sheets
Stained with fresh drops of blood;
He nudged his men,   4750
And, as if suspecting some evil,
He looked toward the seneschal Kay's bed.
There, too, he saw bloodstained
Sheets! (You must know that his wounds
Had reopened during the night.)   4755
"My lady," said Meleagant, "now I've found
The proof I've been wanting!
It is quite true that a man is crazy
To take pains to watch over a woman--
His efforts are all in vain.   4760
And the man who makes the greater effort loses his woman
More quickly than he who does not bother.
My father did a fine job of guarding   4762a
When he watched you because of me!   4762b
He protected you carefully from me,
But in spite of his efforts the seneschal
Kay looked closely upon you this night   4765
And has done all he pleased with you,
Which will easily be proved."
"How?" she asked.--"I have found
Blood on your sheets, clear proof,
Since you must be told.   4770
This is how I know, and this my proof,
For on your sheets and his I have found
Blood which dripped from his wounds.
This evidence is irrefutable!"
Then, for the first time, the queen saw   4775
The bloody sheets on both beds.
She was dumbfounded;
She was ashamed. Blushing,
She said: "As the Lord Almighty protects me,
This blood you see on my sheets   4780
Never came from Kay--
My nose bled last night;
I suppose it came from my nose."
She felt that she was telling the truth.
"By my head," replied Meleagant,   4785
"All your words are worth nothing!
There is no need for lies,
For you are proved guilty,
And the truth will soon be known."

Lors dit: "Seignor, ne vos movez" 4790
(as gardes qui iluec estoient)
"et gardez que osté ne soient
li drap del lit tant que je veigne.
Je voel que li rois droit me teigne
qant la chose veüe avra." 4795
Lors le quist tant qu'il le trova,
si se lesse a ses piez cheoir
et dit: "Sire, venez veoir
ce don garde ne vos prenez.
La reïne veoir venez, 4800
si verroiz mervoilles provees
que j'ai veües et trovees.
Mes ainçois que vos i ailliez,
vos pri que vos ne me failliez
de justise ne de droiture: 4805
bien savez an quel aventure
por la reïne ai mon cors mis,
dom vos estes mes anemis,
que por moi la faites garder.
Hui matin l'alai regarder 4810
an son lit, et si ai veü
tant que j'ai bien aparceü
qu'avoec li gist Kex chasque nuit.
Sire, por Deu, ne vos enuit
s'il m'an poise et se je m'an plaing, 4815
car molt me vient a grant desdaing
qant ele me het et despit
et Kex o li chaque nuit gist."
"Tes!" fet li rois, "je nel croi pas."
"Sire, or venez veoir les dras, 4820
comant Kex les a conreez.
Quant ma parole ne creez,
ençois cuidiez que je vos mante,
les dras et la coute sanglante
des plaies Kex vos mosterrai." 4825
"Or i alons, si le verrai,"
fet li rois, "que veoir le voel:
le voir m'an aprendront mi oel."
Li rois tot maintenant s'an va
jusqu'an la chanbre ou il trova 4830
la reïne qui se levoit.
Les dras sanglanz an son lit voit
et el lit Kex autresimant, *[45d]*
et dist: "Dame, or vet malemant
se c'est voirs que mes filz m'a dit." 4835
Ele respont: "Se Dex m'aït,
onques ne fu neïs de songe
contee si male mançonge!
Je cuit que Kex li seneschax

200

Then he said to the guards   4790
Who were there: "Lords, don't move.
See that the sheets are not taken
From the bed before my return.
I want the king to uphold me
When he has seen this for himself."   4795
Meleagant sought out his father, the king,
Then let himself fall at his feet,
Saying: "Sir, come and see
Something that you would never suspect.
Come and see the queen   4800
And you will be astounded
At what I've found and proved.
But before you go there,
I beg you not to fail me
In justice and righteousness;   4805
You well know the dangers
To which I have been exposed for the queen;
You oppose me in this
And guard her carefully for fear of me.
This morning I went to look at her   4810
In her bed, and I saw
Enough to recognize
That Kay lies with her every night.
By God, sir, don't be upset
If this disturbs me and I complain,   4815
For it is most humiliating to me
That she hates and despises me,
Yet lies every night with Kay."
"Silence!" said the king, "I do not believe it!"
"Sir, just come and see the sheets   4820
And what Kay has done to them.
If you don't believe my word
And think I'm lying to you,
The sheets and spread, covered
With Kay's blood, will prove it to you."   4825
"Let us go then; I will see it,"
Said the king, "for I want to see it myself:
My eyes will teach me the truth."
The king went at once
Into the room where he found   4830
The queen just getting up.
He saw the bloody sheets on her bed
And on Kay's bed as well.
"Lady," he said, "you're in a terrible plight
If what my son says is true."   4835
"So help me God," she answered,
"Not even in nightmares
Has such an awful lie been spread!
I believe the seneschal Kay

201

est si cortois et si leax 4840
que il n'an fet mie a mescroire,
et je ne regiet mie an foire
mon cors, ne n'an faz livreison.
Certes, Kex n'est mie tex hom
qu'il me requeïst tel outrage-- 4845
ne je n'an oi onques corage
del faire, ne ja ne l'avrai."
"Sire, molt boen gré vos savrai,"
fet Meleaganz a son pere,
"se Kex son outrage conpere, 4850
si que la reïne i ait honte.
A vos tient la justise et monte,
et je vos an requier et pri.
Le roi Artus a Kex traï,
son seignor, qui tant le creoit 4855
que comandee li avoit
la rien que plus ainme an cest monde."
"Sire, or sofrez que je responde,"
fet Kex, "et si m'escondirai.
Ja Dex quant de cest siegle irai 4860
ne me face pardon a l'ame,
se onques jui avoec ma dame.
Certes, mialz voldroie estre morz
que tex leidure ne tiex torz
fust par moi quis vers mon seignor. 4865
Et jamés Dex santé graignor
que j'ai orandroit ne me doint,
einz me praigne Morz an cest point,
se je onques le me pansai!
Mes itant de mes plaies sai 4870
qu'annuit m'ont seinnié a planté,
s'an sont mi drap ansanglanté:
por ce vostre filz me mescroit,
mes certes il n'i a nul droit."
Et Meleaganz li respont: 4875
"Si m'aïst Dex, traï vos ont
li deable, li vif maufé! [45e]
Trop fustes enuit eschaufé,
et por ce que trop vos grevastes
voz plaies sanz dote escrevastes. 4880
Ne vos i valt neant contrueve:
li sans d'anbedeus parz le prueve--
bien le veons et bien i pert.
Droiz est que son forfet conpert,
que si est provez et repris. 4885
Einz chevaliers de vostre pris
ne fist si grant descovenue,
si vos an est honte avenue."
"Sire, sire," fet Kex au roi,

Is so courteous and loyal   4840
That it would be wrong to mistrust him,
And I have never offered for sale at market
My body, nor given it away.
Kay is certainly not a man
To insult me like this--   4845
And I have never had the desire
To do such a thing, and never will!"
"Sir, I shall be most grateful to you,"
Said Meleagant to his father,
"If Kay be made to pay for his insult   4850
In such a manner that the queen be shamed.
It is for you to dispense the justice
Which I ask and seek.
Kay has betrayed King Arthur,
His lord, who had faith enough in him   4855
That he entrusted to him
What he most loved in this world."
"Sir, now permit me to reply,"
Said Kay, "and I shall acquit myself.
May God never absolve my soul   4860
After I leave this world
If ever I lay with my lady.
Indeed, I would much rather be dead
Than have committed such a base
And blameworthy act toward my lord.   4865
May God never grant me better health
Than that which I have now,
But may Death take me at once,
If I ever even conceived of such!
I know that my wounds   4870
Bled profusely this night
And soaked my sheets:
This is why your son suspects me,
But he certainly has no right to."
Meleagant answered him: 4875
"So help me God, the demons
And the living devils have betrayed you!
You became too excited last night,
And because you overtaxed yourself,
Your wounds were undoubtedly reopened.   4880
No lies can help you:
The blood in both beds is proof--
It is clearly visible, and we all see it.
One must rightfully pay for a sin
In which he has been so clearly caught.   4885
Never has a knight of your stature
Committed such an impropriety,
And you are shamed by it."
"Sir, sir," said Kay to the king,

203

"je desfandrai ma dame et moi   4890
de ce que vostre filz m'amet.
An poinne et an travail me met,
mes certes a tort me travaille."
"Vos n'avez mestier de bataille,"
fet li rois, "que trop vos dolez."   4895
"Sire, se sofrir le volez,
ensi malades con je sui
me conbatrai ancontre lui
et mosterrai que je n'ai colpe
an cest blasme don il m'ancolpe."   4900
Et la reïne mandé ot
tot celeemant Lancelot,
et dit au roi que ele avra
un chevalier qui desfandra
le seneschal de ceste chose   4905
vers Meleagant, se il ose.
Et Meleaganz dist tantost:
"Nus chevaliers ne vos en ost
vers cui la bataille n'anpraigne
tant que li uns vaincuz remaingne,   4910
nes se ce estoit uns jaianz."
Atant vint Lanceloz leanz;
des chevaliers i ot tel rote
que plainne an fu la sale tote.
Maintenant que il fu venuz,   4915
oïant toz, juenes et chenuz,
la reïne la chose conte.
Et dit: "Lancelot, ceste honte
m'a ci Meleaganz amise;
an mescreance m'an a mise   4920
vers trestoz ces qui l'oënt dire,   [45f]
se vos ne l'an feites desdire.
Enuit--ce dit--a Kex geü
o moi, por ce qu'il a veü
mes dras et les suens de sanc tainz;   4925
et dit que toz an iert atainz,
se vers lui ne se puet desfandre
ou se autres ne vialt anprandre
la bataille por lui aidier."
"Ja ne vos an covient pleidier,"   4930
fet Lanceloz, "la ou je soie.
Ja Deu ne place qu'an mescroie
ne vos ne lui de tel afeire.
Prez sui de la bataille feire
que onques ne le se pansa,   4935
se an moi point de desfanse a.
A mon pooir l'an desfandrai;

4891. mamez   4921. losent dire

204

"I will defend my lady and myself   4890
From your son's accusations.
He causes me grief and torment,
But is clearly in the wrong."
"You cannot do battle,"
Replied the king, "for you are in too great pain."   4895
"Sir, if you will permit,
I am willing to do battle against him
As ill as I am
To prove that I am innocent
Of that shame of which he accuses me."   4900
The queen had sent
Secretly for Lancelot;
She told the king that she will provide
A knight to defend
The seneschal in this affair   4905
Against Meleagant, if he dares.
Meleagant replied quickly:
"I am not afraid to do battle
Against any knight you might select
Until one of us is defeated,   4910
Even were he to be a giant!"
At this moment Lancelot entered the hall;
There was such a mass of knights
That the room was filled to overflowing.
As soon as he arrived,   4915
The queen explained the affair
So that all, young and old, could hear.
She said: "Lancelot, Meleagant
Has accused me of a shameful act;
I am considered guilty   4920
By all who have heard him say it,
Unless you force him to retract his accusation.
He asserts that Kay slept this night
With me because he has seen
Both our sheets stained with blood;   4925
And he says that Kay will be condemned,
Unless he can defend himself
Or unless another will undertake
The battle on his behalf."
"You need not speak in your own defense   4930
As long as I am near," said Lancelot.
"May it never please God to let anyone doubt
Either you or him in such a matter.
If I am worth anything as a knight,
I am prepared to do battle   4935
To prove that Kay never conceived of such a deed:
I will defend him as best I can

por lui la bataille anprandrai."
Et Meleaganz avant saut
et dit: "Se Damedex me saut,⁣   4940
ce voel je bien et molt me siet:
ja ne pant nus que il me griet!"
Et Lanceloz dist: "Sire rois,
je sai de quauses et de lois
et de plez et de jugemanz:⁣   4945
ne doit estre sanz seiremanz
bataille de tel mescreance."
Et Meleaganz sanz dotance
li respont molt isnelemant:
"Bien i soient li seiremant⁣   4950
et veignent li saint orandroit,
que je sai bien que je ai droit."
Et Lanceloz ancontre dit:
"Onques, se Damedex m'aït,
Quex le seneschal ne conut⁣   4955
qui de tel chose le mescrut."
Maintenant lor armes demandent,
lor chevax amener comandent;
l'an lor amainne, armé se sont;
vaslet les arment, armé sont.⁣   4960
Et ja resont li saint fors tret.
Meleaganz avant se tret
et Lanceloz dejoste lui.
Si s'agenoillent anbedui;
et Meleaganz tant sa main⁣   [46a]
aus sainz et jure tot de plain:
"Ensi m'aïst Dex et li sainz,
Kex li seneschaus fu conpainz
enuit la reïne an son lit,
et de li ot tot son delit."⁣   4970
"Et je t'an lief come parjur,"
fet Lanceloz, "et si rejur
qu'il n'i jut ne ne la santi.
Et de celui qui a manti
praigne Dex, se lui plest, vangence⁣   4975
et face voire demostrance.
Mes ancor un autre an ferai
des seiremanz et jurerai,
cui qu'il enuit ne cui qu'il poist,
que se il hui venir me loist⁣   4980
de Meleagant au desus,
tant m'aïst Dex et neant plus
et ces reliques qui sont ci,
que ja de lui n'avrai merci!"
Li rois de rien ne s'esjoï⁣   4985
quant cestui sairemant oï.
    Qant li seiremant furent fet,

And undertake the battle for him."
Meleagant sprang forward
And said: "As God is my Savior,   4940
This suits me, and I'm quite willing;
Let no one ever think otherwise!"
"My lord king," said Lancelot,
"I am knowledgeable in trials, laws,
Suits, and verdicts: 4945
When a man's word is doubted,
An oath is required before entering battle."
Sure of himself, Meleagant
Replied at once:
"I'm quite prepared to swear my oath.   4950
Bring forth the holy relics,
For I know I'm in the right."
Lancelot countered:
"Never, so help me God,
Have I known the seneschal Kay   4955
To speak falsely on such a point."
They asked for their armor at once
And ordered their horses fetched;
They put on the armor when it was brought them,
And their valets armed their horses.   4960
Next, the holy relics were brought out.
Meleagant stepped forward
And Lancelot beside him.
They both knelt;
And Meleagant stretched forth his hand   4965
Toward the relics and swore in a loud voice:
"As God and the saints are my witnesses,
The seneschal Kay slept
This night with the queen in her bed,
And took his full pleasure from her."   4970
"And I swear that you lie,"
Said Lancelot, "and I further swear
That he never slept with her or touched her.
And if it please God, may He
Show His righteousness by taking   4975
Vengeance on him who has lied.
I will take yet another
Oath and swear,
No matter whom it may grieve or hurt,
That if on this day God grant me   4980
The better of Meleagant,
May He alone and these relics here
Give me strength enough
Never to show him mercy!"
The king was deeply saddened   4985
When he heard this oath.
    After the oaths had been sworn,

207

lor cheval lor furent fors tret,
bel et boen de totes bontez;
sor le suen est chascuns montez,   4990
et li uns contre l'autre muet
tant con chevax porter le puet.
Et es plus granz cors des chevax
fiert li uns l'autre des vasax
si qu'il ne lor remaint nes poinz   4995
des deus lances tres qu'anz es poinz.
Et li uns l'autre a terre porte,
mes ne font mie chiere morte,
que tot maintenant se relievent
et tant com il pueent se grievent   5000
aus tranchanz des espees nues.
Les estanceles vers les nues
totes ardanz des hiaumes saillent.
Par si grant ire s'antr'asaillent
as espees que nues tienent,   5005
que si com eles vont et vienent
s'antr'ancontrent et s'antrefierent,
ne tant reposer ne se quierent
qu'aleinne reprandre lor loise.   [46b]
Li rois, cui molt an grieve et poise,   5010
en a la reïne apelee,
qui apoier s'estoit alee
amont as loges de la tor.
Por Deu, li dist, le criator,
que ele departir les lest.   5015
"Tot quanque vos an siet et plest,"
fet la reïne; "a boene foi,
ja n'an feroiz rien contre moi."
Lanceloz a bien antandu
que la reïne a respondu   5020
a ce que li rois li requiert;
ja puis conbatre ne se quiert,
einz a tantost guerpi le chaple.
Et Meleaganz fiert et chaple
sor lui, que reposer ne quiert;   5025
et li rois antredeus se fiert
et tient son fil, qui dit et jure
que il n'a de pes feire cure:
"Bataille voel, n'ai soing de peis!"
Et li rois li dist: "Car te teis   5030
et me croi, si feras que sages.
Ja certes hontes ne domages
ne t'an vandra, se tu me croiz;
mes   fei ice que feire doiz.
Don ne te sovient il que tu   5035

5009. lor *repeated*

208

Their horses, fair and good
In every respect, were led forward;
Each mounted his own;   4990
Then they charged headlong toward each other
As fast as their horses could carry them.
With their steeds rushing full speed,
The two vassals struck each other
Such mighty blows that they were left   4995
Holding only the hafts of their lances.
They forced each other to the ground;
But, not remaining there defeated,
They rose up immediately
With drawn swords to strike   5000
With all the strength of their naked blades.
Burning sparks flew
From their helmets toward the heavens.
So enraged were they in their assaults
With unsheathed blades,   5005
That as they thrust and parried
And met and struck one another
There was no desire to rest,
Not even to catch their breath.
The king, gravely worried,   5010
Summoned the queen,
Who had gone up to the tower loge
To observe the battle.
He asked her in the name of God the Creator
To let them be separated.   5015
"As it suits and pleases you,"
Replied the queen, "in faith,
You would not be doing anything to displease me."
Lancelot clearly heard
What the queen had replied   5020
To King Bademagu's request;
He had no further desire for combat
And abandoned the fight altogether.
Meleagant struck and slashed
Him unceasingly,   5025
Until the king forced his way between them
And restrained his son, who swore and said
That he had no intention of making peace:
"Peace be damned! I want to fight!"
And the king said to him: "You will be wise   5030
To keep silent and do what I say.
Certainly you will never be shamed
Or hurt for believing me.
So do what is right.
Do you not recall that you   5035

209

as an la cort le roi Artu
contre lui bataille arramie?
Et de ce ne dotes tu mie
que il ne te soit granz enors,
se la te vient biens plus qu'aillors?" 5040
Ce dit li rois por essaier
se il le porroit apaier,
tant qu'il l'apeise et ses depart.
Et Lanceloz, cui molt fu tart
de monseignor Gauvain trover, 5045
an vient congié querre et rover
au roi, et puis a la reïne.
Par le congié d'ax s'achemine
vers le Pont soz Eve corrant,
si ot aprés lui rote grant 5050
des chevaliers qui le suioient;
mes assez de tex i aloient
don bel li fust s'il remassissent. [46c]
Lor jornees molt bien fornissent
tant que le Pont soz Eve aprochent, 5055
mes d'une liue ancor n'i tochent.
Ençois que pres del pont venissent
et que il veoir le poïssent,
uns nains a l'encontre lor vint
sor un grant chaceor, et tint 5060
une corgiee por chacier
son chaceor et menacier.
Et maintenant a demandé
si com il li fu comandé:
"Li quex de vos est Lanceloz? 5065
Nel me celez, je sui des voz;
mes dites le seüremant
que por voz granz biens le demant."
Lanceloz li respont por lui
et dit il meïsmes: "Je sui 5070
cil que tu demandes et quiers."
"Ha! Lancelot, frans chevaliers,
leisse ces genz et si me croi.
Vien t'an toz seus ansanble o moi,
qu'an molt boen leu mener te voel. 5075
Ja nus ne t'an siue por l'uel,
einz vos atendent ci androit,
que nos revandrons orandroit."
Cil qui de nul mal ne se dote
a fet remenoir sa gent tote 5080
et siust le nain qui traï l'a.
Et sa gent qui l'atendent la
le puent longuemant atandre,

5042. esmaier

Have arranged to do battle
With Lancelot in the court of King Arthur?
And can you doubt
That it would be a far greater honor
To defeat him there than anywhere else?"   5040
The king said this to try
To quiet his son
Until he could calm him and separate them.
Lancelot, who was very eager
To find my lord Gawain,   5045
Went to seek and ask leave
Of the king, and then of the queen.
With their permission he rode off
Rapidly toward the Underwater Bridge,
Followed by a large crowd   5050
Of knights coming after him;
But many were with him
Whom he would have preferred to have left behind.
They rode all of several days
Until they were about a league   5055
From the Underwater Bridge.
Before they could get near enough
To see the bridge,
A dwarf came forth to meet them
On a huge hunter and brandishing   5060
A whip to encourage
And incite his steed.
Promptly he inquired
As he had been ordered:
"Which of you is Lancelot?   5065
Don't hide him from me, I am one of your party.
Instead tell me with confidence,
Because it is for your profit that I ask."
Lancelot answered for himself,
And said to him: "I am   5070
He about whom you seek and inquire."
"Ah, Lancelot! true knight,
Quit these men and put your faith in me.
Come along alone with me,
For I intend to take you to a very wonderful place. 5075
Let no one observe your departure,
But have them wait at this spot,
For we shall return shortly."
Suspecting no deceit,
He ordered his companions to remain behind,   5080
And himself followed the dwarf, who has betrayed him.
His men who were awaiting him there
Could wait for him forever,

que cil n'ont nul talant del randre
qui l'ont pris et seisi an sont.   5085
Et sa gent si grant duel an font
de ce qu'il ne vient ne repeire
qu'il ne sevent qu'il puissent feire.
Tuit dïent que traïz les a
li nains et si lor an pesa.   5090
Folie seroit de l'anquerre.
Dolant le comancent a querre,
mes ne sevent ou il le truissent
ne quele part querre le puissent.
S'an prenent consoil tuit ansanble: 5095
a ce s'acordent, ce me sanble,
li plus resnable et li plus sage,
qu'il an iront jusqu'au passage   [46d]
del Pont soz Eve, qui est pres,
et querront Lancelot aprés   5100
par le los monseignor Gauvain,
s'il le truevent n'a bois n'a plain.
A cest consoil trestuit s'acordent,
si bien que de rien ne se tordent.
Vers le Pont soz Eve s'an vont,   5105
et tantost qu'il vienent au pont
ont monseignor Gauvain veü,
del pont trabuchié et cheü
an l'eve, qui estoit parfonde;
une ore essort et autre afonde,   5110
or le voient et or le perdent.
Il vienent la et si l'aerdent
a rains, a perches et a cros.
N'avoit que le hauberc el dos,
et sor le chief le hiaume assis,   5115
qui des autres valoit bien dis;
et les chauces de fer chauciees
de sa süor anruïlliees,
car molt avoit sofferz travauz,
et mainz perils et mainz asauz   5120
avoit trespassez et vaincuz.
Sa lance estoit, et ses escuz
et ses chevax, a l'autre rive.
Mes ne cuident pas que il vive
cil qui l'ont tret de l'eve fors,   5125
car il en avoit molt el cors,
ne des que tant qu'il l'ot randue
n'ont de lui parole antandue.
Mes quant sa parole et sa voiz
rot son cuer delivre et sa doiz,   5130
qu'an le pot oïr et antandre,
au plus tost que il s'i pot prandre

212

Since those who had taken him and held him prisoner
Had no intention of returning him.   5085
His men were so distressed
At his failure to return
That they did not know what they could do.
They all agreed that the dwarf had
Deceived them, and were very upset.   5090
It would be useless to seek after him.
They approached the search with heavy hearts,
For they knew not where they might find him
Nor in which direction to seek.
They discussed the situation among themselves: 5095
The wisest and most reasonable men,
It seems, agreed
That they should proceed to
The Underwater Bridge, which was nearby,
Then seek Lancelot afterward   5100
With the aid of my lord Gawain,
Should they find him in wood or plain.
This decision was accepted
Unanimously and without shirking.
They proceeded toward the Underwater Bridge   5105
And upon reaching it
Saw my lord Gawain,
Who had slipped and fallen
Into the deep water;
He was bobbing up and down,   5110
In and out of sight.
They drew near and reached out toward him
With branches, poles, and crooked sticks.
Gawain had only his hauberk on his back,
And on his head his helmet,   5115
Which was worth ten of any others;
He wore chain-mail greaves
Rusted with sweat,
For he had been sorely tried
And had endured and overcome   5120
Many perils and challenges.
His lance, his shield,
And his horse were on the far bank.
Those who dragged him from the water
Feared for his life,   5125
For he had swallowed much water,
And they heard no word from him
Until he had heaved it up.
But when he had cleared his chest and throat,
And had regained his voice and speech   5130
Enough that they could hear and understand him,
As soon as he was again able

a la parole, se s'i prist:
lués de la reïne requist
a ces qui devant lui estoient   5135
se nule novele an savoient.
Et cil qui li ont respondu
d'avoec le roi Bademagu
dïent qu'ele ne part nule ore,
qui molt la sert et molt l'enore.   5140
"Vint la puis nus an ceste terre,"   [46e]
fet messire Gauvains, "requerre?"
Et il respondirent: "Oïl,
Lanceloz del Lac," font se il,
"qui passa au Pont de l'Espee.   5145
Si l'a resqueusse et delivree,
et avoec nos autres trestoz;
mes traïz nos en a uns goz,
uns nains boçuz et rechigniez--
laidemant nos a engigniez,   5150
qui Lancelot nos a fortret.
Nos ne savons qu'il an a fet."
"Et quant?" fet messire Gauvains.
"Sire, hui nos a ce fet li nains,
molt pres de ci, quant il et nos   5155
venïemes ancontre vos."
"Et comant s'est il contenuz
puis qu'an cest païs fu venuz?"
Et cil li comancent a dire;
si li recontent tire a tire   5160
si c'un tot seul mot n'i oblïent;
et de la reïne li dïent
qu'ele l'atant, et dit por voir
que riens ne la feroit movoir
del païs tant qu'ele le voie,   5165
por novele que ele en oie.
Messire Gauvains lor respont:
"Quant nos partirons de cest pont,
irons nos querre Lancelot?"
N'i a un seul qui mialz ne lot   5170
qu'a la reïne aillent ençois:
si le fera querre li rois;
car il cuident qu'an traïson
l'ait fet ses fiiz metre an prison,
Meleaganz, qui molt le het.   5175
Ja an leu, se li rois le set,
ne sera qu'il nel face randre;
des ore se pueent atandre.
A cest consoil tuit s'acorderent

5152. quil a mesfet

214

To speak, he began to talk:
His first question
To those who were before him was   5135
Whether they had any news of the queen.
And those who answered him
Said that she never left
The presence of King Bademagu,
Who served and honored her well.   5140
"Has anyone come lately into this land
To seek her?" my lord Gawain inquired.
And they replied: "Yes,
Lancelot of the Lake," they said,
"Who crossed the Sword Bridge.   5145
He rescued and freed her
And all of us along with her;
But a humpbacked,
Grinning dwarf tricked us--
He deceived us insidiously   5150
By kidnapping Lancelot.
We do not know what he has done with him."
"When was this?" my lord Gawain asked.
"Sir, the dwarf did this today,
Quite near this spot, as we   5155
Were coming with Lancelot to meet you."
"And what has he done
Since coming into this land?"
They began to tell him,
Giving every detail   5160
And not omitting a single word;
And they told Gawain that the queen
Was awaiting him and had sworn
That nothing would make her leave
The land until she had seen him,   5165
So much had she been told about him.
My lord Gawain inquired of them:
"When we leave this bridge,
Will we go to seek Lancelot?"
They all thought it best   5170
To go first to the queen:
Bademagu would have Lancelot sought;
For they believed that his son
Meleagant, who hated him direly,
Had had him imprisoned.   5175
If the king knew his whereabouts,
He would have him freed no matter where he was;
Therefore they could delay their search.
They all accepted this suggestion

et tot maintenant s'aroterent   5180
tant que vers la cort s'aprocherent
ou la reïne et li rois erent,
et Kex avoec, li seneschax,
et s'i estoit li desleax,
de traïson plains et conblez,   *[46 f]*
qui molt laidemant a troblez
por Lancelot toz ces qui vienent.
Por mort et por traï se tienent,
s'an font grant duel, que molt lor poise.
N'est pas la novele cortoise   5190
qui la reïne cest duel porte,
neporquant ele s'an deporte
au plus belemant qu'ele puet;
por monseignor Gauvain l'estuet
auques esjoïr, si fet ele.   5195
Et neporquant mie ne cele
son duel que auques n'i apeire;
et joie et duel li estuet feire:
por Lancelot a le cuer vain,
et contre monseignor Gauvain   5200
mostre sanblant de passejoie.
N'i a nul qui la novele oie,
ne soit dolanz et esperduz
de Lancelot qui est perduz.
De monseignor Gauvain eüst   5205
li rois joie et molt li pleüst
sa venue et sa conuissance;
mes tel duel a et tel pesance
de Lancelot qui est traïz
que maz an est et esbaïz.   5210
Et la reïne le semont
et prie qu'aval et amont
par sa terre querre le face,
tot sanz demore et sanz espace;
et messire Gauvains et Qués   5215
un trestot seul n'i a remés
qui de ce nel prit et semoingne.
"Sor moi lessiez ceste besoigne,"
fet li rois, "si n'an parlez ja,
que j'en fui priez grant piece a.   5220
Tot sanz proiere et sanz requeste
ferai bien feire ceste anqueste."
Chascuns l'en ancline et soploie.
Li rois maintenant i envoie
par son rëaume ses messages--   5225
sergenz bien coneüz et sages--
qui ont par tote la contree

5180. *This line follows 5182 in the MS* 5220. jen preiez

And rode together   5180
Until they neared the court
Where King Bademagu and the queen were.
There with them was the seneschal Kay,
Along with that traitor,
Full to overflowing with deceit,   5185
Who had villainously caused all of those
Approaching to be anxious about Lancelot.
They felt themselves deceived and beaten
And could not hide their grief.
The news was not gracious   5190
That carried this misfortune to the queen,
Yet she tried to act
As cordially as she could;
For the sake of my lord Gawain
She wished to be cheerful, and was.   5195
However, her grief was not so well
Hidden that a little did not appear;
She must express both joy and grief:
Her heart was empty because of Lancelot,
Yet toward my lord Gawain   5200
She showed extreme happiness.
No one who heard
Of the disappearance of Lancelot
Could refrain from grief and sorrow.
The arrival of my lord Gawain   5205
And the pleasure of knowing him
Would have cheered the king
Had he not felt such grief and pain
Over the betrayed Lancelot
That he was overcome and troubled.   5210
The queen urged
And begged the king to have him sought
Without a moment's delay
Both high and low throughout his land.
My lord Gawain, Kay,   5215
And the others without exception
Begged and urged this likewise.
"Leave it to me,"
Said the king, "and say no more about it,
For I am long since persuaded.   5220
Without further urging or request
I will order this search begun."
Every knight inclined and bowed low before him.
The king straightway sent
Messengers--wise and prudent   5225
Men-at-arms--throughout his land
Who asked everywhere they went

de lui novele demandee.
Par tot ont la novele anquise,
mes n'en ont nule voire aprise. 5230
N'an troverent point, si s'an tornent
la ou li chevalier sejornent
(Gauvains, et Kex, et tuit li autre)
qui dïent que lance sor fautre,
trestuit armé, querre l'iront; 5235
ja autrui n'i anvoieront.
Un jor aprés mangier estoient
tuit an la sale ou il s'armoient
(s'estoit venu a l'estovoir
qu'il n'i avoit que del movoir) 5240
quant uns vaslez leanz antra,
et parmi aus oltre passa
tant qu'il vint devant la reïne,
qui n'avoit pas color rosine,
que por Lancelot duel avoit 5245
tel, don noveles ne savoit,
que la color en a müee.
Et li vaslez l'a salüee
et le roi qui de li fu pres,
et puis les autres toz aprés, 5250
et Queus et monseignor Gauvain.
Unes letres tint an sa main,
ses tant le roi et il les prant.
A tel qui de rien n'i mesprant
les fist li rois, oiant toz, lire. 5255
Cil qui les lut lor sot bien dire
ce qu'il vit escrit an l'alue,
et dit que "Lanceloz salue
le roi come son boen seignor,
si le mercie de l'enor 5260
qu'il li a fet et del servise,
come cil qui est a devise
trestoz an son comandemant.
Et sachiez bien certainnemant
qu'il est avoec le roi Artu, 5265
plains de santé et de vertu,
et dit qu'a la reïne mande
c'or s'an vaigne--se le comande--
et messire Gauvains et Ques."
Et s'i a entresaignes tes 5270
qu'il durent croire, et bien le crurent.
Molt lié et molt joiant an furent;
de joie bruit tote la corz,
et l'andemain quant il ert jorz
dïent qu'il s'an voldront torner. 5275
Et quant ce vint a l'ajorner,
si s'aparoillent et atornent;

For news of Lancelot.
They sought information everywhere,
But were unable to learn a thing.   5230
Not finding any news, they returned
To where the knights were staying
(Gawain, Kay, and all the others)
Who said they would go seek him themselves,
With lances fixed and fully armed;   5235
No one will be sent in their stead.
After eating one day, they were
All together in the hall arming themselves
(They had by now reached the moment
Set for their departure)   5240
When a youth entered there.
He passed among them
Until he came before the queen.
She had lost the rosy tint in her cheeks,
And all her color was gone   5245
In her deep sorrow over Lancelot,
Of whom she had heard no news.
The youth greeted her
And the king who was near her,
And afterwards he greeted all the others,   5250
And Kay, and my lord Gawain.
In his hand he held a message
Which he extended towards the king, who took it.
To avoid any misunderstanding,
The king had it read aloud so everyone could hear.   5255
The reader well knew how to communicate
Everything he saw written on the parchment,
And said that "Lancelot greets
The king as his noble lord
And thanks him for the honor   5260
And services he has done him,
Like one who is willingly
And completely at his command.
And he wishes you to know
That he is strong and in good health,   5265
And that he is with King Arthur,
And he bids that the queen
Come there--this he commands--
Along with my lord Gawain and Kay."
The letter bore such seals as to make them   5270
Believe the message, and all did believe.
They were happy and filled with joy;
The whole court resounded with gaiety,
And they planned their departure
For the next day at dawn.   5275
When morning came
They outfitted themselves and made ready;

219

lievent et montent, si s'an tornent.
Et li rois les silt et conduit
a grant joie et a grant deduit   5280
une grant piece de la voie.
Fors de sa terre les convoie,
et quant il les en ot fors mis,
a la reïne a congié pris
et puis a toz comunemant.   5285
La reïne molt sagemant
au congié prandre le mercie
de ce que il l'a tant servie;
et ses deus braz au col li met,
se li offre et si li promet   5290
son servise et le son seignor--
ne li puet prometre graignor.
Et messire Gauvains ausi
com a seignor et a ami,
et Kex ausi; tuit li prometent.   5295
Tantost a la voie se metent.
Si les comande a Deu li rois;
toz les autres aprés ces trois
salue et puis si s'an retorne.
Et la reïne ne sejorne   5300
nul jor de tote la semainne,
ne la rote que ele an mainne,
tant qu'a la cort vient la novele
qui au roi Artus fu molt bele
de la reïne qui aproiche.   5305
Et de son neveu li retoiche
grant joie au cuer et grant leesce,
qu'il cuidoit que par sa proesce
soit la reïne revenue,
et Kex et l'autre genz menue.   5310
Mes autremant est qu'il ne cuident.
Por aus tote la vile vuident,
si lor vont trestuit a l'encontre,
et dit chascuns qui les ancontre,
ou soit chevaliers ou vilains: 5315
"Bien vaingne messire Gauvains,
qui la reïne a ramenee   [47c]
et mainte dame escheitivee,
et maint prison nos a randu."
Et Gauvains lor a respondu: 5320
"Seignor, de neant m'alosez.
Del dire huimés vos reposez,
qu'a moi nule chose n'an monte.
Ceste enors me fet une honte,
que je n'i ving n'a tans n'a ore;   5325
failli i ai par ma demore.
Mes Lanceloz a tans i vint,

220

They arose, mounted, and set forth.
The king escorted them
Amid great joy and exultation   5280
A good bit of the way.
When he had accompanied them
Outside the frontiers of his land,
He took leave first of the queen,
Then of the others together.   5285
On bidding farewell, the queen
Very graciously thanked him
For his many services;
She embraced him,
And offered and pledged him   5290
Her service and that of her husband--
She could make him no greater promise.
My lord Gawain likewise
Pledged to serve him as his lord and friend,
As did Kay; they all promised this.   5295
They set off at once on their way.
The king commended the queen and the two knights to God;
After these three he bid farewell
To all the others, then returned.
The queen and the multitude   5300
Accompanying her did not delay
A single day,
But rode until the welcome news
Reached King Arthur
Of the imminent arrival of his queen.   5305
News of his nephew Gawain kindled
Great joy and happiness in his heart,
For he thought that the queen,
Kay, and all the common people
Were returning because of his daring.   5310
But the truth was quite other than they assumed.
The whole town emptied for them;
Everyone went to greet them,
And each one who met them,
Knight and commoner alike, said: 5315
"Welcome to my lord Gawain
Who has brought back the queen
And many another captive lady,
And returned many a prisoner to us."
Gawain answered them: 5320
"Lords, I am due no praise.
Stop saying so at once,
For none of this is of my doing.
I am ashamed to be honored so,
For I did not get there soon enough,   5325
And failed because of my delay.
But Lancelot was there in time,

221

cui si granz enors i avint
qu'ainz n'ot si grant nus chevaliers."
"Ou est il donc, biax sire chiers,   5330
quant nos nel veons ci elués?
"Ou?" fet messire Gauvains lués.
"A la cort monseignor le roi;
don n'i est il?"--"Nenil, par foi,
ne an tote ceste contree.   5335
Puis que ma dame an fu menee
nule novele n'an oïmes."
Et messire Gauvains lors primes
sot que les letres fausses furent,
qui les traïrent et deçurent;   5340
par les letres sont deceü.
Lors resont a duel esmeü;
a cort vienent lor duel menant,
et li rois trestot maintenant
anquiert noveles de l'afaire.   5345
Assez fu qui li sot retraire
comant Lanceloz a ovré,
comant par lui sont recovré
la reïne et tuit li prison,
comant et par quel traïson   5350
li nains lor anbla et fortrest.
Ceste chose le roi desplest,
et molt l'an poise et molt l'an grieve.
Mes joie le cuer li sozlieve,
qu'il a si grant de la reïne,   5355
que li diax por la joie fine;
quant la rien a que il plus vialt,
del remenant petit se dialt.
Demantres que fors del païs
fu la reïne (ce m'est vis),   5360
pristrent un parlemant antr'eles   [47d]
les dames et les dameiseles
qui desconseilliees estoient,
et distrent qu'eles se voldroient
marïer molt prochienemant.   5365
S'anpristrent a cel parlemant
une ahatine et un tornoi;
vers celi de Pomelegoi
l'anprist la dame de Noauz.
De cels qui le feront noauz   5370
ne tandront parole de rien,
mes de ces qui le feront bien
dïent que les voldront amer.
Sel feront savoir et crïer
par totes les terres prochienes   5375

5341. les *repeated* 5349. si prison 5362. Li dameisel les d.

222

And to him fell greater honor
Than ever any knight received."
"Where is he then, fair sir, 5330
Since we do not see him here with you?"
"Where?" replied my lord Gawain then.
"At the court of my lord King Arthur--
Is he not there?"--"In faith, he is not;
Nor is he anywhere in this land. 5335
Since my lady was taken
We have heard no news of him."
Then for the first time my lord Gawain
Realized that the message
Which had betrayed and tricked them was forged; 5340
They had been deceived by the message.
Once again they were plunged into sadness;
They came grieving to the court,
And the king immediately
Asked what had happened. 5345
Many there were who were able to tell him
What Lancelot had accomplished,
How the queen and all the captives
Were rescued by him,
And through what deceit 5350
The dwarf had stolen him away from them.
This news displeased the king
And caused him much grief and anguish.
But his heart was so elated
At the queen's return 5355
That this grief gave way to joy;
Now that he had what he most desired
He worried little about the rest.
It was while the queen
Was out of the country, I believe, 5360
That the ladies and maidens
Who lacked the comfort of a husband
Came together and decided
That they wished
To be married soon. 5365
They decided in the course of their discussions
To organize a splendid tourney,
In which the lady of Pomelegoi
Was challenged by the lady of Noauz.
The women will refuse to speak 5370
To those who fare poorly,
But to those who do well
They promise to grant their love.
They announced the tourney and made it known
Throughout all the lands nearby, 5375

et autresi par les loingtienes;
et firent a molt lonc termine
crïer le jor de l'ahatine
por ce que plus i eüst genz.
Et la reïne vint dedenz   5380
le termine que mis i orent;
et maintenant qu'eles le sorent
que la reïne estoit venue,
la voie ont cele part tenue
les plusors tant qu'a la cort vindrent   5385
devant le roi, et si le tindrent
molt an grant c'un dun lor donast
et lor voloir lor otreast.
Et il lor a acreanté
ainz qu'il seüst lor volanté   5390
qu'il feroit quanqu'eles voldroient.
Lors li distrent qu'eles voloient
que il sofrist que la reïne
venist veoir lor ahatine.
Et cil qui rien veher ne sialt   5395
dist que lui plest, s'ele le vialt.
Celes qui molt liees an sont
devant la reïne s'an vont,
si li dïent eneslepas:
"Dame, ne nos retolez pas   5400
ce que li rois nos a doné."
Et ele lor a demandé:
"Quex chose est ce? Nel me celez."
Lors li dïent: "Se vos volez
a nostre ahatine venir,   [47e]
ja ne vos an quiert retenir
ne ja nel vos contredira."
Et ele dist qu'ele i ira
des que il le congié l'an done.
Tantost par tote la corone   5410
les dameiseles an envoient
et mandent que eles devoient
amener la reïne au jor
qui estoit crïez de l'estor.
La novele par tot ala,   5415
et loing et pres et ça et la;
s'est tant alee et estandue
qu'el rëaume fu espandue
don nus retorner ne soloit
(mes ore, quiconques voloit   5420
avoit et l'antree et l'issue,
et ja ne li fust desfandue).
Tant est par le rëaume alee

5394. Venir veoir   5406. t *of* quiert *added above line*

224

And those distant as well.
They had the date of the tournament
Heralded far in advance
So that there might be more participants.
The queen returned before   5380
The date they had set;
As soon as they learned
Of the queen's return,
Most of the ladies and maidens
Hastened to appear at court   5385
Before the king and urged him
To grant them a favor
And do their bidding.
Even before learning what they wanted,
He promised them   5390
To grant anything they might desire.
Then they said that they wished
Him to permit the queen
To come observe their tourney.
Unaccustomed to refusal, he said   5395
That if the queen wished it, it would suit him.
Overjoyed at this,
The ladies went before the queen
And stated at once:
"Our lady, do not take from us   5400
What the king has granted."
Whereupon she asked them:
"What is that? Don't keep it from me."
They replied: "If you wish
To come to our tourney,   5405
He will never try to stop you
Nor refuse you his permission."
So she promised to come
Since Arthur had given his permission.
The ladies immediately sent word   5410
Throughout the realm
Saying that the queen
Would accompany them on the day
Set for the tournament.
The news spread everywhere,   5415
Far and wide, and here and there;
It spread so far
That it reached the kingdom
From whence no one had been able to return
(Though now whoever wished   5420
Could enter or leave
And never be challenged).
The news spread through this kingdom

225

la novele, dite et contee,
qu'ele vint chiés un seneschal   5425
Meleagant le desleal--
le traïtor, que max feus arde!
Cil avoit Lancelot an garde:
chiés lui l'avoit an prison mis
Meleaganz ses anemis,   5430
qui le haoit de grant haïne.
La novele de l'anhatine
sot Lanceloz, l'ore et le terme;
puis ne furent si oil sanz lerme
ne ses cuers liez que il le sot.   5435
Dolant et pansif Lancelot
vit la dame de la meison,
sel mist a consoil a reison:
"Sire, por Deu et por vostre ame,
voir me dites," fet li la dame,   5440
"por coi vos estes si changiez.
Vos ne bevez ne ne mangiez,
ne ne vos voi joer ne rire.
Seüremant me poez dire
vostre panser et vostre enui."   5445
"Ha! dame, se je dolanz sui,
por Deu ne vos an merveilliez.
Voir, que trop sui desconseilliez
quant je ne porrai estre la   [47f]
ou toz li biens del mont sera: 5450
a l'ahatine ou toz asanble
li pueples, ensi con moi sanble.
Et neporquant, s'il vos pleisoit
Et Dex tant franche vos feisoit
que vos aler m'i leissessiez,   5455
tot certeinnemant seüssiez
que vers vos si me contanroie
qu'an vostre prison revandroie."
"Certes," fet ele, "jel feïsse
molt volantiers se n'i veïsse   5460
ma destrucïon et ma mort.
Mes je criem mon seignor si fort,
Meleagant le deputaire,
que je ne l'oseroie faire,
qu'il destruiroit mon seignor tot.   5465
N'est mervoille se jel redot,
qu'il est si fel con vos savez."
"Dame, se vos peor avez
que je tantost aprés l'estor
an vostre prison ne retor,   5470
un seiremant vos an ferai
dom ja ne me parjurerai,
que ja n'iert riens qui me detaingne

226

And was recounted far and wide
Until it reached a seneschal   5425
Of the faithless Meleagant--
May hellfires burn the traitor!
This seneschal was guarding Lancelot,
Imprisoned at his castle
By his enemy Meleagant,   5430
Who hated him with a deep hatred.
Lancelot learned of the date
And hour of the tourney,
And from that moment his eyes filled with tears
And all joy left his heart.   5435
The lady of the manor saw
Lancelot sad and pensive,
And privately questioned him:
"Sir, for the love of God and of your soul,
Tell me in truth," said the lady,   5440
"Why you have changed so.
You neither eat nor drink,
Nor do I see you happy or laughing.
You can confide in me
Your thoughts and what troubles you."   5445
"Ah! My lady, for God's sake,
Do not be amazed if I am saddened.
Indeed, I am greatly downcast
Because I cannot be there
Where all that is good in this world will be: 5450
At that tourney where everyone,
I am sure, is gathering.
However, if God has made you kind enough
That you might be pleased
To let me go there,   5455
You can be certain
That I would feel compelled
To return to my imprisonment here."
"Indeed," she answered, "I would
Gladly do this if I did not see   5460
In it my own suffering and death.
But I so fear the strength of my lord,
The despicable Meleagant,
That I dare not do it,
For he would completely destroy my husband.   5465
It is no wonder that I dread him,
For as you know he is most wicked."
"My lady, if you are afraid
That I will not return at once
To your keeping after the tourney,   5470
I shall take an oath
Which I will never break,
And swear that nothing will ever keep me

227

qu'an vostre prison ne revaigne
maintenant aprés le tornoi."   5475
"Par foi," fet ele, "et je l'otroi
par un covant."--"Dame, par quel?"
Ele respont: "Sire, par tel
que le retor me jureroiz,
et avoec m'aseüreroiz   5480
de vostre amor, que je l'avrai."
"Dame, tote celi qui j'ai
vos doing je voir au revenir."
"Or m'an puis a neant tenir,"
fet la dame tot an riant.   5485
"Autrui, par le mien esciant,
avez bailliee et comandee
l'amor que vos ai demandee.
Et neporcant sanz nul desdaing
tant con g'en puis avoir, s'an praing.   5490
A ce que je puis m'an tandrai
et le sairemant an prandrai
que vers moi si vos contendroiz   [48a]
que an ma prison revandroiz."
   Lanceloz tot a sa devise   5495
le sairemant sor sainte eglise
li fet qu'il revandra sanz faille.
Et la dame tantost li baille
les armes son seignor, vermoilles,
et le cheval qui a mervoilles   5500
estoit biax et forz et hardiz.
Cil monte, si s'an est partiz,
armez d'unes armes molt beles,
trestotes fresches et noveles.
S'a tant erré qu'a Noauz vint;   5505
de cele partie se tint
et prist fors de la vile ostel;
einz si prodom n'ot mes itel,
car molt estoit petiz et bas,
mes herbergier ne voloit pas   5510
an leu ou il fust coneüz.
Chevaliers boens et esleüz
ot molt el chastel amassez;
mes plus en ot defors assez,
que por la reïne en i ot   5515
tant venu que li quinz n'i pot
ostel avoir dedanz recet;
que por un seul en i ot set
don ja un tot seul n'i eüst
se por la reïne ne fust.   5520
Bien cinc liues tot anviron

5511 ou *repeated*

228

From returning to imprisonment here
As soon as the tournament has ended."   5475
"In faith," she said, "on one condition
Will I do it."--"My lady, which is that?"
She answered: "Sir, that you
Will swear to return,
And at the same time assure me   5480
That I shall have your love."
"My lady, I will certainly give you
All that I have upon my return."
"Now I see that I am nothing to you,"
The lady answered with a laugh: 5485
"It seems to me that you
Have assigned and given to another
This love I have asked of you.
Nevertheless, without disdain
I shall take all I can have.   5490
I'll hold to what I can,
And accept your oath
That you will honor me
By returning to imprisonment here."
    In accordance with her wishes, Lancelot   5495
Swore by the Holy Church
That he would not fail to return.
Thereupon the lady gave him
Her husband's red armor
And his wonderfully strong,   5500
Brave, and handsome steed.
He mounted and set off,
Armed with magnificent
New and unscarred armor.
He rode until he reached Noauz;   5505
He selected this camp for the tourney,*
And took his lodging outside the town;
Never had such a gentleman chosen
Such poor and lowly lodgings,
But he did not wish to stay   5510
Anywhere he might be recognized.
There were many fine, worthy knights
Assembled in the castle;
But there were even more without,
For so many had come on account of the queen's   5515
Presence that not one in five
Found lodging within:
For every one
Who might ordinarily have come,
There were seven who came only for the queen.   5520
For five leagues round about

se furent logié li baron
es trez, es loges, et es tantes.
Dames et dameiseles gentes
i rot tant que mervoille fu.   5525
Lanceloz ot mis son escu
a l'uis de son ostel defors,
et il, por aeisier son cors,
fu desarmez et se gisoit
en un lit qu'il molt po prisoit,   5530
qu'estroiz ert et la coute tanve
coverte d'un gros drap de chanve.
Lanceloz trestoz desarmez
s'estoit sor ce lit acostez.
La ou il jut si povremant,   5535
atant ez vos un garnemant,*
un hyraut d'armes, an chemise,   [48b]
qui an la taverne avoit mise
sa cote avoec sa chauceüre
et vint nuz piez grant aleüre,   5540
desafublez contre le vant.
L'escu trova a l'uis devant,
si l'esgarda; mes ne pot estre
qu'il coneüst lui ne son mestre;
ne set qui porter le devoit.   5545
l'uis de la meison overt voit,
s'antre anz et vit gesir el lit
Lancelot, et puis qu'il le vit
le conut et si s'an seigna.
Et Lanceloz li anseigna   5550
et desfandi qu'il ne parlast
de lui an leu ou il alast;
que, s'il disoit qu'il le seüst,
mialz li vandroit que il s'eüst
les ialz treiz ou le col brisié.   5555
"Sire, je vos ai molt prisié,"
fet li hyrauz, "et toz jorz pris;
ne ja tant con je soie vis
ne ferai rien por nul avoir
don mal gré me doiez savoir."   5560
Tantost de la meison s'an saut,
si s'an vet criant molt an haut:
"Or est venuz qui l'aunera!
Or est venuz qui l'aunera!"
Ice crioit par tot li garz,   5565
et genz saillent de totes parz,
se li demandent que il crie.
Cil n'est tant hardiz que le die,
einz s'an va criant ce meïsmes;

5550. le regarda

230

The many barons were housed
In tents, shelters, and pavilions.
It was amazing how many
Fair ladies and maidens were present.   5525
Lancelot had put his shield
Outside the door of his lodging-place
And, in order to relax,
Had taken off his armor and was lying
In a rather uncomfortable bed,   5530
Which was too narrow, and had its thin matting
Covered by a coarse hemp cloth.
Lancelot, completely unarmed,
Was resting on his side on this bed.
While he was lying in this hovel,   5535
A barefooted young fellow
In shirt-sleeves came running up:
It was a herald-at-arms
Who had lost his cloak and shoes
Gambling in the tavern,   5540
And who was now unprotected from the cool air.
He noticed the shield before the door
And gazed at it, but there was no way
For him to recognize it
Or to know who was to wear it.   5545
Seeing the open door,
He entered and perceived Lancelot lying
On the bed; and as soon as he saw him,
He recognized him and crossed himself.
And Lancelot instructed   5550
And forbade him to say anything
Anywhere about having seen him.
Should the herald reveal what he knew,
He'd surely prefer to have his eyes put out
Or his neck broken [than receive
          the punishment that would be his.]   5555
"Sir, I have esteemed you highly,"
Said the herald, "and still do so;
Never as long as I live
Would I do anything for any reason
Which might make you unhappy with me."   5560
He hurried out of the house
And ran off shouting:
"The one is come who will take their measure!
The one is come who will take their measure!"*
The youth shouted this everywhere,   5565
And people appeared from all sides
To ask him what this meant.
He was not so rash as to tell them,
But continued shouting as before;

231

et sachiez que dit fu lors primes: 5570
"Or est venuz qui l'aunera!"
Nostre mestre an fu li hyra
qui a dire le nos aprist,
car il premieremant le dist.
    Ja sont assanblees les rotes,   5575
la reïne et les dames totes
et chevalier et autres genz--
car molt i avoit des sergenz
de totes parz destre et senestre.
La ou li tornoiz devoit estre   5580
ot unes granz loges de fust,   *[48c]*
por ce que la reïne i fust
et les dames et les puceles:
einz nus ne vit loges si beles
ne si longues ne si bien faites.   5585
La se sont les dames atraites
trestotes aprés la reïne,
que veoir voldront l'ahatine
et qui mialz le fera ou pis.
Chevalier vienent dis et dis,   5590
et vint et vint, et trante et trante,
ça quatre vint et ça nonante,
ça cent, ça plus et ça deus tanz.
Si est l'asanblee si granz
devant les loges et antor   5595
que il ancomancent l'estor.
Armé et desarmé asanblent;
les lances un grant bois resanblent,
que tant en i font aporter
cil qui s'an vuelent deporter   5600
qu'il n'i paroit se lances non
et banieres et confanon.
Li josteor au joster muevent,
qui conpaignons asez i truevent
qui por joster venu estoient;   5605
et li autre se raprestoient
de faire autres chevaleries.
Si sont plainnes les praeries
et les arees et li sonbre,
que l'an n'en puet esmer le nonbre   5610
des chevaliers, tant en i ot.
Mes n'i ot point de Lancelot
a cele premiere asanblee;
mes quant il vint parmi la pree
et li hirauz le voit venir,   5615
de crier ne se pot tenir:
"Veez celui qui l'aunera!"

5575. La   5586. La si se sont landemain traites

232

This was when the expression was coined: 5570
"The one is come who will take their measure."
The herald who taught us
To say it is our master,
For he was the first to say it.
    Already the crowds were assembled,   5575
The queen and all the ladies
And knights and other men--
For there were men-at-arms
Everywhere, to right and left.
There where the tourney was to be held   5580
Large wooden viewing stands had been erected,
Since the queen and her ladies
And maidens were to be present;
Never had anyone seen more beautiful,
Longer, or more finely constructed stands.   5585
All the women gathered there
After the queen,
For they wished to see the combat
And who would do well or ill in it.
The knights arrived by tens,   5590
By twenties, and by thirties,
Here eighty and there ninety,
A hundred or more here, two hundred there.
So great was the crowd gathered
Before and about the stands   5595
That the combat was begun.
Armed and unarmed knights clashed.
Those who had come for the pleasure of the tourney
Had brought so many lances
That they seemed a dense forest,   5600
In which only lances, banners,
And standards could be perceived.
Those who were to joust moved down the lists,
Where they found a great many companions
Who had likewise come to joust;   5605
And others made ready
To perform different knightly feats.
The meadows, fields, and clearings
Were so covered with knights
That it was impossible to guess   5610
How many were there.
Lancelot did not participate
In this first encounter;
But when he entered the meadow,
And the herald saw him coming onto the field,   5615
He could not refrain from shouting:
"Behold the one who will take their measure!

Veez celui qui l'aunera!"
Et l'an demande: "Qui est il?"
Ne lor an vialt rien dire cil.   5620
Quant Lanceloz an l'estor vint,
il seus valoit des meillors vint,
sel comance si bien a feire
que nus ne puet ses ialz retreire
de lui esgarder, ou qu'il soit.   [48d]
Devers Pomelesglai estoit
uns chevaliers preuz et vaillanz,
et ses chevax estoit saillanz
et corranz plus que cers de lande.
Cil estoit filz le roi d'Irlande   5630
qui molt bien et bel le feisoit,
mes quatre tanz a toz pleisoit
li chevaliers qu'il ne conoissent.
Trestuit de demander s'angoissent:
"Qui est cil qui si bien le fet?"   5635
Et la reïne a consoil tret
une pucele cointe et sage,
et dit: "Dameisele, un message
vos estuet feire, et tost le feites
a paroles briemant retraites.   5640
Jus de ces loges avalez,
a ce chevalier m'an alez
qui porte cel escu vermoil,
et si li dites a consoil
que 'au noauz' que je li mant."   5645
Cele molt tost et saigemant
fet ce que la reïne vialt.
Aprés le chevalier s'aquialt
tant que molt pres de lui s'est jointe,
si li dist come sage et cointe   5650
que ne l'ot veisins ne veisine:
"Sire, ma dame la reïne
par moi vos mande, et jel vos di,
que 'au noauz'. Quant cil l'oï,
si li dist que molt volantiers,   5655
come cil qui est suens antiers.
Et lors contre un chevalier muet
tant con chevax porter le puet,
et faut quant il le dut ferir.
N'onques puis jusqu'a l'anserir   5660
ne fist s'au pis non que il pot,
por ce qu'a la reïne plot.
Et li autres qui le requiert
n'a pas failli, einçois le fiert
grant cop, roidemant s'i apuie,   5665

5651. Quil

234

Behold the one who will take their measure!"
And they asked, "Who is he?"
The herald refused to answer.   5620
When Lancelot entered the contest,
He alone was worth twenty of the best,
And he began to do so well
That no one could take his eyes
From him, wherever he might be.   5625
A bold and valiant knight
Was fighting for Pomelegoi,
Whose steed was spirited
And swifter than a wild stag.
He was the son of the king of Ireland   5630
And fought nobly and well,
But the unknown knight pleased
The onlookers four times as much.
They all troubled over the question:
"Who is this knight who fights so well?"   5635
The queen whispered
To a clever, pretty girl,
And said: "Miss, you must
Take a message, quickly
And without wasting words.   5640
Hurry down from these stands;
Go for me to that knight
Carrying the red shield,
And tell him in secret
That I bid him to do 'his worst.'"*   5645
She quickly and properly
Did as the queen wished.
She followed the knight
Until she was near enough
To tell him quietly,   5650
In a voice which no one might overhear:
"Sir, my lady the queen
Bids me tell you
To do 'your worst.'" The moment he heard her,
He said he would gladly do so,   5655
As one who seeks only to please the queen.
Then he set out against a knight
As fast as his horse would carry him,
And when he should have struck him, he missed.
From this time until dark   5660
He did the worst he could,
Because it was the queen's pleasure.
The knight, attacking in turn,
Did not miss, but struck him
A mighty blow with such violence   5665

et cil se met lors a la fuie;
ne puis cel jor vers chevalier
ne torna le col del destrier.
Por a morir rien ne feïst   [48e]
se sa grant honte n'i veïst   5670
et son leit et sa desenor,
et fet sanblant qu'il ait peor
de toz ces qui vienent et vont.
Et li chevalier de lui font
lor risees et lor gabois,   5675
qui molt le prisoient ainçois.
Et li hirauz qui soloit dire:
"Cil les vaintra trestoz a tire!"
est molt maz et molt desconfiz,
qu'il ot les gas et les afiz   5680
de ces qui dïent: "Or te tes,
amis, cist ne l'aunera mes.
Tant a auné c'or est brisiee
s'aune que tant nos as prisiee!"
Li plusor dïent: "Ce que doit!   5685
Il estoit si preuz orendroit,
et or est si coarde chose
que chevalier atandre n'ose.
Espoir por ce si bien le fist
que mes d'armes ne s'antremist,   5690
se fu si forz a son venir
qu'a lui ne se pooit tenir
nus chevaliers, tant fust senez,
qu'il feroit come forsenez.
Or a tant des armes apris   5695
que jamés tant con il soit vis
n'avra talant d'armes porter.
Ses cuers nes puet plus andurer,
qu'el monde n'a rien si mespoise."
A la reïne pas n'an poise,   5700
einz an est liee et molt li plest,
qu'ele set bien (et si s'an test)
que ce est Lanceloz por voir.
Ensi tot le jor jusqu'au soir*
se fist cil tenir por coart,   5705
mes li bas vespres les depart.
Au departir i ot grant plet
de ces qui mialz l'avoient fet:
li filz le roi d'Irlande pansse
sanz contredit et sanz desfansse   5710
qu'il ait tot le los et le pris;
mes laidemant i a mespris,
qu'asez i ot de ses parauz.   [48f]

5704. tote nuit

236

That Lancelot fled before him
And did not turn his horse
The rest of that day against any knight.
Not on his life would he do anything
Unless he saw that it would bring him shame,   5670
Disgrace, and dishonor,
And he pretended to be afraid
Of all those who approached him.
The knights, who had
Esteemed him before,   5675
Now laughed and joked about him.
And the herald, who was wont to say:
"This one will beat them all, one after another!"
Was very downcast and dejected
On hearing the jibes and jokes   5680
Of the others, who were saying: "Hold your peace now,
Friend; he won't be taking our measure any more.
He's measured so much that he's broken it,
That measuring-stick you bragged so about!"
"What is this!" many said.   5685
"He was so brave just a while ago;
Now he's so cowardly
He dare not face a knight.
Perhaps he did so well
Because he had never jousted before,   5690
And he was so strong at first
That no knight, however expert,
Could stand up to him
Because he struck like a madman.
Now he has learned so much about fighting   5695
That he will never care to bear arms
Again as long as he lives.
His heart can no longer stand it,
For there is none in the world so weak."
This did not upset the queen who,   5700
On the contrary, was pleased and delighted,
For she knew for certain (though she kept it hidden)
That this knight was truly Lancelot.
Thus throughout the day until dark
He let himself be taken for a coward,   5705
Until nightfall separated them.
On parting, there was a great discussion
Over who had fought best:
The son of the king of Ireland felt
That beyond any doubt and without contradiction   5710
He himself deserved all the esteem and renown;
But he was terribly mistaken,
For there were many equal to him.

237

Neïs li chevaliers vermauz
plot as dames et as puceles,
aus plus gentes et aus plus beles,   5715
tant qu'eles n'orent a nelui
le jor bahé tant com a lui;
que bien orent veü comant
il l'avoit fet premieremant   5720
com il estoit preuz et hardiz.
Puis restoit si acoardiz
qu'il n'osoit chevalier atandre,
einz le poïst abatre et prandre
toz li pires, se il volsist.   5725
Mes a totes et a toz sist
que l'andemain tuit revandront
a l'ahatine, et si prandront
ces cui le jor seroit l'enors
les dameiseles a seignors.   5730
Ensi le dïent et atornent;
atant vers les ostex s'an tornent,
et quant il vindrent as ostex
an plusors leus en ot de tex
qui ancomancierent a dire: 5735
"Ou est des chevaliers li pire
et li neanz et li despiz?
Ou est alez? Ou est tapiz?
Ou iert trovez? Ou le querrons?*
Espoir jamés ne le verrons,   5740
que Malvestiez l'en a chacié
dom il a tel fes anbracié
qu'el monde n'a rien si malveise.
N'il n'a pas tort, car plus a eise
est uns malvés cent mile tanz   5745
que n'est uns preuz, uns conbatanz.
Malvestiez est molt aeisiee,
por ce l'a il an pes beisiee,
s'a pris de li quanque il a.
Onques voir tant ne s'avilla   5750
Proesce qu'an lui se meïst
ne que pres de lui s'aseïst;
mes an lui s'est tote reposte
Malvestiez, s'a trové tel oste
qui tant l'ainme et qui tant la sert   5755
que por s'enor la soe pert."
Ensi tote nuit se degenglent   [49a]
cil qui de mal dire s'estrenglent.
Mes tex dit sovant mal d'autrui
qui est molt pires de celui   5760
que il blasme et que il despit;

5739. Ou est alez

238

Even the Red Knight
Pleased the fairest and most beautiful   5715
Of the ladies and maidens,
For they had not kept their eyes on anyone
That day as much as upon him.
They had seen how
He had done at first--   5720
How brave and courageous he had been.
Then he had become so cowardly
That he dared not face another knight,
And even the worst of them, had he wanted,
Could have defeated and captured him.   5725
So the ladies and knights all agreed
That they would return to the lists
The following day, and that
The young girls would marry
Those who won honor then.   5730
With this decided,
They left to return to their lodgings;
And when they had reached them,
There were in many places
Groups of people beginning to ask: 5735
"Where is the worst, the lowliest
And the most despicable of knights?
Where has he gone? Where is he hidden?
Where might we find him? Where shall we seek him?
Perhaps we'll never see him again,   5740
For Cowardice has chased him away,
And he has carried off with himself so much of Cowardice
That there cannot be another so lowly in the world.
And he's not wrong, for a coward
Is a hundred thousand times better off   5745
Than a valorous, fighting knight.
Cowardice is an easy thing,
And that's why he's given her the kiss of peace
And taken from her all he has.
Never, in truth, did Courage   5750
Lower herself enough
To try to lodge in him;
But Cowardice fills him completely
And has found a host
Who loves and serves her so faithfully   5755
That he has lost all his honor for her sake."
All night long those given to slander
Gossiped in this manner.
But often the one who speaks ill of another
Is far worse than the one   5760
He slanders and despises;

chascuns ce que lui plest an dit.
Et quant ce vint a l'anjornee
refu la genz tote atornee,
si s'an vindrent a l'anhatine.   5765
Es loges refu la reïne
et les dames et les puceles,
s'i ot chevaliers avoec eles
assez qui armes ne porterent,
qui prison ou croisié se erent,   5770
et cil lor armes lor devisent
des chevaliers que il plus prisent.
Antr'ax dïent: "Veez vos or
celui a cele bande d'or
parmi cel escu de bernic?*   5775
C'est Governauz de Roberdic.
Et veez vos celui aprés
qui an son escu pres a pres
a mise une aigle et un dragon?
C'est li filz le roi d'Arragon   5780
qui venuz est an ceste terre
por pris et por enor conquerre.
Et veez vos celui dejoste
qui si bien point et si bien joste
a cel escu vert d'une part,   5785
s'a sor le vert point un liepart,
et d'azur est l'autre mitiez?
C'est Ignaurés li covoitiez,
li amoreus et li pleisanz.
Et cil qui porte les feisanz   5790
an son escu poinz bec a bec?
C'est Coguillanz de Mautirec.
Et veez vos ces deus delez
a ces deus chevax pomelez,
as escuz d'or as lÿons bis?   5795
Li uns a non Semiramis
et li autres est ses conpainz,
s'ont d'un sanblant lor escuz tainz.
Et veez vos celui qui porte
an son escu pointe une porte,   5800
si sanble qu'il s'an isse uns cers?   [49b]
Par foi, ce est li rois Yders."
Ensi devisent des les loges:
"Cil escuz fu fez a Lymoges,
si l'an aporta Piladés   5805
qui an estor vialt estre adés
et molt le desirre et golose.
Cil autres fu fez a Tolose
et li lorains et li peitrax,

Everyone had his say.
And when day broke
They rearmed themselves
And returned to the tournament.   5765
The queen, with her ladies and maidens,
Had come back to the stands,
And together with them were
Many unarmed knights,
Who had either been captured or had taken the cross,*   5770
And who were now explaining to them
The heraldry of the knights they most admired.
They said: "Now do you see
The one with the gold band
Across a red shield?   5775
That's Governal of Roberdic.
And do you see the one behind him
Who has placed a dragon and an eagle
Side by side on his shield?
That's the son of the king of Aragon,   5780
Who has come into this land
To win honor and renown.
And do you see the one beside him
Who rides and jousts so well?
On one side of his shield   5785
There is a leopard on a green field,
And the other half is azure.
That's Ignaurés the Covetous,
A handsome man who pleases the ladies.
And the one with the pheasants   5790
Painted beak to beak upon his shield?
That is Coguillant of Mautirec.
And do you see those two knights beside him
On dappled horses,
With dark lions on gilded shields?   5795
One is called Semiramis,
The other is his companion;
They have painted their shields to match.
And do you see the one whose shield
Has a gate painted upon it,   5800
Through which a stag seems to be passing?
In faith, it is King Yder."
Such was the talk in the stands:
"That shield was made in Limoges,
And was brought by Piladés,   5805
Who always wants to be in battle
And is eager and hungry for it.
That shield, with matching harness straps
And stirrups, was made in Toulouse

241

si l'en aporta Keus d'Estrax.*   5810
Cil vint de Lÿon sor le Rosne--
n'a nul si boen desoz le trosne--
si fu por une grant desserte
donez Taulas de la Deserte
qui bel le porte et bien s'an cuevre.   5815
Et cil autres si est de l'uevre
d'Engleterre et fu fez a Londres,
ou vos veez ces deus arondres
qui sanblent que voler s'an doivent,
mes ne se muevent, ainz reçoivent   5820
mainz cos des aciers poitevins.
Sel porte Thoas li meschins."
Ensi devisent et deboissent
les armes de ces qu'il conoissent;
mes de celui mie n'i voient   5825
qu'an tel despit eü avoient,
si cuident qu'il s'an soit anblez
quant a l'estor n'est assanblez.
Quant la reïne point n'an voit,
talanz li prist qu'ele l'anvoit   5830
les rans cerchier tant qu'an le truisse.*
Ne set cui envoier i puisse
qui mialz le quiere de celi
qui hier i ala de par li.
Tot maintenant a li l'apele,   5835
si li dit: "Alez, dameisele,
monter sor vostre palefroi.
Au chevalier d'ier vos envoi,
sel querez tant que vos l'aiez;
por rien ne vos an delaiez,   5840
et tant si li redites or
qu''au noauz' le reface ancor.
Et quant vos l'en avroiz semons,
s'antandez bien a son respons."
Cele de rien ne s'en retarde,   [49c]
qui bien s'estoit donee garde
le soir quel part il torneroit,
por ce que sanz dote savoit
qu'ele i reseroit anvoiee.
Parmi les rans s'est avoiee   5850
tant qu'ele vit le chevalier;
si li vet tantost conseillier
que ancor "au noauz" le face,
s'avoir vialt l'amor et la grace
la reïne, qu'ele li mande.   5855
Et cil: "Des qu'ele le comande,"
li respont, "la soe merci."

5810. cuens destrax 5813. par

242

And is brought here by Kay of Estral.   5810
That one comes from Lyons on the Rhone--
There is none so fine under heaven--
It was awarded to Taulas of the Desert
For a great service,
And he bears it well and uses it skillfully.   5815
And that other shield,
On which you see those two swallows
That seem about to take flight,
But which stay and receive
Many blows of Poitevin steel,   5820
Is an English model, made in London.
It is carried by Thoas the Young."
And so they pointed out and described
The arms of those they recognized;
But they saw nothing of that knight   5825
Whom they had held in such low esteem,
And assumed that he had stolen off
Since he had not returned to the combat.
When the queen failed to see him,
She desired to have him sought   5830
In the lists until he be found.
She knew no one she could trust
To find him more easily than the girl
She had sent the day before with her message.
So she summoned her at once   5835
And told her: "Go, miss,
And mount your palfrey.
I send you to seek that knight
Of yesterday until you find him.
Make no delay,   5840
And tell him once again
To continue doing 'his worst.'
And when you have so instructed him,
Listen carefully to his reply."
The girl left without hesitation,   5845
For the evening before she had carefully
Noticed the direction he took,
Knowing without doubt
That she would once again be sent to him.
She went through the lists   5850
Until she saw the knight,
Then went at once to advise him
To continue doing "his worst"
If he wished to have the love and favor
Of the queen, for such was her command.   5855
"Since she so bids me,"
He replied, "I send her my thanks."

Tantost cele se departi.
Et lors comancent a huier
vaslet, sergent et escuier,   5860
et dïent tuit: "Veez mervoilles
de celui as armes vermoilles!
Revenuz est! Mes que fet il?
Ja n'a el monde rien tant vil,
si despite ne si faillie;   5865
si l'a Malvestiez an baillie
qu'il ne puet rien contre li faire."
Et la pucele s'an repaire,
s'est a la reïne venue,
qui molt l'a corte et pres tenue   5870
tant que la responsse ot oïe
dom ele s'est molt esjoïe,
por ce c'or set ele sanz dote
que ce est cil cui ele est tote
et il toz suens sanz nule faille.   5875
A la pucele dit qu'ele aille
molt tost arriere et si li die
que ele li comande et prie
que "au mialz" face qu'il porra.
Et cele dit qu'ele i ira   5880
tot maintenant sanz respit querre.
Des loges est venue a terre
la ou ses garçons l'atandoit,
qui son palefroi li gardoit.
Et ele monte, si s'an va   5885
tant que le chevalier trova;
si li ala maintenant dire:
"Or vos mande ma dame, sire,
que tot 'le mialz' que vos porroiz."   [49d]
Et il respont: "Or li diroiz   5890
qu'il n'est riens nule qui me griet
a feire, des que il li siet,
que quanque li plest m'atalante."
Lors ne fu mie cele lante
de son message reporter,   5895
que molt an cuide deporter
la reïne et esleescier.
Quanqu'ele se pot adrecier
s'est vers les loges adreciee.
Et la reïne s'est dreciee,   5900
se li est a l'ancontre alee;
mes n'est mie jus avalee,
einz l'atant au chief del degré.
Et cele vient, qui molt a gré
li sot son message conter.   5905

5861. vermoilles   5876. pucel

244

The girl departed at once.
The youths, men-at-arms,
And squires began booing   5860
And saying: "What a surprise!
The knight with the red armor
Has returned! But what can he want?
There's no one in the world so lowly,
So despicable, and so base;   5865
Cowardice has him so firmly in her grip
That he can do nothing to oppose her."
The girl returned
And came to the queen,
Who would not let her go   5870
Until she had heard that reply
Which filled her with great joy,
For now she knew beyond doubt
That this was he to whom she belonged completely,
And she knew that he was fully hers.   5875
She told the girl to return
At once and tell him
That she ordered and begged him
To do "the best" that he could.
The girl said she would go   5880
At once, without delay.
She went down from the stands
To where her serving boy was awaiting her
And tending her palfrey.
She mounted and rode   5885
Until she found the knight;
And she told him quickly:
"Sir, my lady now orders you
To do 'the best' you can."
He replied: "Tell her   5890
That there is nothing it would displease me
To do, if it be pleasing to her,
For I am intent upon doing whatever she may desire."
She was not slow
In returning her message,   5895
Since she was very sure that it would please
The queen and make her happy.
She made her way toward the stands
As rapidly as possible.
The queen stood up   5900
And moved forward to meet her;
But instead of going down to her,
She awaited her at the head of the steps.
The girl approached, eager
To tell her message.   5905

Les degrez comance a monter,
et quant ele est venue a li
si li dist: "Dame, onques ne vi
nul chevalier tant deboneire,
qu'il vialt si oltreemant feire   5910
trestot quanque vos li mandez;
que, se le voir m'an demandez,
autel chiere tot par igal
fet il del bien come del mal."
"Par foi," fet ele, "bien puet estre."   5915
Lors s'an retorne a la fenestre
por les chevaliers esgarder.
Et Lanceloz sanz plus tarder
l'escu par les enarmes prant,
que volentez l'art et esprant   5920
de mostrer tote sa proesce.
Le col de son destrier adresce
et lesse corre antre deus rans.
Tuit seront esbaï par tans
li deceü, li amusé,   5925
qui an lui gaber ont usé
piece del jor et de la nuit--
molt s'an sont grant piece deduit
et deporté et solacié.
Par les enarmes anbracié   5930
tint son escu li filz le roi
d'Irlande, et point a grant desroi
de l'autre part ancontre lui.   [49e]
Si s'antrefierent anbedui
si que li filz le roi d'Irlande   5935
de la joste plus ne demande,
que sa lance fraint et estrosse;
car ne feri mie sor mosse,
mes sor ais molt dures et seches.
Lanceloz une de ses teches   5940
li a aprise a cele joste,
que l'escu au braz li ajoste
et le braz au costé li serre,
sel porte del cheval a terre.
Et tantost chevalier descochent,   5945
d'anbedeus parz poignent et brochent,
li uns por celui desconbrer
et li autres por l'enconbrer.
Li un lor seignors eidier cuident,
et des plusors les seles vuident   5950
an la meslee et an l'estor.
Mes onques an trestot le jor
Gauvains d'armes ne se mesla,

5924. esbaudi   5947. por l'autre d.

She began climbing the steps
And said upon nearing the queen:
"My lady, I have never seen
A more agreeable knight,
For he is totally eager to do 5910
Whatever you command of him.
And, if you ask me the truth,
He accepts the good and the bad
With equal pleasure."
"In faith," said she, "that may well be." 5915
Then she returned to her window
To observe the knights.
Without a moment's hesitation Lancelot
Thrust his arm through the shield straps,
For he was inflamed with a burning desire 5920
To demonstrate all his skill.
He neck-reined his horse
And let it run between two ranks.
Soon all those deluded, mocking men,
Who had spent most of the night and day 5925
Ridiculing him,
Were to be astounded--
They had laughed, sported,
And had their fun long enough.
With his shield over his arm 5930
The son of the king
Of Ireland came charging madly
At Lancelot from across the field.
They met with such violence
That the son of the king of Ireland 5935
Had no further wish to joust,
For his lance was split and broken,
Having struck not moss,
But strong,dry shield boards.
Lancelot taught him a lesson 5940
In this joust,
Striking his shield from his arm
And pinning his arm to his side,
Then knocking him from his horse to the ground.
Immediately other knights rushed forward, 5945
Spurring and charging from both camps,
Some to help the fallen knight
And others to worsen his plight.
Some, thinking to help their lords,
Knocked many knights from the saddles 5950
In the melee and skirmish.
But Gawain, who was there
With the others, never entered

qui ert avoec les autres la;
qu'a esgarder tant li pleisoit   5955
les proesces que cil feisoit
as armes de sinople taintes,
qu'estre li sanbloient estaintes
celes que li autre feisoient:
envers les soes ne paroient.   5960
Et li hyrauz se resbaudist
tant qu'oiant toz cria et dist:
"Or est venuz qui l'aunera!
Huimés verroiz que il fera;
Huimés aparra sa proesce!"   5965
Et lors li chevaliers s'adresce
Son cheval et fet une pointe
ancontre un chevalier molt cointe,
et fiert si qu'il le porte jus
loing del cheval cent piez ou plus.   5970
Si bien a faire le comance
et de l'espee et de la lance,
que il n'est hom qui armes port
qu'a lui veoir ne se deport.
Nes maint de ces qui armes portent   5975
s'i redelitent et deportent,
que granz deporz est de veoir   [49f]
con fet trabuchier et cheoir
chevax et chevaliers ansanble.
Gaires a chevalier n'asanble   5980
qu'an sele de cheval remaingne,
et les chevax que il gaaigne
done a toz ces qui les voloient.
Et cil qui gaber le soloient
dïent: "Honi somes et mort.   5985
Molt avomes eü grant tort
de lui despire et avillier.
Certes il valt bien un millier
de tex a en cest chanp assez,
que il a vaincuz et passez   5990
trestoz les chevaliers del monde,
qu'il n'i a un qu'a lui s'aponde."
Et les dameiseles disoient,
qui a mervoilles l'esgardoient,
que cil les tolt a marïer;   5995
car tant ne s'osoient fïer
en lor biautez n'an lor richeces
n'an lor pooirs n'an lor hauteces,
que por biauté ne por avoir
deignast nule d'eles avoir   6000
cil chevaliers, que trop est prouz.

5984. Et cil ch. le suioient 5990. *first* s *of* passez
added above line

248

The fray all that day,
For he was satisfied to watch   5955
The prowess of that knight
With the red-painted armor,
Whose deeds seemed to outshine
Those of the others,
Making them pale by comparison.   5960
The herald, too, was cheered up
And cried out for all to hear:
"The one is come who will take their measure!
Today you will witness his deeds;
Today you will see his might!"   5965
Thereupon Lancelot wheeled
His horse and charged
Toward a magnificent knight;
He struck him a blow that carried him to the ground
A hundred feet or more from his steed.   5970
Lancelot began performing such feats
Both with his sword and lance
That every armed knight present
Marveled at what he saw.
Even many of those participating in the jousts   5975
Observed with admiration and pleasure,
For it was a pleasure to see
How he caused both men and steeds
To stumble and fall.
There was scarcely a knight he challenged   5980
Who was able to remain in the saddle,
And he gave the horses he won
To any who wanted them.
Those who had been mocking him
Now said: "We are ashamed and mortified.   5985
We made a great mistake
To slander and disdain him.
Truly he is worth a thousand
Of the likes of those on this field,
Since he has vanquished and surpassed   5990
All the knights in the world,
So that now there is no one left to oppose him."
The girls who were watching him
With amazement all said
That he was destroying their marriage hopes.   5995
Their beauty, their wealth,
Their positions and their noble births
They felt to be of little value,
For a knight this brave
Would never deign to marry any of them   6000
For her beauty or wealth alone.

249

Et neporquant se font tex vouz
les plusors d'eles, qu'eles dïent
que s'an cestui ne se marïent
ne seront ouan marïees,   6005
n'a mari n'a seignor donees.
Et la reïne qui antant
ce dom eles se vont vantant,
a soi meïsme an rit et gabe;
bien set que por tot l'or d'Arrabe,   6010
qui trestot devant li metroit,
la meillor d'eles ne prandroit,
la plus bele ne la plus gente,
cil qui a totes atalante.
Et lor volentez est comune   6015
si qu'avoir le voldroit chascune.
Et l'une est de l'autre jalouse
si con s'ele fust ja s'espouse,
por ce que si adroit le voient
qu'eles ne pansent ne ne croient   6020
que nus d'armes, tant lor pleisoit,   [50a]
poïst ce feire qu'il feisoit.
Si bien le fist qu'au departir
d'andeus parz distrent sanz mantir
que n'i avoit eü paroil   6025
cil qui porte l'escu vermoil.
Trestuit le distrent et voirs fu.
Mes au departir son escu
leissa an la presse cheoir,
la ou greignor la pot veoir,   6030
et sa lance et sa coverture;
puis si s'an va grant aleüre.
Si s'an ala si en anblee
que nus de tote l'asanblee
qui la fust garde ne s'an prist.   6035
Et cil a la voie se mist,
si s'an ala molt tost et droit
cele part don venuz estoit
por aquiter son sairemant.
Au partir del tornoiemant   6040
le quierent et demandent tuit;
n'an truevent point, car il s'an fuit,
qu'il n'a cure qu'an le conoisse.
Grant duel en ont et grant angoisse
li chevalier, qui an feïssent   6045
grant joie se il le tenissent.
Et se aus chevaliers pesa
quant il ensi lessiez les a,

6009. meismes *with expunctuating dot under final* s
6044. en a et 6048. il *added above line*

250

Yet most of them
Made vows pledging
That if they did not marry this knight
They would not wed in this year; 6005
They would not give themselves to any lord and husband.
The queen, who overheard
Their boastful vows,
Laughed to herself;
She knew that the one they all desired 6010
Would not take the best,
The most beautiful, nor the fairest,
Even if one were to place before him
All the gold of Arabia.
They all had but one wish: 6015
Each wanted to have that knight.
They were as jealous of one another
As if they had already married him,
Because they believed him so skillful
That they did not think or believe 6020
That any knight, no matter how pleasing he might be,
Could ever have done what he did.
He had fought so well that, when it came time to cease,
Those on both sides said that, without a lie,
There never was an equal 6025
To the knight who carried the red shield.
It was said by all, and it was true.
But as they separated he let
His shield, lance, and trappings
Fall where the press 6030
Seemed to be the thickest,
And he hastened away.
His departure was so furtive
That no one in all the assembled crowd
Took any notice of it. 6035
He set out on his way
As quickly as he could
To keep his pledge
And return directly to that place whence he had come.
After the tournament 6040
Everyone inquired and asked about him;
They found no trace, for he had left,
Not wanting to be recognized.
The knights, who would have been overjoyed
To have had him there, were filled 6045
With great sorrow and pain.
But if the knights were grieved
That he had left them thus,

les dameiseles, quant le sorent,
asez plus grant pesance en orent,   6050
et dïent que par saint Johan
ne se marïeront ouan:
quant celui n'ont qu'eles voloient,
toz les autres quites clamoient.
L'anhatine ensi departi   6055
c'onques nule n'an prist mari.
Et Lanceloz pas ne sejorne,
mes tost an sa prison retorne.
Et li seneschax vint ençois
de Lancelot deus jors ou trois,   6060
si demanda ou il estoit.
Et la dame qui li avoit
ses armes vermoilles baillïees,
bien et beles apareillïees,
et son hernois et son cheval,   [50b]
le voir an dist au seneschal
comant ele l'ot anvoié
la ou en avoit tornoié,
a l'ahatine de Noauz.
"Dame, voir," fet li seneschauz,   6070
"ne poïssiez faire noaus!
Molt m'an vanra, ce cuit, granz maus,
que messire Meleaganz
me fera pis que li jaianz*
se j'avoie esté perilliez.   6075
Morz an serai et essilliez
maintenant que il le savra,
que ja de moi pitié n'avra!"
"Biax sire, or ne vos esmaiez,"
fet la dame, "mie n'aiez   6080
tel peor, qu'il ne vos estuet.
Riens nule retenir nel puet,
que il le me jura sor sainz
qu'il vanroit, ja ne porroit ainz."
Li seneschaus maintenant monte,   6085
a son seignor vint, se li conte
tote la chose et l'avanture;
mes ice molt le raseüre
que il li dit confaitemant
sa fame an prist le sairemant   6090
qu'il revandroit an la prison.
"Il n'an fera ja mesprison,"
fet Meleaganz, "bien le sai,
et neporquant grant duel en ai
de ce que vostre fame a fait;   6095
je nel volsisse por nul plait
qu'il eüst esté an l'estor.
Mes or vos metez au retor

252

The young girls, when they learned of it,
Were far more grieved   6050
And swore by St. John
That they would not marry this year:
If they could not have the one they wanted,
They would have no other.
Thus the tournament ended   6055
Without anyone having taken a husband.
Lancelot did not delay,
But returned quickly to his prison.
The seneschal, in whose charge he was, reached home
Two or three days before Lancelot's return   6060
And inquired after his whereabouts.
The lady who had given Lancelot
The seneschal's magnificent
And well-made red armor,
His trappings and his horse,   6065
Told her husband truthfully
How she had sent her charge
To take part in the jousting
At the tournament of Noauz.
"My wife," said the seneschal, "truly   6070
You could have done no worse!
I am sure that great misfortune will befall me,
For my lord Meleagant
Will treat me worse than would the giant*
If I were shipwrecked.   6075
I shall be dead and ruined
As soon as he discovers it.
He will never have pity on me!"
"Fair sir, do not be distraught,"
Replied the lady, "don't be   6080
So fearful, for there's no need.
Nothing can prevent his return,
For he swore to me by the saints
That he would be back as quickly as possible."
The seneschal mounted at once,   6085
Rode to his lord, and related
The whole adventure to him;
He was reassured, however,
When the seneschal told him how
His wife had made Lancelot swear   6090
To return to prison.
"He will never break his oath,"
Said Meleagant, "this I know;
Yet I am greatly troubled
By what your wife has done;   6095
Not for anything did I want
Him to be at the tournament.
Go back now and be sure

et gardez, quant il iert venuz,
qu'il soit an tel prison tenuz   6100
qu'il n'isse de la prison fors
ne n'ait nul pooir de son cors;
et maintenant le me mandez."
"Fet iert si con vos comandez,"
fet li seneschax. Si s'an va   6105
et Lancelot venu trova
qui prison tenoit an sa cort.
Uns messages arriere cort,
que li seneschax en anvoie   *[50c]*
a Meleagant droite voie,   6110
si li a dit de Lancelot
qu'il est venuz. Et quant il l'ot,
si prist maçons et charpantiers
qui a enviz ou volantiers
firent ce qu'il lor comanda.   6115
Les meillors del païs manda,
si lor a dit qu'il li feïssent
une tor, et poinne i meïssent
ençois qu'ele fust tote feite.
Sor la mer fu la pierre treite;   6120
que pres de Gorre iqui de lez
an cort uns braz et granz et lez;
enmi le braz une isle avoit
que Melïaganz bien savoit;
la comanda la pierre a traire   6125
et le merrien por la tor faire.
An moins de cinquante et set jorz
fu tote parfeite la torz:
forz et espesse et longue et lee.
Quant ele fu ensi fondee,   6130
Lancelot amener i fist
et an la tor ensi le mist.*
Puis comanda les huis murer*
et fist toz les maçons jurer
que ja par aus de cele tor   6135
ne sera parole a nul jor.
Ensi volt qu'ele fust celee,
ne n'i remest huis ne antree
fors c'une petite fenestre.
Leanz covint Lancelot estre;   6140
si li donoit l'an a mangier
molt povremant et a dongier
par cele fenestre petite
a ore devisee et dite,
si con l'ot dit et comandé   6145
li fel plains de desleauté.

6120. mer et la p. 6133. barrer

254

That when he returns
He is guarded so securely   6100
That he will never be able to escape from prison
Nor have any freedom of movement;
And send me word at once."
"It shall be done as you order,"
Said the seneschal. He left   6105
And found Lancelot returned,
A prisoner at his court.
A messenger hurried back,
Sent by the seneschal
To Meleagant by the shortest road   6110
To inform him that Lancelot
Had returned. Upon hearing this,
Meleagant engaged masons and carpenters
Who did as he ordered,
Either willingly or by constraint.   6115
He summoned the best in the country
And told them to make him
A tower, and to work diligently
Until it was completed.
The stone was brought by sea;   6120
On one shore of the land of Gorre
Was a broad, deep arm of the sea;
Set in this inlet was an island
That Meleagant knew well;
He ordered the stone and the wood   6125
For constructing the tower to be brought there.
In less than fifty-seven days
The tower was completed:
Thick-walled and solid, broad and tall.
When it was ready,   6130
He had Lancelot led there
And put within the tower.
Then he ordered that the doorways be walled up
And made all the masons swear
That they would never   6135
Speak of this tower.
He wanted it to be sealed
In such a way that there remained no door nor opening,
Save only a small window.
Lancelot was forced to remain within;   6140
And he was given to eat
Only niggardly portions of poor fare
Through this small embrasure
At fixed hours,
Just as the traitorous felon   6145
Had ordered and stipulated.

Or a tot fet quanque il vialt
Meleaganz. Aprés s'aquialt
droit a la cort le roi Artu;
estes le vos ja la venu.   6150
Et quant il vint devant le roi,
molt plains d'orguel et de desroi
a comanciee sa reison: [50d]
"Rois, devant toi an ta meison
ai une bataille arramie;   6155
mes de Lancelot n'i voi mie,
qui l'a enprise ancontre moi.
Et neporquant, si con je doi,
ma bataille oiant toz presant,
ces que ceanz voi an presant.   6160
Et s'il est ceanz, avant veingne
et soit tex que covant me teigne
an vostre cort d'ui en un an.
Ne sai s'onques le vos dist l'an
an quel meniere et an quel guise   6165
ceste bataille fu anprise;
mes je voi chevaliers ceanz
qui furent a noz covenanz,
et bien dire le vos savroient
se voir reconuistre an voloient.   6170
Mes se il le me vialt noier,
ja n'i loierai soldoier,
einz le mosterrai vers son cors."
La reïne, qui seoit lors
delez le roi, a soi le tire   6175
et si li encomance a dire:
"Sire, savez vos qui est cist?
C'est Meliaganz qui me prist
el conduit Kex le seneschal;
assez li fist et honte et mal."   6180
Et li rois li a respondu:
"Dame, je l'ai bien antendu:
je sai molt bien que ce est cil
qui tenoit ma gent an essil."
La reïne plus n'an parole.   6185
Li rois atorne sa parole
vers Meleagant, si li dit:
"Amis," fet il, "se Dex m'aït,
de Lancelot nos ne savons
noveles, don grant duel avons."   6190
"Sire rois," fet Meleaganz,
"Lanceloz me dist que ceanz
le troveroie je sanz faille,
ne je ne doi ceste bataille
semondre s'an vostre cort non.   6195
Je vuel que trestuit cist baron

Now Meleagant had done all he
Wished. Next he went
Straight to King Arthur's court.
Upon his arrival   6150
He came before the king
And, filled with arrogance and perfidy,
He began to speak:
"O king, I have agreed to single combat
At your court in your presence;   6155
But nowhere do I see Lancelot,
Who was to oppose me.
However, as is proper
I show myself readied for combat
In the sight of all here present.   6160
If he be present, let him come forward
And swear to meet me here
In your court one year from this day.
I do not know if anyone here has told you
How and under what circumstances   6165
This combat was arranged,
But I see knights here
Who were at our pledging,
And who can tell you everything
If they wish to acknowledge the truth.   6170
If Lancelot should attempt to deny it,
I'll not hire any second to defend me,
But oppose him myself."
The queen, who was seated at court
Beside the king, motioned to him   6175
To lean toward her and began to say:
"Sir, do you know who this is?
He is Meleagant, who captured me
When I was being escorted by Kay,
And who shamed and hurt him greatly."   6180
The king answered her:
"My lady, I understand clearly:
I know very well that this is he
Who held my people prisoner."
The queen spoke no further.   6185
The king addressed
Meleagant, saying:
"Friend," said he, "so help me God,
We have heard no news of Lancelot,
Which grieves us deeply."   6190
"My lord king," replied Meleagant,
"Lancelot assured me that I
Would not fail to find him here,
And I am pledged not to undertake
This combat except at your court.   6195
I wish all of the barons

257

qui ci sont m'an portent tesmoing,
que d'ui en un an l'en semoing
par les covanz que nos feïsmes
la ou la bataille anpreïsmes." 6200
    A cest mot an estant se lieve
messire Gauvains, cui molt grieve
de la parole que il ot,
et dit: "Sire, de Lancelot
n'a point an tote ceste terre; 6205
mes nos l'anvoieromes querre,
se Deu plest, sel trovera l'an
ençois que veigne au chief de l'an,
s'il n'est morz ou anprisonez.
Et s'il ne vient, si me donez 6210
la bataille--je la ferai.
Por Lancelot m'an armerai
au jor, se il ne vient ençois."
"Haï! por Deu, biax sire rois,"
fet Meliaganz, "donez li. 6215
Il la vialt et je vos an pri,
qu'el monde chevalier ne sai
a cui si volentiers m'essai,
fors que Lancelot seulemant.
Mes sachiez bien certainnemant, 6220
s'a l'un d'aus deus ne me conbat,
nul eschange ne nul rachat
fors que l'un d'aus deus n'an prandroie."
Et li rois dit que il l'otroie
se Lanceloz ne vient dedanz. 6225
Atant s'an part Meleaganz
et de la cort le roi s'an va;
ne fina tant que il trova
le roi Bademagu son pere.
Devant lui, por ce que il pere 6230
qu'il est preuz et de grant afeire,
comança un sanblant a feire
et une chiere merveilleuse.
Ce jor tenoit cort molt joieuse
li rois a Bade sa cité. 6235
Jorz fu de sa natevité,
por ce la tint grant et pleniere;
si ot gent de mainte meniere
avoec lui venu plus qu'assez.
Toz fu li palés antassez 6240

de chevaliers et de puceles.
Mes une en i ot avoec eles
(cele estoit suer Meleagant)
don bien vos dirai ça avant

6222. rabat 6243-44. *reversed in MS*

Here present to bear witness:
I now summon him to be here one year from this day,
In accord with the pledges we gave
When we first agreed to fight."   6200
    Thereupon my lord Gawain
Arose, for he was exceedingly troubled
By what he had heard.
"Sir," he spoke, "Lancelot
Is nowhere to be found in this land;   6205
But we shall have him sought and,
If it please God, he will be found
Before the year is out,
Unless he is imprisoned or dead.
But if he fails to appear, let me assume   6210
The combat--I am willing.
I will arm myself for Lancelot
At the appointed day, if he is not here before then."
"Ah ha!" said Meleagant. "By God,
King Arthur, grant him this battle.   6215
He wants it and I urge it,
For I know of no knight in the world
I'd rather test myself against,
Unless it is Lancelot himself.
But know for certain   6220
That I will only fight one of those two--
I'll accept no exchange or substitution
And will only engage one of those two."
The king said that he would grant the challenge to Gawain
If Lancelot failed to return in time.   6225
With this promise Meleagant left
King Arthur's court
And rode until he reached
That of his father, King Bademagu.
In order to appear before him   6230
Noble and distinguished,
He began to assume an air of importance
And to act extremely lighthearted.
This day the king was hosting a festive
Celebration at his city of Bath.   6235
The court was open in all its splendor,
For it was the anniversary of his birth;
People of every sort
Came there to be with him.
The palace was overflowing   6240
With knights and maidens.
There was one among them
(She was the sister of Meleagant)
About whom I shall willingly

mon pansser et m'antencĭon;   6245
mes n'an vuel feire mancĭon,
car n'afiert pas a ma matire
que ci androit an doie dire,
ne je ne la vuel boceier
ne corronpre ne forceier,   6250
mes mener boen chemin et droit.
Et si vos dirai orandroit
ou Meleaganz est venuz
qui, oiant toz gros et menuz,
dist a son pere molt en haut: 6255
"Pere," fet il, "se Dex vos saut,
se vos plest, or me dites voir
se cil ne doit grant joie avoir
et se molt n'est de grant vertu
qui a la cort le roi Artu   6260
par ses armes se fet doter."
Li peres, sanz plus escoter,
a sa demande li respont:
"Filz," fet il, "tuit cil qui boen sont
doivent enorer et servir   6265
celui qui ce puet desservir,
et maintenir sa conpaignie."
Lors le blandist et si li prie
et dit c'or ne soit mes teü
por coi a ce amanteü,   6270
qu'il quiert, qu'il vialt et dom il vient.
"Sire, ne sai s'il vos sovient,"
ce dit ses filz Meleaganz,
"des esgarz et des covenanz
qui dit furent et recordé   6275
quant par vos fumes acordé
et moi et Lancelot ansanble.
Bien vos an manbre, ce me sanble,
que devant plusors nos dist l'an
que nos fussiens au chief de l'an   6280
an la cort Artus prest andui.
G'i alai quant aler i dui,
apareilliez et aprestez
de ce por coi g'i ere alez.
Tot ce que je dui faire fis: [51a]
Lancelot demandai et quis,
contre cui je devoie ovrer,
mes nel poi veoir ne trover.
Foïz s'an est et destornez!
Or si m'an sui par tel tornez   6290
que Gauvains m'a sa foi plevie
que se Lanceloz n'est an vie

6270. as *with expunctuating dot under the* s

260

Tell you what I know later;   6245
I do not want to speak further of her now
Since it is not part of my story
To tell of her at this point;
And I do not want to inflate
Or confuse or alter my story,   6250
But develop it in a proper and straightforward manner.
So now I will tell you
That upon his arrival Meleagant
Said to his father in a loud voice,
Which commoner and noble alike could hear: 6255
"Father, as God is your help,
Please tell me truthfully
If one who has made his prowess feared
At King Arthur's court
Is not to be considered worthy   6260
And should not be filled with great joy."
Without waiting to hear more, his father
Answered this question:
"Son," he said, "all good men
Should honor and serve   6265
Him who is worthy,
And keep his company."
Then he flattered him and urged
That he no longer keep secret
The reason he mentioned this,   6270
Or what he was seeking or wanted, and whence he had come.
"Sir, I don't know if you remember,"
Replied his son Meleagant,
"The terms of the agreement
Which was established   6275
When you made peace
Between Lancelot and myself.
But you must recall, I'm sure,
That we were both told before many witnesses
To be ready in one year's time   6280
To meet again at King Arthur's court.
I went there at the appointed time,
Armed and equipped
For what I had gone to do.
All that was required of me I did: 6285
I sought and inquired after Lancelot,
Whom I was to oppose,
But was unable to see or find him.
He had turned and fled!
So I arranged   6290
To have Gawain pledge his word
That there would be no further delay

261

et se dedanz le terme mis
ne vient, bien m'a dit et promis
que ja respiz pris n'an sera,   6295
mes il meïsmes la fera
ancontre moi por Lancelot.
Artus n'a chevalier qu'an lot
tant con cestui--c'est bien seü.
Mes ainz que florissent seü   6300
verrai ge, s'au ferir venons,
s'au fet s'acorde li renons--
et mon vuel seroit orandroit!"
"Filz," fet li peres, "or en droit
te fez ici tenir por sot.   6305
Or set tex qui devant nel sot
par toi meïsmes ta folie.
Voirs est que boens cuers s'umilie,
mes li fos et li descuidiez
n'iert ja de folie vuidiez.   6310
Filz, por toi le di, que tes teches
par sont si dures et si seches
qu'il n'i a dolçor n'amitié;
li tuens cuers est trop sanz pitié,
trop es de la folie espris.   6315
C'est ce por coi   ge te mespris;
c'est ce qui molt t'abeissera.
Se tu es preuz, assez sera
qui le bien an tesmoingnera
a l'ore qui besoingnera;   6320
n'estuet pas prodome loer
son cuer por son fet aloer,
que li fez meïsmes se loe.
Neïs la monte d'une aloe
ne t'aïde a monter an pris   6325
tes los, mes assez mains t'en pris.
Filz, je te chasti; mes cui chaut?
Quanqu'an dit a fol petit vaut,
que cil ne se fet fors debatre
qui de fol vialt folie abatre.   [51b]
Et biens qu'an anseigne et descuevre
ne valt rien, s'an nel met a oevre,
einz est lués alez et perduz."
Lors fu duremant esperduz
Meleaganz et forssené.   6335
Onques home de mere né
(ce vos puis je bien por voir dire)
ne veïstes ausi plain d'ire
com il estoit; et par corroz

6317. *line omitted, then added to end of* 6316
6320. luevre qui   6335. *line repeated*

262

Even if Lancelot were no longer alive
And failed to return
Within the fixed term;   6295
Gawain himself promised
To fight me in Lancelot's stead.
Arthur has no other knight as praiseworthy
As Gawain--that is well known.
But before the elderberries blossom   6300
I will see when we fight
If his deeds match his fame--
And the sooner the better!"
"Son," said his father, "now indeed
You have shown yourself a fool to everyone here.   6305
Those who did not know it before, know it now
Through your own words.
True it is that a great heart is humble,
But the fool and the braggart
Will never be devoid of their folly.   6310
Son, for your own good I am telling you:
Your character is so very hard and dry
That there is no trace of gentility or friendship;
Your heart is too lacking in mercy,
You are too filled with folly.   6315
This is why I find fault with you;
This is what will strike you down.
If you are of noble heart, many
Will bear witness to it
At the appropriate time;   6320
A gentleman need not praise
His courage to magnify his act,
For the act is its own best praise.
Self-flattery does not
Enhance your glory at all,*   6325
Rather it makes me esteem you less.
Son, I chastise you, but to what avail?
It is of little use to advise a fool,
And he who tries to rid a fool of his folly
Wastes his strength.   6330
The goodness which one preaches,
When it is not transformed into works, is wasted--
Wasted, lost, and gone forever."
Meleagant was beside himself
With fury and rage.   6335
No, I can tell you truthfully
That you have never seen any man born of woman
So full of wrath
As he was; and in his anger

fu ilueques li festuz roz,   6340
car de rien nule ne blandist
son pere, mes itant li dist:
"Est ce songes ou vos resvez,
qui dites que je sui desvez
por ce se je vos cont mon estre?   6345
Com a mon seignor cuidoie estre
a vos venuz, com a mon pere;
mes ne sanble pas qu'il apere,
car plus vilmant me leïdoiez,
ce m'est avis, que ne doiez!   6350
Ne reison dire ne savez
por coi ancomancié l'avez."
"Si faz assez."--"Et vos de quoi?"
"Que nule rien an toi ne voi
fors seulemant forssan et rage.   6355
Je conuis molt bien ton corage
qui ancor grant mal te fera.
Et dahait qui ja cuidera
que Lanceloz li bien apris,
qui de toz fors de toi a pris,   6360
s'an soit por ta crieme foïz!
Mes espoir qu'il est anfoïz
ou an tel prison anserrez,
don li huis est si fort serrez
qu'il n'an puet issir sanz congié.   6365
Certes c'est la chose dont gié
seroie duremant iriez
s'il estoit morz ou anpiriez.
Certes trop i avroit grant perte,
se criature si aperte,   6370
si bele, si preuz, si serie,
estoit si a par tans perie.
Mes c'est mançonge, se Deu plest!"   [51c]
Atant Bademaguz se test;
mes quanqu'il ot dit et conté   6375
ot antendu et escouté
une soe fille pucele,
et sachiez bien que ce fu cele
c'or ainz amantui an mon conte,
qui n'est pas liee quant an conte   6380
tex noveles de Lancelot.
Bien aparçoit qu'an le celot,
quant an n'an set ne vant ne voie.
"Ja Dex," fet ele, "ne me voie,
quant je jamés reposerai   6385
jusque tant que je an savrai
novele certainne et veraie."

6343. resbez   6382. quant

264

The last bond between father and son   6340
Was broken, for he did not mince words
With his father, but raged:
"Are you having some sort of dream or nightmare
To say that I'm crazy
When I tell you of my affairs?   6345
I thought to come to you
As to my lord, as to my father;
But that doesn't appear to be the case,
For I think you have insulted me
More vilely than is just!   6350
Nor can you give me any reason
For having done so."
"Indeed I can."--"What then?"
"That I see nothing in you
But lunacy and madness.   6355
I know only too well that heart of yours
Which will yet do you great harm.
Damned be anyone who would believe
That Lancelot, this perfect knight
Who is esteemed by all but yourself,   6360
Would ever flee out of fear of you!
Perhaps he is buried
Or locked up in some prison,
Whose gate is so tightly shut
That he cannot leave without permission.   6365
Indeed it's a fact that I'd
Be sorely angered
If he were injured or dead.
It would be a great loss indeed
If a person so skilled,   6370
So handsome, so valiant, yet so just
Were to perish before his time.
May it please God that this be not so!"
Thereupon Bademagu grew silent;
But all that he had said and related   6375
Had been heard and carefully noted
By one of his daughters--
Know well that she was the one
I mentioned earlier in my story,
And that she was not happy to hear   6380
Such news of Lancelot.
It was evident he was being kept hidden,
Since no one had any trace of news.
"May God," she told herself, "never look
Upon me if ever I rest   6385
Before I shall know
Definite, truthful news of him."

265

Maintenant sanz nule delaie,
sanz noise feire et sanz murmure,
s'an cort monter sor une mure   6390
molt bele et molt soëf portant.
Mes de ma part vos di ge tant,
qu'ele ne set onques quel part
torner quant de la cort se part.
N'ele nel set, n'ele nel rueve,   6395
mes el premier chemin qu'el trueve
s'an antre. Et va grant aleüre
ne set ou, mes par avanture,
sanz chevalier et sanz sergent.
Molt se haste, molt est an grant   6400
d'aconsivre ce qu'ele chace.
Molt se porquiert, molt se porchace,
mes ce n'iert ja mie si tost.
N'estuet pas qu'ele se repost
ne demort an un leu granmant,   6405
s'ele vialt feire avenanmant
ce qu'ele a anpanssé a faire:
c'est Lancelot de prison traire,
s'el le trueve et feire le puisse.
Mes je cuit qu'ainçois qu'el le truisse   6410
en avra maint païs cerchié,
maint alé et maint reverchié,
ainz que nule novele an oie.
Mes que valdroit se je contoie
ne ses gistes ne ses jornees?   6415
Mes tantes voies a tornees
amont, aval, et sus et jus,   [51d]
que passez fu li mois ou plus
c'onques plus aprandre n'an pot
ne moins qu'ele devant an sot--   6420
et c'est neanz tot an travers.
Un jor s'an aloit a travers
un chanp molt dolante et pansive,
et vit bien loing, lez une rive,
pres d'un braz de mer--une tor.   6425
Mes n'avoit d'une liue antor
meison ne buiron ne repeire.
Meleaganz l'ot feite feire
qui Lancelot mis i avoit,
mes cele neant n'an savoit.   6430
Et si tost com el l'ot veüe,
s'i a si mise sa veüe
qu'aillors ne la torne ne met;
et ses cuers tres bien li promet
que c'est ce qu'ele a tant chacié.   6435

6389. murlnure   6395. trueve

She stole noiselessly away
Without a moment's hesitation
And ran to mount   6390
Her comely and smooth-gaited mule.
But for my part I can tell you
That she had no idea which way
To turn upon leaving the court.
She did not know, nor did she inquire,   6395
But the first path she found,
She took. She rode swiftly along,
Uncertain of her destination, guided by chance,
Without servant or knightly escort.
She was in a great hurry and eager   6400
To reach her goal.
She sought far and wide,
But her search was not destined to be brief.
She could not rest
Or stop long in any one place   6405
If she wished to accomplish properly
What she had set out do do:
Release Lancelot from prison
If she could find him and do it.
Yet I believe that before finding him   6410
She will have searched through many a land,
And will have traversed many a country,
Before she will hear anything of him.
But what good is it for me to tell
Of her nightly lodgings and her daily wanderings? 6415
She traveled so many roads
Over mountains, through valleys, high and low,
That a month passed or more
Without her being able to learn
More than she already knew--   6420
Which was less than nothing.
One day as she was riding sad
And pensive through a field,
She saw in the distance beside the shore
Near an inlet--a tower.   6425
But for a league on any side there was
Neither house, nor cabin, nor hut.
Meleagant had had it built
In order to keep Lancelot,
But his sister knew nothing of that.   6430
As soon as she saw it,
She fixed her eyes on it
And never turned away;
And her heart promised her
That this was what she had sought for so long.   6435

Mes ore an est venue a chié,
qu'a droite voie l'a menee
Fortune, qui tant l'a penee.
    La pucele la tor aproche,
et tant a alé qu'ele i toche.   6440
Antor va, oroille et escote,
et s'i met s'antencion tote
savoir mon se ele i oïst
chose dont ele s'esjoïst.
Aval esgarde et amont bee,   6445
si voit la tor et longue et lee.
Mes mervoille a ce que puet estre
qu'ele n'i voit huis ne fenestre,
fors une petite et estroite.
An la tor, qui est haute et droite,   6450
n'avoit eschiele ne degré.
Por ce croit que c'est fet de gré
et que Lanceloz est dedanz;
mes ainz qu'ele manjut des danz
savra se ce est voirs ou non.   6455
Lors le vet apeler par non:
apeler voloit Lancelot,
mes ce la tarde que ele ot
andemantiers que se teisoit
une voiz qui un duel feisoit   6460
an la tor, merveilleuse et fort,   [51e]
qui ne queroit el que la mort.
La mort covoite et trop se diaut:
trop par a mal et morir viaut;
sa vie et son cors despisoit   6465
a la foiee, si disoit
foiblement a voiz basse et roe:
"Haï! Fortune, con ta roe
m'est ore leidemant tornee!
Malemant la m'as bestornee,   6470
car g'iere el mont, or sui el val:
or avoie bien, or ai mal;
or me plores, or me rioies.
Las, cheitis, por coi t'i fioies
quant ele si tost t'a lessié?   6475
An po d'ore m'a abessié
voiremant de si haut si bas.
Fortune, quant tu me gabas,
molt feïs mal--mes toi que chaut?
A neant est comant qu'il aut.   6480
Ha! sainte Croiz, sainz Esperiz,
con sui perduz! Con sui periz!
Con sui del tot an tot alez!

6438. menee   6474. le feisoies   6483-4. *reversed in MS*

Now her search was ended;
After many tribulations Fortune
Had guided her to the right road.
    The girl approached the tower,
Riding right up to it.   6440
She circled it, listening
With perfect attention
To determine whether she might hear
Anything that would bring her joy.
She searched high and low   6445
And saw that the tower was tall and broad.
But she was astonished when
She saw no opening in it--
Except for a small, narrow window.
There was neither ladder nor stair   6450
To enter the high tower.
She reasoned that this was deliberate
And therefore that Lancelot was within;
But before stopping to eat
She was determined to know the truth of it.   6455
She was going to call out his name;
But as she was about to say "Lancelot,"
She was prevented from speaking
By a voice which she heard
Coming from within the tower--   6460
A voice filled with deepest grief,
Seeking only death.
Lamenting piteously, it longed for death:
In its suffering it sought to die;
It no longer valued either life   6465
Or its own body. It said
Feebly, in a low, trembling tone:
"Ah, Fortune, how cruelly your wheel
Has now turned for me!
Your terrible reversal   6470
Has thrown me down from on high:
Once I had everything, now I have nothing;
Once you wept to see me, now you laugh at me.
Poor Lancelot, why did you trust in Fortune
When she abandoned you so soon?   6475
In no time at all she has cast me down
From so high to so low.
By mocking me, Fortune,
You act very badly--but what do you care?
All is turned to naught, no matter what.   6480
Ah! Holy Cross, Holy Spirit,
I am lost! I am damned!
See how far gone I am!

Ha! Gauvain, vos qui tant valez,
qui de bontez n'avez paroil,   6485
certes duremant me mervoil
por coi vos ne me secorez!
Certes trop i par demorez,
si ne feites pas corteisie.
Bien deüst avoir vostre aïe   6490
cil cui tant soliez amer.
Certes deça ne dela mer,
ce puis je bien dire sanz faille,
n'eüst destor ne repostaille
ou je ne vos eüsse quis   6495
a tot le moins set anz ou dis,
se je an prison vos seüsse,
einz que trové ne vos eüsse.
Mes de coi me vois debatant?
Il ne vos an est mie atant   6500
qu'antrer an vuilliez an la poinne.
Li vilains dit bien voir qu'a poinne
puet an mes un ami trover;
de legier puet an esprover
au besoing qui est boens amis.   [51f]
Las! Plus a d'un an qu'an m'a mis
ci an ceste tor an prison!
Gauvain, jel tieng a mesprison
certes quant lessié m'i avez.
Mes espoir--quant vos nel savez--   6510
espoir que je vos blasme a tort.
Certes, voirs est, bien m'an recort!
Et grant oltrage et grant mal fis
quant jel cuidai, car je sui fis
que por quanque cuevrent les nues   6515
ne fust que n'i fussent venues
voz genz et vos por moi fors traire
de cest mal et de cest contraire,
se vos de voir le seüssiez.
Et feire le redeüssiez   6520
par amor et par conpaignie,
qu'autremant nel redi je mie.
Mes c'est neanz--ce ne puet estre!
Ha! de Deu et de saint Cervestre
soit maudiz, et Dex le destine   6525
Qui a tel honte me define!
C'est li pires qui soit an vie,
Meleaganz, qui par envie
m'a fet tot le pis que il pot."
Atant se coise, atant se tot   6530
cil qui a dolor sa vie use.

6522. je *missing in MS*

Ah! most worthy Gawain,
Unequaled in goodness, 6485
How I marvel indeed
That you have not come to my aid!
You have delayed too long indeed
And are quite unchivalrous.
He whom you once so loved 6490
Should be worthy of your help.
Indeed I can say without contradiction
That there is no secluded place nor hideaway
On either side of the sea
For which I would not have searched, 6495
In order to find you,
Seven years or ten at the last,
Had I known you to be imprisoned.
But why am I so distraught?
You are not bold enough 6500
To expose yourself to hardships on my account.
The peasants say truly that in times of hardship*
One can scarcely find a friend;
It is easy in times of trial
To test one's friends. 6505
Alas! It has been over a year now
That I've been kept a prisoner!
Gawain, you are an untrustworthy friend
Indeed to have left me here.
But perhaps--if you do not know I am here-- 6510
Perhaps I am wrong to accuse you so.
Indeed that must be the case, I know it now!
And I was unreasonable and spoke maliciously
When I had such thoughts, for I am certain
That there is nowhere that you and your men 6515
Would not go to rescue me
From this wicked confinement,
Even were I at the ends of the earth,
If you but knew the truth.
And you would do it out of 6520
The love and friendship you bear me--
Yes, that is what I really think.
But it's useless--this can never be!
Ah! may he who has shamed me
Be cursed by God and St. Sylvester-- 6525
And may God damn him!
Meleagant, who out of envy
Has done me all the ill he could,
Is the most wicked man alive."
With these words he took comfort and grew silent, 6530
As grief gnawed away at his life.

Mes lors cele qui aval muse,
quanqu'il ot dit ot entandu;
n'a plus longuemant atandu,
c'or set qu'ele est bien assenee. 6535
Si l'apele come senee
"Lancelot!" quanqu'el puet et plus,
"Amis, vos qui estes lessus,
parlez a une vostre amie."
Mes cil dedanz ne l'oï mie. 6540
Et cele plus et plus s'esforce,
tant que cil qui n'a point de force
l'antroï, si s'an merveilla
que puet estre qui l'apela.
La voiz entant, apeler s'ot, 6545
mes qui l'apele il ne le sot--
fantosme cuide que ce soit.
Tot entor soi garde et porvoit
savoir se il verroit nelui, [52a]
mes ne voit fors la tor et lui. 6550
"Dex," fet il, "qu'est ice que j'oi?
J'oi parler et neant ne voi!
Par foi, ce est plus que mervoille!
Si ne dor je pas, ençois voille.
Espoir, s'il m'avenist an songe 6555
cuidasse que ce fust mançonge;
mes je voil, et por ce me grieve."
Lors a quelque poinne se lieve
et va vers le pertuis petit,
belemant, petit et petit, 6560
et quant il i fu, si s'acoste
sus et jus, de lonc et de coste.
Quant sa veüe a mise fors,
si com il puet esgarde, lors
vit celi qui huchié l'avoit. 6565
Ne la conut, mes il la voit;
mes cele tantost conut lui,
si li dit: "Lanceloz, je sui
por vos querre de loing venue.
Or est si la chose avenue, 6570
Deu merci, c'or vos ai trové.
Je sui cele qui vos rové
quant au Pont de l'Espee alastes
un don, et vos le me donastes
molt volantiers quant jel vos quis: 6575
ce fu del chevalier conquis
le chief, que je vos fis tranchier,
que je nes point n'avoie chier.
Por ce don et por ce servise
me sui an ceste poinne mise; 6580
por ce vos metrai fors de ci."

272

Staring at the ground, the girl
Overheard all that he said;
She hesitated no more
When she recognized that her search had ended.   6535
She called to him as loudly
As she could and more: "Lancelot,
Fair friend, you who are there above,
Speak to one who loves you."
But the one within heard her not.   6540
She shouted louder, and louder still,
Until Lancelot at the end of his strength
Heard her and wondered
Who could be calling him.
He heard the voice calling him,   6545
But could not recognize it--
He thought it might be some ghost.
He searched all about him
To determine if he could perceive anyone,
But saw only the tower and himself.   6550
"My God," he said, "what am I hearing?
I hear words but see nothing!
This is truly amazing!
Yet I am awake, not sleeping.
If it were a dream perhaps   6555
I would think it a lie;
But I am awake, and therefore it troubles me."
Then with some effort Lancelot rose
To his feet and moved slowly, step by step,
Toward the tiny crevice.   6560
When he reached the embrasure he wedged his body in,
From top to bottom and on each side.
Upon looking out,
He stared as best he could, then
He saw the one who had shouted to him.   6565
He saw her, but did not know who she was;
She, however, recognized him at once
And spoke: "Lancelot, I have
Come seeking you from afar.
My search has ended,   6570
Thank God, for now I've found you.
I am she who asked of you
A favor when you were nearing the Sword Bridge.
You granted it to me
Willingly when I asked it of you: 6575
It was the head of the defeated knight,
Which I had you cut off,
Because I had no love for him.
Since you did me that service and gave me that gift,
I have exposed myself to these hardships;   6580
Because of them I will rescue you from here."

273

"Pucele, la vostre merci,"
fet donques li anprisonez.
"Bien me sera guerredonez
li servises que je vos fis,   6585
se je fors de ceanz sui mis.
Se fors de ci me poez metre,
por voir vos puis dire et prometre
que je toz jorz mes serai vostres,
si m'aïst sainz Pos li apostres.   6590
Et se je Deu voie an la face,
jamés n'iert jorz que je ne face
quanque vos pleira comander.   [52b]
Ne me savroiz ja demander
chose nule, por que je l'aie,   6595
que vos ne l'aiez sanz delaie."
"Amis, ja de ce ne dotez
que bien n'an soiez fors botez;
hui seroiz desclos et delivres.
Je nel leiroie por mil livres   6600
que fors n'an soiez ainz le jor.
Lors vos metrai a grant sejor,
a grant repos, et a grant aise:
je n'avrai chose qui vos plaise,
se vos la volez, ne l'aiez.   6605
Ja de rien ne vos esmaiez.
Mes ençois me covient porquerre,
ou que soit ci an ceste terre
aucun engin, se je le truis,
com puisse croistre cest pertuis   6610
tant que vos issir an puissiez."
"Et Dex doint que vos le truissiez,"
fet se cil qui bien s'i acorde.
"Et j'ai ceanz a planté corde
que li sergent bailliee m'ont   6615
por traire le mangier amont--
pain d'orge dur et eve troble
qui le cuer et le cors me troble."
Lors la fille Bademagu
un pic fort, quarré et agu   6620
porquiert, et tantost si le baille
celui qui tant an hurte et maille,
et tant a feru et boté,
neporquant s'il li a grevé,
qu'issuz s'an est legieremant.   6625
Or est a grant alegemant,
or a grant joie (ce sachiez)
quant il est de prison sachiez

6589. jorz *missing in MS*   6605. *line repeated*
6614. p. de corde

"My thanks to you,"
Said the prisoner on hearing that.
"The service I did you
Will be well repaid   6585
If I am freed from here.
If you can get me out,
I can truly affirm and promise
To be yours from this day hence,
With the help of the Apostle Paul.   6590
And as God is my witness,
Never will a day come that I will fail to do
All you may be pleased to request.
Never could you ask of me
A single thing which, if I were able to get it,   6595
You would not have immediately."
"Friend, have no doubt
That you will soon be rescued;
You will be freed this very day.
I would not leave, not even for a thousand pounds,   6600
Without seeing you at liberty before daybreak.
Then I shall put you at ease,
In great comfort and repose:
Whatever I have that is pleasing,
If you want it, will be given to you.   6605
Do not be frightened.
But first I must seek
Where there might be in this land
Some device that I could find
To enlarge this crevice   6610
Enough so that you can escape."
"May God help you find it,"
He said in heartfelt agreement.
"Here within I have plenty of rope
Which the soldiers gave me   6615
To haul up my food--
Stale barley bread and stagnant water
Which have ruined my health."
Then the daughter of King Bademagu
Found a solid pickaxe, as strong as it was sharp.   6620
She brought it to Lancelot,
Who hammered and pounded
And struck and dug,
Though it pained his weakened body,
Until he was able to crawl out easily.   6625
How very relieved
And happy he was--you can be sure--
To be out of confinement

et quant il d'iluec se remue
ou tel piece a esté an mue.   6630
Or est au large et a l'essor;
et sachiez bien que por tot l'or
qui est espanduz par le mont,
qui tot le meïst an un mont
et tot li donast et ofrist,   6635
arrieres estre ne volsist.   [52c]
    Ez vos desserré Lancelot,
qui si ert vains qu'il chancelot
de vanité et de feblece.
Cele si soëf que nel blece   6640
le met devant soi sor sa mure,
puis si s'an vont grant aleüre.
Mes la pucele se desvoie
tot de gré, por ce qu'an nes voie;
et chevalchent celeemant,   6645
car s'ele alast apertemant
espoir assez tost lor neüst
aucuns s'il les reconeüst,
et ce ne volsist ele pas.
Por ce eschive les max pas   6650
et est venue a un repeire
ou sovant sejorne et repeire,
por ce que biax estoit et genz.
Et li repeires et les genz
erent an son comant del tot;   6655
si estoit planteïs de tot
li leus, et sains et molt privez.
La est Lanceloz arivez;
et si tost com il fu venuz,
quant il fu de sa robe nuz,   6660
en une haute et bele couche
la pucele soëf le couche.
Puis le baigne, puis le conroie
si tres bien que je n'an porroie
la mitié deviser ne dire.   6665
Soëf le menoie et atire
si com ele feïst son pere:
tot le renovele et repere,
tot le remue, tot le change.
Or n'est mie moins biax d'un ange,*   6670
n'est mes roigneus n'esgeünez,
mes forz et biax; si s'est levez.
Et la pucele quis li ot
robe plus bele qu'ele pot,
dom au lever le revesti;   6675
et cil lieemant la vesti

6648. que ele coneust 6670. mie *missing in MS*

276

And to be able to leave that place
Where he had been hidden so long.   6630
Now he was free and at large,
And even if all the gold
Scattered throughout the world
Were piled mountain high
And offered and given to him,   6635
He would never want to be back within.
  So Lancelot was freed.
He was so weak that he staggered
On frail and feeble limbs.
Gently, so as not to hurt him,   6640
The girl helped him mount her mule ahead of her,
And they set off in great haste.
She kept off the main roads
Deliberately, so that they would not be seen;
And they rode along cautiously,   6645
For if she travelled openly
Perhaps someone who recognized them
Might do them harm,
And this she was anxious to prevent.
Therefore she avoided narrow valleys   6650
And finally reached a retreat
Where, because of its beauty and charm,
She had often stayed.
The castle and its occupants
Were all in her service;   6655
The place was well-provided,
Safe, and very private.
She brought Lancelot there;
And upon his arrival,
As soon as he was undressed,   6660
She had him gently stretched out
Upon a beautiful, thickly-cushioned couch.
She then bathed and cared for him
So well that I could not
Tell you half of all the good she did.   6665
She handled and treated him
As gently as she would her father,
Completely reviving and restoring him
And giving him new life.
Now he was no less handsome than an angel: 6670
Not starved and weak,
But strong and fair, and able to arise.
The girl found for him
The most beautiful robe she had
And dressed him in it when he arose;   6675
Joyfully he put it on,

277

plus legiers que oisiax qui vole.
La pucele beise et acole,
puis li dist amïablemant: [52d]
"Amie," fet il, "seulemant 6680
a Deu et a vos rant merciz
de ce que sains sui et gariz.
Par vos sui de prison estors,
por ce poez mon cuer, mon cors,
et mon servise et mon avoir, 6685
quant vos pleira, prandre et avoir.
Tant m'avez fet que vostres sui.
Mes grant piece a que je ne sui
a la cort Artus mon seignor,
qui m'a portee grant enor-- 6690
et g'i avroie assez a feire.
Or, douce amie deboneire,
par amors si vos prieroie
congié d'aler; et g'i iroie,
s'il vos pleisoit, molt volantiers." 6695
"Lancelot, biax dolz amis chiers,"
fet la pucele, "jel vuel bien,
que vostre enor et vostre bien
vuel je par tot et ci et la."
Un merveilleus cheval qu'ele a, 6700
le meillor c'onques veïst nus,
li done cele, et cil saut sus
qu'as estriés congié n'an rova:
ne sot mot quant sus se trova.
Lors a Deu qui onques ne mant 6705
s'antrecomandent boenemant.

    Lanceloz s'est mis a la voie
si liez que, se juré l'avoie,
ne porroie por nule painne
dire la joie qu'il demainne 6710
de ce qu'ainsi est eschapez
de la ou il fu antrapez.
Mes or dit sovant et menu
que mar l'a en prison tenu
li traïtres, li forsligniez, 6715
qui est gabez et angigniez.
"Et maugré suen an sui je fors!"
Donc jure le cuer et le cors
Celui qui tot le mont cria,
qu'avoir ne richesce n'en a 6720
des Babiloine jusqu'a Gant
por qu'il leissast Meleagant
eschaper, se il le tenoit [52e]
et de lui au desus venoit--

6679. *repeated at top of [52d]* 6680. fet *repeated*

With more grace than a bird in flight.
He kissed and embraced the girl,
Then said to her fondly:
"My dear," said he, "to God   6680
And to you alone do I give thanks
For being healed and healthy.
Because you have made possible my escape
I give you my heart, my body,
My aid, and my possessions   6685
To take and keep whenever you wish.
Because of all that you have done, I am yours.
Yet I have been absent for a great while now
From the court of my lord Arthur,
Who honored me greatly--   6690
And I have much yet to do there.
Thus, my sweet noble friend,
I would beg your leave with love,
And if it be pleasing to you,
I would go there most willingly."   6695
"Beloved Lancelot, fair gentle friend,"
Replied the girl, "I grant your request,
For I seek that which is to your honor
And good, both now and always."
She gave him a marvelous horse,   6700
The finest ever seen,
And he leapt onto it
Without disturbing the stirrups:
Before one knew it, he was mounted.
Then they sincerely commended one another   6705
To the ever truthful God.
    Lancelot set off on his way,
So overjoyed that, I swear,
Nothing I could ever say
Would convey to you how happy he was   6710
To have escaped from that place
Where he had been imprisoned.
He said over and over to himself
That the unnatural traitor
Who had held him prisoner was now victim   6715
Of his own deceits and damned by his own doing.
"I am free in spite of him!" said Lancelot.
Then he swore by the heart and body
Of this world's Creator
That he would never let Meleagant   6720
Escape with his life if once he managed
To overpower and capture him--
No, not for all the riches
From Babylon to Ghent.

que trop li a fet leit et honte!   6725
Mes li afeires a ce monte
que par tans en iert a meïsmes,
car cil Meleaganz meïsmes,
qu'il menace et tient ja si cort,
estoit ce jor venuz a cort   6730
sanz ce que nus ne le manda.
Quant il i fu, si demanda
tant monseignor Gauvain qu'il l'ot.
Puis li requiert de Lancelot
(li mauvés traïtres provez),   6735
se puis fu veüz ne trovez--
ausi con s'il n'en seüst rien!
(Nel feisoit il, nel sot pas bien,
mes il le cuidoit bien savoir!)
Et Gauvains li a dit por voir   6740
qu'il nel vit ne il ne vint puis.
"Des qu'ainsi est que je vos truis,"
fet Meleaganz, "donc venez
et mon covenant me tenez,
car plus ne vos en atandrai."   6745
Ce fet Gauvains: "Bien vos randrai,
se Deu plest ou j'ai ma creance,
jusqu'a po vostre covenance.
Bien me cuit a vos aquiter.
Mes se vient a plus poinz giter   6750
et g'en giet plus que ne façoiz,
si m'aïst Dex et sainte Foiz
quanqu'avra el geu tot an tasche
prendrai, ja n'en avrai relasche."
Et lors Gauvains sanz plus atandre   6755
comande gitier et estandre
iluec un tapiz devant soi.
Isnelemant font sanz esfroi
tot son comant li escuier,
mes sanz grondre et sanz enuier   6760
de ce qu'il rueve s'antremetent.
Le tapiz prenent, si le metent
cele part ou il comanda;
cil saut sus, einz n'i aresta,
et de desore armer se rueve   6765
aus vaslez que devant soi trueve,
qui ancors desfublé estoient.   [52f]
Trois en i ot qui li estoient
ne sai ou cosin ou neveu,
por voir bien anseignié et preu.   6770
Cil l'armerent bel et si bien
qu'il n'a el monde nule rien
dont nus hom reprendre les puisse
por nule rien que il i truisse

He had shamed him too despicably! 6725
And all was to come to pass
So that Lancelot could avenge himself,
For this very Meleagant,
Whom he had been threatening and was eager to encounter,
Had reached court this day 6730
Without having been summoned.
Upon his arrival he sought
My lord Gawain until he found him.
Then the evil, proven traitor
Asked whether Lancelot 6735
Had been seen or found--
As if he himself knew nothing of him!
(And he did not, in truth,
Though he presumed he did!)
Gawain replied that he had not seen him, 6740
Nor had he come to court since Meleagant had last been there.
"Since it is you whom I have found here,"
Said Meleagant, "come forward
And keep your promise to me--
I will wait for you no longer." 6745
"If it be pleasing to God in whom
I place my trust, I shall soon
Keep my promise to you," replied Gawain.
"I am confident that I shall acquit myself well.
It is like casting dice, 6750
And with God and St. Foy on my side
I shall cast more points than you,
And before I quit I'll pocket
All the bets without delay."
Thereupon Gawain 6755
Ordered a carpet
To be spread out before him.
His squires quickly and quietly
Did as they were asked,
Carrying out his command 6760
Without question or complaint.
When they had taken the carpet and placed it
Where he had ordered,
Gawain immediately stepped upon it,
And from there he asked 6765
Three valets in his suite,
Still unattired themselves,
To bring his armor.
These youths were his cousins
Or nephews, I know not which, 6770
And all were truly doughty and well-bred.
The three youths armed him so well
That there was nothing in the world
That anyone could find to reproach

en chose qu'il en aient fait.   6775
Quant l'ont armé, li uns d'ax vait
amener un destrier d'Espaigne,
tel qui plus tost cort par chanpaigne,
par bois, par tertres et par vax
que ne fist li boens Bucifax.   6780
El cheval tel con vos oez
monta li chevaliers loez,
Gauvains, li plus bien anseigniez
qui onques fust de main seigniez.
Et ja voloit son escu prandre   6785
quant il vit devant lui descendre
Lancelot, don ne se gardoit.
A grant mervoille l'esgardoit
por ce que si soudainnemant
est venuz; et, se je n'an mant,   6790
mervoilles li sont avenues
ausins granz con s'il fust des nues
devant lui cheüz maintenant.
Mes nel va lors rien detenant
ne besoinz qu'il poïst avoir,   6795
quant il voit que c'est il por voir,
qu'a terre ne soit descenduz;
lors li vet ses braz estanduz,
si l'acole et salue et beise.
Or a grant joie, or est a eise   6800
quant son conpaignon a trové.
Et je vos dirai voir prové,
si ne m'an mescreez vos pas,
que Gauvains tot eneslepas
ne volsist pas qu'an l'esleüst   6805
a roi, por ce qu'il ne l'eüst.
    Ja set li rois, ja sevent tuit
que Lanceloz, cui qu'il enuit,
qui tel piece a esté gaitiez,
est venuz toz sains et haitiez.   6810
S'an font grant joie tuit ansanble,   [53a]
et por lui festoier s'asanble
la corz qui lonc tans l'a bahé.
N'i a nul tant de grant ahé
ou de petit, joie n'an face.   6815
Joie depiece et si esface
la dolor, qui ençois i ert;
li diaus s'an fuit, si i apert
joie qui formant les rapele.
Et la reïne n'i est ele   6820
a cele joie qu'an demainne?
Oïl, voir, tote premerainne.

6794. decevant 6807. Va san li r.

282

In all that they had done.   6775
After arming him, one among them went
To fetch a Spanish warhorse,
Which could run more swiftly through countryside,
Wood, hill, and dale
Than did the fine Bucephalus.*   6780
The renowned and worthy
Gawain, the most skilled knight
Ever to be blessed with the sign of the cross,
Mounted this magnificent steed.
He was about to grasp his shield   6785
When he saw Lancelot dismount before him.
He had never expected to see him here!
Gawain stared at him in wonder,
For he had appeared so suddenly,
And I do not exaggerate   6790
If I tell you he was as astonished
As if Lancelot had just fallen
At his feet from a cloud.
When he saw for certain that it was Lancelot,
Nothing he might have had to do   6795
Could have prevented
Gawain, too, from dismounting
And going toward him with outstretched arms.
Gawain greeted him, then embraced and kissed him;
He was filled with joy and relief   6800
At having found his companion.
I shall tell you the proven truth,
And you must never doubt me,
When I say that Gawain would not
Have wanted to be selected   6805
King, if it meant losing Lancelot.
Soon King Arthur and everyone knew
That Lancelot, whom they had been awaiting so long,
Had returned healthy and safe--
To the great displeasure of one among them.   6810
The court, which had long been anxious about him,
Came together in full assembly
To celebrate his return.
There was none so old
Or so young as to not rejoice.   6815
Joy dissipated and obliterated
The grief which had reigned there;
Grief fled and joy appeared,
Eagerly beckoning again to them.
And was the queen not here   6820
To participate in this joy?
Indeed she was, and in the front ranks.

283

Comant? Dex, ou fust ele donques?
Ele n'ot mes si grant joie onques
com or a de sa bienvenue--   6825
et ele a lui ne fust venue?
Si est voir, ele an est si pres
qu'a po se tient--molt s'an va pres--
que li cors le cuer ne sivoit.
Ou est donc li cuers? Il beisoit   6830
et conjoïssoit Lancelot.
Et li cors, por coi se celot?
N'estoit bien la joie anterine?
A y donc corroz ne haïne?
Nenil certes, ne tant ne quant;   6835
mes puet cel estre, li auquant
(li rois, li autre qui la sont,
qui lor ialz espanduz i ont)
aparceüssent tost l'afeire
s'ainsi, veant toz, volsist feire   6840
tot si con li cuers le volsist.
Et se Reisons ne li tolsist
ce fol panser et cele rage,
si veïssent tot son corage.
Lors si fust trop granz la folie!   6845
Por ce Reisons anferme et lie
son fol cuer et son fol pansé,
si l'a un petit racenssé
et a mis la chose an respit
jusque tant que voie et espit   6850
un boen leu et un plus privé,
ou il soient mialz arivé
que il or ne sont a ceste ore.
Li rois Lancelot molt enore,   [53b]
et quant assez l'ot conjoï,
se li dist: "Amis, je n'oï
certes de nul home noveles
piece a qui si me fussent beles
con de vos; mes molt m'esbaïs
an quel terre et an quel païs   6860
vos avez si grant piece esté.
Et tot iver et tot esté
vos ai fet querre et sus et jus,
n'onques trover ne vos pot nus."
"Certes," fet Lanceloz, "biax sire,   6865
a briés paroles vos puis dire
tot si com il m'est avenu.
Meleaganz si m'a tenu,
li fel traïtres, an prison
des cele ore que li prison   6870
de sa terre furent delivre,
si m'a fet a grant honte vivre

284

What? Heavens, where else would she be?
Never had she experienced greater joy
Than that she felt at his return--   6825
How could she have stayed away?
In truth she was so near him
That she could scarcely restrain--and nearly didn't--
Her body from following her heart to him.
Where then was her heart? Welcoming   6830
Lancelot with kisses.
Why then was the body reticent?
Was her joy not total?
Was it laced with anger or hatred?
Indeed, not in the least;   6835
Rather, it was because the others present
(The king and his entourage,
Who were there to see everything)
Would quickly comprehend her love
If, before their eyes, she were to do   6840
All that her heart desired.
And if Reason did not subdue
These foolish thoughts and madness,
Everyone would perceive her feelings.
O! height of folly!   6845
Thus Reason encompassed and bound
Her foolish heart and thoughts
And brought her to her senses,
Delaying her actions
Until she should see and discover   6850
A better and more private place,
Where they might reach safer harbor
Than they would have now.
The king honored Lancelot fully,
And when he had properly welcomed him   6855
Said: "My friend, I've not heard
For many a year such welcome news
Of anyone as that of you
Today; yet I am quite puzzled
As to which land or country   6860
You have been in so long.
All winter and all summer
I've had you sought both high and low,
Yet no one could find you."
"Indeed, fair sir," replied Lancelot,   6865
"In but a few words I can tell you
Everything just as it happened to me.
Meleagant, the wicked traitor,
Has kept me imprisoned
Since the day the prisoners   6870
Were released from his land,
And has made me live shamefully

285

en une tor qui est sor mer.
La me fist metre et anfermer,
la menasse ancor dure vie   6875
se ne fust une moie amie,
une pucele cui ge fis
un petit servise jadis.
Cele por assez petit don
m'a rendu large guerredon;   6880
grant enor m'a feite et grant bien.
Mes celui cui je n'aim de rien,
qui cele honte et cest mesfet
m'a porchacié, porquis et fet,
voldrai randre son paiemant   6885
orandroit sanz delaiemant.
Il l'est venuz querre et il l'ait:
n'estuet pas que il se delait
por l'atandre, car trop est prez.
Et je meïsmes resui prez--   6890
mes ja Dex ne doint qu'il s'an lot!"
Lors dit Gauvains a Lancelot:
"Amis," fet il, "iceste paie
se je vóstre deteur la paie,
c'iert assez petite bontez.   6895
Et ausi sui je ja montez
et toz prez, si con vos veez.
Biax dolz amis, ne me veez
cest don que je requier et vuel."   [53c]
Cil dit qu'il se leiroit ainz l'uel,   6900
voire andeus, de la teste traire
einz qu'a ce le poïst atraire.
Bien jure que ja n'avandra.
Il li doit et il li randra,
car de sa main li afïa.   6905
Gauvains voit bien mestier n'i a
riens nule que dire li sache,
si desvest son hauberc et sache
de son dos, et toz se desarme.
Lanceloz de ces armes s'arme   6910
tot sanz delai et sanz demore;
il ne cuide ja veoir l'ore
qu'aquitez se soit et paiez.
N'avra mes bien s'iert apaiez
Melïaganz, qui se mervoille   6915
oltre reison de la mervoille
qu'il a ses ialz esgarde et voit;
a bien petit qu'il ne desvoit
et par po n'a le san changié.
"Certes," fet il, "fos fui quant gié   6920

6891. s'an *missing in MS*

286

In a tower by the sea.
He had me taken and walled in there,
And there I would still be suffering,   6875
Were it not for a friend of mine,
A girl for whom I had
Done a small favor earlier.
Magnificently has she repaid
That rather tiny favor;   6880
She has done me great honor and great good.
Now, however, without further delay
I would like to repay him
For whom I have no love.
He has long sought and pursued me,   6885
Treating me shamefully and cruelly.
He has come to seek payment, and he shall have it:
He need wait no longer
To receive it, for it is imminent.
I myself am ready, as is he--   6890
May God never give him cause for bragging!
Then Gawain said to Lancelot:
"My friend, it would
Cost me little, were I
To repay your creditor.   6895
I am already mounted
And equipped, as you can see.
Fair gentle friend, do not refuse me
This favor which I want and beg of you."
Lancelot replied that he would rather have one   6900
Or even both eyes plucked from his head
Than to be so persuaded.
He swore never to let Gawain fight for him.
He had given his pledge to fight Meleagant;
He himself would repay what he owed.   6905
Gawain saw that nothing
He might say would be to any avail,
So he loosed his hauberk and lifted it
From his back, then disarmed himself totally.
Lancelot armed himself with these arms   6910
Quickly and without delay;
He thought the hour would never come
When his debt would be repaid and canceled.
He will not rest until he has repaid
Meleagant, who was stunned   6915
Beyond thought at everything
He has just seen with his own eyes;
He felt his heart sinking
And nearly lost his mind.
"Indeed," he said, "what a fool I was   6920

287

n'alai ençois que ça venisse
veoir s'ancore le tenisse
an ma prison et an ma tor,
celui qui or m'a fet un tor.
Ha! Dex, je por coi i alasse? 6925
Comant, por quel reison cuidasse
que il s'an poïst estre issuz?
N'est li murs assez fort tissuz
et la torz assez forz et haute?
N'il n'i avoit pertuis ne faute 6930
par ou il issir an peüst,
s'aïde par defors n'eüst.
Espoir qu'il i fu ancusez?
Or soit que li murs soit usez
et toz cheoiz et toz fonduz, 6935
ne fust il avoec confonduz
et morz, et desmanbrez et roz?
Oïl, si m'aïst Dex, trestoz,
s'il fust cheüz morz fust sanz faille.
Mes je cuit qu'ainz que li murs faille 6940
faudra, ce cuit, la mers trestote
si qu'il n'en i remandra gote,
ne li monz ne durera plus, [53d]
s'a force n'est abatuz jus.
Autremant va, n'est pas issi: 6945
aïde ot quant il en issi,
ne s'an est autremant volez.
Bien sui par consant afolez.
Comant qu'il fust, il an est fors.
Mes se m'an gardasse bien lors, 6950
ja ne fust ne ja n'avenist,
ne ja mes a cort ne venist.
Mes tart an sui au repantir.
Cil qui n'a talant de mantir,
li vilains, dit bien chose estable: 6955
que trop a tart ferme an l'estable
quant li chevax an est menez.
Bien sai c'or serai demenez
a grant honte et a grant laidure,
se assez ne suefre et andure. 6960
Quel sosfrir et quel andurer?
Mes tant con je porrai durer
li donrai je assez antante,
se Deu plest, a cui j'ai m'atante."
Ensi se va reconfortant, 6965
ne ne demande mes fors tant
qu'il an chanp soient mis ansanble.
Et c'iert par tans, si con moi sanble,

6940. cuit quanque

288

Not to go check before coming here
To be certain that Lancelot was still secure
Within my prison tower.
Now he has gotten the better of me.
Ah, God, but why should I have gone there?   6925
Why would I ever have suspected
That he should escape?
Was the wall not solidly built
And the tower not tall and strong?
Nor was there any crevice or flaw   6930
Through which he could slip
Without help from outside.
Perhaps my secret was betrayed?
Even granted that the walls broke
Before their time and crumbled and fell,   6935
Would he not have been buried under them
And killed, his body crushed and dismembered?
Yes, by God, if they had cracked
He would surely have been dead within.
Yet I am certain that   6940
Those walls would never have fallen before
The last drop of water in the sea had been dried up
And the mountains leveled,
Unless they were destroyed by force.
That is impossible; there has to be another answer: 6945
He had help in escaping;
Otherwise he'd not be free.
I have no doubt that I've been betrayed.
Be that as it may, he is out.
If only I'd taken more precautions   6950
It would never have happened
And he would never again have come to court!
But now it is too late to feel sorry for myself.
The peasant, unfamiliar with deception,
Spoke the honest truth in his proverb: 6955
It's too late to lock the barn door
After the horse has been stolen.
I know that I'll be brought
To shame and greatly vilified
Unless I endure great trials and sufferings.   6960
What trials and sufferings?
But so help me God, in whom I place my trust,
I'll fight my best for as long as I am able
Against the knight I have challenged."
Thus he gathered courage   6965
And asked no more than
That they be brought together on the field.
I think their battle will take place soon,

car Lanceloz le va requerre
qui molt tost le cuide conquerre. 6970
Mes ainz que li uns l'autre assaille,
lor dit li rois que chascuns aille
aval soz la tor an la lande--
n'a si bele jusqu'an Irlande.
Et il si font; la sont alé; 6975
molt furent tost jus avalé.
Li rois i va, et tuit et totes,
a granz tropiax et a granz rotes.
La s'an vont tuit; nus n'i remaint.
Et as fenestres revont maint-- 6980
la reïne, dames, puceles,
por Lancelot, gentes et beles.
    En la lande un sagremor ot,
si bel que plus estre ne pot;
molt tenoit place, molt est lez. 6985
S'est tot antor selonc orlez
de menue erbe fresche et bele, [53e]
qui an toz tans estoit novele.
Soz le sagremor gent et bel,
qui fu plantez del tans Abel, 6990
sort une clere fontenele
qui de corre est assez isnele.
Li graviers est et biax et genz
et clers, con se ce fust argenz;
et li tuiax, si con ge cuit, 6995
de fin or esmeré et cuit;
et cort parmi la lande aval,
antre deus bois parmi un val.
Iluec plest le roi qu'il se siee,
qu'il n'i voit rien qui li dessiee. 7000
Les genz fet treire bien ansus;
et Lanceloz molt tost cort sus
Melïagant de grant aïr,
con celui cui molt puet haïr.
Mes avant, einz que il le fiere, 7005
li dist a haute voiz et fiere:
"Traiez vos la, je vos desfi!
Et sachiez bien trestot de fi
que ne vos espargnerai point!"
Lors broche son cheval et point, 7010
et arriers un petit se trait
tant de place con uns ars trait.
Puis lessent l'uns vers l'autre corre
quanque cheval lor porent corre,
si s'antrefierent maintenant 7015
es escuz, qui bien sont taingnant,

6981. chevalier dames et p.

290

For Lancelot is eager to meet him,
Expecting a quick victory.   6970
But before either charged,
The king asked them to go
Down below the tower onto the heath--
The finest from there to Ireland.
They did as he ordered; they went there;   6975
They lost no time going down.
The king followed, accompanied
By milling crowds of knights and ladies.
Everyone went; no one remained behind.
And many returned to the windows--   6980
The queen, the ladies and the maidens,
Fair and beautiful--to watch Lancelot.
   On the heath was a sycamore,
The finest ever grown,
Spreading wide its branches.   6985
About it, like a woven carpet,
Was a beautiful field of fresh grass
That never lost its green.
From beneath the beautiful sycamore,
Which had been planted in the time of Abel,   6990
Gushed a sparkling spring
Of rapid-running water
Over a bed of beautiful stones
That glinted like silver.
The water flowed off through a pipe   6995
Of purest, rarified gold
And ran down across the heath
Into a valley between two woods.
Here it suited the king to take his place,
For he saw nothing there that displeased him.   7000
He ordered his people to keep their distance;
Then Lancelot charged toward
Meleagant angrily
Like a man bursting with hatred.
Yet before striking a blow   7005
He called out in a loud, bold voice:
"Come forward--I challenge you!
And be well assured
That I will not spare you!"
He spurred his horse,   7010
Withdrawing to a spot
A bowshot distant.
Now they charged toward one another
As swiftly as their horses could run;
Each knight struck a lance blow   7015
So forcefully on the other's sturdy shield

291

qu'il les ont troez et perciez,
mes l'uns ne l'autres n'est bleciez
n'an char conseüz a cele ore.
Lors passent oltre sanz demore,   7020
puis se revont granz cos doner,
quanque chevax puet randoner,
es escuz qui boen sont et fort.
Et il resont de grant esfort,
et chevalier preu et vassal,   7025
et fort et isnel li cheval.
Et a ce qu'il fierent granz cos
sor les escuz qu'il ont as cos,
les lances sont oltre passees
qui fraites ne sont ne quassees,   7030
et sont a force parvenues   [53f]
desiqu'a lor charz totes nues.
Par grant vertu l'uns l'autre anpaint
qu'a terre se sont jus anpaint.
Ne peitrax ne cengle n'estriés   7035
n'i pot eidier, que par derriers
chascuns d'ax la sele ne vuide
et chieent a la terre vuide.
Esfreé an sont li cheval
qui s'an vont amont et aval—   7040
li uns regibe, l'autres mort,
que l'uns volsist l'autre avoir mort.
Et li chevalier qui cheïrent
plus tost qu'il porent sus saillirent
et ont tost les espees traites,   7045
qui de letres erent portraites.
Les escuz devant lor vis metent,
et des ore mes s'antremetent
comant se puissent domagier
as espees tranchanz d'acier.   7050
Lanceloz nel redote mie,
car il savoit plus d'escremie
la mitié que cil n'an savoit,
car an s'anfance apris l'avoit.
Andui s'antrefierent granz cos   7055
sor les escuz qu'il ont as cos
et sor les hiaumes d'or barrez,
que fraiz les ont et anbarrez.
Mes Lanceloz le haste fort,
si li done un grant cop et fort   7060
devant l'escu a descovert
el braz destre de fer covert;
si li a colpé et tranchié.
Et quant il se sant domagié

7041. lautre et mort

292

That it was pierced through,
Yet both remained untouched,
Their flesh still whole.
They rode past, then wheeled about   7020
And returned full gallop
To strike mighty blows
On the strong, good shields.
Each was a doughty,
Bold, and valiant knight,   7025
On swift and powerful steeds.
Their mighty thrusts struck
The shields they bore at their sides,
Piercing them through with lances
That, without splitting or breaking,   7030
Now forced their way
Right to the naked flesh.
With great strength they drove
One another to the ground.
Breast-straps, girths, stirrups--   7035
Nothing could prevent each
From being tumbled backward
From his saddle onto the bare earth.
Their frightened horses
Reared and plunged--   7040
Bucking and biting,
For they too wished to kill each other.
The fallen knights
Leapt up as quickly as possible
And drew their swords,   7045
Which had words engraved upon them.*
Their faces protected by shields,
They determined how best
To injure the other
With their sharp steel blades.   7050
Lancelot was unafraid,
Because he had half again as much
Fencing skill as Meleagant,
For he had practiced it since his youth.
Both struck such powerful blows   7055
On the shields suspended from their necks
And on the gold-plated helmets,
That they split and broke.
But Lancelot pursued relentlessly
And gave him a mighty blow   7060
Which split and severed
The steel-covered right arm
Which the imprudent Meleagant had failed to shield.
When he felt the loss

293

de sa destre qu'il a perdue,   7065
dist que chier li sera vandue.
S'il an puet leu ne aise avoir,
ne remanra por nul avoir;
car tant a duel et ire et rage
qu'a bien petit que il n'anrage;   7070
et molt po prise son afeire
s'un malvés geu ne li puet feire.
Vers lui cort, que prendre le cuide,
mes Lanceloz bien se porcuide;
car a s'espee qui bien taille   [54a]
li a fet tele osche an s'antraille
dom il ne respassera mais,
einz iert passez avrix et mais;
que le nasal li hurte as danz
que trois l'en a brisiez dedanz.   7080
Et Melïaganz a tele ire
qu'il ne puet parler ne mot dire;
ne merci demander ne daingne,
car ses fos cuers li desansaingne,
qui trop l'enprisone et anlace.   7085
Lanceloz vient, si li deslace
le hiaume et la teste li tranche.
Jamés cist ne li fera ganche:
morz est cheüz, fet est de lui.
Mes or vos di, n'i a celui   7090
qu'ilueques fust qui ce veïst
cui nule pitiez an preïst.
Li rois et tuit cil qui i sont
grant joie an demainnent et font.
Lancelot desarment adonques   7095
cil qui plus lié an furent onques,
si l'en ont mené a grant joie.
    Seignor, se j'avant an disoie,*
ce seroit oltre la matire.
Por ce au definer m'atire: 7100
ci faut li romanz an travers.
Godefroiz de Leigni, li clers,
a parfinee la Charrete;
mes nus hom blasme ne l'an mete
se sor Crestïen a ovré,   7105
car ç'a il fet par le boen gré
Crestïen, qui le comança.
Tant en a fet des lors an ça
ou Lanceloz fu anmurez,
tant con li contes est durez.   7110
Tant en a fet. N'i vialt plus metre
ne moins, por le conte malmetre.

Ci faut li romans de Lancelot de la Charrete.

Of his right arm,   7065
He determined to sell his life dearly.
If he could find the chance
He would avenge himself,
For he was nearly insane with anger,
Spite, and suffering.   7070
His situation was hopeless
If he could not find some evil trick to harm Lancelot.
He ran toward him, thinking to surprise him,
But Lancelot was on his guard
And with his trenchant sword   7075
Opened Meleagant's belly so wide
That he would not be healed
Before April and May had passed.
A second blow slashed his helmet, knocking the nasal
Into his mouth, breaking three teeth.   7080
Meleagant was so enraged
That he could not utter a word;
Nor would he ask for mercy,
Because his foolish heart, which bound
And held him prisoner, had so besotted him.   7085
Lancelot approached, unlaced
Meleagant's helmet and cut off his head.
Never again would Meleagant deceive him:
He had fallen in death, finished.
But I assure you now that no one   7090
Who was there and witnessed this
Felt any pity whatsoever.
The king and all the others there
Rejoiced greatly over it.
Then the happiest among them   7095
Helped Lancelot remove his arms
And led him off amid great joy.
   My lords, if I were to tell more
I would be going beyond my matter.
Therefore I draw to a close: 7100
The romance ends here.
The clerk Godefroy de Leigni
Has put the final touches on the Knight of the Cart;
Let no one blame him
For completing the work of Chrétien,   7105
Since he did it with the approval
Of Chrétien, who began it.
He worked on the story from the point
At which Lancelot was walled into the tower
And finished it.   7110
This much only has he done. He wishes to add nothing further,
Nor omit anything, for this would harm the story.

Here ends the romance of Lancelot of the Cart.

295

TEXTUAL NOTES

1. "My lady of Champagne" is Marie of Champagne, daughter of the French king Louis VII by his first wife, Eleanor of Aquitaine. Marie was married by 1159 to Henry I of Champagne and was the patroness of Chrétien de Troyes, Andreas Capellanus, Conon de Béthune, and a number of other important writers of both Latin and vernacular literature. Hers was the principal literary court of twelfth-century France, and was rivaled in Europe only by that of her mother Eleanor and Henry II Plantagenet in Norman England. Marie was widowed in 1181. Since Chrétien was from Troyes in Champagne, she was truly his *dame*.

12. A warm, dry mountain wind in Europe, which is especially prevalent in the springtime months of April and May.

17. With Foerster (1899) and Frappier (1969), I prefer *pelles* "pearls" to Guiot and Roques' *pailes* "silk cloths". The opposition here, as noted by Holmes (1963), is between the polished gem (*jame*) and unpolished stones (*pelles, sardines*).

18. Like Frappier (1969) I end the quotation here rather than after line 20, as did Roques (1958).

24-29. The precise meanings of the principal terms in this passage are the subject of much scholarly dispute. The countess is, of course, "my lady of Champagne" of the opening line. *Matiere* is usually interpreted to refer to Chrétien's source matter or story--be it Celtic, classical, or contemporary (see Introduction); while *san*, furnished (like the *matiere*) by the countess, is seen as the meaning or interpretation given the source material--and refers therefore to the thematic interpretation of the entire poem. This traditional viewpoint is best expressed in Paris (1883), Frappier (1968), and Kelly (1966). The received opinion was challenged by Rychner (1967, 1968, 1972), and by Tony Hunt (1972). For them, *matiere* refers to the occasion to write, while *san* is the inspiration or desire to write. Thus, Hunt translates: "Chrestien begins his tale of the knight of the cart. The countess inspires and prompts him to do it, and he puts his mind to it and simply applies his effort and understanding" (pp. 327-328). The *painne* may "include all the steps of composition from the conception of the matter and order of the poem to the final organization" (Kelly, p. 94). For Kelly, pp. 36-39, *antancion* refers to the care and attention that Chrétien showed in his elaboration of the *matiere* so as to reveal the *san* intended by the countess. But for Robertson (1951), *antancion* is the equivalent of "intention (sententia)." It is quite possible that Chrétien leaves this passage, as he does many another in his romances, purposefully enigmatic. My translation adheres most closely to the discussion by Kelly.

29a, 30a. These lines are omitted by Guiot, but the mention of Camelot is found in all the other manuscripts that contain this passage, including Garrett 125, which alone has the correct reading, Chamaalot. While perhaps not indispensable, it is to be noted that Chrétien characteristically begins his romances with an indication of both time and place (see *Yvain*, lines 7-8; *Erec*, lines 27-28).

106. The *seneschal* in a medieval court was a sort of *majordomo* with full responsibility for the overseeing of feasts, ceremonies, domestic arrangements, and the administration of justice. Chrétien's Kay (Old French *Keu*), perhaps because his name translated "cook," is a consistently weak, rash, and boastful character. Here, as elsewhere, he displays the principal medieval sin of *desmesure*.

112. An old French volume measure equalling 0.446 liters.

168-170. The motif of the "rash boon," whereby a person swears to grant a wish before it is expressed, is popular in Arthurian romance. The boon to be granted frequently goes against the grantor's deepest wishes, or even his moral principles, but to fail to grant it would involve a loss of honor. The moral dilemma thus created has been studied by Frappier (1969) and Köhler (1974).

209. *Ha! amis, se le seüssiez.* Guiot wrote *Ha! rois* (king), which is an absurdity since the king already does know. The lines must be addressed to Lancelot, as Kelly(1966) has shown. Foerster (1899), Frappier (1969), Foulet (1977), and others prefer the reading of T (Paris B.N. fr. 12560): *Ha! Ha! se vos le seüssiez*, defending it on the ground that it is characteristic of Chrétien's style to "keep his readers in the dark" as long as possible. There is certainly merit in this argument, but I have nonetheless chosen the reading of A since the mutual love of Lancelot and Guinevere, and the irony that the feelings of each are withheld from the other, seems central to Chrétien's conception of his story.

303. I have indicated a suspension after this line, for a considerable amount of time must pass at this point after Gawain loses sight of the unknown knight and before he reaches the scene of the battle.

328. Guiot wrote: *a ces qui murtre et larron sont* (for those who are murderers and thieves). But theft is adequately covered by lines 330-31, authenticated in all MSS; and Shirt (1973) has shown in two perceptive socio-historical studies of the role of the cart that Chrétien was here listing the major crimes punishable by death.

360a, b. Although Roques passes over Guiot's omission of these lines without even a note, Vinaver (1969) has shown that without Lancelot's two steps, Guinevere's later treatment of him and her words in lines 4484-89 would be incomprehensible.

458. Literally "all night long." But it is clear from what follows that it is to be understood as "all evening." For the metonomy, see also Foerster, p. 368.

461. As Gallais (1963) quite correctly points out, castles of the period generally had only a single large hall, and beds were usually set up in the same room in which dinner was served.

503-07. The passage is garbled in the MSS. Although Foerster, 1899, eventually chose the reading of T, he acknowledged its weaknesses (p. 368). The principal difficulty in accepting C is that Lancelot must lie under the cover (see line 511), not upon it. Although no MS has *soz*, I agree with Frappier (1969) in presuming a scribal error and restoring *soz* for *sor* in line 506.

504. A measure of length equivalent to approximately four feet. Thus the bed would have been about two feet longer and higher than the others.

639. It is quite possible that *Gorre* refers to the Celtic Underworld, sometimes referred to as the Ile de Voirre, "Isle of Glass." False etymology identified this in turn with Glastonbury, Somerset. In the poem it is the land into which Meleagant will take the queen and where he will hold her captive along with many others. Its capital city is Bade (Bath).

752. Following this second warning I add a third, clearly alluded to in line 780. The lines added are 757-62 in Foerster's edition.

759. The hauberk was the basic piece of twelfth-century armor: a chain-link tunic with full sleeves, extending to the knee. It was usually split from the waist down to facilitate riding. Similar to it, but composed of small, generally

circular plates of metal sewn onto leather, was the *broigne* (burney). Under one or the other of these the knight generally wore a quilted tunic (*gambison* or *auqueton*) for padding. Over them he wore his *bliaut* (the principal medieval outer garment, long-sleeved, knee-length, fastened at the neck with a brooch) or a *mantel* (cloak). Many fine illustrations of these fashions can be found in the Bayeux tapestry and in contemporary illuminations and sculpture.

766, 842. A French knight's shield was losenge-shaped-- rounded above and faintly pointed below. When not in battle, it hung loosely at the knight's side by a strap (*guiche*) fastened over his shoulder and around his neck. When challenged, he thrust his left forearm through the armstraps (*enarmes*) and pulled the shield into position before him.

967. The bailey refers to either the stone walls surrounding a courtyard, or to the courtyard itself. The latter meaning is obviously intended here. This bailey thus separated the outer defensive walls from the *donjon* (tower keep) within, and was the scene of constant activity in the Middle Ages. Stone castles were being constructed in France as early as the late tenth century, but wooden castles of the motte-and-bailey type remained the more popular well into the twelfth century.

972. *ele atandoit.* Most critics prefer the reading in other MSS: *ele i amenoit* (she was bringing there), but C seems defendable, even preferable. That she has been expecting the knight's arrival implies for her a mysterious and preordained role in the adventure, the sort of mystifying detail of which Chrétien was fond.

1072a, b. These lines are found in all copies except Guiot's and appear to be original.

1085-86. This passage is confused in the MSS. See the variants in Foerster and his note, p. 371. The reading in C is somewhat repetitive, but more logical than that chosen by Foerster: *ne sera cos* (he[Lancelot] will not be cuckolded).

1126-29. This passage is at best unclear. In line 1128 Guiot wrote: *et garde amont par la fenestre*; MS A has: *Et esgarde avant vers la fenestre.* Roques saw the *fenestre* as "designating not an opening in the wall, but a movable, unclosed part of the door, such as a peephole, or the upper part of a French door" (p. 322). Holmes (1963), on the other hand, considered it to be "a small window opening beside the door between the two *chambres*" (p. 336). I prefer the reading of T, in which Lancelot looks up just in time to see the swords descending toward his head.

1203. The principal medieval undergarment was the *chemise* (*chainse*), worn by both male and female. It was generally of linen and had tight-fitted sleeves. On the male it came about to the knees, while on the female it trailed to the ground. Though one was not considered improperly attired in only a *chemise*, the *bliaut* or *mantel* was more commonly worn over it (see above, note to 759). People normally slept naked in the Middle Ages, so the girl's and Lancelot's failure to remove their *chemises* here is significant. Later, when her testing of Lancelot is completed and the girl is ready to sleep in truth, she removes the *chemise* (1263).

1273. The *angevin* was the denier of Anjou--a small silver coin worth the equivalent of a little less than a dime today.

1300. *Logres* is the mythical kingdom of Arthur. A fascinating account of its founding is given in the opening chapters of Geoffrey of Monmouth's *History of the Kings of Britain*. He recounts how Brutus, great-grandson of the legendary Aeneas, fled Italy after slaying his father and eventually reached Albion, which he renamed Briton in honor of himself. He divided the land among his three sons: Kamber received Wales (Kambria), Albanactus took Scotland (Albany), and Locrinus was given what is now England proper (Loegria). The precise geographical boundaries of Logres varied through the centuries. In the time of Arthur it seems to have included the land east of the Severn and south of the Humber (excepting Cornwall).

1343. A relative clause on the order of "who caused this wound and who alone could heal it" seems to be missing from all MSS at this point. See Foerster, p. 372.

1346. Foerster's reading, *qu'il vienent pres d'une fontaine* is preferable to Guiot and Roques' *Que il voient une f.* (until they see a f.) because it is certain from lines 1359-60 that the Knight of the Cart does not see the spring at the same time as the maiden does.

1352. Indicates a long and imprecise period of time. Ysoré is the name of a Saracen king mentioned in several of the epics of the Old French William of Orange cycle and in some Arthurian romances.

1475. *Theriaca* (or *theriac*) is a paste made from many different drugs pulverized and mixed with honey which was formerly used as an antidote to poison.

1478. Many of the stones discussed in the medieval lapidaries, as well as relics of the many saints, were used sympathetically and superstitiously to ward off various dangers and diseases. The Knight of the Cart, like other courtly lovers, creates here his own "religion of love," in which the strands of hair are the magical "relics" of his lady.

1482. The great fair called *Lendi* or *Lendit* was held annually at St. Denis, near Paris, between the eleventh and the twenty-fourth of June. This, and the four great fairs held in Champagne (Provins, Troyes, Lagny-sur-Marne, and Bar-sur-Aube), were at the very center of medieval commerce, and travelers and merchants brought goods to them from every corner of the known world.

1561. That is, she set no store by what she said and was only answering in order to be properly courteous.

1641-42. The dice-games mentioned in these lines have no precise modern parallels. Albert Henry (1962) has shown that *mine* refers principally to the metal tray into which the dice were cast, but was extended to refer to the game played. In 2703 the original meaning seems intended, while the extended interpretation fits 1642. Foerster did not believe that *san* could refer to a game of dice since it would repeat the meaning of *dez* (p. 376). I see no problem here, however, for Chrétien was fond of redundance, and frequently used nouns, adjectives, or verbs with similar meanings in parallel situations. Philippe Ménard (1970) takes the same position, directly counter to that of Foerster (p. 401). He suggests that *san* can be derived from SENI (Latin for "doubles in sixes"--the winning throw in *trictrac* or backgammon).

1657. For *chemise*, see note to 1203.

1719. *chose lige. Lige* ("liege") is an important feudal term signifying principally a vassal who has sworn unreserved fidelity to an overlord. Clearly the maiden has not promised fidelity to Meleagant and the expression seems in context to imply a type of one-sided possessiveness rather than a reciprocal arrangement.

1747. In Old French there is an anacoluthon, passing from the third person in 1745-46 to the first person here, which I have avoided in my translation.

1855-56. The passage is garbled in all MSS; see Foerster, pp. 376-77. Since no MS has a totally acceptable reading, we have retained that of C, but recognize that the rhyming of a word with itself is uncharacteristic of Chrétien.

1858. Dombes was a small principality in Burgundy, between the Rhône, the Saône, and the Ain. It forms part of the present-day Department of Ain. No doubt it was chosen here for rhyme, rather than for any unusually fine medieval tombs.

1866. Preceding *Yvains*, each MS has a different name, all equally unknown. The context implies that he is a celebrated knight of Arthur's court. *Aloens* (T), *Leones* (A), and *Looys* (C) point to either Leones or Lionel, or possibly to Arthur's son Loholt, mentioned in the *Parzival* and *Lanzelet*.

302

1888. Since Chrétien has just completed a description of the exterior, the reading of the other MSS is preferable.

1904. It is tempting to adopt the reading *ne sers ne jantis hon* (serf and nobleman) in Foerster, since the opposition seems more evident. Nevertheless, Guiot's *clers* is quite possible.

2022. A *vavasor* was the vassal of an important noble, rather than of the king. Although he might serve at court, this role was traditionally that of the seneschal (see above, note to 106). The vavasor generally held an outlying fief and lived in the sort of manor house which formed an important stop along the routes of itinerant knights.

2226. How he could strike *beneath* the edge and yet hit the neck is unclear, so I have followed Frappier (1969) in adopting Herbert K. Stone's (1937) reading, *par desus*.

2240-41. These lines were in indirect address in C. The direct address should begin at 2240, as in the other MSS, rather than at 2242.

2326-31. The entire passage is faulty in C. The main verb is missing in the first three lines, which I have supplied by following T and Foerster. From 2332ff, it is clear that Lancelot and his companions have been trapped by descending gates both behind (2320-23) and before them. These gates were shut upon the heels of the fleeting knight, which I have indicated by choosing the reading preferred by Foerster.

2362. I have adopted Foerster's reading to eliminate the anacoluthon of C.

2422. After this verse Foerster includes two lines which are missing only in C, but which even he regards as superfluous and repetitious:

Quant ceste novele ont oïe,
Mout an est lor janz esjoïe.

(When they had heard this news their people were extremely happy).

2566. Literally: there came the gift of a knight; probably with ironic meaning.

2677-79. The syntax is confused in all versions. Foerster creates a composite text; however, C can be defended since Old French relative clauses are frequently separated from their antecedents. Cf. 2894-95 and Foerster's note, p. 386 (to his lines 2908-09).

2739. The helmet of the period was not fully enclosed, but when attached to the coif and ventail covered nearly the entire face and could successfully hide the knight's identity. See, for examples, illustrations 39 and 41 in Hindley (1971).

It was attached to the neck-band (*coler*) by laces or straps (*laz, corroie*; and see 2670) which Lancelot here severs. The ventail appears to have been "a separate triangular, or rectangular, strip of mail which was fastened to the coif on both sides and to the hauberk, across the mouth---by leather thongs." (Holmes, 1969). And see Foerster, p. 384. It allowed the knight to breathe, yet to be fully protected.

2848-51. The passage is awkward, but clear. On the one hand, Generosity urges him to reward the head to the girl who has requested it (I read *la pucele* as an oblique case, functioning as a dative); on the other, the defeated knight begs to be spared. The parallels one would anticipate (Generosity: Mercy; or maiden: knight) have been lost, probably through faulty MS transmission; I have restored it in my translation.

2854-60. The passage presents an anacoluthon in Old French which is, nonetheless, easily understandable. No MS gives a fully satisfactory text (see Foerster, pp. 385-86).

2863. Although C's *vialt* is possible, rhyming the same word is uncharacteristic of Chrétien.

3016. Other versions read *la mer salee* (the salty sea), but C's *betee* (frozen, congealed), a *lectio difficilior*, offers an image which appears less banal and more appropriate.

3104. *souler ne chauce n'avanpié.* Following Holmes (1963), I translate *chauce* as "mail-leggings" and *avanpié* as "socklet," being a type of protection for the upper part of the foot against the rubbing of the leather shoes (*souler*).

3125. The Knight of the Cart had been given a magic ring by his fairy mother, the Lady of the Lake (see 2335-50).

3227ff. The passage is confused in the MSS. Those other than C and V add two lines after 3228, which are redundant and probably a later edition by a scribe who felt that the omission of the direct object pronoun (*la*) was unfortunate. This omission, however, is syntactically normal in Old French (Ménard, 50.1; Moignet, p. 140).

3248. The line in C repeats verbatim 3236. It is in error here and has been replaced by the reading found in the other MSS and printed already by Foerster.

3277. I have extended the meaning of *prodon* to conform better to the context and tone of Meleagant's tirade.

3358. "The ointment of the Three Marys" was a purportedly miraculous ointment widely attested in medieval texts. The Three Marys are mentioned in the Gospel account of Easter Sunday. "When the sabbath was over, Mary of Magdala, Mary the mother of James, and [Mary] Salome, brought spices with which to go and anoint [the body of Jesus]" (Mark 16:1). The most widespread medieval legend of the Three Marys, studied by V. F. Koenig (1960), replaces Mary of Magdala with Mary the Mother of Christ, and makes all three the daughters of St. Anne, one by each of her husbands.

According to a legend recounted in the *Mort Aimeri de Narbonne*, the ointment used by the Three Marys to anoint the body of Christ after his burial became part of the relics of the Passion which were brought by Longinus into Femenie. The composition of the ointment is not mentioned in Mark, but there is likely confusion with the spices myrrh and aloes used by Nicodemus in the burial of Jesus (John 19:39). King Bademagu could be offering the Knight of the Cart either a few drops of the miraculous ointment of the Passion itself, or a portion of any ointment composed, like it, of myrrh and aloes.

3485. The most important medical schools in the Middle Ages were at Salerno in Italy and Montpellier in France.

3505. Some of the best early medieval steel armor seems to have been produced in the region of Poitou, since there are frequent references to Poitevin arms. For example, these lines from *La Geste des Loherans*: "li quens Guillaumes son compere feri, / grant cop li done de l'acier poitevin"(Count William struck his companion a mighty blow with his Poitevin steel). In the *Chevalier de la Charrete* there is a further reference to these fine arms in 5821, *mainz cos des aciers poitevins*.

3674. Old French *loge* carried three principal meanings. When, as here (and later, 5013), it indicates a gallery or bay at the top of a wall or tower, I have translated it "loge." Later, at the tournament, when it refers to temporary wooden viewing stands or *tribunes* (5581, 5584, etc.), I translate "stands." Finally, it can be used to indicate a rustic arbor or bower, or perhaps just a tent (5523). The following observations by Holmes (1969), one of the principal authorities on medieval housing and construction, will help clarify the problem: "Usually it (*loge*) was a room (of wood) completely open on the façade or having there a series of wide window arches extending low to the floor. This last was called a *loge fenestree*... Such a loge could be a gallery, an upper room, an entry into a house, or a viewing stand (perhaps of two or three stories). The essential was that it was mostly open on the front side." It was from such a *loge fenestree* that Bademagu and Queen Guinevere observed the combat between Meleagant and the Knight of the Cart. Bademagu placed the Queen *a une fenestre* (3750), then took his place, probably reclining, in one of the adjacent arches *(couchiez sor une autre fenestre*, 3572). At the tournament of Noauz, the Queen and her ladies observe the combat from viewing stands, which

305

likewise have *fenestres* (5916).

3700a, b. These two lines, which seem essential to a complete understanding of the passage, are missing only in C.

3740. The meaning of this line remains obscure to me, in spite of Roques' suggestion "that one could understand that, if Lancelot goes toward the tower in which the queen is, he does not do so as ordinarily he would to offer her his services, for he was obliged to stop Meleagant's flight by stopping his own pursuit, in order to remain at a sufficient distance from the tower in order to keep the queen in sight" (223). See the discussion by Foerster, pp. 392-93, and Rahilly (1974), p. 397.

3803. Ovid's tale of the tragic love of *Piramus and Thisbe (Metamorphoses,* 4: 55-166) was well known in twelfth-century France through the beautiful adaptation into octosyllabic couplets (with laments in irregular *stances*) by an unknown poet around mid-century.

3857-58. These lines are in direct address in C and V. However, the movement from indirect address (3856) to direct within the same sentence is foreign to Chrétien's style and betrays an error in these MSS.

4029. Foerster supposes a lacuna after the preceding line; Roques gives no indication of any problem. In spite of Foerster's objections, the difficulty seems easily resolved by A's reading, which I have adopted.

4219. *Breibançon* are "plündernde und mordende Söldner-banden, urspr. aus Brabant," according to Foerster (p. 396): that is, "hired killers." Brabant is that region in central Belgium of which Brussels is the principal city.

4276. As at 3248, Guiot inadvertently repeated 4270. (See note for 3248). I therefore substitute Foerster's *Morz qui onques ne desirra / Se ceus non,* etc. (his 4294-95).

4287. Literally, "And in order to do himself ill," which, with Foerster, I understand as euphemistic.

4372. I correct this line in accord with Stone (1937), p. 401. See also Foerster's note to 4390, p. 398.

4434-35. Might also be understood: "Never would she have wished that any great harm befall him."

4523. It was not unusual in the Middle Ages for males and females to share the same sleeping quarters. In this instance, where both are titular captives of King Bademagu, they are no doubt kept guarded in the same chamber for convenience.

4699. Although Guiot's *sanc* (blood) is acceptable, it destroys the image begun in 4697 and seems therefore less satisfactory than *cors* in the other MSS.

4739. The room in which the queen is kept was, like many medieval quarters, hung with tapestries or heavy cloths to reduce drafts and retain warmth, as well as for decoration.

4762a, b. Omitted by Guiot alone; the omission is not noted by Roques. They seem essential, however, for they both extend Meleagant's sarcasm and introduce the subject to which *il* in 4763 must refer back.

5506. Since, for this tournament, the towns of Noauz and Pomelegoi were the opposing camps, Lancelot, in order to participate in the tourney, must choose one of the two sides. His choice is Noauz, for a reason which will become evident shortly. (See note to line 5645.)

5536. *Garnement* today implies "scamp" or "rogue" and is somewhat pejorative. In the present context it seems to imply no more than the fact that the person is not of the upper class and is improperly dressed, having lost most of his clothes gambling.

5563-64. Chrétien treats the line   *Or est venuz qui l'aunera!* (var.: *or est venuz qui aunera*) / "The one is come who will take their measure!", as a proverbial expression (see 5572-74) which he later interprets himself (5678: *Cil les vaintra trestoz a tire!* / This one will beat them all, one after another). The expression means, quite simply, "The one is come who will win the tournament!" It has been likened by Archer Taylor (1950), I think correctly, to the English expression "To take his measure." In context in the *Chevalier de la Charrete,* the expression appears clearly to mean what it does in English today: "to get the best of someone," i.e., to defeat, better, or otherwise prove superior to another. The translation which Chrétien himself gives, quoted above, certainly supports such a conclusion.

One of the main roles of the *heraut* (herald) at the medieval tournament was, as his name implies, to announce the arrival and presence of the principal knights. He did this by a formula which often began, *Or est venuz...* A good example can be found in Sarrasin's *Le Roman du Hem* (ed. A. Henry), 3686: *"Or est venus Gaste forest!"* For further discussion of heralds' cries, see the introduction to Henry's edition, pp. xxxviii-xxxix, under "Gaste de gastebois."

5645. Chrétien employs a pun which it is impossible to convey without changing the name of the town, Noauz. The expression, *au noauz,* can mean "Do one's worst" or "Onward for Noauz!" When Guinevere sends the girl to the unknown knight with this message, she knows that Lancelot alone, being the model lover that he is, will interpret it "Do your worst," whereas any ordinary knight would understand it simply as "Onward for Noauz!" That the knight does understand it as "do your worst," coupled with his unhesitating obedience to this dictum, is proof for the queen that he is indeed Lancelot.

5704. Roques concedes the difficulty of Guiot's *tote nuit jusqu'au soir* (all night until evening). All other MSS give *tote jor* or *tot le jor*, which I adopt.

5739. To avoid repetition of the first part of 5738, I prefer Foerster's reading.

5770. Two classes of knights were not permitted to take part in the tournament—those who had been defeated previously, and those who had sworn to take up the Holy Cross of the Crusade and who thus could fight in no such lower, more frivolous cause. These knights joined the ladies in the stands and on the sidelines, explaining the rules and identifying the "players" for them. The use here of personal and family devices for decoration and identification is remarkable, for this was not widespread until the thirteenth century.

5775. *bernic*. For a discussion of this unusual word, see Foerster, p. 414 *(bellic)*.

5810. Quex d'Estraus is among the knights of Arthur's court mentioned in Chrétien's *Erec*, line 1695. MS C's *cuens*, without an article, is grammatically unusual.

5831, 5850. Old French *rans*, which I have translated "lists" in both instances, can refer either to the enclosed area in which the organized combat is held, or to the formation made by the knights of the opposing camps as they line up abreast (English "rank," as opposed to "file"). The context permits some doubt as to the precise meaning intended, but I have understood *Parmi les rans* to mean that the maiden is searching *through* an enclosed area rather than *along* a formation.

6074. *li jaianz*; cf. MS T, *li jeanz*. Roques suggests that the giant might be Dinabuc, killed by Arthur at Mont-Saint-Michel. The account of this feat is found in Geoffrey of Monmouth, pp. 237-40, and Wace, lines 11288-11318. Foerster rejected the reading of TC in favor of *li laganz* of MSS VF, in spite of linguistic and logical difficulties, since he could not identify the giant. OF *lagan* means "shipwrecked goods" which could be kept by the finder; extended meanings might be "destruction, ruin" or "abundance, excess". None fits the context.

6132. According to Godefroy of Leigni's witness at the end of the work (7098-7112), Chrétien abandoned his poem at

about this point. Godefroy completed it by carefully following
Chrétien's outline (see 6246-51 and 7104ff.); he, too, was no
doubt concerned to relate accurately the *matiere* and *san* given
by Marie of Champagne. Foerster, p. 465, suggested that
Chrétien stopped at 6107.

6133. To complete the rhyme, and following the sense of
the passage, I prefer *murer* from the other MSS to C's *barrer*.

6325. Old French frequently reinforces the negation by
referring to items of little value (see Moignet, 1973, p. 277):
a nut, a leek, a button, a glove, etc. Here, I have translated the literal "not even the value of an aloe" as "not...
at all."

6502. The reference to the peasant and his proverbs is
typical of Godefroy of Leigni (see also 6955). Mario Roques
lists eight proverbs in *The Knight of the Cart*, all from the
part attributed to Godefroy of Leigni. Chrétien occasionally
uses proverbs in his other works, but nowhere does he directly
attribute the use of them to the peasant class, as many
twelfth- and thirteenth-century writers did. In *Yvain*, 594,
Chrétien introduces a proverb with *l'en dit*; in *Erec et Enide*
he uses *Bien est voirs que* (3342) and *ceste parole est veri-
table* (1218); most frequently, however, Chrétien unobtrusively
weaves his proverb into the fabric of the sentence. The use
of peasant proverbs in a work clearly intended for a courtly
audience is a noteworthy social phenomenon, and one to which
no doubt Chrétien did not desire to call particular attention.
A famous collection entitled *Li Proverbe au Vilain*
(Tobler, 1895) was compiled in the last quarter of the twelfth
century at the court of Philip of Flanders, for whom Chrétien
composed his *Story of the Grail*. After each adage (of which
there were originally two hundred and eighty) there follows
a commentary in six-syllable verse with the refrain, *Ce dist
li vilains*. An unpublished study of Chrétien's use of proverbs
was prepared by Margery Ellis as a Master's thesis at the
University of Chicago in 1927; she counted 57 proverbs in his
works.

6670. After this line, other MSS add a couplet which
does not seem essential: *Or est plus tornanz et plus vistes
/ Qu'onques rien aussi ne veïstes* (Now he is so agile and
lively / That you've never seen anything like him).

6780. Bucephalus was the horse used by Alexander the
Great on most of his campaigns. It was attributed magic powers
in the twelfth-century Old French *Romance of Alexander*.

7046. There is unfortunately no indication of precisely
what was engraved upon their swords; perhaps individual
mottoes.

INDEX OF NAMES

The Garland Library
of Medieval Literature

Chrétien de Troyes. *Lancelot, or The Knight of the Cart*. Edited and translated by William W. Kibler

Walter Burley. *On the Lives and Characters of the Philosophers*. Edited and translated by Paul Theiner

The Poetry of Arnaut Daniel. Edited and translated by James J. Wilhelm

Waltharius and *Ruodlieb*. Edited and translated by Dennis Kratz

The Poetry of Duke William IX of Aquitaine (Guilhem, Count of Poitiers). Edited and translated by Gerald A. Bond

Brunetto Latini. *Il Tesoretto (The Little Treasure)*. Edited and translated by Julia Bolton Holloway

The Poetry of Cercamon and Jaufre Rudel. Edited and translated by George Wolf and Roy Rosenstein